The sight of her filled Veleda's eyes. *Goddess*, the girl thought, the word filling her mind with an absolute certainty. Just as this building could be called nothing other than a temple, so could this awesome figure be identified only as what she was.

"Yes, I am Bast, She Who Protects the Two Lands, lands unknown to you, My Daughter. In me glow the living force and the gentle warmth of sunlight. My power is that of the moon: light and dark, waxing and waning but ever-present, source of wisdom, giver of dreams and visions. For I am She: Silver Shining, Mother of Life. All that lives is sacred to Me. Those who seek Me with true hearts will find joy, protection against evil, and happiness in all their days. I bid you welcome, child."

The words rang in Veleda's ears. The deep, rich voice was the same one that had drawn her to this place, and, wrapped within a holding spell, she listened to it. The question came to her lips naturally, springing out before she was quite aware that she was asking it.

"Am I truly dead, then, Lady?" she whispered.

THE DAUGHTERS OF BAST
The Hidden Land

SARAH ISIDORE

AVON · EOS

AVON BOOKS, INC.
1350 Avenue of the Americas
New York, New York 10019

Copyright © 1999 by Sarah Isidore
Cover art by Rowena
Published by arrangement with the author
Library of Congress Catalog Card Number: 99-94756
ISBN: 0-380-80318-6
www.avonbooks.com/eos

First Avon Eos Printing: September 1999

AVON EOS TRADEMARK REG. U.S. PAT. OFF. AND IN OTHER COUNTRIES, MARCA REGISTRADA, HECHO EN U.S.A.

Printed in the U.S.A.

WCD   10 9 8 7 6 5 4 3 2 1

To the Goddesses who inspired me...
May my words find favor with them.

And in memory of Sheldon Miller
and
Ervin Chudnow

I

THE NEED-FIRES LIT UP THE horizon. From the cleared spaces atop every hill they blazed, their jagged fingers painting the night sky with streaks of bloody orange.

Hidden within the sheltering groves of beech and alder that lined the slopes below, the girl watched the leaping flames. This was the third night that the great fires had been lit, but so far the sacred flames had failed either to heal or to drive the evil away. The dying still continued. Those stricken with the mysterious sickness had not benefited from the magic contained in the flames. Or perhaps, the gods were not listening.

At the girl's feet, a large cat also watched the fires, his orange-gold eyes a lambent glow in the darkness. A wicker cage held him prisoner, but despite his confinement, he was quiet, and very calm. Unnaturally so, the girl thought. Frowning, she glanced down at him. She had seen other cats caught as he was, and invariably they fought, yowling piteously and struggling to get free, as if they sensed all too clearly the fate that awaited them.

This one, though, was different. He puzzled her, made her uneasy with the calm way in which he stared back and forth between her and the blazing hills. He was an unusually large cat, completely black save for his glowing eyes and a splash of white on his chest. Indeed, but for those eyes, he would have been all but invisible in the wicker cage. That yellow-orange gaze held the girl's, as flame-bright as the need-fires burning in the distance.

A faery cat, the girl thought suddenly. Her aunt said they were always completely black, except for a patch of white on their chests, just as this cat was. And yet, if the animal were truly a faery cat, she should not have been able to entice him into her cage with a large piece of dried fish.

"I'm sorry," she said to the cat. "I would spare you if I could."

She picked up the cage with its silent occupant, and started down the slope. Despite the cat's weight, she moved easily, her bare feet following the dim pathways between the great trees without conscious effort. The woods were very dark. The moon was in her crone aspect and the only light came from the distant stars filtering through occasional openings in the vast canopy of interwoven branches.

Truly, one had to possess the eyes of a cat to travel through the forests which clothed these lands at night; either that, or be born into the tribes who had lived here since the beginning of memory. The scent of woodsmoke drifted on the wind, stinging the girl's nose. Grief stabbed her for those who had died, and those who might still die. Yesterday, one of her friends had passed into the Otherworld. The souls of two more, both girls her own age, were preparing to follow, unless tonight's ritual proved successful.

The weight of the cat in his wicker cage pulled her gaze downward. Others with far more years and wisdom had decided on the ritual to be held this night, but to the girl there was an oppressiveness in the air, a certainty that the sacrifice of this cat or any other would not bring about the results her people desired so desperately.

The cat stared up at her, his eyes brilliant and intent in the darkness. The girl's steps slowed. A faery cat was a creature of powerful magic, an animal who could travel between the mortal world and the Otherworld: the realm where gods and Goddesses dwelled. If this cat were indeed such an animal, then using him in the sacrifice would add greatly to its power.

But even as she told herself this, the girl felt her uneasiness grow. Power or not, the cat would suffer a slow and painful death, and increasingly, she was struck by the sense that this was a deed that should not be.

Just ahead of her lay the track that led to the *nemeton*, the sanctuary where the ritual would take place. People would already be gathering there, at least those who were not too ill to attend. Her mother's sister, a respected Druid, had been selected to officiate over the lengthy sacrifice and perform the complex and all-important divinations. As her foster-daughter, the equally important task of finding a cat had been entrusted to the girl. What would happen if she failed in that task by releasing the object of the sacrifice?

The girl squared her shoulders and stepped onto the narrow trail. Her pace quickened. The cat made no sound, no attempt to free himself from the confines of his prison as he swung along at her side, yet the girl knew that those gold-orange eyes were still fixed upon her.

The track widened and began to climb, twisting as it wound its way along the first of several slopes it would follow before ending at the sacred grove. In the vast territory of the girl's people, holy places existed beyond number, but this roofless sanctuary was among the most hallowed. The forest which surrounded it was imbued with power and the grove itself was a place of awe, entered only by the Druids unless a ceremony such as this one was decreed. Then the people were allowed to enter, crowding into the consecrated clearing until they overflowed into the trees beyond.

The girl marched on. As she drew closer to the grove, the first sounds of voices started to carry, faint and drifting on the breeze. Muted and soft, she could hear that someone was crying. Now the girl's resolute strides faltered. She hesitated, strode forward and stopped, took another few steps, then paused again.

Abruptly she made up her mind. Lowering the wicker cage to the ground, she swiftly untied the thongs that held the door closed. In spite of this sudden and unexpected freedom, the cat remained where he was, staring at her with those disconcerting eyes.

"Hurry," the girl said impatiently. "Before I change my mind." She beckoned at the dark woods around them. "Flee, while you have the chance!"

The cat rose, stretched himself in a single luxurious movement, and stepped out of the cage. Yet he still made no attempt to leave. Instead, he raised his tail in that universal feline gesture of friendliness and twined gracefully about the girl's ankles.

The girl looked down at the animal in dismay. She nudged him away with her foot, not hard, but firmly enough to discourage any further overtures. "Go," she repeated. "If you are indeed a faery cat, then you know what awaits you. And if you are only a mortal cat, you still should have sense enough to run."

The cat's sleek body curved lithely away from her foot. He gave her an affronted look and rolled onto his back. Waving all four paws in the air, he rubbed himself back and forth against the star-silvered grass, a loud purr rumbling in his chest.

"What are you doing?" The girl was nearly pleading. "Do you want to die?"

Still on his back, the cat craned his neck and vigorously began to groom himself.

The girl's consternation flared into anger. Cats, originally brought by traders, were still rare in the country of the five tribes of Belgae. One thing people had quickly discovered about them, though, was that they could be maddening creatures. And this one was surely the most maddening of all cats ever born.

"By the spirits of earth and sky," she muttered. "So this is my reward for trying to spare you."

Stooping, she snatched up a large stick and tossed it. Her aim was good; the stick did not strike the cat, but it landed close enough to startle him.

In the blink of an eye, the animal regained his feet, the long black tail lashing against his sides. But incredibly, he still refused to run. He stared at the girl, and the expression in those glowing orange eyes was so eloquent, she expected him to speak at any moment. Nervously the girl grabbed another stick and raised it. Only then did the creature burst into a fluid streak of motion, vanishing like liquid smoke amongst the huge bodies of the trees.

The girl heaved a sigh of relief as she picked up the empty cage and went on toward the sanctuary. All at once she felt lighter in her heart, in harmony again, as if her spirit-self approved the rightness of what her physical-self had done.

But as she drew nearer to the sound of voices, the reality of what she had indeed done—and the necessity for explaining it—returned. People were gathering in greater numbers now, coming along the nine sacred pathways that led to the grove. The power of the sanctuary itself was already reaching out, drawing her in even before she reached the first of the trees carved into mystical representations of the Great Mother Anu, Dagda, the Father of the Gods, and all their attendant deities. They were the Shining Ones, these holy images, and always had they protected and guided those who honored and revered them.

Torches had been placed all along the pathways and set in a ring about the grassy inner space of the grove. Their flaring light merged into the greater illumination of a large bonfire that blazed in the center of the glade. Druids were gathered about the fire, the long white robes they donned for ceremonies tinted orange and gold by the leaping flames. From their circle, a lone figure detached itself and came toward Veleda. The girl paused, then forced herself to go forward to meet her foster-mother, Ancamna, one of the most important Druids of their tribe.

Ancamna was a tall, stern-faced woman with the deep-seeing eyes characteristic of all those initiated into the sacred mysteries. As a child she had wandered across the path of an ill-tempered bull and been badly trampled. Only the great healing skill of the Druids had kept her from crossing over into the Otherworld, but the accident had left her partially crippled, forcing her to walk with the aid of a long wooden staff from that time on.

However, there were few who now noticed her limp or the way she had to lean on the polished staff with its carved designs for support. In a subtle way she had incorporated her handicap into the mantle of dignity and power her Druid training had given her, and if she had suddenly become able-bodied and thrown away her staff, she would have seemed less without it, instead of more.

It was the custom for well-born children to be given foster-parents to guide and nurture them, and Veleda had always known that it was a particular honor to have a foster-mother such as Ancamna for hers. But there were certain drawbacks in having a Druid as one's foster-mother, the chief drawback being that it was impossible to hide anything from her.

Veleda had difficulty meeting those deep-set eyes as Ancamna first perused the empty cage and then studied the face of her sister's child. "I sense the presence of a cat within the wicker bars of your basket, Foster-Daughter," the Druid said at last. "But my outer gaze shows me that the cage is now empty. Tell me, why is that?"

Veleda swallowed. She straightened her shoulders and made herself meet those penetrating eyes. "Yes, Mother's Sister, I did have a cat. But I let him go."

"You let him go?" Veleda's true mother had joined them just in time to hear this. She gasped out the question as if she were certain she had not heard correctly.

"I had to!" Veleda looked from her mother's face to her foster-mother's. "I know he was needed for the sacrifice, but—I had to free him."

"Daughter, do you understand what you have—"

Ancamna laid a hand on the other's shoulder, cutting her off. "I think she understands, indeed, Bormana," she said gently. "Veleda." Her dark eyes searched the girl's face. "Why did you have to free the cat?"

Veleda struggled to find the words. Haltingly, she described the cat and the way he had willingly surrendered himself to the trap. She told of how he had stared at her, of the increasingly powerful conviction she had felt that she must let him go. Finally, she described his bewildering refusal to leave when she did release him.

Ancamna listened intently as her foster-daughter spoke, her face impassive. She said nothing when Veleda had fallen silent, but stood like a tall, white-garbed statue, leaning on her staff, her eyes thoughtful. Just beyond the two women and the girl, people continued to gather, crowding in amongst the huge oak trees, adding their own patterns to the circles in the intricately landscaped spiral design as they assembled. The empty wicker cage and the fact that the officiating Druid was deep in conversation with Veleda escaped no person's notice, but at the same time, no one dared come near enough to overhear what was being said.

"Well?" Bormana prodded after several moments had passed, and her sister had still not spoken. "What does your sight tell you about this, Ancamna?"

The Druid turned her dark gaze on the tree that held the image of Anu in its depths. The light from the torches flickered over the abstractly depicted features of the Goddess, animating them so that it seemed as if she was speaking to her priestess.

"The cat was a gift from Anu," Ancamna said suddenly. "The Great Mother sent him to us for tonight's purpose, and it is not well, my foster-daughter, that you have refused to accept him."

Bormana went rigid, her hand convulsively clutching Veleda's. "I feared as much," she whispered. "Oh, Sister, how can we protect her from the Goddess's anger?"

"She must find the cat and bring him here. It should be easy enough to do, for he offered himself willingly to her before." Ancamna fixed her stern eyes on Veleda's. "Do you understand me, girl? You must not hesitate this time. I think the evil demon that brought this sickness to our tribe has tricked you into refusing Anu's gift so that tonight's ritual would be prevented. You must not let this happen. The burden is upon your shoulders to see that it does not.''

"But what if the cat does not come to her a second time?'' Bormana broke in. "What if the Goddess is so insulted that She takes back her gift?''

These were horrifying questions, and their implications even more so, but for the sake of her daughter, Bormana had to ask. She saw the stubborn set of Veleda's jaw, and her anxiety increased. Veleda was hardheaded, even among the Belgae, who were notorious for that quality. But to be hardheaded in the face of a Goddess, when a crisis was upon the land was dangerous, as well as foolhardy. If Anu did not react with displeasure, then their people certainly would.

Ancamna was also familiar with Veleda's expression. "Anu is our Mother,'' she said simply, her voice deep and gentle. "Always has She been patient with Her children, and She will be patient again. If,'' she added, and her tone changed as she stared at her foster-daughter, "Veleda does not insult her a second time.''

Veleda lowered her eyes. "I will do as you think best, Mother's Sister.''

"Will you?'' Her foster-mother's Druid-seeing gaze pierced the girl's outward show of obedience and saw into the rebellious doubts that lay underneath.

"Yes—'' Veleda closed her lips over the protest bubbling up inside her, bit back the words that tried to fight their way out. Her certainty that the cat's death would serve nothing, least of all the purpose of the ritual was still strong, but how could she explain that to Ancamna? And in any case, would not a Druid priestess know far more about such matters than an untried girl would? "I will do my best to find the cat and bring him back,'' she muttered, and glanced at her true mother's worried face. "Truly,'' she added, seeking to ease that troubled expression. "I will find him."

"You must." Ancamna's voice grew stern. "Remember your obligations, child. The Goddess has singled you out and laid a sacred task upon you. I see your doubtful thoughts, but you have mistaken mercy for duty. A daughter of the Belgae puts the welfare of her tribe above all else. Go now, and return quickly."

Veleda nodded and picked up the wicker container. She went back along the spiral path lit by the torches, through the growing crowds of people, her pace quickening so that she would not have to answer the questions aroused by the empty cage swinging at her side. But there was one whose attention she was not swift enough to escape.

"Veleda!" A tall, broad-boned girl was running after her. "Wait, it is I, Sattia!" She panted as she drew up to Veleda. "What has happened? I saw you speaking with your foster-mother. Where are you going?" She peered at the empty cage. "Maiden of Waters, where is the cat?"

She was a big girl, even among the six tribes of the Belgae, where few grew up to be small. In contrast to the light hair of her people, Sattia's hair was dark, cut straight across her forehead in a bang that flopped with every movement. She and Veleda had been soul-friends since the time they were weaned, and never had they held secrets from one another. Until now.

"I must go back out into the woods," Veleda said evasively. "I'll return soon." She kept walking as she spoke, hoping that Sattia would drop behind.

"But how can you leave now?" Sattia stubbornly kept pace with her. "What about the sacrifice?"

Veleda sighed. "If I don't go," she said, "there will not be a sacrifice."

She broke into a run, passing beyond the sacred ring of the *nemeton* and leaving her soul-friend behind to stare after her in confusion. She took care not to glance at the carved images of the Shining Ones as she passed through the sacred grove and into the vast unsilent night forest.

The crackle of flames and the voices and rustling of her people faded into the chirring music of the night. In the distance wolves howled, gathering together for the hunt, foxes barked in the thickets, and deer rustled through the trees heading away from the sound of those who would seek their flesh before the night was through. Close by an owl hooted, sending shivers up Veleda's spine; the cry of an owl was never a good omen. On a night such as this, it could not be worse.

The cat was waiting for her.

Her eyes had adjusted from the flare of torchlight to the deep shadows of the woods, allowing her to start searching for the long sleek shape and glowing orange eyes of the cat. Suddenly she heard a soft miaow. She stared in the direction of the sound, and at that moment, a shaft of moonlight slanted through the canopy of leaves as if sent by Anu Herself, revealing the black and white form beneath an immense grandmother of an alder tree. Ancamna had said he would not be difficult to find, and here he was! Perhaps the feeling that had so powerfully bade her let him go was indeed nothing more than the merciful impulse to save him from a painful death.

"If you are truly a gift from Anu, then come," she said. Kneeling, she opened the wicker cage and waited, her breath stilling in her throat.

The cat's eyes blazed like two small fires. He glided toward her, straight to the opening in the cage. Delicately, he raised a paw, and just as delicately, placed it within the cage. Veleda held her breath. Her hand hovered above the wicker bars, ready to drop the door the moment his body was fully inside. Suddenly—almost as if he were teasing her—the animal danced backward several paces and sat down, curling his tail neatly about his feet.

For an instant Veleda remained in place, hardly able to believe she had come so close to regaining her prey, only to lose him yet another time. From the small distance that separated them the cat regarded her; in the hazy moonlight she could have sworn he was smiling.

And thus, a strange little dance between the two of them began. Again and again the same scene repeated itself: the cat drawing tantalizingly close, Veleda holding herself still, trying to entice him inside the cage with sweet words, only to watch in frustration as he leaped away, drawing her ever deeper into the forest each time he did.

Nine times, Veleda thought, straightening up wearily after another failed attempt. A sacred number. Abruptly she froze, her eyes widening until her eyebrows climbed into her hair. A few paces away, the cat sat and watched her, but he was all that was familiar. The woods she had wandered in all her short life were gone. Trees still loomed all about her, but they were like no trees that grew in the territory of the Belgae. Veleda stared and stared as the truth bloomed slowly in her mind.

The cat had led her into the Otherworld.

2

COLORS DAZZLED VELEDA'S eyes, bathing the trees that rose all about her in brilliant shades that glimmered and changed from one hue to another even as she looked. The grass beneath her cowhide sandals was deep and soft, and glancing down, she saw that it was silver, a luminescent silver so rich it seemed as though the moon had come down from the sky to gild each blade.

The moon. She looked up and there it was, filling her vision, huge and silver and perfectly round, hanging low in a sky that was painted with rainbows, each one arching over the other, and so many of them that the sky itself seemed to be one endless rainbow.

A soft miaow recalled her attention to the one responsible for bringing her here. The faery cat had drawn closer, his flame-bright eyes fixed upon her face. Transfixed, she returned his gaze. He had changed, as different now as the woods, which had once been so familiar. A large cat before, he now appeared even larger.

He stood watching her, utterly still but for the very tip of his long black tail that twitched slowly back and forth. The sleek body was enfolded in a mist that seemed to rise from the silver grass, or perhaps it was the moon flowing down to paint him in hues of silver and black. Regardless, he was truly a magical creature now, just as she had suspected from the first.

She could scarcely return that alien and powerful gaze.

An awareness looked out at her from those orange eyes, a knowledge both human and animal and so far beyond both that there was no reckoning with it.

Locked in that gaze, Veleda hugged her arms across her chest in a vain attempt to stop shivering.

"What have you done to me?" Her voice quaked. "I know I meant you harm, but it was needful. And why did you have to do this! With all your power, you could have just escaped!"

The cat said nothing.

Veleda folded her arms tighter. "I am dead, aren't I?" she demanded, terror making her angry, and anger strengthening her terror.

The cat merely looked at her.

In truth, she must surely be gone from the world of the living, and Veleda now fell silent, afraid and angry still, but shamed more than either by her reaction to this fate.

Always, from the time she was old enough to grasp such things, she had been taught that death was nothing to fear. The borders beyond the worlds were thin and easily breached. The domain of those who had passed from flesh-and-blood life was beautiful beyond any dream for those who had conducted their lives with honor. It was a belief that went to the core of not only the Belgae, but every one of the innumerable tribes that made up the proud fierce people known as the Keltoi, or "the hidden people."

Beyond counting were the nights in the clan long-house when Veleda had listened to her foster-mother speak warmly of the Otherworld, as if it were a beautiful grove waiting just over the next hill. Many were the occasions when she had heard someone cheerfully assuring a friend not to worry about an owed debt, that it could easily be repaid when they both met in the Otherworld.

So, in knowing all of this, why was she standing among these jeweled trees, bathed in the glow of silver, and awash in grief and anger and fear?

Because I don't want to be dead! I'm not yet ready!

The words cried themselves out in her mind, and dropping her head, Veleda acknowledged their truth. For she was yet young. Only fourteen winters had she spent in the land of the living, and though it was commonplace for many of that age and even younger to die, Veleda had always been strong and healthy, confident, as all the young and strong are, that death might come for others but not for them.

But it had come, brought to her by this cat who was far more than a cat, and who had surely had this fate in mind for her all along. Worse, still, she had died having failed in the task laid so carefully upon her by Ancamna. Now the ritual could not be held, or—even if another cat was found this night—it would lack the power the faery cat would have given it. So many had died already of the sickness, and now more would die. And all because a foolish girl had given in to pity and released the sacrifice which could have saved them.

The cat was still looking at her, the white patch on his chest glimmering like frost under the moon. Veleda could have sworn there was sympathy in that enigmatic glowing gaze. She watched dully as he glided a few paces off, then paused, tail held high, staring back at her.

His paws were touching a path. She had not noticed it before, but now, even without the cat, the trail was unmistakable. Shimmering and dark against the paler silver of the grass, it wound away through the trees, beckoning to her. The cat's tail twitched impatiently, and opening his jaws wide, he yowled, his fangs catching the sheen of light rising from the ground and pouring from the sky.

The cry took Veleda aback. She had almost expected him to speak, but his meaning was clear nonetheless. She followed the cat as he set off down the narrow road of the Otherworld. Responsible though he was for her being here, the idea of not following was unthinkable. He was all that remained that was somewhat familiar. If she railed at him and he left her behind, she would be alone, a possibility too awful to contemplate.

Girl and cat walked silently, Veleda's feet treading along the beaten silvery-dark earth as though they had come this way countless times before. But she did not notice, too caught up in what had befallen her to pay heed to this strange familiarity.

Her throat felt bruised, as if she had been choked. Images of those she loved formed in her mind: her true mother's face bearing that familiar look of pride and exasperation as she scolded her headstrong eldest child; her father, jovial and brooding by turns when he sat with her by the hearth fire, telling stories of the bloody raids and counter-raids for cattle he had taken part in; the proud way Ancamna held herself on her tall stick, her voice low and compelling as she talked of the world's mysteries to her foster-daughter. And there were so many others: friends, cousins, aunts and uncles, especially her four younger brothers, who had the irritating habit of following her about in dogged devotion.

The path entered a stand of trees thicker than any Veleda had ever seen. Their wide trunks closed in about her, their multihued crowns obscuring the night sky. Yet even in the depths of this unworldly forest, the light from the giant moon and that rainbow sky penetrated. But it was not just the light that gave the trees their colors, she realized; the colors came from the trees themselves, and the light only intensified their brilliance. On she walked, through these jeweled woods unlike any that could ever exist on earth, her eyes darting about but always returning to the faery cat, keeping him in sight as devotedly as her brothers had once trailed after her in the life that was now gone.

What would happen to them now? Would the sickness take them, as it was taking so many of the very young and the very old?

The trees thinned, and the path narrowed and began to climb. They were among a series of low hills clothed in flowers of silver and gold. The faery cat grew playful as he led Veleda through these flowers, capering as if he were a kitten, stalking and pouncing so that silver-gold dust sprayed about him in glittering clouds. Flower petals kissed Veleda's feet and ankles, leaving trails of gilded pollen. Their fragrance was unlike anything she had ever smelled.

If the moon and sun had a scent, she thought, surely it would be like this. The aroma teased at her, tempting her to linger, to lie down and snuggle deep into a bed of flowers while she gazed up at the moon and the shimmering sky.

But the cat was moving on, drifting over the flowers like a wraith of smoke, and she hurried to keep him in sight.

She glanced out over the hills, at a landscape carved from magic and, for the first time, wondered why she had seen no creature other than herself and the cat. She knew so many who had crossed into this domain before her: grandparents, uncles killed in skirmishes resulting from cattle raids, two brothers and a sister who had all died before the age of five, and of course the many who had died more recently in the plague. But none of these friends and kin had come forth to greet her, to welcome her to the Otherworld.

Veleda's heart clenched with shame as she realized why. Of all things, a person must care for the welfare of her people and act honorably in all matters. In failing to bring back the faery cat, Veleda had done neither.

"That is why they are staying away," she muttered, not sure if she was talking to herself or the cat, who had halted at the sound of her voice. "For not only did I fail our people, but I am afraid on top of everything else, when everyone knows that death is nothing to fear."

You have not failed your people, Daughter. And there is no shame in fear, but only courage, for one who has the strength to face her fear and continue on in spite of it.

The deep female voice tolled through the core of Veleda's being. Her muscles froze, awe filling every vein, her eyes unconsciously searching for the source of those ringing tones. The words had held music within them, beating in her heart like the drums of Beltain, imbuing her with the same sense of peace and reverence she felt when Ancamna and the other Druids sang chants to Anu in the sacred groves.

The faery cat had stopped his capering. He stood alertly, ears pricked, his whiskers twitching, as if he, too, had heard the voice. His sharp feline gaze drilled through her for a moment, then he started forward again. Instead of hurrying after him as she had done, Veleda hesitated. Staring ahead of him she saw that the path led to a mountain. The massive peak loomed up against the rainbow sky; the winding path glittering against steep slopes as it twisted its way up to the crest.

The sight of the mountain, vast and foreign, held her. It aroused the same awe and reverence as the mysterious voice had, but also a surge of terror that stampeded through her souls, pounding in her mind as blindly as a team of runaway chariot ponies.

Nothing was as it seemed in the Otherworld; this journey with its distant destination was no exception. In the realms of magic, climbing up to those heights was far more than a walk up to the top of a mountain. To follow where that path led would set events in motion—Veleda knew this as she had never known anything before—and the consequences of what those events might be paralyzed her.

Had she not done enough harm as it was? What if there was evil here? Her people were dying as it was; she could not bear the thought of any new action of hers contributing to what they were suffering already.

Mysteries lay atop that peak, and answers. Portents hovered about the rocky slopes and that pinnacle gilded in brilliant hues by moon and sky. The fear Veleda had felt before was as nothing to what she felt now, and even the cat's impatient cry could not move her.

Come ahead, Daughter. For I am waiting.

The voice reached out, enfolding the girl in warmth as real as an embrace. A deep rumbling touched Veleda's ears. It took a moment for her to realize what it was: the faery cat had come very close and was purring.

Veleda let out a long shaky breath. "Very well," she said, speaking to him as well as the mystical voice. "Let us go, then. After all, I've come this far; I may as well go the rest of the way." She took a quick and bleak pride in the fact that her voice was not quaking as much as it had before.

They went ahead quickly. The faery cat seemed eager to reach their destination, flowing over the rocks and difficult places in the trail as the ascent grew steeper and rougher. But to her surprise, Veleda easily kept pace with him. Her strides were long and effortless, her legs carrying her with a speed beyond that of the physical world. Wonderingly she became aware that her fear had left her; she was drawn forward now by a longing she could not name, inexplicable, but as strong as her earlier fear had been.

Then she saw it. The mountain's steep crags gave way to a broad plateau, and upon this flat plain a building of pink stone gleamed under the enormous hovering moon. It blazed like a jewel as Veleda gazed at it in the silvery light. This was a sacred place. There was no other way to describe the graceful structure with its soaring columns and the air of sanctity that reached out even from the path, stretching out with invisible arms to draw her in.

Veleda's people worshipped beneath the open sky, in holy groves of ancient oak or in great roofless enclosures built by human hands. Temples, however, were not unknown among the tribes.

The Keltoi possessed wealth beyond measure in their rich lands, and they thrived on trade. Anu had gifted Her children with cattle, timber, precious metals, fur, and above all, gold and silver. Over uncounted generations, the tribes had built an extensive trading network with merchants in distant lands, men willing to brave the long and dangerous water routes in order to make their own fortunes by acquiring those riches. For the tribes who made up the Belgae—some of whose territories lay near the sea—there were always interesting things to be learned about life in these far-off places.

Veleda had often heard traders speak of "temples," holy edifices built as dwelling places for the gods and Goddesses they worshipped. It was a strange idea, this practice of confining ones' deities to a house of stone, but in watching the reverence that shone on the traders' faces when they talked of the temples, she knew it did not seem strange to them at all. And the places they described sounded beautiful, constructed of the most magnificent materials possible so that the god or Goddess who lived there would be pleased.

Surely, this soaring structure of luminous pink stone was a temple. And that could only mean one thing: that the Shining Ones were not the only deities present in the Otherworld. Whatever presence was calling to her from this lonely peak was not one of the familiar Goddesses of her tribe.

The thought of being summoned by a foreign Goddess almost made Veleda stop again. But she was being borne ahead on that tide of inexplicable longing, and even the thought of facing an unknown deity was not enough to halt her.

They passed through another grove of rainbow-colored trees. The brilliance of the building's pink stones grew brighter and brighter as Veleda approached. The luster was so blinding that she had to glance away, and so it was her feet, rather than her eyes, that guided her after the cat. They arrived at an outer courtyard, paved with large flat stones of a deep silvery gray. A miaow stroked her ears as gently as the pawing of kittens; the tickle of fur brushed against her legs, and looking down, she caught her breath.

Cats were everywhere. She had been so entranced by the pink edifice she had not noticed them; now she wondered how she could have missed their presence. Cats of every color and description gathered about her, a wave of fur. Some were black as night, others white as snow; there were brown tabbies, silver tabbies, and orange, blacks with white faces and paws, or whites spotted with gray or black or brown; there were calicos and tortoise-shells, and the deep ancient brown an Egyptian trader had once told her was the oldest cat color of all.

Eyes stared up at Veleda, catching the light in shades of green and gold and blue. She tried to count, but quickly gave up. There were so many they seemed to have no end. They perched all along the low walls that enclosed the courtyard, crowded the gray flagstones, rubbed themselves against her, or sat and watched the human visitor with the clear enigmatic gaze that was the hallmark of all felines.

Suddenly the cats drew apart. The tapestry of multihued fur shifted and patterned itself, the bodies at last forming a pathway. At the end of it stood the faery cat.

In this dense crowd of waving tails and gleaming eyes, he still retained an air that set him apart from all the others. And now he was even more different than he had been. His coat was no longer black with a splash of white on the chest, but brown, a deep glowing hue that burned somewhere between silver and gold under the enormous moon's light. Had it not been for his eyes—large and slanted and gleaming as golden-orange as the flowers on the hills over which he had led her—she would not have known it was he.

Once she would have been frightened by this change in him, but too much had already happened for her to react. She watched the shimmer of the silver stripes encircling his tail as he held that tail up and advanced toward the girl he had brought so far. When he had reached the human, he did not rub against her as his companions had, but stood as though waiting.

Intuitively Veleda understood. Silently, she and the animal entered the temple.

The halls were empty and wide, echoing to the sound of Veleda's feet. Torches flickered against the pink walls, casting long shadows that mingled the shapes of girl and cat into one restless being. The air was very still, but the odor of incense was sweet and heavy, wafting through the halls despite the lack of any breeze.

Soundlessly the faery cat led Veleda on. She saw that they were coming to what appeared to be an inner sanctuary. Doors inlaid in gold and silver and set with glittering gemstones stood open. Through the doorway Veleda saw an enormous throne, a magnificent chair of gold. She and her guide entered, and as they drew nearer to the throne, she saw unfamiliar symbols carved into its base.

The low murmur of words rippled through the quiet air, floating about her like voices drifting in the wind.

> *Hail to thee, Lady of Silver Magic, Lady of Spells*
> *Protect us now and always*
> *Direct our feet on the true path.*

And threading through that soft unseen chorus came a sound older than time: the rhythmic tinkle of bells and the gentle strains of a stringed instrument.

Veleda stopped in her tracks. Something in the tuneless music, in the low measured chant, called out to her, held her entranced, while she listened. Slowly, compelled by the longing that had enfolded her from the moment she first heard the mysterious voice, she looked up.

There before her, seated on the glittering throne, was a figure bathed in clouds of shimmering silver light. At first, Veleda thought she was looking at a great cat, then at a woman, its outlines wavered so. Finally, the figure solidified into a combination of both.

The sight of her filled Veleda's eyes. The giant body was that of a woman, sleek and elegant and powerful, draped in a tight-fitting garment of gossamer linen that bathed Her in a glow of silver and gold. Radiant, She sat in a shimmer of light. Her head was not that of a woman, but of a cat, yet the expression on that face and in those huge golden eyes was neither human nor feline. It was something so far beyond both, so deep and all-seeing that Veleda had to turn her own eyes away, unable to meet that gaze.

Goddess, the girl thought, the word filling her mind with an absolute certainty. Just as this building could be called nothing other than a temple, so could this awesome figure be identified only as what She was.

Yes, I am Bast, She Who Protects the Two Lands, lands which are unknown to you, My Daughter. In Me glow the living force and the gentle warmth of sunlight. My power is that of the moon: light and dark, waxing and waning but ever-present, source of wisdom, giver of dreams and visions. For I am She: Silver Shining, Mother of Life. All that lives is sacred to Me. Those who seek Me with true hearts will find joy, protection against evil, and happiness in all their days. I bid you welcome, child.

The words rang in Veleda's head. The deep rich voice was the same one that had drawn her to this place, and, wrapped within a holding spell, she listened to it with each of her souls, hearing the words with something other than her ears.

The question came to her lips naturally, springing out before she was quite aware that she was asking it. Yet there was no doubt that here in this sanctified place, before this shining being, she would receive an answer to her question.

"Am I am truly dead, then, Lady?" she whispered.

3

HER VOICE SOUNDED UNNAT-
urally loud above the soft music.
The chanting had stopped, although
she could still hear the gentle strains
of the bells and the harp.

A glimmer of amusement rippled
through her mind. *Far from it,
child. Life is still strong within you
and will be for some time. For you have tasks to fulfill.*

"Then I am dreaming."

Yes, of course, Veleda told herself. Should she feel relieved or concerned that she was still alive? Yet if a Goddess said it were so, then it was. And, since she was not
dead, that would explain this unworldly place, as well as
her own unquestioning acceptance of all she had seen.

The glimmering amusement fragmented into laughter.
*Dreams are many things, child, and they can be seen in
many different ways. But there are worlds upon worlds, and
asleep or awake, they exist beyond that which you experience with your mortal senses.*

In her mind, Veleda nodded agreement; the Goddess may
be alien, but the words She spoke could not be more familiar if Ancamna herself had said them to her. The inner
voice seemed to chime throughout her entire mind and soul,
lulling her as if she were listening to a healing chant.

The Goddess raised a luminous hand to the cat, who had
settled himself at Her feet and was absorbed in grooming
the back of his head with a busy paw.

You have helped one of My children and in so doing,

23

*you have shown your heart to be true and wise, faithful to
the older wisdoms rather than the new. I am old, too,
Daughter; old beyond knowing, ancient beyond the memory
of mortals. All animals are sacred to Me and have been so
always, but the most sacred to Me of all are those who
belong to the nation of cats. There is no power, no magic,
to be gained, in tormenting and murdering one of my beloved ones as your elders wished to do. Indeed, in the lands
from which I come, the most severe penalties mortals can
inflict would punish any who tried.*

The faery cat had progressed to washing his face, but at
this, he lowered his paw, drew whiskers back from gleaming fangs, and let out a hiss that plainly indicated his opinion of such practices.

Veleda found her voice again. "What lands are those,
Lady?" she asked timidly.

A deeper sort of glow infused those all-seeing eyes. *Kemet, My Daughter, is the name of My country, although
you know it by the Greek word, Egypt. But Kemet is the
true name. It means "Black Land," and that is as it should
be, for the River of Life, She Who Is Mother Nile, gives
Kemet its name. Each year the river's holy water stands
and fails not, carrying the high flood, which leaves black
soil in its wake. The gift of life is in that black earth, for
it holds fertility in its darkness. Rich are the grains Mother
Nile gives birth to; long and sweet are the days; the soft
warm nights have the months come aright. That is life in
Kemet, and has been for long and long.*

Bast's words sent pictures parading before Veleda's inner eye; hot and colorful and utterly unlike anything she
had ever seen. A golden land appeared before her, blazing
under an anvil of sun that burned with a heat more fierce
than any sunlight she had ever experienced. She saw a great
river that surged like a very current of life across the boundaries of space and time. She felt in her own pores the unfamiliar heat and grit of sand, felt her skin cooled by the
delicate touch of night breezes. She sensed the rightness of

an ancient land flowing through season after season as it had since the beginnings of time.

"Your land is beautiful, Lady," she said in wonder. "But why have you left it?"

Once again there was that glimmer of amusement. *Is that not obvious, child? Why to seek you out, of course.*

Veleda's throat closed. The faery cat was watching her, his eyes slitted, a purr rumbling steadily in his chest.

You have proven yourself worthy, the Goddess said. *And now, I offer you help in return. The plague attacking your people is the doing of My Sister, She Who is called Sekhmet.*

"Sek—" Veleda stumbled over the unfamiliar word.

She is a Goddess of death and destruction. Her very breath brings disease in its wake. So has it always been, even in the greatest days of the Black Land. And now, She has breathed upon your land.

"Lady, I do not understand." Veleda was genuinely puzzled. "If She is a Goddess of Egypt, why would She come here?"

The long green eyes with their wealth of wisdom looked into those of the human woman. There was such sadness in their depths that Veleda had to glance away.

A new time is sweeping down upon us, Bast said at last. *The old ways are giving way before it, and there is great confusion amongst We Ancient Ones, We who have been worshipped since the earliest days of humankind. The world is not the same. The mortal folk who once revered Us are turning away from Our sacred shrines, and My Sister is angry because of it.*

"But what has this to do with the Belgae?" At her question Veleda imagined that the faery cat's expression changed, that he was regarding her with disapproval, but she understood his censure no better than she understood anything else.

Why should she care about what happened in far-off places? The Belgae were the center of the world; nothing

else mattered except in how it pertained to them. Not even
the welfare of other Keltoi tribes was of consequence, unless it was a tribe with whom the Belgae had an alliance,
and even then, whatever befell them was viewed only in
relation to the significance it held for the continued well-
being of the Belgae.

Yes, that is so. Bast's clear voice cut through Veleda's
thoughts as though She had seen directly into the girl's
mind. *In such a way do your people look at the world, and
they are not unique. It has ever been the practice of mortals
to see no further than their own borders, to care only about
what happens to their own kin and country.*

Her crystalline gaze grew more piercing. *Once it would
not have mattered, to be so insular, so unconcerned with
the fate of others. But a new power has arisen, and the
world is becoming a smaller place because of it. That
power is hungry; soon it will turn its appetite to the lands
of your people, and neither the Belgae nor any other tribe
in your realms can afford to continue as they have. Anu
and the other Goddesses of the Keltoi know this. As do I.
Now you must learn it too.*

Veleda stared up at that shimmering presence. Confusion
roiled through her, billowing up in a cloud that obscured
all attempts at comprehension. She had no idea what this
foreign Goddess meant, and hearing her invoke the name
of Great Mother Anu only added to the disorder of her
thoughts.

Oh, why was Ancamna not here instead of her! Ancamna
or some other great Druid who could understand and interpret the Goddess's words. She was too young, too inexperienced to be standing before this Shining One. If this
was all a dream then she was more than ready to wake.
Whatever Bast wanted, how could the Goddess possibly
think that Veleda could provide it?

*You can, My daughter. In time. My Sisters and I have
need of you. On your shoulders will We place a great and
terrible burden: the future.*

For the first time since the faery cat had led her into Bast's presence, fear touched Veleda with cold dank hands. She knew a response was required. But to answer was the last thing she wanted to do. If she did, she would be accepting the great and terrible burden the Goddess was speaking of. The muscles in her legs twitched as if urging her to flee; but she stood where she was. Enigmatic as Bast's words were, she had not only hinted at a threat to the Belgae, but had offered to cure the sickness ravaging the tribes. Veleda could not ignore these things for the sake of safety, no matter how much she might wish to.

She swallowed, tried to speak, and swallowed again. "You are a Goddess," she whispered at last. "How can you have need of one such as I?" The question came out weakly, and her voice sounded as dusty as the sands of the golden land Bast had shown her. But at least she had spoken, rather than running away like a craven coward.

From the height of Her throne, Bast gazed down at her. Veleda felt a sweeping warmth, an affinity and acceptance so far beyond any emotion she had ever experienced that the very definition of love seemed a poor thin word. The faery cat had not taken his orange-fire eyes from her. She fancied now that he was smiling at her.

Yes, you will do, Bast said, and the Goddess's voice rumbled throughout the sanctuary, as if a giant purring cat were speaking. She tilted Her shining head to the faery cat. *Mau, you have chosen well.*

Sister!

Veleda clapped her hands to her ears. The angry shout, and the new voice that had uttered it, reverberated in her mind. The force of both word and voice made her stagger. She felt a blast of heat that seared her like living flame. Her flesh burned as though it was about to blister, but there was coldness behind the burning, a chill as dark and irrevocable as the true death.

Unaware of her actions, she turned to the source of that savage cry. A red-tinged darkness was swirling into the sanctuary. At first, all she saw was an ominous cloud, but it rapidly coalesced, coiling and turning in upon itself until it became something else.

The shape of a human female formed out of that twisting blackness, then the cloud parted, revealing the figure itself.

She was enormous, as tall as Bast would be if She rose from Her throne. A red linen garment clung to Her limbs, although it was not Her body that held Veleda frozen, but Her face. This Goddess, too, possessed a feline head, but there was no resemblance between the benevolence and wisdom in Bast's countenance and the expression on this intruder's face. Lions did not inhabit Keltoi lands, but Veleda had seen depictions of the great cats on pottery brought by traders, and she recognized the lioness head that rose from the figure's powerful shoulders.

Opening those fearsome jaws, the creature snarled at the Cat-Goddess. The faery cat snarled back, crouching as if he were about to spring at the newcomer in spite of the difference in their sizes. But Bast remained seated on Her golden throne, watching the other Goddess calmly.

The intruder snarled again, and then turned Her pale yellow gaze to Veleda. Her long fangs gleamed in the light. Veleda's heart slammed in her chest as she met that stare. There was nothing impersonal about the way this being was glaring at her. Malevolent purpose stamped every line of that unearthly body. But what could she possibly have done to arouse this new Goddess's wrath against her?

Have no fear, child. Bast's gentle strong voice was as serene as Her posture upon the throne. *She cannot harm you. Not here.*

The Lion-Goddess snapped Her jaws together and let out a harsh crack of laughter. *You have the truth of that, Sister. But once she leaves Your protection, I will have My will. Do not doubt it! Do you know who I am, girl?* She demanded of Veleda.

Veleda was motionless, unable to move the constricted

muscles of her throat, any more than she could move her body.

I am Sekhmet the Destroyer. Slayer of Men. Uncounted are the ages mortals have feared and respected My power. Mighty temples have been raised to Me, great festivals held in My honor. Priests serve Me faithfully, spending the length of their days seeking the ways in which I might be propitiated. For I am the bringer of plague and disease. Every year when the Nile is low, My breath scorches the Black Land in the Harvest Season, and thousands die.

She thrust out Her hand. In that giant fist a bunch of arrows were clutched. Her voice slashed at Veleda. *Look upon the Seven Arrows of Sekhmet, mortal. They represent the strength of My will. Through them I send evil fortune, and no one may escape. No one!*

Lower your weapons!

The voice of Bast was no longer gentle. Her command hurled through the sanctuary and with an involuntary jerk, Sekhmet's hand instantly obeyed. It was obvious, even to Veleda, that She did not wish to, but She had no choice.

Bast rose from Her throne, towering in Her anger. The other Goddess took several steps back, retreating as the cat-deity's fierceness pursued Her. *This is My holy place. How dare You profane it with Your threats and Your violence. In these realms, Your dark force has no power to harm mortals, and well You know it.*

For a quivering instant, Sekhmet glared at Her Sister. The gazes of the two Goddesses clashed: the deep green eyes of Bast and the pale yellow ones of Sekhmet. Abruptly, the lioness head turned back to Veleda.

What is your name, girl? There was a silkiness in the growling voice that had not been present before, as if a giant cat were rubbing against Veleda, urging her to draw nearer to the source of that voice. The muscles of the girl's throat moved in an impulsive eagerness to provide the answer. *What are you called?* the silky voice persisted.

Something rose up in Veleda then, halting the speaking of her name, stifling it far down in her throat. Sweat broke out on her forehead, but she clamped her lips shut and did not reply.

You see? Triumph rang in Bast's melodic voice. *Untaught and unawakened though she is, she still has power. Bending her to Your will is not so easy as You think.*

Sekhmet's frightening gaze went from the girl to the Goddess's Sister. *Here in Your temple, perhaps. But She must leave this place, and when She does, She will return to the world of mortals. Then We shall see.*

Her fiery eyes fixed on those of Veleda. *Yes, We shall see,* She repeated. The words were more of a hiss than true spoken words, and they sizzled through the girl's mind.

The blackness swirled up again, obscuring the Goddess's tall figure. When it cleared, She was gone.

Veleda shivered in the sudden release of tension. Her muscles slowly loosened as the peace of the sanctuary restored itself. She looked up to meet Bast's powerful, gentle gaze through the shimmering light. The great cat face was utterly alien, and yet Veleda felt recognition, a sense of familiarity, deep in her bones, that jarred her.

"Who was She?" Her throat felt as if she had swallowed an entire country of sand again, and she felt the fear return.

She Whom you must be protected from and against Whom you must learn to protect yourself. The green eyes with their wealth of love and wisdom were sad as they looked into those of the girl. *It is a great deal to ask of one so young and so mortal, so unawakened to her gifts. But the fates have left no other way. The burden lies upon you.*

"I don't understand."

All will be explained by the one who came to you.

Veleda frowned. "The faery cat?"

He is one of Mine. But for now, his place will be in the world of mortals, not these Realms. And as for you, My daughter, the time for you to leave My domain draws nigh.

"But Lady, there is so much I don't know. You have to tell me—"

The questions filled Veleda's mind, but Bast forestalled them. *Sekhmet spoke true about one thing, child. You must depart from this place. With Mau to guide and protect you, you may return safely to the mortal world. Take these with you.*

She made a gesture. The glimmering light parted, revealing a long sleek arm, gleaming with muscle and magic. Two long thin rods appeared in Her hand. Even as Veleda's eyes saw them, they disappeared. Suddenly she felt the weight of something in her own hand. Looking down she saw that she was now holding the rods. They were very light, carved from ivory and elaborately decorated with images of unfamiliar animals and creatures that were clearly magical.

She stared at them. The two long wands were made from glazed steatite, in several sections that fit together. The sides were decorated with brightly painted eyes that returned her stare as if they could truly see her. They were joined by equally bright depictions of a lion, a panther, a cat, and several fantastic looking animals she could not recognize. Silver pegs to the topside of each rod fixed small figurines of turtles and long-legged birds that looked to her like some sort of crane. A turtle was fastened to each of the bottom ends. Various other signs and symbols were prominent on both rods.

They are yours, Bast said. *The symbols contain great magic, and, as with all magic, that power can be turned either to good or to ill. However, with the skills you will learn from Mau and with the true heart which you already possess, their aggressive force can be turned into the magic of protection. Mau will show you certain herbs; they, along with these rods, will heal your people of the sickness. But, after you have done that, you must guard them well, for you will have need of them.*

Veleda looked up at that vast feline face with its unfathomable wisdom. The rods were warm in her hands, throbbing as though they possessed a life of their own. She clutched them tighter, her bones and flesh understanding instinctively the profound feeling of magic. "Why will I need them, Lady Bast?" she asked.

The long slanted eyes regarded her gravely. *To protect yourself. And that is their most important task of all. Now you must leave.*

Leave? Veleda's whole being protested the idea. "But there is more I must know!" she protested. "Lady, why does She wish me harm—"

There is no time. The Goddess spoke as if She had not heard. *Mortals may not bide in these Realms for long. Already, you have gone beyond what is safe. Mau will help you to understand the tasks I have set upon you. Farewell, My daughter. My blessings go with you.*

A gentle mist tinted with silver came out of nowhere and encircled Veleda. A great sense of peace wrapped itself about her like the softest of furs, banishing all the questions and fears. Her eyes closed, she lost track of either sensation or thought. When her eyes opened, she was outside, in the familiar moonlit darkness of deep woods. In her hands the rods were still clutched, warm and throbbing to her touch.

She was staring at them dazedly, when a dry precise voice said, "Well, we have herbs to gather, human girl. Unless you would rather stand here lost in your fancies, while your people sicken and die."

Veleda's head jerked around. The faery cat was standing next to her. It was he who had spoken.

4

VELEDA'S THOUGHTS WERE whirling. Her body felt as insubstantial as the mist that Bast had called to bring her home. The face of the Cat-headed Goddess still filled the inner landscape of her mind, bathing her in the glory of the Goddess's presence. She was sanctified and dazed, ecstatic and bewildered, and now a cat was addressing her as clearly as if he were human. She blurted out the first words that came to her mind. "You can speak."

The faery cat had regained his jet-black color and his long dark tail jerked with impatience. "By my Lady's sistrum, of course I can. Though not to just anyone. Humans, by and large, are not worthy of the effort. And you babble in so many different tongues it makes my ears hurt just to remember them all. Among my kind, conversations are simple and so much more elegant. It doesn't matter where in this great world an animal comes from, we all speak the same language."

As he spoke, the cat enunciated the words of the Belgae tongue with careful correctness. His voice was light and concise, with a musical lilt to it. Certainly Veleda had never thought about how a cat would sound if one could talk, yet this creature somehow sounded just the way she would have expected a cat who talked to sound.

"The herbs," she said suddenly. "You will show me?" The mysteries of the Otherworld—one of which was this cat—had not yet loosened their grip. They still surrounded her but the solidity of her own world was now intruding, equally as strong, and with that awareness, the weight of her people's plight descended as well. "We must hurry."

"That," the cat said with exaggerated patience, "is why I am here." He padded soundlessly off among the dark massive shapes of the trees. "You may call me Mau," he added over his shoulder. "And keep a good hold on those wands. You are far from ready to encounter Sekhmet or any of Her minions."

Veleda shuddered at the mention of the other Goddess. Her mind had sought to protect her by walling away the terror of her encounter with that lion-headed deity. But this talking cat—deliberately it seemed—had brought all the malevolence of that brief ordeal back to haunt her.

"Who was She?" It was the same question she had asked of Bast in the Goddess's sanctuary; perhaps Mau would provide a more satisfactory answer than the Cat-headed Goddess had.

"She is Bast's Sister," Mau said. "Though sisterhood is the only thing They bear in common. Lady Bast is a Goddess of light. Sekhmet is a Goddess of darkness, and She takes joy in that darkness. Blood and death are like food and wine to Her. She cannot thrive without either."

He paused, his orange eyes resting knowingly upon her face. "But what you really wish to know is the reason She was so filled with hatred toward you. Is that not so?"

Veleda found it difficult to meet his gaze. There was magic in those glowing depths, an echo of the deep all-seeing wisdom she had seen in the green eyes of Bast. "Why would Ba-Bast"—the Goddess's foreign name rolled awkwardly off Veleda's tongue—"not tell me? She spoke only in riddles."

The cat made an odd little chirring noise, a blending of a miaow and a purr. To Veleda it sounded suspiciously like a laugh. "You know very little about cats, don't you? To speak in riddles is our nature. Why give a straight answer to a question, when a curved one is so much more interesting? And as for Lady Bast, She is the Mother of all cats, and a Goddess besides. You can hardly expect Her to tell you everything at once. That is why She sent me back with you."

"But you're a cat." Veleda did not attempt to keep the irritation from her tone. Magical this strange animal may be, but after all that she had experienced she was ill minded to play guessing games, even with a talking cat. "Does that mean you will answer me in riddles as well?"

He made that chirring noise again. "If it suits me."

A small creature—a mouse or a chipmunk—darted across the forest track in a blur of frantic movement. Mau leaped after it, even though the tiny animal had already escaped into the deep undergrowth. He appeared some distance further up the path and called out, "Come along, human girl. I know how slow you are with your two legs, but it's you who wanted to hurry, remember?"

Veleda ran after him, her annoyance increasing as fast as her pace. This being who called himself Mau was as frustrating now as he had been when she had thought he was only a cat. Considering that she had saved his life, she thought angrily, he could show a little more gratitude.

"Se-Sekhmet said that She is worshipped and feared by Her own folk in Egypt," she snapped when she had caught up to Mau. "By the sacred fires of Beltain, why would She want to come to these lands making trouble for my tribe, causing us to sicken and die? It makes no sense."

If a cat could shrug, Mau surely did so then. "We all take what we have for granted. Even a Goddess. It is when the things which we take for granted are gone that we come to realize how important those things were. The people here are no different, only in your case, it's freedom that you take for granted. In their way, the tribes of this vast land of yours are as arrogant as Sekhmet."

Veleda stiffened. "Freedom is the same as honor to the tribes of the Belgae," she said indignantly. "And we take neither one for granted."

Mau stretched his jaws in a yawn that showed all of his pink tongue. "Well, human girl," he said unconcernedly. "Both your people's freedom and their honor will disappear as quickly as river mist in summer if you don't heed Bast's warning about the Romans."

Veleda stared at him. "Romans? Your Goddess gave me no warning about the Romans."

Mau spread his front legs and vigorously groomed his belly fur. "Yes," he said between licks. "She did. That is one of your first lessons: to pay better attention. And here is another." He straightened up, wrapping his long tail about his paws in a graceful curve. "The herbs."

Veleda peered down. The night was far advanced and the light from the moon was waning. The forest was a blur of shadows and undergrowth. Whatever herbs he was referring to, she certainly could not see them.

"I do not have cat eyes," she said testily. "Just what am I supposed to be paying attention to?"

Mau sighed. "Great Mother protect me from the ignorance of mortals," he muttered. "Very well, look closely." He arose, glided past Veleda, and nosed at a clump of shrubs. "These have been used by the people of Kemet to heal Sekhmet's plague for uncounted ages. Your Druids would not know this, of course, for such a sickness has never been seen in this land. Get out your knife and cut off as many of the stems as you can, then start picking the berries. I will tell you what to do with all of it when you're done."

Carefully Veleda laid the rods beside the cat. Pulling her knife from the belt at her waist, she did as he bade her. The clump of shrubs stood taller than a man and the older plants had sent out a large quantity of suckers to begin new clumps, so cutting off stems was a fairly easy task. The mature shrubs were covered in small berries of a fine red color, oblong and slightly curved, and as she began plucking them off the branches and piling them in a heap, Veleda let out an exclamation.

"I recognize this plant," she told Mau. "We call it barberry, and it causes wheat blight! The farmers say that any crop planted near bushes like these will rot in the fields."

Mau made a disgusted little noise in his throat. "That does not surprise me in the least. A people who believe that placing me in a wicker cage and slowly roasting me to death will cure a plague are certainly not the busiest bees in the hive when it comes to cleverness. But the juice I will teach you how to make from the stem bark and the berries of this bush will cure this foolish tribe of yours, human girl; you may believe that."

"All of them?" Veleda glanced over her shoulder at the lithe dark shape beside her, as she cut off yet another stem and added it to the pile she had already collected.

"Most of them. And those for whom this remedy comes too late will be healed by the magic in the wands Lady Bast gave you. I will teach you how to use those, as well."

Veleda continued to work under the cat's unblinking gaze. Her mind moved as quickly as her hands, her thoughts swirling with excitement. Could this unpopular shrub that farmers hastily cut out from the earth whenever they found it growing near their precious grain actually contain healing secrets that would save her people? Yes, she told herself. Mau had to be speaking the truth, for had not that enigmatic and glorious Goddess Herself sent him back to help her?

Mau stopped her when the heap of stems and berries stood as tall as her knees. "That is enough for now. Any more, and you'll have too big a load to carry back to the dwellings of your people."

Veleda saw that he was right. She set about the next task of fashioning a way to tote the ungainly pile along the dim narrow forest tracks. For the stems, she wove a net out of heavy vines yanked off of nearby tree trunks and slung the bag over her shoulders; for the berries, she fashioned a pouch from half a dozen broad oak leaves, painstakingly placed each of the berries within its folds, then nestled the pouch in her tunic, where it rested against her small young breasts.

She turned to Mau. "I'm ready."

As they made their way through the woods, Mau's words about the Romans came back to Veleda. She had so much else to think on that she wished she could forget what he had said. But she could not. Nothing a magical cat said concerning so important a people as the Romans could afford to be forgotten.

"What did you mean about the Romans, Mau?" she demanded. "What have they to do with any of this?"

"The true question," his light feline voice corrected her, "is what does Sekhmet have to do with the Romans."

The packet of leaf-wrapped berries tickled the sensitive skin between Veleda's breasts. She frowned. "But the Romans have their own gods, and She is a Goddess of Egypt."

"The Romans neither know nor care about Sekhmet. It is She who is drawn to them."

"I still do not understand."

Mau let out a soft hiss. "I do not wonder at that, human girl. It is a sad and difficult business. Kemet has long been under the foot of foreign rulers from Greece, you see, and the ancient gods and Goddesses—even my own Mistress, Lady Bast—no longer possess the power they once did. The hearts of the people are turning away from them and toward other gods."

Veleda shook her head. To hear that such a wondrous Goddess was being forgotten by her own people sent a pain through her heart. Yet, that was the way of the world. People conquered each other and the weaker generally took on the customs of the stronger. She did not want to say this to Mau, though, for fear he would become offended and lapse back into his maddening behavior of before. Since he had ceased his frustrating antics and was explaining things to her openly, she had to keep him talking this way.

He was already continuing, his voice containing the same

note she heard in her aunt's voice when Ancamna explained some matter of Druid knowledge. "Once Kemet was a land where the Mother in all Her incarnations was revered, and that includes Sekhmet, for She, too, is but another face of the Mother, and therefore sacred."

Mau made a growling noise deep in his throat. "But Greece and Rome are places of men. Everything in the Roman world is based on the power of the cock, and they are busy reshaping the rest of the world into that image."

Veleda was listening so intently that she stumbled over a root. Instantly her hands flew to the packet of herbs, making sure they were safely in place. "Yes," she said quickly. "I know the Romans worship war, but so do the Belgae, and so does every other tribe in the lands of the Keltoi."

"True enough. Yet the Mother has not lost Her place among your tribes. Look at your customs: women serve as Druids, the Goddess is revered above all other gods, and your men are wise enough to know that mortal women are sacred, more sacred than any man. They know that only women hold the gifts of magic within them, something the Romans have long forgotten, if indeed, they ever knew it in the first place."

"So," Veleda exclaimed in a burst of horrified understanding. "Sekhmet wants to come to our lands and have us worship Her?"

Mau hissed again. "Sekhmet does not care a whisker for your people, girl. No more than She cares whether the Mother is losing Her place in the world or not. She cares only about slaking Her thirst for blood and death. Kemet can no longer give Her that. Once, in the time of the Pharaohs, it could. The Black Land was powerful then. There were always wars to be fought and other peoples to be conquered. And when there weren't the wars, there were the plagues She brought. She feasted on the deaths She caused, and people would flood Her temples to worship and make sacrifices in hopes of saving themselves."

"Well, She will not get such worship here," Veleda told him in a low, fierce tone. "We Belgae do not reward foreign gods who come to do us harm."

Mau made that chirring noise she now recognized as a laugh. But his light voice held no humor in it. "Sekhmet does not want your people's worship, Veleda," he said, using her name for the first time. "She wants your blood."

Veleda's steps slowed, and she stared down at the cat beside her. It was odd, but though their acquaintance as two beings who could talk to each other was so brief, she was already coming to feel that she could read Mau's expressions, as if he were a person and not a cat. His expression now was somber.

"But the herbs . . ." She clutched the packet tighter against her chest, and her voice was no longer fierce but young again, and uncertain. "The Goddess said they would stop the dying. The sick will be cured . . ."

"They will," Mau agreed. "But that will not be the end of it. Why do you think I am telling you about the Romans? Sekhmet sent this plague only to amuse Herself, though of course, the joke lost its humor once She discovered that my Lady Bast favors you. Now She will try to do away with you, to see that you enter the Otherworld again, this time for good."

"Because your Goddess gave me the secret of these?" Veleda indicated both the herbs and the wands.

"In part." They had both drawn to a halt, and the cat came near her. He brushed against Veleda's legs, the long tail curving about her calves. The touch of his fur against her skin was luxurious, softer than the pelt of a fox taken in winter.

"Pay heed, human girl." Mau's light dry voice was low. "Sekhmet's real purpose is to ally Herself with the new power in the world: the gods of Rome. They will provide Her with the blood She craves. But now, you stand in Her way. Lady Bast has touched you, girl. You have been chosen. There are gifts within you that have yet to be awakened. You do not see them, but Sekhmet does. She has to be rid of you before. . . ."

"What?" Veleda wanted to shake the creature when he fell silent, and she wanted to dash off through the trees so that she would not hear what he said. "Before what, Mau?"

His orange eyes glowed up at her, brighter than the moon that was sinking slowly beneath the broad heads of the trees as it began to set in preparation for the still distant dawn. "The legions shed blood wherever they march. And the next place to hear the tread of their sandals will be these rich lands. The home of your people."

Silence fell between them again, silence as deep as the woods, as vast as the oceans which separated these lands from Kemet, the alien country from which Bast and Sekhmet had come. The night denizens rustled and flew and cried out, immersed in their own dramas of life and death, unconcerned with what befell any other creature besides them.

"But I am only an untried girl," Veleda whispered at last. "I've not gone into battle. I'm not Druid-chosen. What can I do?"

Mau gazed up at her. Slowly, he half closed his eyes, then opened them again, an oddly affectionate gesture. "Everything," he said calmly. "You, Veleda, are the hope of your people; not just your tribe, but all the tribes that live amongst these enormous woodlands and mountains. And, if you learn how to use Lady Bast's gifts, you will be their salvation."

The man in the bed tossed and turned in his delirium, weakly struggling to toss off the many furs that had been wrapped about him. He was a young man, only recently turned warrior age, and Ancamna regarded him with a sad and bitter twist to her mouth.

Here in this very hall, in the month of *Elembiuos*, she had officiated at the feast this new warrior's parents had held to honor his bravery in his first battle, a cattle raid into the territory of the Arverni. How proud his mother and father had been then. Ancamna's Druid-trained memory called up with flawless skill their laughter and smiles as they recounted the boy's part in the battle, the bright gleam in their eyes when others praised his courage.

Now the great long-house was empty. Despite the lateness of the hour, the rows of box beds that lined the walls were unoccupied. Those who occupied them: servants, warriors, even other family members, had all been barred because of the sickness. Only the parents hovered about their son's bedside, helpless, appearing far older than their years, watching him prepare for another journey, not this time into the territory of the Arverni, but to the Otherworld.

The father paced back and forth, pausing every few moments to stare down at the sick youth. The young man's mother patiently kept replacing the fur coverings, as if the repetition would somehow prevent that journey, would keep him here and accomplish what all the other attempts at healing had not.

Brucettus, the boy's father, was a big man, heavy-muscled and tall, as all men of the Belgae were. But tonight he seemed shrunken. The light from the central hearth-fire scored deep lines around his pale blue eyes, and there was a greater amount of gray in his auburn beard and shoulder-length hair than Ancamna had ever seen as he came toward her.

"Priestess." The noble laid a wide callused hand on Ancamna's arm, drawing her towards the fire. "Lady Ancamna, I beg you. Save him. Save my boy." His voice thickened in his throat. "He is my only living son."

A young serving woman entered, bearing a large bowl of water and an armful of clean cloths. "It came on him so suddenly, Lady," she whispered, setting the bowl down. "Yesterday, he was as full of fire as a young stallion"—an involuntary smile crossed her features at some private memory—"he went hunting and brought home a fat buck for the roasting spit. Last night, he ate and drank and was a man . . . in all ways. Then he awoke this morning and could not leave his bed. He could barely lift his head.''

"Yes," Ancamna said, nodding. "That is the nature of the sickness. I have seen it before." She did not add what else she had seen: that those so afflicted took ill in the morning, and by nightfall, were often dead. This young man, by the looks of him, would soon be among them.

Brucettus persisted. "Can't you do something for him, Priestess? You have skills; the healing arts of the gods are known to you—"

"And because I am a Druid, Brucettus, I cannot lie to you," Ancamna said gently. "Whatever this illness is which attacks our folk, the Mother has not shown me, or any other Druid, how to cure it."

The warrior's mother, a strongly built, firm-featured woman even taller than Ancamna, looked up from her place beside the bed. "If the cat ritual had been held," she said in a low, ragged voice, "my son would even now be recovering."

The unspoken accusation hung in the air. People had dispersed from the Holy Circle hours ago when Veleda failed to return with the sacrifice. Few blamed Ancamna for this fiasco, but Veleda was her niece, and the dishonor which the girl had brought on herself could not help but touch all the members of her clan, even one of the holy Druids. Ancamna herself, in spite of the love she felt for her sister's daughter, was finding it difficult to excuse the enormity of what Veleda had done.

"Perhaps he would be, Aleria," she said to the mother. "And perhaps he would not. It was my hope that the ritual would have brought a cleansing of this evil, but none of us can truly know the will of the gods in these matters."

"No one blames you, Lady," Brucettus put in swiftly. Privately he agreed with his wife, but he was desperate not to offend the powerful Druid who represented his son's only chance for survival.

Ancamna walked over to the bed. The taste of failure

was already in her mouth, sour and sad with the knowledge that here was another journey to the Otherworld she would not be able to prevent. To end one's life in the glory of battle was a joyous thing. To die like this, wasted away to nothing in the grip of an evil fever, was an abomination.

Still, she was bound by her vows; it was her sacred duty to try to save this suffering young warrior. She took several packets of herbs from the belt around her patterned tunic and set them near the hearth. Then, clearing her mind of anger and frustration, of the pain of yet another loss, she raised her arms and began to chant.

5

"IT'S AS GOOD A PLACE TO BE-
gin as any, and your aunt is there."
Mau sat beside Veleda on a small
knoll. Across from them the torches
of the hill fortress wavered in a fit-
ful breeze. Clouds were drifting
over the sky, carried by the wind
which promised rain before morn-
ing, and a chill had clamped its fingers into the air.

"I wonder who is sick," Veleda muttered. It did not
occur to her to question how the cat knew Ancamna was
in the fortress; by now, he had quite convinced her of his
powers. "It has to be Brucettus or Aleria. Garkol, their son,
is young and strong, and the plague seems to attack the
very old and the very young first."

"Well, if you go there," Mau said in his matter-of-fact
way. "You will find out. Go ahead now. You don't have
a lot of time. Or perhaps I should say that the one who is
sick does not have a lot of time."

Veleda looked at him in consternation. "You're not coming with me?" Her mouth went dry at the thought of climbing up to the hill fortress alone, of convincing the people
there, including her aunt—a noted healer herself—that she
possessed the cure for this terrible sickness.

Her companion made that familiar chirring sound. "My
thanks but no, human girl, I will be fine right where I am.
I don't care to end up twisting over a slow fire in a cage;
that would be very unpleasant, even for a magical cat, and
until the slow-witted folk around here realize that burning

45

me is not the answer to their problems, it is far too distinct
of a possibility. Anyway, I have shown you what you need
to know. You're a quick learner; you'll do fine.''

Veleda's hands tightened about the objects she carried:
the two wands and the small gourd. The gourd had been
hollow when Mau told her to pick it up from the forest
floor; now it was full of the juice he had taught her to
render from the fruit and bark of the barberry bush. Her
fingers tightened still more at the memory of these last
hours. The cat had done more than teach her how to make
a healing remedy. He had shown her magic, and the reality
of it now pulsated in the wands she held.

She shivered, her skin icy with apprehension, while behind her eyes a fever raged, burning her with the fire of
magic. All of this was still too new to her. Mau had revealed secrets, he had taught her true magic, yet she was
an infant in the face of what he had shown her. Never had
she felt more powerful as when she held these gifts from
Bast, and never had she felt more inexperienced.

"But what if they don't believe me?" she asked qua-
veringly. "I thought you would be there, you being a
magical cat and all. When they heard you talk it would
prove—"

"Ah, but they won't hear that. Did I not tell you most
humans are not worthy of my speaking with them? If you
go around telling people I can talk, they will not only think
your wits are addled, but you'll distract them from what is
really important, which is to take the medicine you offer.''

Veleda tried to think of some response and could not.
She swallowed several times, calling up her resolve. So she
would have to do this alone. Well, that should come as no
surprise; she had been in Mau's company long enough to
learn how unpredictable he could be.

She jumped. Mau had reached out a big paw and patted
at her. His claws were sheathed, but just barely; beneath
the delicate softness of paw pads she felt the prick of them
as he spoke.

"Listen to me," he said, continuing to press his paw against her leg. "This is another test, and, as with all the tests you will face from now on, there can be no failing of it. I have given you great weapons, human girl. Weapons of magic and weapons of healing. As for the rest, the strength is already within you. Use that power to convince these people to listen to you."

Veleda stared down at him. Something in her awakened at the cat's words, came blazing to life as fiercely and suddenly as a hawk swooping down from the sky. Perhaps it was a result of the magic Mau had shown her, or perhaps, as he had said, it had always been within her, sleeping, waiting for this precise moment. The fears and doubts of herself vanished between one breath and the next, and she gripped the tools of power and healing with new hands. Purposes burned in her, bright and clean, sweeping away all uncertainty, pointing her like an arrow at what she must do.

"I understand," she said softly, and even her voice seemed changed.

Mau did not need to hear her speak to see that change. He lowered his paw, his eyes slitted in satisfaction. To those familiar with them, cats always seem to be smiling, but even one unschooled in feline emotion could not have missed that pleased expression. He watched as Veleda set off down the slope. Her strides were long and swift, the thin wands moving in rhythm with her steps, a part of her now rather than the awkward burden they had been.

"Ah," he murmured, speaking not only to himself, but also to his Goddess. "It has begun."

Ancamna tipped the rest of the liquid down the young warrior's throat. A thin line of saliva dribbled down each side of his mouth and she carefully blotted the fluid away before lowering his head back to the roll of stuffed hide that served as a pillow. Her handling of the boy was deft, each motion skilled and kind. But the bleakness was in her face when she looked up to meet the worried eyes of the parents.

"He can no longer swallow," she said quietly.

Their gazes fixed on hers, as if by sheer intensity they could alter the implication of what she had told them. They knew what it meant; everyone in the tribe did. Enough people had died for them to know that when an afflicted one stopped swallowing, the end was very near.

Brucettus himself swallowed and swallowed, unable to speak. It was Aleria, schooled in matters of life far more demanding than any warrior discipline, who took charge. Leaning forward, she stroked the young man's hair back from his forehead.

"Then I will see to it that my son is prepared as a warrior should be for his journey to the Otherworld," she said in a calm firm tone. "Lady, can you not ease him until that time comes?"

Ancamna started to answer, but the words never left her lips. The serving-woman had come back into the bedchamber. Her face bore a strange expression, disapproving and hopeful at once. An instant later, Ancamna saw the reason. A small figure slipped out from behind the slave and came swiftly towards the bed.

Veleda.

At sight of her Brucettus regained his voice in a roar of outraged anguish. "How dare you enter this hall?" He threw himself from the bed, barring the girl's way. "Druid," he went on hoarsely, glancing back over his shoulder. "Forgive me for speaking harshly to your foster-daughter. But this child of your sister has not behaved with honor. She refused to discharge the task you laid upon her, and because of it my own boy lies dying!"

"Garkol is not dying because the ritual was not held." Veleda's young voice was low and determined, not at all the voice of one whose winters numbered only fourteen. "Hear me, lord; what I say to you is true. Yes, I did not do as my aunt bade me, but there were reasons. And I have come back to heal your son."

Ancamna rose to her feet. Behind her Aleria hovered over the sickbed, as if to protect her son from this new development. But Brucettus raged on. "What can you, a disobedient girl accomplish? A girl who does not care about the fate of her own tribe! Your aunt is the most powerful of our Druids, and she is unable to heal my son. Pah, you are not content with dishonoring yourself, now you must seek to dishonor your aunt as well."

"Brucettus." Ancamna's voice rang out in an inflection possessed only by those versed in Druidcraft. "Do not presume to speak for my honor. I am quite able to do that myself."

The burly noble fell silent, seeming to shrink in upon himself. Only a fool would challenge the mysteries which lay behind the power heard in that tone. And Brucettus, for all his grief and pain and rage, was not a fool.

Veleda spoke into the silence, not to the noble, but to her aunt. "Things have happened, Mother's Sister. That is why I did not return with the cat. I have been given the secret which will heal the illness striking down our people." She thrust the gourd up so that the firelight illuminated it. "I know how to save Garkol—"

"How could you learn healing secrets that the Druids don't know?" Unable to contain himself Brucettus hurled the question at her. He would have said more, but again clamped his lips shut at a single quelling glance from Ancamna.

The Druid turned her intense stare on her niece. "What is in the gourd, child?" Her eyes went to the wands in Veleda's other hand and her eyebrows rose. Tools of magic; they were imbued with it. The glimmer of power surrounded those two long rods, a power that was unfamiliar to her, but one as strong as any she had ever encountered. In the name of Anu, where had the girl gotten them?

That same force was in Veleda's voice as she answered her aunt's question. She met Ancamna's eyes. Her stare was direct, unfaltering before the strength of the woman's

Druid gaze. "It holds an herb tincture, Aunt. I will mix it with a little water and give it to Garkol to drink. It will heal him."

From her place by the bed, Aleria spoke. "My son cannot swallow, girl. Your aunt has already tried to dose him. It just trickles out of his mouth."

"We can try again."

Aleria and Brucettus looked at Ancamna in amazement, and she glanced back at them. For a moment she was as surprised as they were at what she had just said. But the hesitation passed quickly. Magic thrummed in the smoky firelit chamber, billowing about Veleda and clothing the girl in a mantle of power. Ancamna could see colors swirling in the air, colors of strength and colors of healing. Later she would find out what had happened to her niece, but now, there was a life to be saved.

"Your son is dying," she said to them. "The Otherworld is waiting for him, and even if the tincture does nothing, it will make no difference. If there is any chance at all to save him, we must take it. I would have no right to call myself Healer if I told you otherwise."

Brucettus shifted his weight. Apprehension and fear clouded his features, blending into the emotion he found most comfortable: anger. But Aleria forestalled him, making the decision before he could.

"Give him the tincture," she ordered. "I would have no right to call myself a mother if I told you otherwise."

Veleda completed the preparations quickly. As she worked, she came to understand how foolish it had been to worry about whether she could follow Mau's instructions. The knowledge of what to do was a part of her, as natural as throwing a spear or saddling and bridling a horse. The magic that had begun earlier this night, when she had first trapped the faery cat, was no longer a force that eddied in the outside boundaries about her; it had entered her, become a part of her souls.

Under four pairs of watchful eyes—for the serving

woman was till there, huddled in a corner by the fire—she measured out the dose in the shallow drinking bowl Ancamna handed her and carefully stirred in a small amount of water. She was aware of her aunt's keen gaze scrutinizing every move, but even that did not deter her. Her hands were as steady as her gaze when she went to the bed.

Garkol's breathing was labored. His mouth had gone slack, and Veleda could see that getting even a small amount of the tincture down his throat would not be easy. But suddenly Ancamna was there beside her. The Druid's skillful hands lifted and steadied the boy's head and gently she massaged his throat to make him swallow as she gave low-voiced instructions for the most effective means of administering the medicine. Even so, despite all their efforts, Garkol ingested only a small amount.

Ancamna shook her head. "Unless the power which has visited you this night is very strong, I do not think he has taken enough to help him."

Veleda bit her lip. What her aunt said was true. Mau had told her the sick must drink the entire dose in order for the healing process to begin. That left only one alternative. She bent to retrieve the two long rods from where she had lain them beside the bed.

Aleria, Brucettus, and their slave shifted nervously as Veleda picked them up. Aware of their unease, Ancamna hid her own. She knew Veleda as well as her own mother did; indeed she had assisted at the girl's birth. Veleda had never exhibited any of the subtle signs that showed that one was Druid-called. Yet there was power in her now; that was undeniable.

Turning to Aleria and Brucettus, Ancamna put all the reassurance at her command into both voice and gaze. "The girl has brought no evil here," she said. "Let her try this one last thing."

She spoke the truth. Her finely attuned awareness could detect no trace of evil in the forces swirling about her niece. Yet, by the same token, she did not know the source of this power which had allied itself with her niece. That alone was reason enough to be cautious.

However, the downward spiral to death had begun. Unless action were taken quickly, no magic on earth would be able to halt that spiral. The consequences of failure were equally clear. If the boy died now, his grief-stricken parents would not only focus their rage at his loss even more directly on Veleda, but word of her part in the sad events here would spread as swiftly as the disease itself.

Ancamna laid a hand on Veleda's arm. She said nothing, yet her thoughts communicated love and encouragement as clearly as if she had spoken aloud. Veleda gave her a small grateful smile in response, and then a look that was deep and grave. For she saw something else in her aunt's gaze: a warning.

In silence, the girl raised the wands up and pointed them east, in the direction of their source: Kemet and the ancient temple of the Goddess who had given them to her. The magic in them sprang out to enfold her. It rushed through her, throbbing and pulsing, racing from her fingers to her arms and all the way up to her heart, warming her like honey-sweet mead on a cold night. She was no longer aware of Ancamna's keen gaze or the dark apprehensive stares of Brucettus and Aleria. She knew only this force, sweet and hot, imbuing her with power. This was more than magic, more than spells; this was life, the very essence that burns in all that lives.

The strength of it was limitless. She was smiling, and had no idea that she was. She lowered the wands, tracing them in careful patterns over Garkol's prone form. Softly, so softly that not even Ancamna who was closest to her could hear, she murmured the words Mau had so painstakingly taught her. Not that it would have mattered if her aunt could hear them; the words did not belong to any Keltoi tongue, but to a language as old as the alien and distant land from which it came.

There was absolute silence in the long-house. The only sounds were Veleda's indistinct murmur, the hiss and snap of the fire, and the labored breathing of Garkol.

This last sound, the painful noise of someone struggling in his last throes, ceased quite suddenly. The boy's chest rose and fell in a single deep breath. He sighed again, shifted in the piled up furs, and opened his eyes.

"By my stallion's balls," he said fretfully. "I am thirsty enough to drink a lake. Is there any mead or beer about?"

Out in the night Mau crouched on the knoll, front paws curled neatly against his chest. His eyes glowed, miniature replicas of the great fire blazing inside the hall. He watched the hill fortress of the humans, and a deep purr rumbled within him, vibrating his sleek flanks.

Abruptly the purring stopped. An instant later Mau was on his feet. He lowered his body into the posture of hunting, extending himself until he seemed even longer than he was. His tail stretched out, rigid but for the very tip which jerked slowly back and forth.

"I see you," he snarled, his fangs gleaming like wind-blasted bone in the shadowy darkness. "Do not think you can hide from me."

Something moved amongst the trees, then something else. Misshapen forms revealed themselves in brief glimpses, each set off by a single yellow eye that fixed on the cat in burning malevolence.

Mau glared back. When he spoke his voice was not light, as it had been with Veleda, but a deep throaty growl vibrating with menace. "Go back to She Who sent you," he hissed. "I guard her, and you can do no harm to her while I do."

A cluster of moments passed. The distorted shapes moved again, but restlessly now, as though in anger. Slowly the movements lessened, the burning yellow eyes faded, and, one by one, the intruders disappeared, back into the dark space from which they had come.

But even when they were gone, Mau did not relax his guard. For the rest of the night he stayed in his hunting posture, alert and vigilant, his orange eyes blazing. When dawn grayed the trees and picked out the fortress's rough massive lines, he was still there, unmoving, watchful.

6

THE PLAGUE DISAPPEARED AS rapidly as Veleda's ability to travel. She was young and strong, yet by the end of three weeks even her youthful vigor was tested. The territory of the six tribes who made up the country of Belgae was vast, encompassing great forests of pine, spruce, birch, and alder, alternating with fields cleared for corn, barley, and rye. Their lands stretched all the way to the great Rhine River, beyond which lay the even denser forests of the fierce Germanic tribes, who preferred to wander with their flocks and herds, rather than staying in one place as the Belgae did. Accompanied by Ancamna and sometimes other Druids, Veleda began traveling through the countries of the Bellovaci, Nervii, Suessiones, Aduatuci, Remi, and her own people, the Eburones. They went from solitary farmsteads to bustling villages and walled towns where dozens of clans lived clustered together for protection, to the great hill fortresses of the noble class to which the Druid class itself belonged.

Noble, commoner, or slave, it made no difference; Veleda healed them all. As there were too many sick, and the area was too large for her to do this alone, she quickly shared the making of the tincture with the Druids and they, too, dispersed over the land to help those who required only the tincture to bring them back to health. The potion alone would have drawn attention from these priests and priestesses, for they were great healers themselves and here was a remedy whose properties were unknown, a medicine that healed where all their own cures had failed. But when the full-blown magic of the wands was called for, then whatever Druids were not traveling with the tincture joined their sister Ancamna to watch these puzzling healings take place.

Tinctures were one thing; the magic of the mysterious rods was quite another. When Veleda called upon the force contained in those colorful staffs carved and decorated with alien signs and symbols, the Druids, well-versed in their own magic, would stare silently, observing her with an intent and frowning concentration that verged on subtle, and sometimes not so subtle, suspicion.

Because this was no magic born of any Druid skills, many were tempted to reject it. They could not. There was too much at stake. The miraculous healing of one person after another—some at the point of death—could not be denied. To refuse to allow the girl to heal would mean a return of the sickness, a dire possibility that could mean the destruction of the entire tribe. Not even the strangeness of these outland spells was more of a threat than that.

As Veleda restored her people to the robust health that was their natural state, Ancamna found herself drawn aside with increasing frequency by her holy brethren. In the shadow of a giant alder or oak, near the hearth-fire of some noble's hall, or beside the bubbling waters of a sacred spring, Druids would grip Ancamna's arm and start to whisper.

"The girl is not Druid-called," they would say. "She has not been touched by Anu, or Lugh or any other of our gods. Yet some Divine One has clearly blessed her. She may not have possessed an affinity for magic before, but she does now. She is your foster-daughter, Ancamna. What shall we do with her?"

Ancamna understood their concerns; they were her concerns as well. But each time she could only respond in the same way. "When the healing is done and all the sick among us are restored, then will we meet together. The girl herself will tell us how she came to be given these gifts.''

It was not how Ancamna would have chosen to handle matters. Her own desire to understand the mysteries Veleda had brought with her ate at her as virulently as the plague had eaten at the Belgae. But Veleda had asked this of her, and Ancamna could not refuse. Her niece was profoundly changed; she bore the unmistakable stamp of power. Yet there had been a look in the girl's eyes when she asked her aunt to wait for an explanation, an expression that for just a moment had transformed her back into the child she really was. For the sake of that child, Ancamna had agreed.

The month of *Simivisonios* came smiling upon the land and those who lived in the country of the Belgae smiled back in greeting. People called these days the Time of Brightness, for now was when the sun was at her zenith and Anu favored the seeds placed in her lovely dark breast. Only weeks ago, it had seemed that Anu would look down upon abandoned cattle and sheep and neglected fields where tender young shoots had died for want of care, but thanks to Veleda, all that had changed. Men and women who had been tottering about their farmsteads or lying in their beds at the brink of death were now up and at their daily tasks. Most were strong enough to start tending their beasts and the seeds they had planted in the month before the sickness struck. They sang and laughed as they worked, and murmurs of thanks to Veleda and whatever mysterious god or Goddess had blessed her with the power to help them, rose up into the clear warm air.

It was in this month, on a clear bright evening just as dusk was falling, that the Druids of the entire Eburones tribe came together to finally receive answers to all their questions. In this they were joined by delegations of fellow Druids from each of the neighboring tribes of Belgae.

Even without these other delegations swelling their numbers, the gathering of Druids would have been great. The Eburones themselves were large and prosperous, and the Druids who attended to the people's needs were many.

Clothed in colorful robes, armlets and torques gleaming, their tall figures squeezed with relentless patience into the holy grove near Veleda and Ancamna's family hall. The rustle of their voices drowned out the evening breezes soughing through the trees. Both men and women came, some of them young, in the first flush of their powers, others filled with age and experience, their hair white as the first snow of winter. They jostled politely, and sometimes not so politely, for position. Their numbers threatened to overflow the grove, large though it was, and still they came.

From a raised wooden dais in the center of the circular clearing, Veleda watched them assemble. A fist had entered her stomach, clenching and unclenching with each breath, yet she was not nervous.

Once she would have been. Once the mere thought of standing before all these Sons and Daughters of the Oak would have made her knees quake and her voice clog in her throat. They were a class unto themselves, these Druids. The very title they bore was synonymous with wisdom. The most powerful chieftain was less intimidating than the least of them. Deep within their rigorously trained minds rested all the wisdom, history, and law of the Eburones and all the gifts of the sacred mysteries as well. They were walkers between the worlds, seers of the unseen, and on this day they had come to see her.

Veleda gazed at them calmly, meeting the many penetrating glances thrown her way with an unshakable directness. Excitement tightened her belly now, not fear. She could hardly wait for all the holy ones to assemble so she could begin. She knew that many of them were uneasy with a power they had had no part of, and thus no control over. Many of them had come to interrogate her, perhaps to even reduce her back to the status of an untried girl. But that would not happen. Veleda, too, was a seer of the unseen, a walker between the worlds. Bast—a Goddess totally unknown to these powerful Druids—had come to her and her alone. And that mighty Cat-headed Goddess had helped the tribe, just as She had said She would. Now Veleda, touched by Bast's serene strength, had a task to fulfill as sacred as that of any Druid. She looked down at the gathering men and women, not as a trembling girl, but as an equal.

Standing beside Veleda, Ancamna leaned on her staff and watched her. "Anu, bless us," she said at last. "You are not afraid to face them, are you? Not in the least." There was no need to lower her voice. No one spoke loudly in the hushed atmosphere of the grove, but the din of so many softly murmuring voices was enough to override her words, even had she shouted.

Veleda smiled at her. She could not know that even her smile had changed, or what it told to someone versed in the magic arts as Ancamna was. The power that coursed through her, the link to her mysterious deity who had come to her, revealed itself in that smile. Ancamna drew in her breath. Over these last weeks she had watched the girl perform countless healings with the two rods she had been given. Ancamna herself had administered the tincture and seen its efficacy over and over.

But she had wondered if once the healing was done the uncanny power of both tincture and rods would disappear as inexplicably as it had appeared. With both her inner and outer eyes she saw now that this would not happen. If anything, Veleda had grown in strength as she herself became more at ease with her gifts. This pleased Ancamna, and it worried her. *There is a larger purpose behind these events,* she thought. *Where will it lead?*

A gruff voice rang out, rising over the sibilant murmuring. "Sister, we are all here. Let us begin."

Axiounis, the one who had spoken, was a venerable figure, gnarled and powerful as one of the oaks that ringed the grove. His beard and hair were dark as iron, save where age had painted them with wide streaks of snowy white. He stepped forward, holding a heavy staff girdled with gold and as gnarled as his body. The gaze he fixed on Ancamna was straight and deep.

Most Druids found and pursued an area of learning in which he or she excelled; Ancamna's was healing, Axiounis's was lawgiving. Ancamna could feel the questions bubbling up inside her colleague, and she knew he would interrogate Veleda with the probing intensity he showed whenever his vast knowledge of the law was required to settle a dispute between tribal members.

"Yes, Axiounis," she called back to him. "I think it is time."

An abrupt silence fell. The voices of the massive old oaks reasserted themselves. The wind muttered through their leafy crowns as each Druid made his or her private prayer to Mother Anu and all the gods and Goddesses who watched over the tribe.

As swiftly as it had fallen, the silence ended with another voice. It was Quelia, known as She of the Many Tongues for her unique ability to sing in a glorious range that went from the highest notes to the very lowest. Indeed, she always sounded as if she were singing, and she did now, as she said, "Well, then, I will ask the first question. Tell us, Veleda, where did you go on the night your foster-mother sent you to fetch back the cat you had caught and then freed? We searched for you, in both the seen and the unseen worlds, yet not even magic could reveal you to us. Where were you?"

Emotions flowed up and over the assembly, slapping at Veleda like waves. Expectation, curiosity, distrust, the need to understand—even jealousy—all these feelings washed over Veleda, and for an instant she swayed in the strength of it.

She recovered immediately, but everyone in this keen-eyed gathering had seen. More than a few nodded, whispering to each other in satisfaction. Just as they had suspected, whatever power the girl had been given was already fading. Soon she would be as she had been, and life would return to normal. This disturbing shift in the world, with its mysterious sickness and equally mysterious healing, would soon be a thing of the past.

Ancamna's lips tightened. She, too, felt the myriad emotions bombarding Veleda, and her own perceptions added to it. She was angry. The need for knowledge on the part of her companions she understood. The distrust, even the jealousy, were also reactions she could identify with; every man and woman here had spent twenty years and more honing their craft, and this girl had eclipsed them all. But to hope for her to become less than she now was? That was wrong.

She was about to say so, when Veleda spoke. "If you could not find me," she said. "It was because She who called me did not wish you to."

Her voice was as calm as her eyes. The intensity of all these powerful ones had caught her off guard, but that was over. Bast was with her. She could feel the Goddess's presence wrapping itself about her, as soft and reassuring as Mau rubbing against her legs, and at the same time, as vast and far-reaching as an ocean composed solely of power. The temple of Bast spread itself across the inner landscape of her mind, its rose-pink stone gleaming in the rainbow light of the Otherworld. Within Her sanctuary Bast Herself sat on Her throne looking at Veleda, beautiful, utterly outland, and yet, deeply familiar. The great cat face was smiling.

"But the time has come to speak of where I was, and why," she went on. "I was in the Otherworld."

The new silence that fell at her words was profound. Veleda spoke into it, her voice deepening as she went on. She recounted the faery cat's luring of her, how he had led her out of this world and into the realms of magic. She told them of Bast's temple, and of the Goddess Herself. Barely repressing a shudder, she described Sekhmet and the Lion-headed Goddess's sending of the plague. Then she spoke of returning to the world, of Mau coming with her, and the way the faery cat had taught her the secrets of the tincture and the wands.

At this point in the narrative, the Druids could no longer keep silent. A discussion began, as fluid and swift as river currents, the words flowing back and forth between one speaker and the next.

Veleda listened as the assembled Druids debated what they had heard. She was not entirely surprised to hear the quick acceptance of outland Goddesses such as Bast and Sekhmet. Egyptian traders had been traveling to the lands of various tribes for centuries; it was only logical that their deities might also decide to visit. However, what the Druids could not so easily accept—also not surprising—was Veleda's part in all of this.

Her contribution to the tribe's welfare was undeniable and many spoke of this, praising her for what she had done, insisting that the end result was far more important than the mysteries that had led her to accomplish it. Others did not agree, pointing out the troubling aspects of all this. Yes, the girl had done a wondrous thing; however, she had gone beyond the natural order of things to do so. She had bypassed the boundaries of Druid authority and Druid knowledge; the magic she had worked was not a result of anything familiar, and therefore, it was suspect.

Throughout this discussion Ancamna remained beside Veleda, listening intently, although she took no part in the comments and arguments her brothers and sisters hurled at each other. "Let them talk," she whispered to Veleda. "Their attention will turn back to you soon enough."

No sooner had she spoken than the questions began, pelting at Veleda like hail.

"By Wind and Oak, why would a Goddess from the land of Egypt call a girl of the Belgae to Her?"

"Yes, and why would another Goddess from such a far-off land desire to send a plague upon our country?"

"Where is this faery cat you speak of? No Druid has

ever seen him. Are you certain it was he who taught you the healing secrets?''

Ancamna finally had enough. Her sharp voice cut through the din. "Peace," she shouted, striking her staff down on the dais for emphasis. "Is this the way of our assemblies? Give my niece a chance to answer one of you, before the rest rush in to drown her out.''

"Ancamna speaks the truth of it," Axiounus the law-giver agreed. "How can we learn anything unless we allow the girl to speak?''

Grudgingly the gathering quieted. Scores of eyes, each with that piercing quality peculiar only to Druids, trained themselves on Veleda. It was enough to make any uninitiated one cringe, and for the length of a heartbeat something in Veleda quailed. But the moment was quickly gone. Strengthened by Bast and by her own growth over these last weeks, she met all those stares unflinchingly. Her voice was still calm.

"I cannot tell you why Bast chose someone like me, rather than one of you, who all know so much more of these matters than I do. Yet She did make me Her choice and now I have obligations to Her, as well as to our people. And there is more to tell you. Bast says that the old ways are passing, that the Mother is being forgotten. Only here, in the lands of the Eburones and all the other tribes, is She still venerated as is proper. Because of this, Bast sent us a warning. I did not understand it at first, but the faery cat helped me—''

"The cat again," someone interrupted. "Maiden of Waters, where is this creature?''

Ancamna glared the speaker into silence. "Go on," she said to Veleda, encouragement in her tone.

Veleda drew a breath. In truth, she could not have said where Mau was, not precisely, but she did know that he was nearby. He had shadowed her throughout these weeks of travel and healing. She had caught continual glimpses of his dark shape and had tried repeatedly to call him to her. But with the maddening independence of his kind, he had refused to come. He had been equally adamant in refusing to show himself to Ancamna or anyone else.

However, this was not the time to be thinking about where Mau was. Veleda's gaze did not falter before the Druids, but for the first time since the gathering began, anxiety twinged through her. What she had to say next was a difficult thing. She, who had actually seen Bast and Sekhmet, who had listened to Mau talk in a human voice and performed magic, still found it difficult to believe that Romans would dare penetrate into the territory of the powerful tribes who made their homes in these remote lands. How would the Druids, who thus far had received no proof other than her word, react on hearing such a thing?

"Rome has set its eyes upon our country," she said at last. "They are no longer content with the southern territory they now call Gallia Provincia. Their legions will march beyond those stolen lands, and seek to take our own freedom and country from us."

The people in the grove stared at her. A thunderstruck expression took over the features of Axiounis and spread, traveling from one face to another, until every man and woman looked the same. Even Ancamna was not immune. Frowning deeply, she turned to her foster-daughter, fixing her eyes on Veleda's face as if she were waiting for the girl to correct herself, to retract the words and say something else instead.

But Veleda could not pull back what she had said. She stared back at her aunt, and Ancamna saw that she could not. The tall Druid swept her gaze back out over the gathering.

"I have seen no omens about a threat from the Romans," she said in a low voice. "Not in dreams or in divinations. Can any of you, my Brothers and Sisters of the Oak, say differently? Has anyone here been shown something I have not?"

The responses flowed back to her, spoken and unspoken. Chief among them was disbelief. The tribes of Belgae were the greatest fighters in the world, and not only did they know it, but their enemies knew as well. No people could forge better weapons or match them in horsemanship. Their cavalry was unmatched in its swiftness and maneuverability, and above all, their warriors showed an absolute dedication to warfare that no opponent could hope to compete with. Rome was a force in the world; in truth, the Druids realized that. But the notion that Roman soldiers could ever triumph over the all-consuming bravery of the tribes was an idea that no one in this grove could support, certainly not without better proof than they had seen thus far.

And in any case, there had been clashes between the tribes of the Keltoi and the Romans before. The bards still sang songs of glory about the centuries-old exploits of the army of warriors who had crossed over the mountains and gone on to sack Rome itself. More confrontations had erupted some two hundred years later, leading to savage battles in which the tribes crushed four Roman armies in four years. Rome might have grown in her own power since then, but the reputation of the northern giants who stiffened their hair with lime and fought naked had not faded. Even in modern times, and despite the fact that a Roman province encroached on lands that had once been free, that reputation remained.

"I have been given no signs that would support what the girl says," Quelia said in her musical voice. "And yet, could not the sickness itself have been an omen?"

Ancamna nodded, as did many others. "I have been thinking so myself."

She was about to say more, but Axiounis suddenly shouldered forward. His eyes were blazing, and he had raised his staff high to command attention, although with his age and his reputation, he needed no emblem of authority.

"I have listened to this girl talk of outland Goddesses," he said impatiently. "And I have continued to listen, even as she warned us about the Romans, when we, with all our combined powers, have seen no hint, no trace of trouble, in either dreams or omens. If all that she says is true, then why has this cat, this creature of Bast who taught her how to make the tincture and use the magic in the wands not shown himself? Where is he, this magical helper of hers? If I saw him, perhaps I might then be inclined to take these warnings about the Romans more seriously."

A dark blur streaked out of the canopy of trees. It landed with a soft thud on the dais next to Veleda, a large cat, entirely black but for a splash of white on his chest. His orange eyes narrowed and widened as he stared out over the assembled Druids.

A grin broke over Veleda's face, suddenly making her look as young as she really was. "Here he is," she said happily. "This is Mau."

The cat brushed his sleek body against her legs. There was affection in the movement, but nothing ingratiating, rather it was a gesture among equals, a greeting that he expected to be returned. Veleda stooped and ran a hand over the thick silken fur of his back. "Will you not say something to them?" she whispered. "They do not believe me about the Romans."

Mau's clear eyes fastened on Ancamna. She had moved closer, and as she leaned on her carved staff, she stared down at Mau with such concentrated intensity it seemed that she would divine all his secrets, whether he spoke to her or not.

They will believe you in time. The cat did not say the words aloud, but Veleda heard them clearly in her head; in just the same manner had first Bast, and then the horrible Sekhmet, communicated with her. *After all,* Mau said, that soundless mental voice still managing to convey dryness. *They are trained in the mysteries, are they not? I should not have to talk like one of you two-leggeds in order for them to realize I am made of magic. All they need do is look at me, as your aunt is doing.*

Others were indeed looking at him that way. And for this reason, when Ancamna took her fierce gaze away from Mau and addressed the assembly, no one, not even Axiounis, contradicted her. "The sickness was an omen," she said firmly. "And so was the healing of it. The cat is yet another sign. Whether all these things mean we should fear the Romans, I cannot say; certainly none of us here have been given reason to think so. But even without magic the Romans would be fools to cross into these lands and challenge our swords."

Heads were nodding and voices were murmuring in agreement.

Ancamna went on. "What is clear to me is this: Veleda was not Druid-called before, but she is now. I acknowledge my niece"—she laid a hand on Veleda's head—"as Druid-called, and I say that she should be sent to the Island of the Mighty for her training, so that she may enter our order."

Veleda looked up at her aunt in astonishment. "But this is about the Romans," she burst out. "It has nothing to do with me. I am only the messenger. The Romans will come, and we must be prepared when they do. We must ready ourselves—"

"And how shall we do that?" Axiounis asked her in his most precise lawgiver tone. "Explain to us what your outland Goddess said we must do."

Veleda glanced at Mau He slitted his eyes and purred softly, but offered no help. "There is only one way," she finally said, feeling the weight of Axiounis's gaze and that of every other Druid in the grove. "The tribes must unite into one force. Tribe by tribe we can be defeated, but standing together, we cannot. That is what Bast said."

In fact, it was what Mau had said, but there was no point in trying to explain that. In any case, it did not matter; no one would have heard her. The cacophony of voices was deafening. To Veleda's dismay, many in the grove had actually begun laughing. Others were plainly horrified. Still others were angry. But everyone, regardless of his or her reaction, was expressing that reaction aloud. Ancamna was calling again for quiet, but few were listening. What Veleda had suggested was so outrageous, so beyond belief, that at least for the moment, Druid discipline was set aside.

Do not concern yourself. Mau's inner voice was reassuring. *When dealing with humans you can never expect too much. No offense to you, girl, but your kind does not exactly shine as the brightest apples on the tree. Lady Bast knew they would not believe you at first.*

Veleda glared at him. "She knew?" The uproar was still going on, which was fortunate, for she paid no heed to how loud her voice had become. "Then why, in the name of the Mother, did She allow me to face them all—"

The cat's unruffled reply broke into her anger. *You will be sent to be trained in the mysteries of your people, girl. That is what is important. You will become a Druid. It was what we wanted.*

"I don't understand." She had mysteries enough to deal with already, Veleda thought to herself. Suddenly the excitement of being a part of those mysteries was no longer as bright. Gods and Goddesses commonly used humans to further their own divine plans; this was well known. But that did not mean one had to like the feeling of being used. "Why can you not go on teaching me?" she demanded. "Are not the powers of you and Bast enough? Anyway, I doubt they will accept me into their school, not after what I just said."

Mau's eyes grew huge as he looked at her. This time he spoke aloud, knowing that no one would pay attention. "You will have need of what these Druids can teach you," he told her quietly. "Your people will pay no heed to what you tell them about the Romans unless you have the authority of Druid office behind you. And as for accepting you: they will take you into their school. Believe that."

And he was correct. When the furor died down, the gathering did just that.

7

RARICUS CHEWED ABSENTLY on a slice of roasted boar haunch and looked across the low wooden table at his daughter. Tonight's feast was an important event, held in Veleda's honor to celebrate both her healing of the people and her being called to the order of the Druids. Amborix himself, king of the Eburones, had come with all his train. As befitted the most important man here, he sat in the center of several great circles of diners. Raricus the host sat next to him, with the other chieftains ranged about them in order of distinction. Around these most important of men sat their wives and older children. Behind the nobles and their families, the warriors who served as their shields-men formed their own circle, and their spears-men beyond that. Ranged around the warriors on the thick mat of dried grass that covered the hall's earthen floor were the rest of the tribe: artisans, farmers and their families, even slaves, all come to enjoy Raricus's largesse.

Two stags, a boar, an entire ox, and a host of smaller game had been roasted on spits over the huge hearth-fire. Small loaves of bread, the staple food at any meal, had been baked by the dozens and were sending their fragrant odor up to mingle with the rich meat smells. An astonishing number of fish, flavored with vinegar and cumin, wrapped in leaves and placed in the hot coals of the hearth-fire to bake, were hurriedly being unwrapped by the house-slaves. Other servants were scurrying back and forth, bearing platters laden with meat and bread or large pitchers brimming with cormu: a honey-sweetened mead ladled from the enormous mead bowl that stood in one corner of the hall.

Roughly the feasters snatched the food and drink from the hands of the harried slaves, shouting at them and each other, breaking into brief joyous quarrels over who deserved the better cut of meat or the first cup of cormu from a new jug. Children raced back and forth, eating and drinking as they ran, and followed by dogs that roved about, snatching up scraps wherever they fell. Occasionally a man or woman would break into song, gesturing at the bard who sat in a place of honor at Raricus's table, the latter smiling back, though he remained silent; his portion of the feast— the entertainment—would come later. Around Raricus the great long-house was heavy with sound, with voices raised in oaths and laughter that pounded at one's ears. The air swirled with the bright colors of checked and patterned clothing, dense with smoke that stung the eye and wreathed up toward the rafters in filmy strands of ashy silver. But Raricus paid no heed to either the noise or the smoke. He had spent his life in noisy firelit halls; all the fathers before them had once been ruled over by his father. Now they were ruled over by Raricus. One day, the eldest of his sons would sit in the place of honor in this hall, watching over the feasters as Raricus was doing now.

Yet it was not his sons who claimed Raricus's attention this night; it was Veleda, his only daughter. She was dressed in her best clothing: a long gloriously patterned tunic of deep blue. Gold was one of the great treasures of the Belgae and they loved to adorn themselves with it. Tonight it glittered all about Veleda. A finely worked belt of the burnished metal encircled her waist, and earrings and bracelets, also of gold, gleamed at her ears and on her upper arms. The light from the torches burnished her unbound hair, making it look even redder than usual, dancing in her large slightly tilted green eyes, and casting its glow over the broad features so similar to Bormana's.

She had always resembled to her mother, Raricus mused to himself. His wife was a big woman, tall and muscular, but he had known Bormana all her life and he remembered how she had looked at this age, just like Veleda. The girl was gangly and awkward now, but one day she would grow into herself and then she would come to possess the same air of dignity as her mother.

Raricus narrowed his eyes. For perhaps the first time since her soul had been reborn into this world, Raricus thought he saw himself in his daughter, in the firm set of her jaw and the steady way she returned his gaze. He stared at her and felt a wave of pride wash through him. It was an unaccustomed feeling. Raricus was an affectionate man, and in his own way he loved this girl who was his only daughter. But, like most men with their daughters, he had remained a distant presence in her life.

Women were, and had always been, an enigma to Raricus; they possessed gifts unique only to them. Magic touched women in ways that it did not touch men. The wisest man who became a Druid could not equal the wisest woman who likewise joined the order. Women alone could prophesy. Only they could understand and use the mysteries that to men could never be anything but unknowable. Thus had it always been, and thus, if the gods were willing, would it remain. But there was a distance between men and women because of the latter's gifts, a gulf of magic which neither sex questioned. Raricus and the men with whom he surrounded himself rarely spoke of this distance; it was an element of nature as unquestioned as the Goddess waxing from maiden to crone in the three phases of the sacred moon.

Yet for Raricus himself, the distance from at least one woman was not so great. Over the years shared between them he had come to love Bormana deeply, and not only for the children she had given him. He cherished her for herself. Unlike her Druid sister, Bormana showed no affin-

ity for magic, and this lessened that otherwise natural gap
and made him feel easy with her.

Now here was his daughter, who he had been thinking
it was time to arrange a marriage for, revealing abilities he
had never suspected, abilities which would place her irrev-
ocably within the ranks of mysterious women. Ancamna
was sitting on one side of her while Bormana sat on the
other. Wife and sister-in-law also returned his stare, and
Raricus, seasoned warrior though he was, found it difficult
to meet all three pairs of those eyes, the green of Bormana
and Veleda's, and the enigmatic dark depths of Ancamna's.

He took refuge in raising his own voice above the din.
"Hear me, my guests," he roared. "Kindred and fellow
nobles, before we are all too drunk, let us not forget the
reason for this feast. Let us not forget how my daughter
went to the Otherworld and came back with the means of
taking away the sickness that was attacking our people. The
Eburones are healthy and strong again, as the gods meant
us to be, and there"—he thrust an arm out in Veleda's
direction—"sits the reason for our good fortune. My
daughter!"

The crowded long house erupted in a burst of cheering
agreement. People waved drinking goblets, knives, and
slabs of venison or pork in the air, craning their necks and
pushing at each other to catch a glimpse of Veleda through
the haze of the torches and the smoke from the hearth-fire.
She looked out at them, bearing their roaring approval with
the same ambivalence she had felt at being seated in this
prominent place of honor. Her soul-friend Sattia caught her
eye from her place at another table and gave her a wide
smile. But there was something tentative in the black-haired
girl's grin. Like so many others Sattia had changed toward
Veleda, treating her with a blend of gratitude and awkwardness that bordered unmistakably on awe.

Veleda returned her soul-friend's smile and stared at the
silver goblet of wine before her. To be treated with such
respect was a heady sensation and part of her could not

help but react with pleasure. After all, she had received no more notice during her fourteen winters than any other well-born girl her age, which was not a great deal. But there was something uncomfortable in all the attention. She should not be the object of all this grateful and warm-hearted acknowledgement. Mau should be here, too, sitting beside her at this table, though of course he was not; he had disappeared right after the Druid gathering had ended. She knew he had not gone far, yet she wished he had stayed with her. There was so much she still wanted to ask him. And lying within her, weighing like a stone, was the sense that her people were celebrating too soon.

Ancamna raised her hand in a gesture for silence. "Do not forget the outland Goddess," she said sternly. "She came to our aid unasked. Would you ignore her now?"

"Let us not forget something else." Veleda's voice sounded strange to her father's ears, distant, and far older than the young girl he had always seen her as. "The warning she gave us."

Raricus frowned at her in a silent command to keep quiet, but she returned his gaze, and then stared out over the people packed into the hall, knowing that she could not. "Can you not see?" A note of pleading entered her voice. "The healing will mean nothing if you ignore what Bast commanded me to tell you."

The mood of the hall had changed. People were muttering and shaking their heads, turning away as if that would protect them from hearing any more. Everyone here knew what Veleda was referring to. Druids were bound by their oaths to tell the truth, and they had not hidden what had gone on in the grove. What the nobles and chieftains heard had not been popularly received. First the sickness and now this dire warning about Romans. It was too much. Life was finally getting back to normal, and no one was anxious to see it disrupted yet again.

Amborix's deep measured voice rose over the mumbling. "I am grateful to you, Veleda, as we all are. But you are not a seer. You are not yet trained as a Druid.''

The king's comment encouraged others. "This Goddess you speak of is outland," a woman called out. "Why should we believe Her?"

"Perhaps the girl is mistaken," someone else suggested, and many leaped to agree. "Yes, that must be so. The Romans would not dare come here."

"They will." Veleda rose to her feet. "They will." Her voice was shaking and her green eyes held a distant expression, fixed on some point far beyond the smoky hall. "The Great God Lugh will look down from the sun and cause that sun to cast her shining gaze down off their helmets and breastplates. But no light will glow from their swords, for those will be dull, crusted with dried blood. Dusk will fall as another day begins, and She Who Lives in the Sacred Moon will look down and weep over the bodies of the dead. . . .''

Her words trailed off. Dazedly she returned to herself, glancing about her as if uncertain of where she was. Ancamna put a gentle hand on her shoulder. "All is well, child," she said softly. "You are back with us."

Veleda's eyes regained their focus. She realized that the hall had gone unnaturally still. Hands that held drinking horns or pieces of meat and bread were poised in the air, midway to people's mouths. The servants stood motionless, frozen in the act of carrying platters or pouring mead. The huge fire popped and chattered in the silence and in its bright glow people watched her, their faces no longer joyous, but guarded and uneasy. Her own family was watching her, staring at her as if they had never seen her before. The bard, a stocky gray-haired man with faded blue eyes, glanced from Veleda to Ancamna, frowned and shook his head.

Veleda turned to Ancamna. "What happened?"

"You had a vision." Her aunt's face was thoughtful. "Your outland Goddess has apparently given you the gift of seeing, as well as the ability to heal. This will change where you go for the first part of your training."

"What did I see?" Veleda furrowed her brow, trying to remember. All she had been left with were sensations, and they were not pleasant ones. The chill of death crawled through her bones, the coppery scent of blood was a heavy reek in her nostrils. She wanted to shudder and she fought against it as she asked again. "What did I see?"

"You spoke of death," her mother said before Ancamna could answer. "Of bodies lying in the sun, and weapons red with blood. Do you not recall it?"

"No." Veleda looked anxiously at Ancamna. "No."

But even as she spoke, a deep awareness spread through her. Bast's warning trembled in her ears. She could not remember the vision itself, but she understood the meaning of it.

"It's to be expected." Ancamna's voice was reassuring in its calmness. "Those who have been blessed with the gift of seeing often do not recall what the Shining Ones choose to show them. They speak their vision aloud and other Druids interpret its meaning."

"But I understand its meaning." Veleda's eyes were blazing. Her voice cracked with pain as she cried out to her gathered people. "Why will you not believe the warning Bast keeps trying to give you? Can't you see we are in danger? All of us!"

Here and there mutterings arose as the feasters whispered to each other. People shifted nervously, their appetite for food and drink gone as they brooded over this latest surprise from Raricus's daughter. Prophecy was no light matter. The girl had seen something; that much was evident—but what had she actually seen? She was not yet a Druid. Truly, how much could her assertions about the Romans be believed? The enormous service she had done her tribe had not been forgotten, but in the way of all people, now that the danger was past the memories of the plague were already dimming, and Veleda's contribution along with it. The girl was young, and were not these things better left to the Druids, whose province they were? Perhaps once she started her own training as a Druid, her insistence would change.

"Wait!" A thought occurred to Raricus, blazing across his mind as if the hand of a Shining One had placed it there. "Could it not be that the dead my daughter saw were Romans?" He slammed his drinking horn down on the table, sending honey-mead splashing up his arm. "Yes!" he cried, and wheeled to face Ancamna. "The girl is not trained, she has no idea of what she saw. It could as easily be one as the other."

His excitement was infectious. Amborix jumped to his feet. "Raricus speaks the truth," the burly king shouted. "Let the Romans come to Belgae, if that be their wish. The Eburones will prepare a welcome for them!"

Others added their voices to those of the two men, and the hall rapidly grew as noisy as before. Boasts filled the air, mingling with threats of what the Romans' fate would be if they came to these lands, until the roaring shouts became so loud that no one could hear anything else.

Veleda watched in dismay. "No, you don't understand," she shouted in a futile attempt to make herself heard. But even her own parents paid her no heed. Bormana's eyes were shining as she pounded the table with the hilt of her dagger, and Raricus had climbed atop his bench, the better to make his own voice carry over the uproar. Sattia and several others friends were nearby, fists raised, throats vibrating with battle-yells. Always had Sattia loved the arts of war; she would far rather practice with a sword than learn any of the skills ascribed to women. Still, as entranced as she was, she was also a soul-friend, and Veleda called out to her, trying to get her attention.

"It's no use," Ancamna said to her. "They are too caught up to listen to you, or to their fears. It is far easier to look forward to battle, especially one they think they will win."

"But that's just it! They won't win. They have it all wrong."

Ancamna sighed. "You won't convince them of that. Not now anyway."

"Aunt." Veleda leaned close, staring up into the woman's enigmatic dark eyes. "Do you believe me? Do you see the warning Bast sent back with me?"

"I am not a seer, child. That was never my gift."

"Foster-Mother, please!"

Ancamna looked away for a moment, her eyes drifting over the exultant display their people were putting on. She turned back to Veleda. "I think," she said quietly, "that our people had best be prepared."

Dawn broke over the great forests of Belgae, bathing the mighty trees in shifting patterns of purple and rose. Mist rose from the broad winding river of the Mother Goddess, the Rhine, first leg on the route Veleda would take on her long journey to the Druid school on the island of Eire. Ancamna would accompany her on that journey, but now the time had come to bid farewell to all those who would not be going with her: family, friends, even the dogs she had raised from puppies and the horses she had helped to train.

As the morning brightened, Veleda walked beside the Rhine with her mother. The river glittered under the strengthening sun, shimmering as though the Goddess whose namesake it was had dressed it in silver. Mother and daughter held each other's hands as they walked, but they moved in silence along the grassy bank, listening to the birds announce the new day. In the deepest part of the river fish leaped from the water to snap at flies, regaining the depths with a sharp splash. On the far bank a group of deer came down to drink, raising their heads to watch the humans across the water. On their side of the river Veleda and Bormana could hear the sounds of the nearby village

stirring into life. Off in the distance the long square plank-
boat Veleda would travel on was already being loaded with
furs, bars of gold and silver, bushels of wheat, and finely
worked iron tools that would be traded further on down the
coast.

Bormana paused to stare at the boat "I love you, my
only daughter," she said at last. "You are the child of my
body and my heart. Sons are a blessing to any mother, but
daughters are a gift from Anu. Here''—she pointed to her
head, the residing place of the three souls—"we are the
same. But you have always been closer to Ancamna than
to me. Even if I had not named her as your foster-mother,
I think it would have been the same. Perhaps it's because
you were always Druid-called, and the Goddess did not
wish us to know it before now."

"I haven't always been Druid-called." Veleda was looking not at the boat, but at her mother. How could she explain the extent to which her life had changed? The
importance of the message she carried? "Mother, what I
have been saying is the truth. The Goddess Bast came from
a very long way to help us and warn us. Can you not believe me?"

Bormana sighed. "I believe you were given a great gift
that healed our people. And I believe that if the Romans
do come to our lands we will make them wish they hadn't.
You have a great deal of learning ahead of you, my daughter. In time you may come to look at all of this differently."

Veleda shook her head. "No," she said quietly. "That
will not happen, Mother."

Her mother eyed her thoughtfully. "Did the outland
Goddess tell you when the Romans would come?" She
nodded in satisfaction when Veleda shook her head again.
"You see? It may be that you did not understand what she
told you. That is why Ancamna is taking you to the school
on Eire, so the Druids can teach you about your gifts."

"The Mother's blessings upon you." Ancamna offered
the traditional Druid greeting as she came towards them.

"Are you ready to depart, Veleda? It is almost time."

"Does she have to go this day?" Bormana knew the answer even as she asked the question, but she could not help herself. The enormity of the separation from her only daughter was looming before her; twenty years would Veleda be gone, an endless time in which the seasons would change, festivals be celebrated, harvests gathered, all without the face of her daughter to brighten the nights and days. Suddenly the honor given to Veleda was to her mother no longer something to rejoice in.

Ancamna touched her younger sister's arm in sympathy. "Yes, my sister, we must. Aiua read the omens and they are favorable for starting the journey. And as the new day began at dusk, she saw nine wrens flying in the direction of Eire. Nothing could be clearer than that. We have to leave today."

Bormana nodded in resignation. In the face of such an obvious sign, there was nothing one could say or do to argue any further. "Of course," she said, and squared her shoulders. "Come then," she added briskly to her daughter. "Let us get you to the boat."

Together, they walked back along the bank, to where the plank-boat was moored. On such boats was the tribe's commerce conducted. This one was piled high with trade goods, the last of which was being lashed into place. Except for the magical rods, which she always carried with her in a pouch attached to her belt, Veleda's belongings were already on board. A small group had gathered beside the boat, her father and brothers among them. As Veleda drew closer, more people began to arrive: running down the paths that led from the river to the village, trotting through the woods, converging steadily until the boat was all but obscured by the tall brightly clad bodies of adults and the restless darting forms of children. The everpresent dogs ran to join in the excitement, barking and snapping at each other as they raced along the bank.

Veleda noted this in wonder. "Are they all here for me?" she asked her mother and aunt.

"They are indeed." Ancamna smiled. "Why are you surprised? You have been of great service to our tribe. You healed many people. Why would they not come to bid you a safe journey?"

Bormana swelled with pride as she looked upon this honor being done to her daughter. It did not ease the pain of being separated, but it helped.

The final farewells began in earnest, flowing past in a flurry of hugs, well wishes, and calls of thanks and good fortune. Veleda's eyes searched for and found Sattia. Her soul-friend elbowed her way to the front of the crowd and the two girls caught each other up in a fierce embrace.

"I am going to work hard at my training as a warrior," Sattia whispered. "And when you come back, we can practice our swordcraft together. After all, Druids can still use a sword."

Before Veleda could answer, others took Sattia's place. The rest of the leavetaking became a blur: of faces both smiling and weeping, of warm arms gripping her in affection and sadness, of voices ringing in her ears so loudly that the many sounded like one. Her father's rough cheek brushed her own, her mother embraced her so fiercely that her ribs hurt. Her brothers hung back, rushing forward at the last moment to pile into her arms. She felt a dog's cold wet nose thrust into her palm, and then she was aboard the boat. Ancamna was beside her, and the rough wooden deck was swaying beneath her feet as the boatmen set their shoulders against the long poles to push off from the shore.

"Look well upon your home, child," Ancamna said to her as the sturdy plank-boat moved out into the current. "Long and long will it be before you set eyes upon it again."

Veleda said nothing. It was painful to swallow past the great lump that had formed in her throat. Her people lined the banks, waving and smiling and calling out. Not a single mention had been made of the warning she had tried to give last night. Other Druids had made their own divinations and had still discovered no confirming signs. Even Ancamna was still reserving judgement. Without the all-important Druidic approval, chieftains, craftsmen, farmers, and warriors alike felt confident that what Veleda had seen was not a prediction of a Roman threat, but of their own victory. Yet this did not lessen anyone's gratitude to her for her vanquishing of the sickness.

Veleda's people crowded along the shimmering Rhine, as glorious as the river itself, glowing in the full flower of their pride and strength. The sunlight caught in the gold and silver of their arm-rings and torques and earrings gave a sheen to the many hues of red and blonde and brown hair. It shone in the colorful green and red and blue patterns of their cloaks and tunics and danced off their bright faces as they grinned and laughed. They were indeed a sight to behold. Years later, when it had all become blood and anguish and death, when so many of these folk who were calling to her now had gone to the Otherworld, Veleda would look back down the pathways of memory, and remember them as they had been on this day. The Eburones. Proud and strong, and above all—free.

But at this moment, She was thinking of Mau. She had not seen the cat since the assembly in the sacred grove. There had been no sign of him at the feast, or this morning when she had been making her last preparations. Had he deserted her? It would not be surprising, Veleda told herself. After the way she had failed to convince even the smallest child of Bast's warning, the Cat-headed Goddess had, in all likelihood, called the faery cat back to Her. The thought left her with an empty feeling in her heart. In truth, Mau was an annoying creature, but, by Oak and Ash, she was growing accustomed to him. And he was supposed to protect her. If Bast had indeed deserted her, did that mean that Sekhmet would leave her in peace as well?

"No, she will not," a familiar voice said. "And neither will I."

She spun around. Mau was standing behind her, his huge orange eyes like twin reflections of the sun. When he saw that he had her attention he sat down, curling his tail fastidiously about his paws. "I may as well tell you I have never liked boats," he went on conversationally. "Any more than I like water. The thought of swaying along a river cooped up with a gaggle of humans who won't wash for weeks is not my idea of pleasure. Ah, well." He stretched out a front paw, extended his claws, and regarded them critically. "There are always rats and mice to hunt on a boat. At least I won't be bored."

"Where have you been?" Veleda was caught between irritation and the desire to laugh. "And aren't you worried that someone will hear you? My aunt"—she glanced about and realized that neither Ancamna nor the boatmen were paying attention to them. Ancamna was standing with the lead boatman consulting with him about the journey, and the other men were occupied with maneuvering the long unwieldy vessel into the tricky river currents.

"Don't worry." Mau lowered his paw and extended his entire body in a luxurious stretch. "Ahh, that feels good." His eyes narrowed with delight, his light voice rising with the effort of elongating himself. "When she comes over here," he added. "She'll see a cat, but not a talking one."

"We could tell her, you know," Veleda said. "She may be trusted."

"I do not trust any two-legged." Mau replied. "Neither birds nor people. You, human girl, are the one exception."

Veleda sighed. "So be it. But tell me, where have you been?"

Mau ended his stretch and looked at her, his eyes wide. "Where I am supposed to be," he said simply. "Guarding you."

"Has something happened?" Veleda felt her own eyes

widen until it seemed as though they had grown as large as those of Mau himself.

"You did not notice? Well, I shouldn't be surprised. You are untaught, in spite of your gifts. Last night Sekhmet gained a small victory, and I had to make certain it did not grow into a larger one. It was She who was responsible for your people mistaking the meaning of what you tried to tell them at that feast."

A chill went through Veleda. "How?"

"It was easy for Her. In their love of battle, your people are far too susceptible. All She had to do was place the thought in the mind of your father and it was done."

"My father?" The chill within Veleda caught fire, blazing into a white-hot rage. "She tried to harm my father?"

Mau made an impatient sound. "No, girl, She tried to harm you, and She sought to do it through your father, and everyone else in the hall last night. It was Her intent to turn them against you, to make your own people attack and destroy you for what they thought was a false and evil prophecy. I must admit: had She succeeded it would have been a neat bit of irony. You, the hope of your people, killed by them."

Stunned, Veleda stared at him. Her own kith and kin kill her? Even under the influence of Sekhmet, it was an idea her conscious mind could not take in. "How—how did you stop them?" she finally managed to ask.

Mau's feline gaze seemed more enigmatic than ever. "That," he said, "is why I am here. To protect you. I could not make them accept the truth of what Lady Bast wants you to tell them, but at least I could turn their love of blood away from you and toward the Romans. It was not the best solution, but it foiled Sekhmet, and it kept you alive."

Veleda was silent for several long moments, remembering the faces of her parents and brothers as they shouted and rattled their weapons. "My aunt," she said at last. "She was not taken in."

"No, she wasn't. She is powerful as Druids go, but don't

hold too much confidence in that; not all Druids are as strong as she is. You will have to be careful, very careful, until you have grown in strength yourself—''

Abruptly Mau fell silent. Veleda looked up and saw Ancamna approaching, her tall body swaying awkwardly with the movement of the boat, her staff thumping on the wooden planking with every step. "I vow the first few hours on a boat are hard for me," she confided as she came closer. "Thank the gods, I'll soon be used to it." She stared thoughtfully at Mau, who returned her gaze in continued unblinking silence. "I see another traveling companion has joined us," she said.

"He will be going with me to Eire," Veleda explained quickly. "Bast—the outland Goddess I told you of— wishes it."

Ancamna nodded, her eyes fixed on Mau in the same manner she had studied him when he leaped up on the platform to join Veleda at the Druid gathering. The cat sat motionless, his flame-bright eyes looking intently into the Druid's dark ones. They remained that way for several moments while Veleda watched, afraid to speak lest she disturb whatever wordless communication was taking place.

Finally Ancamna broke the silence. "You will not reveal your powers to me, will you?" She asked this softly, without taking her eyes from Mau's.

The cat made no sound.

"I expected not." Ancamna turned at last to her niece. "It appears you have a powerful protector, my foster-daughter." Her deep seeing gaze searched Veleda's face. "The question is, what is he here to protect you from."

Veleda looked back at her, and she did not realize how her eyes burned. "What is important is that I must protect our people," she said.

She was only a girl, but the words were those of a grown woman, a warrior, on fire with purpose. Ancamna took note of that fire, listened closely to the tone in her niece's voice.

She looked again at the cat, and then back at Veleda. She said nothing more.

Wrapped in the mists of early evening, the island of Eire rose up from the sea as if appearing from a dream.

Swaying in the sturdy round hide boat that could weather the sea's capricious winds and waves with ease, Veleda stared, unaware that her mouth had fallen open, utterly caught up in the beauty of her destination. Now she saw why Eire was also called Island of the Woods. From her vantage point on the water, this country appeared to be one vast and lush woodland. The green of it was a sight to mesmerize the eye and enchant the soul. Mountains tipped toward the sky, as fertile as the Mother's breasts, and crowned with trees that still glittered from a recent rain shower. As Veleda looked out over this land where she would be spending at least the next twelve years of her life in the initial part of her training, the lowering sun sent long fingers shimmering out through the mists, calling up a rainbow that curved gracefully about the island in the damp air.

Beside her Ancamna watched her niece and smiled. "Magic is strong on Eire," she said. "And so are learning and the ancient wisdoms. They keep to the old ways here. You will be taught well."

"It's beautiful," Veleda breathed. "I had not thought it would be so beautiful."

"Beauty is but a reflection of what lies within. When you leave this island you will carry the beauty of the land within you forever." Ancamna turned her gaze from Eire to Veleda. "Had it not been for the vision that came to you the night of the feast, you would be going to Albion now, to one of the Druid schools there. But on Eire, you can begin learning the arts of divination and prophecy. The woman who will teach you is a great Mistress of these arts. She will show you how to use the gifts the outland Goddess gave you."

SARAH ISIDORE

Veleda nodded. She knew, as all her people did, of the mysterious Druid colleges situated on Albion, also called the Island of the Mighty, and on Eire. She also knew that the training she was about to embark upon would be more difficult and demanding beyond measure.

"Other teachers will come to examine you through your schooling," Ancamna continued. "To see how you are progressing. After twelve years have passed, you will be examined once again, and if all goes well, then will you go to the Island of the Mighty for the remainder of your training."

"Will I see you during that time, Mother's Sister?" The question had gnawed at Veleda during the long nights of the journey. Now, as the round boat bounced over the choppy waves, bearing them steadily closer to the moment when she would bid farewell to this woman whom she loved as a second mother, Veleda could hold it back no longer.

Ancamna's smile held understanding in its warmth. Yet her answer was typically Druid. "Who can say? If it is meant for us to, then we shall. In the meantime"—her gaze went to Mau, who crouched in front of them, his sleek fur ruffled, clearly put out by the continuation of this interminable water journey—"you will have someone to watch over you."

Veleda's gaze followed Ancamna's, and she, too, smiled. "Yes," she said softly, and tentatively reached out to touch the cat's back.

The hide boat was soon nosing its way onto a flat stony beach. It was a natural landing place where cargo was routinely unloaded from the mainland or Albion. But on this evening the beach was deserted. Only one figure stood there waiting for the boat to land, a woman dressed in Druid robes.

"Is that her?" Veleda whispered to Ancamna. "My teacher?"

Ancamna was watching the distant figure with a fond

expression. "She is called Nuadu, and nowhere will you encounter a man or woman who is wiser in the sacred ways of divination. She is a seer without peer and it is a great honor that she has agreed to take you on as one of her students. But then"—her fond expression favored Veleda—"you are special indeed, my foster-daughter."

Mau was the first to leave the boat, departing in a long arching leap that brought him well onto dry land. In spite of her nervousness, Veleda had to hide a grin. If they had been alone, she was certain that she would, at this moment, be hearing an acerbic discourse on boats and travel over any body of water in general.

One of the boatmen jumped out to help Veleda and Ancamna onto the beach, while the other man pushed the boat farther up onto the stones. The lone woman came toward them. Bright red hair flowed unbound over her shoulders, partially hiding the gold Druid's torque. As she drew closer, Veleda realized that her red hair and long swinging stride disguised the fact that she was actually quite old. Deep lines had marked their pathways over a face of the most extraordinary sweetness the girl had ever seen.

The gentleness of her countenance was both striking and unexpected. Veleda had seen other Druids skilled in the arts of divination and they had never impressed her as either gentle or sweet. These were the Druids whose skills included the art of sacrifice, of bringing death so that the living might be protected. There were other ways to accomplish this, but sacrifice was chief among them. The men and women whose province this was were wise beyond dispute, but along with that wisdom, they bore the stern implacability of death, an aura that made them intimidating and almost feared.

There was nothing fearful or intimidating about Nuadu. The smile she gave Veleda and Ancamna was as open as the sunrise and she advanced toward the latter with her arms outstretched. The two women embraced and when they drew apart, Nuadu approached Veleda and took her hands. The older woman's hands were dry and strong, callused from a lifetime of work. She stared at the girl for some moments in silence. Her light hazel eyes sparkled into Veleda's, probing with a kindly yet searching scrutiny. Veleda looked back, feeling as if each of her souls had been laid bare to that gentle gaze.

"So she is the one." Nuadu addressed Ancamna, though her gaze remained on Veleda. "I see that she has been gifted."

"Yes, and now she must be taught how to use those gifts."

Nuadu turned her wise eyes on Ancamna and studied Veleda again. "It will not be easy," she said.

8

 AND IT WAS NOT EASY.

Nuadu took Veleda under her wing the way a mother duck shepherds her young, adding her to the eleven students who already attended her, all of them young women, for women were thought to make the best seers. But Nuadu's kindness did not disguise the fact that the days and years ahead would be arduous ones.

Veleda had grown up in the *oppidum* of her father, with all the comforts that went along with being the daughter of a chieftain. She had always taken for granted the fine tunics, glittering jewelry, and thick furs upon her bed, not loving them unduly but still accepting them as her due. With Nuadu these things vanished like snow beneath a spring sun. Physical amenities were a distraction, the seer explained to her. Luxuries interfered with learning. Therefore the accommodations for both herself and her students were sparse in the extreme. The school lay near a large settlement, north, as was the sacred direction for all such schools. Learning was conducted mostly by rote, in order to strengthen the memory, and much of that learning was done in total darkness.

The places where this happened were secret, forbidden to all but the initiated and those they taught. They were called "Houses of Darkness," and that was precisely what they were: small stone huts hidden in wooded hills or valleys overlooking the sea, black as a grave once a student had crawled into one and lay down to recite the day's lessons, repeating them over and over and over again, until the knowledge was engraved in the mind as indelibly as carving upon stone.

The duty of a seer was to divine the affairs of humankind from a close observation of nature, something that could be done only through the holy mysteries of dreams, augury, and sacrifice. The study of each of these arts was highly complex. Each student had to learn the meaning of the sun in all its forms; such as a brilliant sun denoting blood; a dark sun denoting danger; two suns in one night denoting disgrace; and the sun and moon in the same course denoting battle. There was the infinitely detailed study of bird flight and bird song. Divination was inextricably bound up with the favorable or unfavorable nature of days, a subject that took years to master. There were magical postures and complex patterns of ritual invocations to be learned, so the distractions of the outer world would not interfere with one's inner vision. There was Composing on One's Finger Ends: a seer's ability to touch someone with his staff or pick up an object and by means of an invocation, discover the history of that person or object.

And then there was the Inspiration of Tradition: the art of sacrifice. In this all-important method, the seer would chew upon flesh of certain animals, and, after the proper invocations, cast herself into sleep of incubation during which she would give a true augury through access to the wisdom guarded by the totemic beast thus consumed. It was here that the profound differences between Veleda and the other students first began to emerge.

When Nuadu had said to Ancamna that it would not be easy, both women had known that she was speaking of more than rigorous learning and lack of comfort. Veleda soon discovered this for herself. There was a price for the gifts she had been given. As this period of her teaching began, the paying of that price began also.

Even in these early stages of her training, Veleda excelled. Her mind was sharp and focused, able to take in and grasp vast amounts of information, then memorize it in the darkness of the stone huts where the final phase of each day's lessons took place. Her abilities did not go unnoticed by the other students, all of whom had advanced further along the path of learning than this latest arrival to their ranks. They were not sure what to make of either her or the large black cat who accompanied her everywhere but to the Houses of Darkness, where even the glow of his eyes would be enough to break the absolute blackness of the study environment. Veleda found herself set apart from her companions, as much by her own feelings as by theirs.

She alone was under the hand of an outland Goddess. She carried the memory of Bast within her constantly; the warning she had thus far failed to deliver successfully weighed upon her like one of the great green mountains of Eire. Bast had said She would gift her with prophecy, but Veleda's own sense of urgency to progress as far and as fast she could added to whatever gifts the Cat-Goddess had bestowed.

On the day Nuadu started teaching the ways of sacrifice, these differences became even more profound. When the students gathered on a hill after their plain morning meal of porridge, bread, and mead, the Druid came to join them. She was dressed in her ceremonial white robe and trotting along behind her on a short tether followed a small brown and white nanny goat. A soft wind toyed with the folds of the woman's snowy white robe as she led the animal in a circle to her right. They went sunwise, for to go to the left was a contrary direction and against the order of the universe, certain to bring the worst of luck upon any action thus taken.

Nuadu brought the goat to a halt and stood for a moment, looking at each student's face. She started to speak, stroking the goat lightly as she talked. "The duty of sacrifice is no light matter. It is an awesome responsibility, laid upon us by the gods. We who are learned in its ways must ever be mindful that the one offering up his life does so that we might learn from his wisdom. Therefore we are bound to treat any creature destined for sacrifice—be they human or animal—with the greatest of respect."

A strange feeling came over Veleda as she listened. She was keenly aware of Mau's presence. The cat was sitting beside her, and though he would not speak to her before all these people she could feel his thoughts swirling around her like heavy smoke. He disapproved. And yet surely the people of Egypt used sacrifice to honor their gods and ask for guidance? She herself had watched the Druids conduct sacrifices all her life, although she had never guessed that one day she would be the one learning to perform that sacred task. Granted, Mau himself had once been destined for sacrifice, but that had been before Veleda discovered he was a magical being. He was impervious to any such fate, therefore why was she sensing this condemnation?

Nuadu continued with her lecture, calming the fidgety goat with a gentle hand. "The death must always be painless. There is no merit in causing agony to the body of a creature about to share her soul with you. And remember: in the moment of this goat's death, she will be reborn in the Otherworld."

"Mistress," one the students said. Her name was Eponina, in honor of the horse-Goddess Epona, and of all the students she had been the friendliest to Veleda. She possessed a bright and shining intelligence and she asked a great many questions. "We all know that sacrifice must serve a higher purpose," Eponina said. "Is the sole purpose here to teach us? It seems a poor way to use the life of this creature."

"It would be," Nuadu answered gravely. "But it is not. There is a dispute between two farmers over their flocks and this goat will be used to render a judgement. A sacrifice is meaningless unless the object being sacrificed has meaning to those who offer it. This goat is a most valuable milker and both farmers claim her. You, my students, will participate in determining the man she belongs to. I will sacrifice the animal, then each of us will eat of her flesh. After that, we will recite the invocations and cast ourselves into the ritual sleep. Then will I see how well you are learning.''

Veleda shifted her feet, as restless and fidgety as the goat. The feelings prickling over her had grown stronger, and now she recognized them clearly. This was how she had felt the night she had found Mau and set him free, when she had gone against Ancamna and all those older and wiser than she to prevent the sacrifice. She glanced down to find that Mau was staring up at her. For a long heartbeat their eyes met. Suddenly Veleda understood. It was not Mau she was sensing. It was Bast.

The truth struck her, enveloping her in warmth. The presence of the Goddess was all around her, speaking to her without words, calling to her, instructing her. The brightness of early morning faded, the faces of Nuadu and the other students receding as if night had fallen. Bast's face took shape before Veleda's transfixed gaze, filling her vision. In the border between time and space, the enormous eyes looked into hers, intimate and unknowable at once. The cat face smiled, and the voice thrummed through Veleda's being. *I have given you gifts. Use them.*

Nuadu pulled on the tether, drawing the nanny goat closer. Gesturing to Camma, another of the students, she bestowed upon her the honor of holding the silver basin that would be used to catch the blood when the goat's throat had been cut. Then she drew a curved long-bladed knife from her robes and held it up. Her sweet voice rang out, chanting the invocations before sacrifice. She lowered the knife, positioning it carefully for the stroke that would slice through the goat's jugular vein.

''No.'' Veleda's voice cracked out as sharply as the smack of a sword against a shield.

Nuadu's hand froze in midair, the knife suspended over the goat's throat. Next to her Camma's head swiveled

around. Still holding the basin she stared at Veleda in astonished horror, her mouth hanging open. Her expression was
mirrored by each of the other students. To interrupt a sacrifice was undreamed of, so far beyond the realms of accepted behavior that the implications could not be
imagined. That the most evil of luck would follow such a
deed was certain. If Veleda had done this not as one going
through the process of being initiated into the mysteries,
she would have risked banishment or death. Even with her
status as a student, her fate was highly uncertain at best.

Veleda realized that she was trembling. She knew as well
as anyone else the seriousness of what she had done. For
her to have freed Mau before the sacrifice that night was
grave enough. But Ancamna had given her a way to salvage
the situation and thus save herself. For this, there could be
no excuse. She grew aware that those who had been standing near her were stepping away, as if they feared that being
close to her would bring her ill fortune upon them. Only
Mau remained beside her, calm and unmoving, his orange
eyes fixed unwaveringly on Nuadu.

Slowly the Druid lowered the knife. Veleda tried to interpret her expression, but the woman's serene face and
light hazel eyes were unreadable.

"Why have you done this?" Nuadu's voice was low and
calm, not raging, as Veleda would have expected. Her companions clearly expected the same; they glanced at each
other in surprise.

"There is no need." Veleda spoke tentatively. But even
as she said the words, a certainty as absolute as Anu's three
phases swept over her and she repeated herself emphati-
cally. "There is no need."

"What mean you?" Nuadu's voice was still quiet, but
frown lines had appeared between her eyes. She kept the
knife lowered although she continued to hold the goat's
tether firmly in one hand.

"I mean"—Veleda hesitated for the barest instant—"I
mean that there is no need for the goat to die. She can share

her wisdom with us without giving up her life to do it."

The students exchanged incredulous whispers. "In truth, Veleda?" Eponina gasped out excitedly, and was promptly hushed by the others.

"Child," Nuadu said in her gentle voice. "Do you understand the gravity of the deed you have committed? Sacrifice is a holy act. In interfering with what is to happen here, you have committed sacrilege. You have set yourself apart from what is sacred."

"No, Mistress, I have not." That same certainty carried Veleda forward, enabling her to ignore the shocked stares of her companions and meet Nuadu's gaze without flinching. "I know that sacrifice is holy. It is sacred to me, as well; you must believe that. For you and other Druids it is the path to wisdom—"

Nuadu cut her off, and for the first time there was anger in her tone. "This cannot pass without consequences. You understand that much, do you not?"

Veleda kept her eyes squarely on those of her teacher. "I do, Lady. But—I have been given a gift. I can speak with this goat; I can learn her wisdom. Please, will you not let me show you? If you are not satisfied, then you may inflict any punishment on me that you deem fit, and I will accept it."

Nuadu said nothing. She stood there, her students gathered behind her, her light hazel gaze scrutinizing Veleda from head to foot. Clouds began to drift across the sky, throwing the hill into bars of sunlight followed by bars of shade. High overhead a hawk rode the currents, wings lazily outstretched as it searched for game. The silence stretched on, and, except for a brief searching look at Mau, Nuadu continued to stare at Veleda. It was impossible to know what she was thinking. Whatever gifts Bast had given her, Veleda thought ruefully, they did not include seeing the thoughts of a Druid.

The lengthy silence was suddenly broken by the nanny goat. She let out a loud bleat and tugged at the tether, trying to move toward Veleda. The animal's movement seemed to decide Nuadu. "Very well," she said abruptly. "You have already disrupted the universal order with your actions. Now we will see if you can put things right."

She released the tether. Without hesitation the goat trotted to Veleda, the tether trailing loosely behind her. She stopped in front of the girl and stood motionless, the restlessness that had filled her earlier completely gone. Her eyes were a pale golden color and they looked into Veleda's, bright and fearless and utterly knowing. For a moment Veleda had no idea what she should do next. Then she felt Mau brush against her, and sure and swift, the knowledge came to her.

She knelt before the goat and stretched out her hands. The nanny's ears were long and silky and she stroked them gently. She ran her fingers through the thick brown and white coat, then caressed the animal's face. At last her gaze locked with that of the goat and she fell into the creature's mind. It happened so swiftly that she was not aware of it. Nuadu and her students saw a blankness come over her face. Nuadu understood that expression instantly. The girl had the same look that seers took on when they entered the ritual sleep. But that state of inner wisdom could not occur until after one had eaten of the sacrificial animal's flesh; at least, it had never been known to before. This was something utterly new, outside of the powers she was familiar with. The Druid leaned forward, intent on what was happening before her.

Beyond human eyes, Veleda and the goat danced together. The goat spoke to Veleda in that vast whirling space. She knew that she had almost died and that Veleda's interruption had saved her. She was grateful, but she was still a goat, with all the contrariness of a goat's nature. She butted Veleda playfully, darted around her, and teased her by running off into the mists. Finally, she came to the human, leaned her head against Veleda's, and shared her wisdom.

The goat did not think as humans did, in cumbersome words and ideas. Her wisdom revealed itself in pictures. She showed Veleda what she needed to know, the images spreading before her. When she was through, she butted the girl again, as if unable to resist a final indulgence in her nature, but also to tell her that the communication was finished.

"The dispute is settled."

The wide-eyed students started at the sound of Veleda's voice. It sounded strangely disconnected, as if it was coming from somewhere else, even though her lips moved and the words were plainly hers. She went on, her eyes open, although to everyone watching, it was clear that she was seeing only what lay within.

"Seven of the goats belong with the farmer east of the river. The remaining thirteen, along with this one, must go to the flocks of the farmer to the west. That is where their proper home lies."

Very slowly she dropped her hands from the goat. The animal shook herself, nosed gently at Veleda's face, lowered her head to sniff at Mau, then finally wandered off and started to graze on the bushes nearby. As she moved away, Veleda's eyes regained their focus. She swayed a little, and Nuadu swiftly stepped forward to steady her.

Veleda looked into the older woman's face. "What I have seen is true," she said. Her voice sounded like her own again, and she stood very straight, meeting Nuadu's piercing gaze without difficulty. Mau sat beside her, as motionless as the goat had been, his luminous eyes studying the Druid as intently as she herself had studied Veleda while the latter was communing with the goat.

Nuadu regarded Veleda in silence. The other students neither moved nor spoke, their eyes flicking nervously between their teacher and their fellow student. Only the goat had lost all interest in the proceedings. She rustled amongst the brush and saplings, busily yanking leaves off branches, her tail twitching in rhythm with her chewing. A hare, disturbed by her progress, darted out from the brush and raced past. But no one, not even Mau, paid it the slightest heed.

All at once a great smile bloomed upon Nuadu's age-marked features. The sleeves of her robe fell back as she reached out to grasp Veleda's shoulders. "Yes," she said happily. "I know it well. You, my fledgling, have a true gift. The gods have indeed favored you with *eicse*, wisdom." She stepped back, and just as swiftly as it had appeared the smile was gone. "Are you tired?" she asked.

Veleda nodded. "A little." This surprised her; she had not noticed that she was, until Nuadu asked her.

Nuadu was not surprised. "Walk with me," she said. "We must return the goat to her rightful owner and tell both men of the judgement." She retrieved the goat's tether and gestured for the rest of the students to accompany them.

They all set off; Nuadu and Veleda first, the goat behind them, and the students following. Mau, in his own independent way, trailed along, disappearing and reappearing from amongst the woods that lined either side of the path.

To walk beside the teacher was a favored position, and Veleda was well aware of it. But it was a bittersweet sign of approval. She was equally aware of her companions, whispering and staring, as they traipsed along in a close group behind their teacher and this favored one who possessed such mysterious gifts. Veleda struggled against the impulse to turn around. It seemed as if eleven pairs of eyes burned holes in her back, and it was not a pleasant sensation. Never had she found a problem in making friends; all her life she had felt easy with those of her age, playing and practicing weaponscraft together, riding horses, exploring the woods, and in short, doing all the things a young tribeswoman did.

She should be exultant over what had just happened, she told herself. And yet, instead of the joy and pride anyone would expect her to take in this latest demonstration of Bast's gifts, she felt unexpectedly lonely, and deeply set apart from her peers. She walked beside Nuadu and self-criticism added its weight to her loneliness. She should be thanking the Cat-Goddess for this wondrous ability instead of brooding because she had no friends. She should be spinning with joy over this incredible capacity to speak with animals, and not a magical animal such as Mau, but real animals, on their own terms. She did not deserve Bast's favor; she was not worthy.

"It is not easy, is it?" Nuadu's gentle voice jerked Veleda from her painful reverie.

"Lady?" she responded hesitantly.

"Your companions watch you now. They do not know what to make of you. You are different, special, not like them. And that is never an easy thing to bear."

A shaky sigh heaved itself involuntarily from Veleda's breast. "Oh, Mistress," she breathed. "How did you know?"

Nuadu's smile held sadness in its warmth. "It is the way of such gifts, fledgling. Nothing comes without a price, Veleda, in this world or any other. What came to you today was an extraordinary blessing from the gods, but you must pay for it nonetheless. Your aunt said that you were favored, and she saw true. But I see true, as well, and what I see is a high price to be paid. A very high price."

Veleda's steps faltered. "Lady," she said in a low voice. "You are a great seer. Do you believe me about the Romans? No one else does, but surely you must, especially after"—she gestured at the goat—"this."

The Druid walked for some moments in silence. "Ah, the Romans," she murmured at last. "A most interesting and a most troubling people."

Mau wandered out of a copse of silvery birch trees. On noiseless pads he paced alongside Veleda, his tail held high, appearing in every way a simple cat but for his remarkable all-too-knowing eyes. He turned those eyes on Veleda, and she knew at once that his sudden appearance had not been coincidence. Nuadu gazed at him thoughtfully. She had been curiously silent when it came to this large black cat.

Veleda was certain that her aunt had spoken to her about Mau, but still, she would have expected the seer to question her about his presence, or at least remark upon it. So far she had done neither.

"Ancamna spoke to me about your prophecy, of course." Nuadu turned her gaze back to Veleda. "It is one of the reasons you are here, after all. But then, you must know that."

Veleda resisted the sudden desire to seize the woman's sleeve. "They will not listen to me," she burst out. Behind her, the soft murmurs of the other students abruptly stopped, and hastily she lowered her voice. "Not my people, and not the Brothers and Sisters of the Oak, the wise ones, who should know that I went to the Otherworld and that Bast charged me with a true warning to bring back to them."

Ah, what a relief it was to finally say these words aloud! She had not realized until now, how much the anger and frustration had been swirling around inside her.

Nuadu's slight sad smile had not changed. "It is a Druid teaching that a person who visits the Otherworld comes back as an immortal. Do you believe that you are now immortal, fledgling?"

"No." It was a shocking question, and Veleda had to look away before answering. "I know that I am not." If such an enormous thing as everlasting life had been among Bast's gifts, she thought to herself, Mau would have certainly said so. She caught his gaze, and knew that she was right.

"Then perhaps you were not in the Otherworld, but somewhere else. And that could be why the Druids of your tribe have difficulty believing your warnings."

"They do not want to believe!" Veleda's anger was returning with new force, and she had to struggle to keep her voice down, lest the others overhear. "They have no faith in the words of an outland Goddess, even though it was Her outland magic which cured them. They would rather go to war than prepare themselves for war. Their pride rules them, not their sense—''

"And you, fledgling," Nuadu asked gently. "What rules you at this moment?"

Caught up in her anger, Veleda glared at her teacher. Nuadu returned her stare calmly, and after a moment the girl's eyes fell. "How can I make them believe me, Mistress?" she whispered.

They had descended the twisting path and were walking past fields planted in corn, the young plants stretching up toward the cloud-speckled sky. Ahead lay the first of the farmsteads they were to visit, its thatched house and outbuildings neat and well cared for. Someone had already brought word to the farmer of the seer's coming, and he, his wife, and several other people were hurrying through the fields to meet her.

Nuadu laid her free hand on Veleda's arm. "A person who understands others must first learn to understand herself. And she can never lead others, unless she can first lead herself. All the gifts and all the *eicse*, from your outland Goddess or any of our own Shining Ones, can never matter if those lessons are not learned." She took away her hand and waved to acknowledge the approaching farmer.

"But Lady." Veleda hurried to get the words out before the farmer and his family reached them. "Time flows away from us like a stream in the spring melting. What if there is not enough time to learn what must be learned?"

Nuadu's serene smile shone on the girl's agonized face. "Then you will just have to work all the harder. And whatever time the Shining Ones see fit to bestow upon us is the time we will have."

As the farmer came within hailing distance, Veleda grew aware that Nuadu had never answered the question she had asked her when they first began this conversation. She had never said whether she believed the prophecy about the Romans.

*   *   *

In the afternoon of that same day, the time came for the students to enter the Houses of Darkness, where they would recite the day's lessons until the words had been carved into their minds.

The house assigned to Veleda was a particularly remote one. Squat and small, it huddled in a thick copse of beech trees, hidden from view. The sea was a roaring presence outside, but once one had crawled through that narrow opening and blocked it with the piece of wood that lay just inside, the stone walls blocked out the voices of even the largest waves breaking upon the strand.

Inside Veleda lay on her back, her palms over either eye, crossways across her face, in the now familiar posture of learning. The quiet which surrounded her was absolute, disturbed only by the rhythmic droning of her voice as she repeated the different meanings and symbols of sacrifice. Unlike her companions, who regarded these daily periods as a necessary means to an end, Veleda had come to look forward to the lengthy hours spent in the Houses of Darkness. Only here, wrapped all around by the darkness for which the houses were named, did time stand still, easing for a while the constant pressure that never allowed her to forget that she had left the sacred tasks laid upon her unfulfilled.

Today, though, it was more difficult to reach the proper level of concentration. Veleda'a thoughts were still caught up in what had happened this morning. The beauty of her communication with the goat still lingered, filling her with wonder. Bast had said She was the guardian of animals, therefore, it made sense that She would bestow such a gift. But there were so many questions that needed answering, and Mau, the one who could answer them, was not here. With his usual unpredictability, he had vanished when the first farmer came to meet Nuadu and her students, and Veleda had not seen him since.

With an effort, she cleared her mind, determined to sink into her studies. Slowly she succeeded, and so caught up was she that she did not notice the difference in the atmosphere of the stone house. It was subtle at first, so slight that even had her concentration not been so intense, Veleda would not have been aware of any change in the dense blackness. Gradually, though, something began to prick at the outer edges of her consciousness, disturbing the power of her concentration. She tried to ignore it, certain that this was but a test of her ability to focus. Yet the very act of her ignoring the change in the hut's atmosphere seemed only to make it stronger. Still, she kept on with her recitations, her voice filling up the blackness.

Then she heard the first rustle, followed by a stamp, as though something had taken a single heavy step.

Her voice faltered, losing its steady rhythm. Could she have imagined it? Storms sometimes blew up from the sea this time of day; perhaps she had just heard the wind. Yet, even as she suggested this to herself, she knew it was not possible. The stone house's opening was blocked by the wood which acted as a makeshift door, and in any case, the entrance was too low and narrow to let in gusts of wind, much less another person; it was barely large enough for her to squeeze through.

The noise came again, and now Veleda could no longer ignore the change in the tiny hut's atmosphere. A foul odor wafted into her nostrils, slapping up against her face with the unmistakable reek of rotting flesh. Evil had crawled into the stone house, laying itself with thick power over the aura of learning that should have prevailed. She was not alone in here. Something was with her, something malevolent, something that meant her harm.

Veleda's breath caught in her throat. She gave up all pretense of continuing with her lessons. Her heart had begun to pound, its beating so loud it drowned all else. Slowly she lowered her hands from her eyes. She had to fight against an almost overwhelming urge to keep them there, to shut out whatever it was that had so mysteriously joined her in the darkness.

But once she moved her hands away her eyes insisted on opening. She saw nothing but black, familiar and unrelieved as always. Her heart beat ever faster when she realized it was not unrelieved after all. In one corner of the hut there was a glow, shifting and nebulous, like the spirit lights one saw in the far-off deepest parts of the forest on Samhain eve. Only now the glow was not far away. Even as she looked a shape began to form within the glow. As it did, another glow appeared, and then another, until each corner of the House of Darkness was occupied.

Within those four glows there were forms, each one exactly the same. Naked, the bodies were male in all respects save one: none bore the slightest sign of genitalia. The faces revealed in the yellow-green light were hideous beyond the very meaning of the word, bearded caricatures of men, their features twisted and livid with malevolence.

Veleda wanted to flee with every shred of nerve and bone, but she was caught in the glow of eyes that burned red and yellow and green, until the colors all blurred into one evil flame multiplied eight times. Unable to move, frozen on the earthen floor, she stared, while her mind gibbered in horror at one other observation. Each of the creatures possessed only one arm and one leg, and on the side of the body where the other limbs should have been, there was not even a suggestion of stumps to indicate that an arm or leg had ever been present.

Balancing with impossible ease on their single legs, the four nightmares each took a single hop toward her, moving with an eerie and terrifying grace. Their mouths opened in soundless snarls, revealing long sets of upper and lower fangs stained the color of old blood. The odor of rot intensified until Veleda could scarcely breathe. The ancient instinct to survive rose up, and she struggled to gain her feet, to flee before those death-colored fangs could rip into her flesh. It was useless; a holding spell had been placed upon her by those terrible eyes, and she was bound to the floor as surely as if chains encircled all her limbs. A scream bubbled up in her throat, but even that escaped as nothing more than a sort of strangled gurgle. Her eyes bulged helplessly, as one of the creatures lunged for her throat.

And clicked together on empty air.

In the instant before those jaws could close a black shape swirled up between Veleda and the creature. A furious yowl erupted, the sound scraping across her nerve endings. After that, the hut's enclosed space became a spinning snarling mass of thuds and claws and teeth and arms grasping at the air. Through it all Veleda lay as one dead, frozen on her back, miraculously untouched, although the battle raged right over her. In these close quarters it seemed impossible that the combatants would not land atop her, but somehow they did not.

Suddenly all was still. The fetid odor was abruptly gone. Veleda's lungs expanded, gratefully drawing in a deep breath of the close but clean air. The light from the hideous creatures had also vanished, although two eyes still glowed at her through the darkness. They were familiar eyes, though, and Veleda swallowed several times, hoping that her voice had returned.

"Mau?" she finally gasped out.

"Who else would it be?" his dry voice replied.

She swallowed again, experimentally moving her arms and legs, discovering that she was able to sit up. "Did—did they hurt you?"

"Of course not," he said, sounding inordinately cheerful. "I am a magical being. It would take more than Sekhmet's demons to harm me." His cheerful tone vanished. "The same cannot be said of you, however." Busily he began to clean himself, the rough sound of his tongue the only noise now, aside from Veleda's ragged breathing. "Foul things," he growled between licks. "They taste as loathsome as they smell."

Velleda shuddered. "Is that what they were? Demons?"

"What else?" Mau sounded impatient. "And you know as well as I do who sent them. It's why I'm here, after all.

To protect you from the likes of demons or any other magic Sekhmet tries to work."

"In truth?" Anger put a sudden stop to Veleda's shuddering. "Then why did it take you so long to perform your task? By the Ninth Wave, Cat, one of those creatures was about to plunge his fangs into my throat!"

If she expected Mau to be abashed, he was not. "Yes, well," he said calmly. "That could not be helped."

"And why could it not be helped? Were you waiting to see my throat torn out before you decided to "protect" me?"

"I was waiting," Mau said in that same unperturbed tone, "to see what you would do."

Veleda struggled to her knees. The roof of the stone house was too low to permit her to stand, so she remained on her knees, shaking with rage and the aftermath of the absolute terror that had gripped her. "Then I hope you are happy with what you saw. I could do nothing! Nothing!"

"Why do you think the demons came to you today?" Mau asked quietly.

"I—what difference does that make!"

"They came because of what you did this morning. It is a great gift my Lady Bast gave to you, and it has been sleeping inside you ever since, waiting for the proper time to come forth. Now that it has, Sekhmet will seek even harder to destroy you. She will look for your weaknesses, and when She sees them, as She did this afternoon, when you lay here distracted and thinking of other things, She will send those who do Her bidding to attack you."

Veleda's anger was leaving her. "Without you they would have killed me," she admitted miserably. "I was not strong enough to keep them from me."

Mau resumed his washing. "Then you must see to it that you become so," he said.

9

Twelve years later in the territory of the Aedui tribe in Gaul

"IT WILL WORK, I TELL YOU. They have said they will come."

The speaker turned excitedly to his companion, his green-and-red checked cloak swirling about broad shoulders. It was warm for a day in the month of Seed-Fall, and the frost that had whitened the morning was rapidly fading, darkening the grass in patches of moisture beneath the sun. The lake beside the two men had not yet frozen for the winter, and men were out on its waters and along its banks, hunting birds and netting fish in preparation for the long cold months that lay ahead.

"That," said the other man, "is precisely what I fear, that they *will* come. Do you know what you do here, Divitiacus?"

"Oh, yes, I know." Divitiacus's blue eyes glittered, fixing themselves on the lake. Several hide-covered boats were out on the water, but the fishermen were too far distant for any risk of the conversation being overheard. "I have gained the most powerful ally in the world for our tribe. The legions of Rome will push back those filthy Germans from across the Rhine. Ha!" He slapped a thick-muscled thigh. "Ariovistus boasts to the Otherworld itself about the valor of his warriors, but he and those warriors will have an unpleasant surprise when the Roman eagle swoops down upon them."

The other man turned to him. He was younger than Divitiacus, but they were much the same height and the family resemblance between them was strong. However, in contrast to the other's enthusiasm, the younger man's features were heavy with doubt, his blue eyes troubled. "We are both of us Druids, as well as chieftains," he said quietly. "What has happened to the clearness of your gaze that you cannot see the doom hovering about your deeds? The rich foods and wines of Rome have blinded your vision. You have allowed yourself to fall into the softness of perfumed cushions and have forgotten your duty to our people."

Divitiacus's blue eyes narrowed. "If any man but you, my brother, had spoken those words to me, his head would already be rolling in the grass." His hand went to the hilt of his sword as if to confirm this. "Heed me, Dumonorix," he went on harshly. "I journeyed to Rome out of duty to the Aedui. For no other reason than that did I go—"

"Although the honors they heaped upon you did nothing to shorten your stay, did they," interrupted Dumonorix, his tone equally harsh.

"I received the honors that were due me as King of the Aedui!" Divitiacus bit out each word, his clenched teeth gleaming beneath the sweeping blonde moustaches that adorned each side of his mouth. "And as for softness, I was a guest in the house of Quintus Tullius Cicero, who is himself a valiant soldier, as well as of noble blood. He is a fighting man, and yet he knows how to enjoy his comforts. And where is the harm in that, I ask you?"

His expression changed as he looked out over the lake. "Ah, Brother, how can I describe it to you. Rome is a wondrous place, a city beyond dreams. The buildings, the markets, the games, the food and wine, and the women— so unlike our own women. I tell you, Dumonorix, never have you seen the like. If only you had journeyed there with me, then would you understand."

Dumonorix stood in silence, arms folded across his chest, waiting for Divitiacus to turn back to him before he answered. "And what would I understand?" he asked coldly. "That I, too, should slaver after the luxuries of Rome like a dog lurking about a freshly slaughtered pig? No, Brother, I have no desire to visit Rome. I am a man of the Aedui, and with that, I am well content. As you should be, even more than I, for you are the king of our people. Yet here I stand, listening to you prate on and on about the glories of Rome, instead of concerning yourself with matters of importance to your tribe."

"I addressed the Senate!" Divitiacus snapped. "The Senate of Rome itself. There is no more important council of men in the world, and they sat there, in their white togas, in that glorious marble chamber, listening to *me*. The words flowed from my tongue, given to me by great Lugh, the Divine Poet Himself, convincing those senators to do my will. And I succeeded. The Senate has given me promises of an alliance. With Rome's soldiers, we will sweep away the Germans' incursions into our lands."

"You may succeed too well," Dumonorix warned. "Your Roman eagle may indeed swoop down upon the Germans. And then will she sweep down upon us."

"She will not." Divitiacus grinned, in possession of himself once more. "I have been given promises, and I intend to use them to our advantage. I am in control here, not the Romans."

Dumonorix shook his head. "Have you learned nothing? Roman promises cannot be trusted. They are not bound by oaths as we are. Honor-price means nothing to them. If the Senate promised you aid, it was because they saw value in it for Rome, and Rome alone."

His brother laughed. "You are the one who has learned nothing, Dumonorix. Self-interest is the way of all men in pledging alliances. I am a king, and well do I know the paths of kingship. Let you practice your Druidcraft, Brother, and leave the complexities of statecraft to me." He touched the heavy golden torque that curved about his neck. "That is the reason I wear this." Proudly his fingers traced the ends of the torque, each one ending in an intricately carved boar's head, an animal sacred to the Aedui.

The boastfulness in the gesture was too much for Dumonorix. He stepped close to Divitiacus, meeting him eye-to-eye, his jaw so tight the muscles along it bulged and jumped. "You are not the only one who wears a torque of gold." He yanked aside his cloak to reveal the burnished yellow metal gleaming about his own throat. "But while we both may wear this emblem of our noble blood, it seems that I alone remember what it means."

"And I do not? This torque is my birthright, the sign of our noble blood and my claim to the rule of the Aedui. How dare you speak to me like some milk-fed babe who does not know its worth!"

"I speak as the truth bids me." Dumonorix had not moved. "And if you view your torque as only a sign of your kingship, then you bear reminding, indeed." Reverently he laid his hand on the torque about his neck. "This is more than a sign of kingship or noble blood. This is a symbol that we are free men. Without it we are nothing; no better than those men who have fallen from their dignity, forfeited their honor-price, and become slaves. Freedom carries its own price, and the torque serves to reminds us of that. We are bound to protect our tribe, to put its welfare above all else. On no man does that burden rest heavier than upon the peoples' king—"

"Enough," snarled Divitiacus. "Even a king must listen to a Druid, but I, too, am a Druid, and I will listen no more. I know my duty. In bringing Rome to our country, I have worked a great deed, one that the bards will sing about for generations. Rome is a power in the world, brother; you cannot change that. Better that we welcome her as an ally than an enemy. You may not thank me for what I have done, but the people will praise me. For I have acted in their interests."

"No," Dumonorix said softly. "You have acted according to your ambition. And we shall all suffer for it.''

At last he stepped back from his brother and started to walk away. Suddenly he paused and wheeled around. "Look well upon your torque, Brother. When the Romans come, they will strip it from you and place a slave-collar on your neck in its stead. Then you will heed my words, but it will be too late.''

Veleda lay awake, listening to the breathing of the women around her. Over the years they had grown so familiar she could distinguish the sleep-sounds made by each one. Eponina, for example, always snored, a fact she vociferously denied when awake. Camma talked in her sleep, uttering things that were truly prophetic; indeed that was the very reason she had been brought here for training so long ago.

And then there was Mau. He had become a great comfort to Veleda during this peaceful yet busy time of her training. During the long days of learning he would sit next to her, looking, the other women would whisper to Veleda, as if he understood every word Nuadu spoke, which, of course, he did. Often he disappeared for lengthy periods to wander in the thick woods that lay all about the school, but every night he came back, curling up next to his human charge, his deep rumbling purr lulling her back into sleep.

Tonight, though, he had not yet returned from the hunt he so often made during the dark hours. Although Veleda was usually asleep when the cat slipped back into the student's house, she had developed a sense of when this should happen. It was long past that time.

Mau's absence was one of the reasons she was wakeful this night, but it was not the only reason. From the moment she lay down, Veleda had been gripped by the certainty that some knowledge was waiting to make itself known to her. The feeling no longer disconcerted her, as it would have when she first came here. She had grown immeasurably during these years, in confidence as well as in power. But in order for the knowledge to be revealed she would need to sleep, and sleep would not come.

Eponina rolled over in her furs, snuffled a little, and resumed snoring more vigorously than ever. Veleda sat up in her own furs, staring into the shadows. The hearth-fire had long since died, breaking apart into chunks of blackened wood. Every so often a weak flame would spring up from the charred embers; in one of these brief glows two eyes appeared, blazing brighter than the flame. A paw tapped at Veleda's knee. Without surprise, she brought her gaze down from the smoke-hole through which she had been studying the stars.

Mau said nothing. He would not speak around others, even while they lay deep in sleep. But Veleda knew that he was waiting for her to accompany him. Silently she eased out from her bed. Moving with care, she drew on her under-shift and then her tunic. The cat's long lithe shape slid ahead of her, barely visible in the gloom.

Outside, it was far brighter than in the house. The nights on Eire were often cloudy, but this night was clear. The moon was halfway to the fullness of her maiden aspect and a river of pale light streamed down, further brightened by the stars twinkling in the moon's train.

The low round shape of the student house was softened in the glimmering light, its thatched roof seeming to glow in the night. Veleda glanced at it over her shoulder as she followed Mau into the woods. He darted ahead of her, then paused to wait beside the massive trunk of an ancient ash. Nearby something rustled in the bushes and the cat cocked his head, listening intently.

"So," Veleda said. "We are far enough away from the ears of any who would hear us."

"We would have to be," Mau grumbled in his dry precise voice. "Who could speak loud enough to be heard in your house with the way that one roars on and on through the night."

Veleda smiled. "Do not be so harsh toward Eponina. She is not the only one who snores, you know. So do you."

Mau drew himself up. "Cats," he said with enormous dignity, "do not snore."

She pointed a finger at him. "The one I am looking at does. You make a little noise like this"—she made a sound between a soft miaow and a grunting murmur—"and you only do it when you're deeply asleep. It's actually rather endearing."

Mau's whiskers stiffened and his eyes narrowed to slits: his way of expressing displeasure. "Enough of this," he said sharply. "We did not come out here to talk nonsense, but of something important."

"Which is?" Veleda leaned against a beech tree.

"It is time for you to leave this place and return home."

She straightened abruptly. "But my training is not over yet. Eight more years of studying the mysteries lie ahead of me before I may be named Druid."

"Your people do not have eight more years, which means that neither do you. You have become a seer, and that will have to suffice."

"What do you mean, my people do not have eight more years"—Veleda caught herself. She stared at Mau in the moonlight, and her heart began to pound.

"Yes," he said quietly. "You begin to understand."

"Then I must go indeed." Veleda felt as if her mind had suddenly caught flame. She had dreaded this moment, yet waited for it to arrive. Now that it had she was curiously relieved, and galvanized with eagerness as well. There were a great many plans and preparations to be made if she were to leave quickly. Before anything else, she must speak with Nuadu. As soon as she thought of her teacher she also recalled the foundation of Nuadu's teachings: a seer's most important responsibility was to pay close heed to all things. She frowned. "I was studying the stars before you came to me. They showed me nothing amiss, they reveal no ill-fortune that we should be warned of."

"And they won't. What you need to know will be revealed to you in the House of Darkness. Come, you will need to purify yourself first."

Swiftly he glided off in the direction of the well-trodden path that led to the *tigh 'n allus*, the sweating house. Veleda hesitated a moment, and then followed after him. She knew he was not in the mood to answer questions. There was a sense of urgency about him that communicated itself to her clearly, and caught up in the portents of what lay ahead, she went along in the cat's wake, silent and thoughtful.

The house where Nuadu and her students bathed was half again the length of a tall man. It was low and round and the bathers entered through a small door. Inside a great turf fire was kindled until the place became heated; the embers were then swept out and the bathhouse was ready. It was the custom for several people to bathe together and Veleda felt strange in preparing the house only for herself. Mau watched silently as she stooped to go in and out with pieces of turf. The white patch of fur on his chest gleamed like frost under the silver light.

Veleda was already drawing into herself in preparation for entering the bathhouse. This was far more than a simple cleansing of the body. Used in this way, the *tigh 'n allus* was a means of purification, a mystical ritual, during which the bather sought *sitchain*, the state of inner peace essential to receiving visions. Any distraction, such as speech, would interfere, and so she and the cat did not speak while they waited for the fire to be ready.

When Veleda pulled off her clothing and entered the "sweating house" the temperature was so intense that the air itself seemed to brand her lungs with its fiery touch and the bath stones around the remains of the turf-fire glowed red. She seated herself near the stones, gasping in the relentless heat. She would remain here until the sweat poured from her body like water down a cliff, until the thoughts no longer whirled about in her head and her mind floated free as a cloud.

It took roughly an hour. When the moment finally came, she got to her feet, swaying slightly, and pushed open the door. Rushing out she headed straight for the cold water spring near the bathhouse. Gasping, she dunked herself several times before emerging refreshed and prepared for what lay ahead. When she was dressed again, they went on to the House of Darkness.

This House of Darkness was the same one that Sekhmet's demons had attacked Veleda in on that afternoon twelve years ago. She had known without Mau having to tell her that she should not speak of this incident to Nuadu; thus it had remained assigned to her as her place of learning. But in all these many seasons, the demons had not come back. Veleda had practiced her lessons, lying alone in the darkness, secure in the knowledge that Mau crouched outside, guarding and protecting her. Indeed, as with many terrible happenings, the memory of the demons had faded over time, until she rarely thought of the hideous creatures that had lurched at her out of the gloom.

Now, as they arrived at the little hut, Veleda stared at Mau, and it was as if a haze had been lifted from her eyes. She should have stayed in the state of *sitchain*, but the question pushing at her would not allow it. "They have never truly gone away, have they?" she asked, and they both knew what she meant.

Mau sat down in front of the hut's entrance. "They have not. I have merely kept them from you on all the other times they tried to seek you out. The Lion-Headed Goddess does not turn away so easily from those whom She has set Her face against."

Veleda stood very still. She was surprised to find that rather than being shocked, she was angry. "Why?" she demanded, her voice low and tight. "Even now, after all my training, and the gifts which Lady Bast gave to me, do you think me so weak that I can never defend myself without your aid?"

"You needed time to grow into those gifts," Mau answered calmly. "My task was to guard you while you did. Tonight, we shall see if you have grown enough. It is time for you to stand alone. If you are to leave this island and help your people, we must be certain that your powers are great enough for you to pass this final test unaided."

Veleda gazed into the doorway to the hut. It was utterly black, as dark as the entrances to the burial chambers of the dead. She looked back at the cat. "And if I fail?"

"If you fail, then my Mistress made the wrong choice." As if he recognized the harshness of that statement, Mau's dry tone softened. "But you will not fail." Suddenly he was beside Veleda, rubbing his long silky length against her legs, purring as he spoke. "You were strong when I found you, and you are stronger now. You have had good teachers and you have learned well. The ordeal that lies ahead is difficult, but not impossible, and at the end of it, Bast and I will be waiting."

He stood aside. Veleda looked again at the entrance to the House of Darkness, and when she looked back, Mau was gone. She stood for a moment, shutting out fear, pushing away the overwhelming sense of being totally alone. She gathered in upon herself, allowing the secret place of power deep within, that Nuadu had helped her create and nurture, to expand throughout her being. Then she lowered herself to hands and knees and crawled slowly inside.

Instantly dampness and dark surrounded her. She had to command herself to push the block of wood against the entry hole, shutting herself in. It took an equal effort to lie down on the earthen floor in the classic position of learning. She crossed her arms over her chest, placed her palms over her eyes, and waited.

During her training she had only been in the stone house a few times after dark, and then for specific rituals with Nuadu and the other students nearby. This was different. The sense of isolation was complete, far stronger than it was during the day, although it should not make any difference, for not even a finger of sunlight could make its way inside these squat stone walls. And while stone walls could keep out light, they welcomed the damp; after a short time Velleda felt the chill of wet rock seeping into her very bones. And still, she waited.

Slowly her mind spiraled upward, drifting and coalescing into the floating sensation of *seeing* that had become so familiar. Then the images began to form. She had expected Sekhmet's demons; all her senses were attuned to that, and to the need to protect herself from danger. But what came instead were visions.

She saw two men—chieftains by their gold torques, and Druids by their dress—walking beside a lake. The sun was shining, but the land wore the look of Seed-Fall and frosty air whitened the men's breath as they talked. The tension between them was obvious. The features of the older man were flushed and tight with anger, and he jabbed the air with a finger as he talked. Veleda felt her own body tense as she watched him. A smoky gray nimbus twisted about the man, heavy with menace and portents of doom. Even as she looked that murky cloud grew shot with crimson, and despite the hold of the trance-state, Veleda shuddered with revulsion, knowing that those spidery red tendrils symbolized blood, the blood of her people.

By contrast, the nimbus of the other man was a swirling shining mist of silver and gold. As repulsed as she was by the older man, was she drawn to the younger. He resembled his companion so much that the two must be brothers, and yet the younger man was very different. As angry as he was, there was still a calm about him, a self-containment that came only with great discipline. He was bright and bold, honest and deep, a man schooled in the paths of wisdom. But the color of scarlet was also winding its way through the silver and gold mist that wreathed about him. . . .

The image of the two men faded. The older one now stood inside a magnificent chamber of marble that Veleda somehow knew was Roman. He towered over the men about him, who, even though they were seated, she could see were all of small stature. He stood out in other ways as well; his flowing yellow hair presented a sharp contrast to the short dark curls of those around him and the distinctive white togas of the high-born Romans looked plain against his gold jewelry and brightly patterned tunic, cloak, and trousers. The chieftain preened under their attention, gesturing grandly as he orated in the eloquent time-honored tradition beloved by all the tribes.

The words that flowed from his mouth were without sound, but Veleda well understood the expressions of the men who listened. Their faces were disdainful: sly, and filled with condescension. They leaned over, whispering to each other, obviously more interested in their thoughts than those of their visitor. It was a wonder that the chieftain could not see the Romans' contempt for himself, but he did not. He orated on, caught up in his own self-importance, and Veleda felt apprehension slither along her bones. There was ill fortune here.

The glistening marble walls dissolved into a rich green haze that formed itself into the great forests of home. She saw the same man again, but now he stood before a gathering of his tribe. Men and women crowded together, their gazes fixed intently on the face of the yellow-haired chieftain. Other chieftains stood at the front of the crowd, and a number of Druids, both male and female, stood with them. The faces of the Druids were grave. The younger man Veleda had seen in the first vision at the lake was also there. His face was the gravest of all.

For the first time, Veleda could hear words. The chieftain's voice rolled out over her ears, rich and strong. But her flesh crawled with disgust and rage as she heard him speak. "This is how I counsel you, my people," he cried. "We must submit to the Romans. We must give them our oaths of peace and friendship. In that way will our tribe not only survive, but it will prosper. Blessed will we be when we bide under the protection of Roman gods, as well as our own Shining Ones.'' He beamed at the people, a smile as bright as his hair lighting his comely features—until the younger man leaped forward to stand beside him.

"Prosper?" this one shouted. "Do you think we may do so when we are no longer free men and women? *You* have brought the Romans to our shores, Brother. And just as I warned you, now that they have come, they will not leave. They turn their eyes to their own purpose, which includes making us their slaves, and you, a noble of the Aedui, ask us to tamely bend our necks to the Roman yoke!"

"I ask you to do what is expedient!" the other roared back. "Let other tribes clash their shields and batter their swords against the legions. They will be crushed, their towns laid waste, and their fields put to the torch. They and their kindred will be the ones taken into slavery, sent to Rome in chains to be sold in the marketplaces, never to see these lands again. Yet will the Aedui, under my wise counsel, go on tending their fields and cattle, increasing their goods while Rome smiles upon us." He raised his hands to the sky, the pale winter sun glinting off the gold bracelets on his arms. "That is what I foresee for our people!"

The assembled people shouted and muttered, their individual voices losing themselves in the general uproar. But to Veleda one voice stood out, throbbing in her ears with grief and certainty. "No," the younger brother said. "That is not how it shall be."

A shriek of laughter billowed up, drowning out the clamor of the tribal assemblage. So sudden was it Veleda thought at first that someone in the crowd was laughing. She quickly grasped the truth. That hideous sound did not belong to the voice of any mortal. Under its power the voices and the images of the people vanished, hurled away by waves of crimson that spilled and frothed like blood from a freshly cut throat.

Indeed, he speaks well, a deep female voice hissed,

and each of Veleda's three souls froze, for she recognized that voice. *That is not how it shall be. But the truth shall be far worse than even he foresees!*

The laughter came again, and, as if the laughter itself was forming them, so came the demons.

The odor of rot was overwhelming in the close confines of the tiny hut. A treacherous weight descended upon Veleda's limbs, the same sensation that had bound her into helplessness and terror when these creatures had appeared before. But this time Mau could not help her. This time she would have to protect herself alone.

Claws scraped against the packed earthen floor. The desire to lower her hands and force her eyes open was instinctive, but Veleda fought against it. She looked within herself, to the source of her strength. And it was there for her, waiting. It had always been there, but Bast had introduced her to this core of power, and Nuadu had taught her how to use it. A glow began to warm the darkness behind her eyes. It shimmered and danced, reaching out for her souls, enfolding her in an embrace as comforting as the breath of Anu, as brilliant as the light in the eyes of Bast.

Bathed in that glow Veleda's fear left her. She had not moved from the position that left her so vulnerable to the demons, but even though her eyes were still closed, it was as if she could see the demons at the outer edges of her vision. The shimmering light was preventing them from drawing any closer to her. Their twisted jaws slavered, fangs gnashing in frustration, as they hopped on their single legs, beating at the shining barrier that kept them from their quarry. She watched them serenely.

A snarl roared out. The sound was deafening in the tiny hut, reverberating off the stone walls. The demons looked up eagerly and ceased their attempts to break through the barrier.

Your puny magic cannot keep My minions from you, Sekhmet's deep voice hissed. *Let us see if you can withstand this!*

THE HIDDEN LAND 121

The face of the Lion-Goddess loomed up in a vision of red, blocking out everything: the walls of the house, the slavering demons, and the shimmering glow that kept Veleda within its safe embrace. A shattering noise composed of a roar and a laugh exploded in her ears, and when it was gone, so was the light.

The demons leaped forward.

10

BUT VELEDA WAS NOT UNPRE-
pared. In the instant before the
boundary that had kept the creatures
from her disappeared, the power
that had been coiling deep within
her shot forth.

The demons were taken completely by surprise. The hungry an-
ticipation on their distorted faces was replaced by an almost
comical look of astonishment as all four of them flew backward to impact against the unyielding stone with murderous
force.

A man of mortal flesh and blood would have been badly
injured, even killed, by such a violent contact, but these
creatures were not human. They bounced up, snarling ferociously, and lunged again. And again they were hurled
back against the walls. Two more times they tried, and with
each attack, Veleda felt herself grow stronger.

But neither the demons nor their mistress had yet given
up. The creatures were suddenly gone from the hut. Veleda
did not need open her eyes to know this; the abrupt absence
of the odor of death and rotting told her. She came very
close to relaxing the position of seeing, but an inner voice
so subtle she could not tell whether it was hers or Bast's
hissed a warning. Regardless of the voice's origin, she listened to it.

An instant later the demons were back. But they were
no longer in the hut. They had left the physical world and
were battering at the walls of Veleda's mind.

She saw them clearly. They loomed up against the dark plane of her inner consciousness, their shapes the color of dried blood. This was a battle on another level and it would have to be fought as such. Now, for the first time since this had begun, the wands that Veleda always wore in the belt around her waist came into play. In this inner world she saw them as vividly as she saw the demons; long and glittering they affixed themselves to her hands, warm and pulsating, as if they were alive. She held to that image and added to it; calling up a fierce cry in her mind, she raised the wands and charged her enemies before they could leap at her.

Sweat beaded on Veleda's forehead, rolling along her hair and into the dirt, drop after drop, until the hard-packed floor beneath her head was damp with it. And still the silent battle raged. It was not a fight of flesh and bone crashing against flesh and bone, but the effort was no less great. In her mind's eye she saw herself, whirling and leaping with a wand in each hand, defending against the four-pronged attack with flames of light that blazed along her arms, onto her outstretched hands, and then out through the wands.

She would never know how long she fought; time in this inner world was not the same as it was in the outer. As swiftly as it had begun, it was over. The twisted demon shapes suddenly began to dwindle. Once started, the process became faster and faster until, with an odd little popping sound, they were gone.

Veleda was not aware that she was holding her breath. She waited for another roaring threat from Sekhmet. But no savage noise rose up to batter at her ears. The moments dragged by, and finally she opened her eyes and slowly sat up. Her muscles were stiff and sore, as though she had been wielding a sword from sunset to sunset for months on end. It was an effort to crawl to the entrance, an even greater effort to roll away the block of wood. She did both as if she was a grandmother heavy in years, rather than a young woman in the flush of her strength.

Outside, the moon had sunk low in the blue-black sky, lightening to a dim reflection of herself in the approaching dawn. The stars still glittered palely, even though a purple tinge was glowing above the trees to the east. In the distance the sea was unusually quiet, rolling up onto the strand and back again with a gentle murmur.

Veleda drew a deep breath and slowly straightened to her full height. She was alive. The beat of her heart was a sweet song in her breast, the flow of blood in her veins more beautiful than the rivers lived in by the Maiden of Waters. She gulped in breath after breath of the air from the dying night, savoring it like imported Roman wine, cool and clean and rich in her mouth. Life in all its different poems throbbed within her and about her, and she rejoiced that she could share in it. Raising her hands to the far-off moon, a prayer of thanksgiving burst, unbidden, from her lips. She sang to Anu, to Bast, to all the gods and Goddesses of her people, and when she was done she lowered her hands and looked for Mau.

He was not in the long grass outside the House of Darkness, nor in the copse of bushes that ringed the grass. She walked over to the trees, her eyes searching amongst the massive trunks. Her eyes were well accustomed to the darkness by now; indeed the woods seemed almost bright after the utter black of the stone hut.

"You see?" a familiar voice said from above her head. "I said you would not fail."

Surprised, Veleda looked up. She had not thought to search for Mau above rather than below. His orange eyes shone at her and her gaze picked the rest of him out. He was lying on the branch of a dogwood tree, stretched out to his full length, his tail fluffed to twice its size. He never climbed trees unless he was upset; he had told her that several times. The sight of him up there, his tail bristling, touched a warm spot in Veleda's heart and made her smile. He must have been very worried about her.

"Sekhmet came to me, Mau," she said in a quiet voice.

"And She called upon Her demons to destroy me. But with the help of the Shining Ones, I sent Her and them away."

Mau blinked his great eyes deliberately, the way in which he always greeted her when he was feeling affectionate. "Sekhmet is a Goddess, human girl. She may have left, but you did not send Her away. No mortal, no matter how great her powers, can ever send away a Goddess. She is still there, waiting, along with those creatures of Hers." His tail was slowly regaining its normal shape. "What else did you see?"

Veleda told him of the two chieftains beside the lake, of the scene in Rome, and the two men's confrontation before the gathering of their tribe. "They were true prophecies," she concluded grimly. "And the worst of it is that a man of the tribes has offered his own people's honor-price up to the Romans. Of course, what could we expect from the Aedui; they have ever been untrustworthy and lacking in honor."

Mau's tail lashed against the tree limb. "That is ill spoken of you, human girl. Have you forgotten your task to bring *all* the tribes, including the Aedui, together into one force? Thoth's Feather, the dislikes all you tribes bear toward one another makes my head swim. Your people need to turn that dislike against the Romans, instead of each other. And how can you lead them in doing so, if you are no better than the rest?"

"You have the right of it," Veleda said seriously. "And I have not forgotten."

She fell silent, brooding on what she had said to Mau, and he to her. His observation was all too accurate, but she, too, had spoken truth in her answer to him. The daunting and perhaps impossible task of bringing about a union between the tribes was what she had set her eyes upon during these long years of her training. Never was it far from her thoughts, and yet, in the space of a single breath she herself had given voice to the quarrelsome nature of her people, the very nature that made alliances between them so difficult to achieve or maintain. These animosities were ancient, as deeply ingrained in the blood of the six tribes of the Belgae, the Aedui, and all other tribes, as their love of warfare. Perhaps, she reflected uneasily, there could not be one without the other.

"Never mind," said Mau. "You have done well, and you have proved that you are ready." He rose up, poking his hindquarters into the air, while lowering his head and shoulders and stretching out his front paws, digging rhythmically into the bark with long curved claws. "This means"—his claws worked more savagely at the bark— "that I will have to bounce around in one of those accursed boats yet again."

Veleda placed her hands upon the wands at her waist. "Which of the gods sent the visions to me?" she asked softly. "Was it Bast, or Anu, or one of our *Teutates*, our tribal Shining Ones?"

Mau twitched his whiskers, his equivalent of a shrug. "Bast has a hand in all deeds of magic which visit you, human girl. But as for the rest, who can say? Your folk worship as many gods as do the people of Kemet. For that matter," he added darkly, "it could have been Sekhmet who showed you the face of this man who seeks to betray his own."

"It is not a question of his seeking to betray us." Veleda's tone was equally dark. "He *will* betray us. Ill fortune surrounded him like flies buzzing about a week-old wolf kill. Sekhmet would take pleasure in one such as he."

"She will take even greater pleasure if he succeeds," said Mau. He lifted a front paw and gave it half a dozen swift distracted licks. "Did you see an answer to that?"

"I did not." Veleda sighed, then studied the cat thoughtfully. "But you yourself told me the Romans are on their way, and you are a creature of magic besides. You should be able to see more than I."

"Not in this," Mau told her. He extended his claws and

cleaned between them furiously. "That is why you are necessary."

Nuadu's brows drew together in a frown as she regarded the woman who stood before her. "How can you speak to me of leaving? You have not yet passed your ordeal. Until you have done so, you may not be named a seer."

"Lady," Veleda said quietly. "I have."

There was a long silence between them.

Nuadu's eyes swept back and forth over Veleda's face and her expression slowly altered. "So." She spoke in a soft whisper, more to herself than to Veleda. "They have come to you. It is sooner than I had expected."

"Lady?" Veleda stared at her sharply. "What do you mean?"

"What do you think I mean? The purpose that sent you to me has now come forth to call you back. I would have preferred to keep you with me longer, but we are mere humans, and rarely do things go as we wish in these matters."

Veleda continued to look at her teacher. Had Nuadu seen the two chieftains of the Aedui? And had she seen the demons? "But you said they had come to me," she reminded Nuadu. "Do you know what I have seen?"

Nuadu did not answer at once. "I can catch glimpses of it in your eyes," she said in a distant tone. "And the images of what was and what will be hover about you. I seem them like smoke drifting in a silver mirror."

"What will be, Lady?" Veleda stepped closer. Nuadu's power was as deep and swift as the sea that ringed the rocky shores of Eire. They had never spoken of Bast and the task the Cat-Goddess had set for her, but Veleda had always sensed that her teacher knew a great deal more than she let on. Perhaps Nuadu's enormous abilities as a seer were enabling her to envision a future as yet withheld from Veleda herself.

"The two will strive together while the invaders come,"
the far-off voice went on. "Bitter will their fighting be, and
bitterer still will be the outcome. Goddess and mortal alike,
there is no end to the battle."

Veleda drew in her breath. Not only had Nuadu seen the
Aedui chieftains, but she knew of Bast and Sekhmet as
well. But before she could speak, her teacher shook herself,
and her light hazel gaze regained its focus. "Yes, you must
return to your homelands, indeed," she said in her normal
voice. "There is nothing more I can do for you here. You
have learned all you can, and the need of others is too
great."

"Lady." Veleda grasped the older woman's forearm, her
fingers digging into the wiry muscles. "You must tell me.
What have you seen? What do you know?"

Nuadu gave her a smile, and there was both sadness and
knowledge in it. She had to look up to meet Veleda's eyes,
for the latter had grown over the years and now stood taller
than her teacher. She put her free hand over Veleda's where
it gripped her arm. "I have already told you, child," she
said in gentle reproof. "I caught only glimpses. These are
your visions, not mine, just as the task you carry is yours
and not mine. I know more than you think, and less than I
wish. I cannot help you."

"But you saw the future," Veleda persisted. "Divitiacus
seeks to betray the honor-price of his tribe by calling Rome
to our shores. His brother is trying to prevent that. You
spoke of what will be and the bitterness of it—"

Nuadu cut her off, withdrawing her arm with gentle firm-
ness. "I spoke of what *could* be," she corrected. "As you
should realize. You are no longer a fledgling studying to
be a seer; you have attained what you came to me for. And
well do you know the language of seeing. I spoke in that
tongue when I described what hovers about you." She was
no longer smiling as she looked at Veleda. "But bitter indeed will it be, when brother goes against brother, and Roman legions set their sandals upon the sacred lands of

freedom. Blood will soak the ground like rain in early winter. Neither you nor I require the gift of seeing to know that.''

Veleda was silent. Nuadu could not help her. But within the core of wisdom she carried inside her, she had already known that. Time was as capricious and ever-changing as the wind. Even to the most gifted, the future did not reveal itself easily. The true outcome of events was never certain, it was always subject to change, and not even a mistress of the art such as her teacher could control how those events might change. Nor, for that matter, could a Goddess.

She gazed at Nuadu thoughtfully. ''Have you always known of Bast, then?''

''Bast,'' Nuadu said. She nodded. ''So that is her name. Her presence has been with you since the day your Mother's Sister first brought you to me.''

''Yet you never spoke of it.''

Nuadu smiled. ''*She* never spoke to me. And neither did the cat she sent along as your guardian. It was not my place to speak of such things, when I did not know the wishes of the outland Goddess in the matter. My task was to teach you, and this I have done.''

Veleda returned her smile. ''Yes,'' she said gently. ''And you have taught me well. I am grateful, Lady.''

Nuadu's glance traveled to the woods that fringed the meadow. Mau had just come out into the sun-dappled grass and was basking in the midday heat, looking for all the world like nothing more than a large cat settling down to take a nap. Nuadu's gaze lingered on the creature's dark form as he lolled in the grass, the black of his coat contrasting against the deep sparkling green. ''I pray that I have done enough,'' she said at last, and was silent again. ''Ah well, it's too late now.'' Turning back to Veleda, she gave herself a little shake. ''But I wonder how grateful you will be when the training I have given you bears fruit.''

''It has already borne fruit,'' Veleda told her with a puzzled look. "Else you would not be giving me leave to travel home."

Nuadu's eyes had returned to Mau. The cat was rolling on his back in a posture most unbefitting to a creature of magic. Nuadu watched him for a moment. "No," she said gravely. "When what awaits you comes to pass, then we shall see if you have cause to be grateful. Now come, we must arrange for your journey."

Julius Caesar, governor of Illyricum, and the provinces of Nearer Gaul and Further Gaul, was a spare man, honed for war and the ruling of men. He was tall for a Roman, and of fair complexion, another unusual trait in this race of dark-skinned people. His face was broad, contrasting somewhat with his thin lips and the shape of his nose, which was sharp as a legionary's shortsword. He possessed dark brown eyes that were keen with knowledge he had gained from surviving political intrigues and bids for power since the age of sixteen.

On this overcast afternoon, under a heavy slate sky, he was preparing for yet another power bid, the greatest of his career. If successful, he would become the most important man in Rome. And he was determined to be successful.

Caesar had a great fondness for colorful and fine clothes. The red cloak he always wore on campaigns was a bright spot in the dreary light as he reined his stallion to a halt. His thin lips pursed into an even tighter line as he surveyed the unruly horde before him. *These people truly are barbarians*, he thought disdainfully. The gods had wasted the riches of this land on such a race of primitives. By Jupiter, they did not even know enough to water their wine!

And yet, he was developing a certain fondness for Divitiacus, king of the Aedui. The man was enthralled with anything Roman and he was especially eager to ingratiate himself with Caesar himself, whom he plainly considered the most illustrious of men. Even more to his favor, he had spoken the truth when he addressed the Senate. The Germanic tribes were indeed causing problems. They had left their own lands and in a relentless and warlike advance, they had now driven the tribe known as the Helvetti from their own ancestral territory.

For two years the Helvetti had been setting aside grain and other supplies in preparation for a move. Now they had put their own farms and fields to the torch in order to deny them to the advancing Germans and to strengthen their resolve not to be turned back, and were massing for a gigantic migration across the western lands. They had even persuaded several tribes whose lands bordered theirs to join them. The migrants now measured in the hundreds of thousands, over a quarter of them men bearing arms.

The enormous caravan had gathered on the banks of the Rhone River, opposite the Roman garrison at Lacus Lemannus, the deep blue body of water that would one day be known as Lake Geneva. This was the northernmost border of Further Gaul. If the migration were to be prevented, it would have to be here. Julius Caesar was a man who saw opportunities where others did not. He was quick to take advantage of them, for through such openings were careers made. He had decided that this exodus by the Helvetti must be prevented, and he was determined that the credit for doing so would be his.

The stallion curvetted, his tail swishing with impatience. Caesar controlled him absently, balancing easily in the stirrupless Roman saddle. His dark brown eyes swept out over the legions gathered before him. He had positioned them in order to take the best advantage of the terrain. A series of low hills stood on this side of the river and he had placed the legions along one of them.

The men stood quietly, wrapped in the peculiar stillness that clothes all soldiers before a battle. Like most armies, Caesar's legions were composed mainly of heavily armed infantry. To the untrained eye, there was an anonymous quality about this gigantic mass of neatly organized men. Each legionary looked the same in his knee-length woolen tunic, heavy leather jerkin, and thick leather sandals tied with thongs up to the shins. Their bronze helmets gleamed in row after ordered row, the horsehair plumes fluttering. Interspersed above them waved the red or black feathers that topped the helmets of officers, all of whom were mounted. Above the helmets the two javelins that each legionary carried into battle thrust straight into the air, their points glittering beyond counting.

Caesar looked on them with pride. This was the look of a proper army, disciplined, orderly, and prepared for the orders of its commander. Only Roman legions possessed this appearance, and that was why they were the greatest soldiers in the world. Compared to the nobility of these men, the warriors across the river were a rabble. Caesar's eyes roved over them with contempt. The Helvetti men were as different from the Romans in their silent legions as wine was from water. Among them there was no uniformity, no control. Each man was clothed differently in garishly patterned tunics and *bracae*, the peculiar trousers they were so fond of. The clothing was as brightly patterned as it was colorful and from a distance the scene they presented was one of eye-blinding and dizzying movement.

Legionaries carried sturdy oblong shields, made of wood, rimmed with iron and covered with heavy leather. Every shield looked exactly the same, a sharp contrast to the Helvetti shields with their vivid array of personal decorations. Few of the tribal warriors wore helmets, apparently disdaining them in favor of elaborate hairstyles that had been coated with lime to make the hair stand straight up and appear as blond and stiff as possible. Before the eyes of the watching Romans, they danced and gyrated on the grassy river bank, waving those outlandishly long swords, beating them against the wooden shields, and shouting and singing in their incomprehensible tongue.

Caesar regarded this display without expression. He was forty-one years old and this would be the first pitched battle he had ever commanded. He intended to win.

He gave the stallion his head and cantered down the low rise toward his waiting troops. What he said to them in the moments before this battle was of critical importance. The ferocity of these barbarian tribes in combat was legendary. Divitiacus had explained that his people had no fear of death, because those who died bravely went to the Otherworld, a place where they would continue to live on in eternal bliss. Romans, on the other hand, were civilized men, and they knew enough to fear death. If the Helvetti's initial charge succeeded in wreaking terror among the legionaries and causing them to break ranks, not only the battle but Caesar's own future would be lost. He would have to pick his words carefully.

He rode to the front of the ranks, his crimson cloak fluttering in the breeze. His personal staff joined him, cantering their horses just behind his. He pulled up before his men, and beneath the rows of helmets, thousands of eyes fixed on their commander, waiting for him to speak.

"Men," Caesar called out. "Remember who you are this day. You are *Romans*!" He guided his prancing mount up and down the lines so that all might hear him. "There is no better fighter in the world than a good Roman legionary. Our foes across the river are barbarians. As fearsome as they may look and sound, they are undisciplined and un-schooled in the arts of war. They are overgrown children, impulsive and disorganized in the manner of all children."

He could feel the men's attention wrapping itself about him like an enormous hand. They were absorbing each word, the plumes on their helmets quivering as they nodded in agreement. Now was the time to begin cautioning them about the cost of defeat.

"I am a prudent man," he shouted. "Always have I sought to protect my legions by choosing to fight Rome's enemies with the advantage of either surprise or darkness to aid me. But on this day we do not have those advantages. What we do have is this: our bravery!"

A spontaneous cheer rose up, dying away only when Caesar raised his hand for silence. "Heed me well, Romans," he continued. "Each of us will have need of our bravery. We must fight this battle before us and rise up as the victors. Anything less will mean falling into the hands of the barbarians, and any man who finds himself their captive will suffer the cruelest and most hideous of deaths. That much is certain."

This was a threat that required scarce reminding. Every man here—officer and legionary alike—dreaded that very fate. Caesar could sense their apprehension on the dank air, and he prepared to alleviate it and strengthen them in one final step.

He raised his voice as loud as it would go. "This is a day that calls for great measures, from myself as well as from each of you. So that the danger will be the same for us all, and no man will have any hope of escape, I, along with every officer here, will dismount and fight on foot, shoulder to shoulder with each of you!"

There was a stunned moment, and then the legions erupted. Their cheers buffeted Caesar like storm winds as he swung off the stallion's back, motioning for his officers to do the same. His keen eye took note of the reactions among his personal staff, as well as the expressions on the faces of the officers scattered at regular intervals among the ranks of infantry. Most were as filled with fervor as the men they commanded, but here and there, the face of an officer bore a look of shock and apprehension. Caesar filed away that information for later, as grooms came running up to lead the horses back behind the lines.

It was early in the afternoon when the Helvetti made their charge. The battle fever among them had been building for hours, the blood lust steadily rising, until they could wait no longer. They surged up the hill toward the legions, coming in a phalanx, their ranks close and deep, swords or spears gripped in one hand, their shields joined so that they overlapped on each other. They were ninety paces away from the target of their charge, when a wave of javelins flew at them, hurled by the legionaries in the front ranks. The javelins shot straight into the mass of charging, roaring men, driving deep into the overlapped shields.

Now Caesar's earlier foresight in the orders he had given to his armorers bore fruit. He had instructed them to make the tips of the javelins out of soft iron that would bend when it pierced a shield. The armorers had done their work well; the javelins struck deep into the wood and wicker framework of the enemies' shields, and they would not come out.

The single-minded fury of the Helvetti's charge disintegrated into confusion. The warriors yanked futilely at the embedded javelins, and when they were unable to pull them out, they were forced to drop their shields. But by that time, the Romans had made their own charge. Protected behind their sturdy oblong shields, they broke and scattered the tight phalanx of giant barbarians. Stabbing and slashing with short swords and daggers, the first rank of eight rows of legionaries tore through the disorganized warriors. When they finally grew tired, the officers, fighting side by side with their men, shouted out orders to fall back, and the next rank stepped up into their places.

The fighting was savage. In actuality, disorganization was a more natural battle state to the tribes than carefully thought out strategy was. In battle it was every man for himself, and individual bravery was the ideal, not the anonymous faceless discipline of Roman legions. The warriors swung their great swords, roaring out their terrible war cries. The air sang with the clash of metal against metal and the sounds of death, blood, and fury. But the remorseless ordered ranks of the Romans pushed the Helvetti steadily back down the slope.

The impulse to withdraw came as swiftly as the original decision to attack. Suddenly the Helvetti forces were in full retreat, scrambling back across the narrow valley. Shouting in triumph, the trumpets of each cohort blaring out signals,

the legionaries pursued them. But the impulse to flee was
only temporary. The warriors ceased their flight and, shouting encouragement to each other, they began taking up new
positions on another hill. The Romans came charging after
them, and as they did, the armies of the Helvetti allies, the
Boii and Tulingi, impatiently waiting their own turn to join
the battle, swept out and attacked the Romans' right flank
like wolves seeking to scatter a herd of cattle.

The tactic might have worked but for Caesar's watch-
fulness. Bellowing out commands, he kept the main body
of his men after the Helvetti, while at the same time he
detached the rear third of the legions to deal with this new
threat.

Now the battle was truly joined, and once joined, it
seemed as though it would go on forever, trapped in a timeless space of swinging arms, contorted faces, groans and
screams, and the bitter scents of sweat and blood and
spilled entrails. The long afternoon wore on, and still the
once-quiet valley shrieked with the clatter of swords smashing against shields. The warriors of the three tribes fought
like those possessed by the Raven Goddess of War. Many
were deep into the coveted trance that comes upon men at
such times: the mystical battle state that possessed a man
with a divine rage so great it enabled him to fight like ten
warriors instead of one.

It was not enough. Aside from the Helvetti's initial
charge and the tactic of keeping the Boii and Tulingi back
to attack the Roman's flank, the tribes had no strategy or
battle plan to keep them cohesive. The discipline of the legionaries, on the other hand, was unshakable. Against the
iron wall of stabbing swords, identical bronze helmets, and
utter obedience to orders, even the glorious frenzy of the battle trance had no chance of succeeding. Inexorably the Roman troops wore the Helvetti and their allies down. The
afternoon light faded into the colors of evening and the lowering sun looked down at the continued retreat of the tribes.

They had fallen back again, this time to the ridge of the

opposite hill. Here the women, children and those too old to fight were waiting for them. Hastily a barricade out of wagons and carts was thrown together, and with their families sheltering behind the crude barrier, the warriors of the Helvetti, Boii, and Tulingi made their last desperate stand.

Darkness had long since fallen and the combatants were fighting by starlight when the Romans broke past the barricade and into the temporary encampment. New sounds added themselves to the clamor: the battle cries of women as they fought to defend their children, the screams of the dying, and the helpless roaring of the doomed warriors as they battled to save the families being cut down before their eyes.

The Romans were pitiless. Children, infants, white-haired old ones, all were slashed and hacked into quivering piles of bloody flesh, without regard to age or sex. Women fell beside their men, parents beside their sons and daughters, and still the slaughter went on.

Those who were not already dead fled from the carnage. But the legionaries were not content to let them go. Racing after the escaping tribespeople, they ruthlessly hunted down any fugitives they could find. It was far into the night when Caesar finally called off the pursuit. Many thousands of paces away from the scene of the battle, the shaken survivors slowly gathered together, and set off on a march to safety that would last until well past dawn.

I I

FOR CAESAR THE DAY'S
events were a triumph, the taste of
which would linger sweet as honey
in his mouth for days. For the Helvetti and their allies, the day had
been a disaster, and the bitterness of
it was worse than gall. Word of the
defeat reached far across the deep
forests, the wide green valleys, and broad sweeping rivers
of the land, into the territory of the six tribes of the Belgae.

The Eburones had already learned of it on the day that
Veleda returned home. All the way upriver, on the last leg
of their journey under a lowering sky heavy with the prom-
ise of rain, the boatmen had spoken of little else. They were
Eburones themselves, and all but one, who had been a child
when Veleda left the tribe, remembered her warnings about
the Romans. And they remembered also that those warnings
had not been heeded.

"You should have taken your prophecy to the Helvetti,"
one of the boatmen told Veleda in a somber tone. "For
they had need of it, did they not, Lady?"

"They did," Veleda answered quietly, looking at him.
"But they would have listened no better than our own people."

The man nodded, turning his gaze away from hers. "That
is true enough, Lady," he said respectfully, and directed
his attention back to his poling.

Veleda watched him for a moment. She was still not
accustomed to the deference with which her fellow tribes-

men treated her. Twelve years ago she had left as a girl; now she was returning as a grown woman and a seer, a learned Sister of the Oak, with woods knowledge and magical abilities that would forever set her apart from the uninitiated. She would have been treated with respect in any case, but the fact that her long-ago prophecy was beginning to prove itself added immeasurably to the esteem in which these boatmen clearly held her.

And they did not know the half of it. This was not a joyous homecoming. The blood of the slain Helvetti stained the breast of Anu and the tread of Roman legions scarred Her sacred body. But even with the shame of that Roman-inflicted defeat hanging in the air like an evil miasma, the essential nature of people remained unchanged. The whole day long Veleda had listened to the boatmen argue about the battle and its conclusion.

"The Helvetti should have stayed in their own lands and fought the Germans like warriors," one insisted. "They were fools to run with their tails between their legs, and the Tulingi and the Boii were even greater fools to join them."

"Nonsense," another argued. "It has ever been the custom for tribes to go in search of new lands. If they wanted to pass through, or even take the lands of the Aedui for themselves, they had every right to. Let the Aedui fight for their homes like men have always done. The better warriors would have decided the matter and that would have been the end of it. But instead, their king dishonored himself by going to the governor of that Roman province and begging for his help. It is the Aedui and their groveling for Roman interference that caused this, not the Helvetti."

"Pah," snorted a third boatman, and spat over the side. "What difference does any of this make? By the spirits of Samhain, my ears ache from listening to all this talk. The doings you keep pulling apart and examining so closely are no concern of the Eburones or any of the six tribes of the Belgae. Lugh's harp, let them all fight until their sword blades are dull; it's of no consequence to us. They did not seek to cross our lands, and no king of the Eburones would ever go crawling to the Romans if they did. Helvetti, Aedui, they can tend to their own affairs, as we have always tended to ours.''

It was a familiar and troubling refrain. The boatman's comrades may have had different opinions about the causes of the battle, but on this one point they all agreed: shameful as the defeat had been, it ultimately had nothing to do with the Eburones. Veleda listened to them talk, holding her own thoughts to herself. Mau crouched beside her, his ears flattened in distaste at this watery journey, and she stroked his thick sleek fur, knowing that he alone knew what she was thinking. Her people might accord her great esteem for the truth of her long-ago prophecy, but they had yet to realize the danger to themselves.

A steady rain had begun to fall when the longboat pulled into the mooring place to deliver its lone important passenger. Veleda's kin, along with many other folk, had assembled to welcome their tribal daughter home. It was traditional to greet one who had been trained in the mysteries with joy and celebration. But two factors swelled the number of people on the wet riverbanks even more: the recent Helvetti defeat, and the fact that Ancamna, her own foster-mother, was now High Priestess of the Eburones.

Shouts went up as Veleda jumped out of the boat. She was promptly engulfed in embraces and greetings. Her mother and father gripped her tightly, then stood back, smiling with pride and love. Her brothers crowded about her, shy and eager at the arrival of this learned and powerful woman who was still their sister. All of them looked older; gray streaked the hair of Bormana and Raricus, and her brothers had grown into men, tall and muscular, with the mustaches worn by warriors sweeping each side of their faces.

Then Ancamna came striding through the throng, leaning

on her distinctive familiar staff. Except for the heavy and intricately carved gold torque that marked her status as High Priestess, she alone seemed unchanged. Her hair was as black as ever, her eyes the same deep burning brown. The people parted respectfully to let her pass, and only when they had come face to face did Veleda realize that something had indeed changed. She and Ancamna were now the same height.

The High Priestess studied her gravely while those gathered on the riverbanks stood silent. The everpresent dogs capered about in the rain, some still barking, although not one of them came near the large black cat sitting in the tall grass. All at once a smile beamed out from Ancamna, so bright and warm it suddenly seemed that they all stood in the high heat of summer.

"Mother's Sister," Veleda said softly, unaware that a smile as bright as her foster-mother's was glowing on her face. Tears pricked her eyelids as they embraced. "Forgive me," she said when they drew apart, her smile widening. "I should call you by your title, Lady, that of High Druid."

Ancamna laughed. "To you I will always be your Foster-Mother, and now, we have become sisters in our holy order, as well as through blood."

Their kinfolk called out in agreement, their voices joined by those of all the others. Bormana and Raricus shouted that everyone must attend the feast that the servants had laid out in celebration of their daughter's homecoming, and the people's enthusiasm grew even greater. The rain was still steady, slanting down across people's heads under the force of the wind that had sprung up. No one paid any heed. The reds and blues and greens and yellows of their clothing were the only bright spots in the dankness of the late afternoon, as they trooped off in the direction of Raricus's hall.

An escort of smiling Druids waited to accompany the High Priestess and her foster-daughter, but Ancamna gestured for them to go ahead. When they stood alone in the pouring rain, she laid her hands on Veleda's shoulders. "You saw rightly all these years ago," she said quietly. "We should have listened to you."

"Perhaps." Veleda looked into her foster-mother's eyes with sadness. "But who can say? It may not have made any difference. The only question is whether people will begin to listen now." She sighed. "Judging from the way the boatmen talked, I have my doubts. People respect me now; they look up to me as a seer, but is it enough to convince them that all the tribes must band together to stop the Romans?"

Ancamna gazed off into the distance as if her eyes could pierce the heavy mists that lay over the river and see the Helvetti fugitives on their futile march to avoid the legions. "The governor known as Caesar has forbidden the tribes across whose territory the Helvetti are fleeing to offer them aid of any sort. He has let it be known that any who give them food or horses or supplies will be dealt with as harshly as the Helvetti and their allies were."

Veleda's jaw tightened. "And have they done the bidding of this Roman who dares to pronounce such edicts over lands he does not govern? Lands that are held by free people?"

"The Druids of the tribes there have sent me word that the governor's demand is being heeded." Ancamna's voice was grim. "But our Brothers and Sisters of the Oak are working hard to convince the nobles to do otherwise. From freeman to chieftain, there are those who are already doing what is right. They are secretly bringing food and other aid to the Helvetti, but those willing to help are few in number. Most folk are bloodless with fear at the threat of Roman legions falling upon them and destroying their farms and fields."

Veleda listened without surprise. "As bloodless as Divitiacus, the shameless one who brought Roman soldiers to these sacred lands in the first place."

Ancamna eyed her, also without surprise. "So you know

of that." Her dark gaze grew wide, deepening as it fixed itself on the face of her foster-daughter. "Yes, of course you do," she went on in a slow distant voice. "Visions were sent to you, were they not? Of both he and his brother?"

At Veleda's nod, Ancamna's eyes regained their customary focus. She laid a hand on the younger woman's arm. "Come," she said. "There will be time to speak of these matters later. Everyone will be waiting for us. This feast has been laid in your honor. It would not be seemly for you to be late."

They started back along the path that led to the village, a path Veleda had not trod in so many seasons, and yet one that her feet still followed as easily as if she had never left. Smiling slightly, Ancamna looked at Mau. "I see that your companion is still with you. The outland Goddess must still deem his presence necessary."

Veleda's eyes softened as she met the cat's unblinking gaze. "Oh yes, he is always with me. It is because of him that I have learned the craft of seer so well. He is very important to me, Mother's Sister."

Ancamna studied Mau intently, as the cat paced alongside them. After a few moments, she shook her head, still smiling. "High Priestess I may be, with powers greater than when this creature came to you twelve seasons ago. And yet I can still not pierce his armor."

Veleda glanced at her sideways. "Is it so important that you do?"

"Apparently not," Ancamna answered with a shrug. "For if the gods meant me to know his secrets, I would."

Veleda fell silent as they walked on towards the feasting place. Great awnings made of tanned hides that had been stitched together were spread out over the open area so the people could eat and drink out of the rain. The wind toyed with her, bringing the tantalizing odors of roasting meat to her nostrils, even as it tugged irritably at the awnings as if determined to ruin the feast by pulling them away from their moorings.

Veleda stared at the flapping hides, not hearing the sounds of laughter and shouting and barking dogs, all the noises that were the hallmark of a contented and prosperous tribe. It seemed to her that the wind was not the wind; it was the legions of Rome, sweeping over the protections that had always covered her people.

The rain pelted at the awnings and they strained at their ropes. But in spite of the tugging wind, they stubbornly held their shape and kept those beneath them reasonably dry. Veleda looked up at the hides snapping fiercely in the wind. Was it an omen? Would the protections that sheltered her people be as strong as these hides?

The following summer, in Equos, the Month of the Horse, Caesar would lead his legions into the lands of the Belgae.

Divitiacus was a man greatly pleased with himself. From the capital of the Aedui, the hill fort called Bibracte, he surveyed the realms of his people and laughed aloud.

The harvest would be rich this year. Summer was yet young, but already the corn and wheat stood tall, and the Mother had blessed the flocks and herds with many new lambs and calves. There would be meat and grain in plenty to keep the people fed throughout the long cold months when they arrived as they always did. But for now, the endless snows of winter had melted under the warm breath of yet another spring. Spring had bloomed into early summer, and the season for making war had arrived.

The events of the summer before had gone even better than Divitiacus could have hoped. The Helvetti and their unfortunate allies had been so badly defeated by the Romans that they had finally sued for peace. Then another longtime enemy of the Aedui, the German chieftain Ariovistus, made the mistake of setting his will against that of the Roman governor.

Years ago, at the request of the Sequani, another tribe hostile to the Aedui, Ariovistus had crossed the Rhine River with his army to fight against them. But afterward, instead of returning home, Ariovistus and his army had stayed on in the pleasant lands of the Sequani, eventually joined by the rest of the tribe. More battles were fought and more Aedui nobles were slain. Then the Germans turned against their former allies and seized a third of the Sequani land. Not content with the territory he had planted his people upon, Ariovistus soon demanded that his unwilling hosts vacate even more land so that yet another German tribe could join him.

It was at this point that the neighboring tribes, even the Sequani, saw the wisdom of Divitiacus's befriending of the Romans. The Roman governor had turned back the Helvetti; perhaps he could force the Germans to do the same.

Caesar had not disappointed them. After a continual march of seven days he had led his six legions, still flushed with their victory over the massive Helvetti army, into the Sequani lands west of the Rhine now occupied by the Germans. Ariovistus, however, had not been intimidated by the speed of the legions, or by their feat against the Helvetti. He had boasted of his warriors' prowess and threatened the Roman governor, warning him to leave this place, lest he and his legions suffer the same fate as every other foe who had ever dared to set their swords against those of the Germans.

Divitiacus had accompanied Caesar on this venture, and he had heard and seen for himself the Germain chieftain's taunting. But the pride of Ariovistus was misplaced. His going against the will of Caesar proved as disastrous as the Helvetti's attempted migration had been. Ariovistus and his Germans were resoundingly vanquished and driven back across the Rhine. Both wives of Ariovistus were killed and the chieftain himself barely escaped with his life.

By then, it was early fall, and the end of the warmaking season. In six months Caesar had inflicted severe defeats on two major tribes. And Divitiacus, king of the Aedui, was the friend of this important Roman.

Divitiacus laughed again, as he looked down upon the fields of sprouting corn. He and the Roman governor got on well together; Caesar turned to him for advice and sought out his counsel about the customs and practices of the tribes. It was Divitiacus who had spoken to a group of German prisoners and discovered that Ariovistus was avoiding a pitched battle because the omens had warned him not to fight before the new moon. Armed with that psychological advantage Caesar had immediately forced and won that very battle.

The Roman leader had not forgotten the part Divitiacus played in making this second great victory possible, and the Aeduian chieftain now basked in the governor's favor. If only Dumonorix and those who supported his brother in his anti-Roman beliefs could be won over as easily!

But they could not. Divitiacus's smile faded as he thought on this. If anything, the triumphs over the Helvetti and the Germans had only hardened Dumonorix's resolve that the Romans would bring nothing but disaster to this entire land. The resulting factions between the followers of Dumonorix and those who remained faithful to Divitiacus were tearing the Aedui apart. It was not a good situation, and with Caeser returning to Aedui territory, matters were not likely to improve.

Days later, this prediction was borne out. As Caesar led his legions from Nearer Gaul, where they had wintered, into Aedui territory, the welcome they had been expecting did not materialize. People disappeared at their approach, and those who did not vanish met the Romans' arrival with scowling faces and smoldering eyes. Soon scattered pockets of resistance flamed up, directed at any individual legionary or small group of men foolish enough to let themselves be found alone.

Caesar could not allow such attacks to continue. On the third day of his coming to Aedui lands, he summoned Divitiacus to his tent.

"My friend," Caesar said when the Aeduian king and

his escort arrived. "Come, have a cup of wine with me. And you, good nobles," he added with a courteous nod to the chieftains who had accompanied Divitiacus. "Please allow my servants to extend my hospitality to you, while I speak with your king."

He made a polite gesture for Divitiacus to precede him into the tent. The latter had to stoop in order to enter; Caesar's quarters were sumptuous, as befitted the quarters of the Governor of the Gaulish provinces, but they were designed for Romans, not the men of the northern tribes. Two couches piled with cushions had been set near a large brazier. Other smaller braziers burned nearby, and numerous lamps added their light, throwing shadows up on the tent walls. A large table stood in one corner, its top almost obscured by the heaps of scrolls that lay scattered across it. A young slave stood waiting in another corner, holding a large wine jug in both hands.

Divitiacus took the couch his host proffered and stretched out on it with more than a little awkwardness. In spite of the time he had spent in Rome, this custom of lying upon a couch to hold conversations did not come easily to him. A man lay down when he was going to sleep, make love, or die, not when he was going to talk with another man. And these Roman couches were so accursedly small he felt like a pig trussed for the spit whenever he tried to recline upon one. Still, he was determined to master this Roman habit, as he was set upon mastering all things Roman. He did his best to settle himself on the cushions, unaware of the slight smile that flitted over Caesar's face. He watched enviously as the governor took the other couch, moving with complete grace.

The slave came forward, his feet padding soundlessly on the thick fur rugs that lay over the earthen floor. He poured wine for the two men and retired back to his corner. Divitiacus saluted his host with the goblet. "To you, great Caesar," he cried boisterously. "Your feats against the enemies of the Aedui will be sung of until the end of time. May the gods smile upon all your days and all your endeavors."

Caesar returned the salute. "And to you, noble Divitiacus. A successful man does not forget his friends, and you, great king, are counted among my friends."

Divitiacus beamed at the compliment then eagerly quaffed the good Roman wine. Like all his people, he adored wine and regarded it as one of the most precious commodities for trade. He drank great quantities of it whenever he could, although the Roman habit of watering their wine appealed to him no more than their sprawling on couches did.

Caesar flicked a hand at the slave and the boy hurried forward to refill Divitiacus's goblet. The Aeduian emptied this as quickly as he had the first, and the slave poured out a third measure. Divitiacus restrained himself from drinking this goblet full as quickly; Caesar had only taken a few sips from his goblet and Divitiacus wanted to emulate Roman manners as much as possible.

"So, Governor," he said conversationally. "Are you comfortably settled? Is there anything I may do for you?"

A delicately carved table inlaid with gold and mother-of-pearl had been set between the couches and laid with platters of fruit and small pastries. Caesar picked at a clump of grapes as he considered his answer.

"In truth, noble Divitiacus," he said at last. "There is." His dark brown eyes met the blue eyes of his guest. "You can put a stop to the attacks upon my men."

"Ah." Divitiacus shook his head, taking a deep swallow of wine. "I am your friend, good Caesar, and I give you my sacred oath as a king and a Druid, that those unfortunate incidents were none of my doing. You understand this, do you not?"

"I understand it well," the other man replied. "For you are a man clothed in honor, and these attacks are the acts of cowards and men without honor."

Divitiacus was silent. His face was expressionless as he drank again, but inwardly he was cursing Dumonorix. A movement to drive the Romans out of Aeduian territory was smoldering like a poorly put out fire and his brother was at the heart of it. They had fought over this issue ferociously when the legions were first sighted on the border, but neither brother had succeeded in convincing the other of the rightness of his opinion. Divitiacus was fully aware of each act of aggression that had occurred, and he had fervently hoped that Caesar would find the culprits and put a stop to their activities on his own. It was the only way Divitiacus himself could remain uninvolved; the only way he could avoid deepening the factions that were already splitting his tribe apart so deeply.

It appeared, however, that Caesar was not going to deal with this problem in so advantageous a manner. "You are the ruler of your people," the Roman said, and there was a hint of iron beneath his cordial tone. "You are also a wise man, as well as an astute one. You know the man responsible for instigating these attacks, and so do I."

Divitiacus held out his empty goblet for the slave to refill. "More than one man was responsible, Caesar. King I may be, but I have told you about the nature of our people. Our warriors love battle, and when their blood is heated with the desire to fight, they pay no heed to any authority but their own. Likely the assaults upon your legionaries were committed by some of our young men: brave but foolish warriors caught up in the moment and blind to any of the consequences."

He selected a meat-filled pastry from the platter and ate it in a single bite. Fastidiously he brushed the crumbs from his flowing moustaches. "Do not mistake me, my good friend," he said, meeting Caesar's eyes. "Hospitality is sacred among us, and I am shamed by these breaches of it. The men who have done these things have cost you lives, but they have cost me honor. I will do everything in my power to find the guilty ones and punish them."

Caesar regarded him with steady dark eyes. "My good friend," he said in a crisp quiet voice. "Because we are friends, let us speak plainly, the way wise men speak to one another. These acts were not random skirmishes by young hotheads; they were part of an organized resistance to our presence here. I know it, and you know it. Just as we both know that your brother Dumonorix is the man leading that resistance.''

"Dumonorix?" Divitiacus's scoffing tone was forced. "Caesar, he is as young and foolish as any of them! I will not deny that his sentiments towards Romans are not entirely—favorable, but an organized resistance? I fear you give him more credit than he deserves.''

"Continue to deny it and I will begin to think that I give you more credit than you deserve," Caesar said shortly. He paused a moment to let his words sink in. "I must request that you arrest him.''

Divitiacus stared at him. "I cannot. Dumonorix is not only my brother; he is a chieftain and a Druid, as I am. He is my brother in more than blood. Such an action would alienate me from the good opinion of my people.''

"Divitiacus," Caesar said. "I must insist. If you truly count yourself as my friend, then you will do this. And more importantly, if you count yourself as a friend of Rome, you will do this.''

Divitiacus was silent. The governor's tone was even, but the threat beneath his quiet words was as clear as a mountain pool. Caesar and the empire he represented were powerful friends—and equally powerful enemies; the Helvetti and the Germans could certainly attest to the latter. The Aedui, on the other hand, were basking in the glow of Rome's favor. Their enemies licked the wounds of utter defeat, while wine and other luxury goods flowed into Aedui territory. They would continue to flow so long as that favor continued. There was nothing but benefit to be gained by remaining in Rome's good graces. Divitiacus saw the truth of this so clearly; why could his brother not see it also?

But Dumonorix did not see it, and it was unlikely that

he ever would. Worse, there were other men who had openly embraced his belief that Caesar and his legions must be driven out of Aedui lands. His brother was courting disaster, and not only for himself. But Dumonorix was blood kin. There could be no worse crime than to turn against one's own blood. As King and Druid, Divitiacus would sentence any man who committed such a heinous act to exile beyond the Ninth Wave. Could he do no less to himself? Would his people expect no less when they learned of it?

Divitiacus slowly untangled himself from his awkward reclining position on the too small couch and stood up. He drew himself up to his full height, gazing down at Caesar with steady blue eyes. "I cannot do this thing, Governor," he said quietly. "Ask anything else of me and I will do it, and gladly. But Dumonorix is my brother, and among the Aedui, blood is the strongest tie of all. I will not be the cause of harm to my brother, not for any power or favor that you or any other man in the empire of Rome can grant me."

He turned, sweeping his cloak about him, and strode from the tent.

It would count as the one truly brave deed of his life.

12

VELEDA STOOD WITH THE other Druids as Dumonorix paced back and forth in the grove. He looked precisely as he had in her vision, even to the aura that still clung to him, rippling with the colors of bravery and sacrifice and misfortune. He had been orating passionately for some time, but among these listeners there was little need for his persuasions.

The fact that Dumonorix addressed such an attentive audience was due in large part to Veleda. Her rise in status had begun more than twelve years ago and since her return, it had risen still more. Memory among all Keltoi people was strong, and Veleda's banishing of the mysterious illness that had attacked so many remained vivid. Word of the prophecies she had made at that time had also spread among the six tribes of the Belgae and only added to her mystique.

Now the events of the previous summer had borne out her warnings of long ago. The fires had finally been lit. People were stirring at last to the danger Rome represented to their freedom. Veleda, who had seen that danger and tried to warn them of it so long ago, found herself elevated to a status approaching that of Ancamna herself. The tribes of Belgae were uniting, drawing together to face a common threat. It was not the massive coalition of tribes Bast had told Veleda must be formed, but it was a beginning, and an important one.

"The tribes of Belgae are strong fighters," Dumonorix called out. "I, who have fought against you myself, can swear to this. Everyone knows of your reputation, even the Romans. With the six tribes standing together, Caesar will take note. He is not a fool, this Roman who calls himself 'Governor.' He will not challenge so powerful a confederation, and when the time is right, your warriors and the true men among the Aedui will join together to drive this abomination from our lands."

Ancamna raised her carved staff. "The Remi will not join the confederation," she said. "The tales of what the legions did to the Helvetti and the Germans last summer have cooled their blood. I spoke to their Chief Druid myself, and he, too, sought to persuade the nobles, but still they refuse."

"Then let them cower about Caesar's heels like whipped dogs," Dumonorix snarled. "They will have the King of the Aedui, my own brother, to bear them company."

His handsome features distorted in a grimace of rage and pain, and the words seemed to tear at his throat as he spoke. It was difficult for him to speak of Divitiacus. He had fled from his people's lands at his brother's own urging, but never would he forget that last meeting between them. Divitiacus had told Dumonorix of Caesar's request, and his own refusal. And yet, despite the courage that he had shown by refusing to arrest his brother, Divitiacus still remained adamant in his determination to support Rome. They had argued savagely, nearly coming to blows. In the end, Dumonorix had left his ancestral lands, but only to gain support from other tribes.

He had taken a highly unusual step in coming to the lands of the Belgae. There was no friendship between the Belgaic tribes and the Aedui, and there never had been. But these were new times, calling for new measures. Veleda was not the only one who looked at the world with far-seeing eyes. Dumonorix saw the future, and he was more than willing to alter that future by seeking help from old enemies. It was an unexpected boon to come into the Belgaic territories and discover that the minds of the nobles and the Druids in these remote lands were not only receptive to his pleas, but that they were taking action already to protect themselves.

The young seer called Veleda was responsible for this foresight, and Dumonorix was deeply grateful to her. He looked over at her. She stood in a position of honor near the High Priestess, who, he had been told, was her fostermother. Her green eyes were fixed on him, but even with his Druid sight he could not decipher her expression.

A large black cat sat beside her. The cat accompanied her everywhere, and the Druids here had told Dumonorix that the animal was a faery cat and a magical bond linked them. Dumonorix did not need to be told; this much his Druid sight revealed clearly.

Dumonorix's features smoothed out as he glanced at Veleda. She was not among the fairest women he had ever seen: a strong hand had traced her features and she was spare and big-boned at the same time. Yet there was a quality about her that drew him. The gods had touched her with their shining hands and power glittered all about her, flaming in her red hair and burning in her eyes so that it seemed as if a great fire blazed inside her. He sensed her determination, a determination that drove her as fiercely—perhaps even more fiercely—than his own, and that drew him even more.

Veleda continued to study him with those mysterious eyes, as the High Priestess and the other Druids spoke in turn about the alliance of the five remaining tribes. Dumonorix listened carefully, but did not take part in the discussion. He had accomplished his task; an army would be formed, the size of which would send a clear message to Caesar that he had best be content with the portions of land Rome had already stolen and now called her provinces. In time, Dumonorix would utilize his newly forged friendship with these Belgaic tribes to drive the Romans out of Aedui territory forever.

At length, everyone who had something to say had said it. Ancamna chanted the ritual blessing that brought the council to an end, and as the Druids began to leave the grove, Dumonorix took the opportunity to approach Veleda.

"I have much to thank you for, Lady, and so do my people," he said seriously, then added in a soft bitter tone. "At least, those among them who still prize their freedom above all else,"

Veleda shook her head. "It was your own courage that brought you here and led you to fight against Rome, Dumonorix, and that was none of my doing."

"Ah, that is not so," the chieftain insisted. "You have opened your people's eyes with your visions. If you had not, then I would not have been welcomed in these lands." He let out a short laugh. "Indeed, had I been an ordinary man and no Druid, I would have likely gotten my head taken before I could invoke the law of hospitality."

Veleda smiled. "It's true enough our warriors have clashed swords with yours a time or two. But only when you have tried to steal our cattle."

Dumonorix laughed again. "And now our tribes will fight together, and this time, the heads that roll from the blades of our swords will be Roman heads."

Raucous shouts echoed through the grove, drawing the attention of them both. A group of chieftains were coming along one of the paths. They had been waiting for the Druid's council to end, and now that it was over they were arriving to claim Dumonorix as their guest.

Veleda's father was in the forefront of the group. "Come and drink with us, Dumonorix," he called out. "And then we will escort you to our king. We shall feast to the alliance between us."

Dumonorix's eyes flashed, taking on the blue-white tint

of lightning when it sparks across the night sky in high summer. "By the Raven Goddess of Battle," he roared. "I will feast with you and your king. And not only will I drink to our alliance, but I'll drink to the Roman defeat as well!"

He took courteous leave of Veleda and was promptly swept up by the chieftains, heading off down the path in a swirl of brightly colored cloaks, shouts, and laughter. Veleda looked after him, a slight smile curving her lips.

"You like him," Mau observed, slipping up beside her.

Veleda continued to smile. "I do. He is pleasing on the eyes, he is wise and honest, and he feels as we do about the Romans. In truth, he saw the threat of Rome all on his own, without any help from Lady Bast. Perhaps she should have chosen him for this task, instead of me."

She was teasing a little. Suddenly she felt more lighthearted than she had in many days. The Druid gathering had been a success, and her talk with Dumonorix, brief though it was, had left her feeling warm and oddly happy.

But Mau did not respond in the same vein. "Bast chose you because she chose you," he said. "And you see as clearly as I do what the colors about Dumonorix portend. It would be well if you did not grow to like him too much."

Veleda's happiness left her in a rush as swift as a blast of wind-driven sleet. The truth of her vision returned with full force, haunting her, weighing like a stone deep in her belly. In spite of his strength and courage, Dumonorix was marked. How could she have forgotten that, even for a few moments? Her heart twisted with grief for the young chieftain; anger choked her at the fate that awaited him.

Ancamna walked over to her. "You are distressed, Foster-Daughter," she observed. "The tribes are uniting against the Romans. This is what your Goddess told you to strive for. Why are you not more joyful?" Her keen dark eyes studied Veleda, and a frown creased her forehead.

Veleda said nothing. Ancamna was right; Dumonorix's ill fortune aside, she should be joyful, but she was not. Remembering the fate that hovered about the young chieftain made her spirit heavy. She could not rid herself of the feeling that much blood would be spilled. Far too much blood. The air already stank of death.

"What has your sight shown you?" Ancamna persisted.

Mau made a noise deep in his throat. Veleda stared down at him. "Nothing," she said at last. "Only my own fears, Mother's Sister. Nothing more."

Ancamna laid her hands upon Veleda's shoulders, her eyes probing the younger woman's face. "You have strong powers, Foster-Daughter. Ask them to help you in your seeing."

That night Veleda did as Ancamna requested. She asked for guidance in her dreams. The serene cat face of Lady Bast came to her, but the Goddess whispered one word only: *Wait.* "For what?" Veleda cried out into the deep silence of sleep. But Bast said nothing more.

Instead Sekhmet's cruel laughter swirled through her dreams, and her laughter was the color of blood.

The events of that summer did not go as either Dumonorix or the tribes of the Belgae expected. Supreme in their confidence, the kings from each of the five tribes that formed the alliance ordered a special set of gold coins struck, both to finance the military enterprise and to commemorate their certain victory over Rome, should Caesar be so foolish as to enter Belgae territory. A great army was assembled on the southern border of Belgaic territory, some two hundred leagues from the northern edge of Caesar's Provincia. Yet, despite the size of the warrior gathering, there was no attempt to go beyond the tribal boundaries. The intention of the confederation was not so much to attack Rome as to warn.

However, when reports of the army reached Caesar, he took it as the opportunity he had been waiting for. This was a declaration of war, he wrote in his dispatches to Rome. He gave a liberal slant to his writings, depicting the massing of the barbarians as the first step in an offensive to drive the Romans out of Gaul entirely. In order to protect the province, the only possible response was a second campaign, this time against the powerful Belgae.

Caesar ordered two additional legions recruited from Nearer Gaul, and as spring lengthened into early summer, he ordered them to march across the Alps and head north to join his commander Labienus in the town of Vesontio. A few weeks later, he traveled there himself to resume command of his army: a force that had now swelled to forty thousand men in eight legions. Within days he led them out of the town's north gate. Joining him was Divitiacus with a large force of men loyal to him, and therefore to Rome. The army kept up a steady march, and in two weeks they had crossed the River Marne, the southern limit of Belgaic territory.

Here Caesar was met by representatives of the Remi, the one Belgaic tribe that had refused to join the alliance. To his surprise, these men asked to be placed under the protection of Rome. It was a request not in keeping with all that he had heard about the savage tribes of Belgae. Divitiacus had told him much about the tribes of this region. They were legendary fighters, reputed to be the fiercest warriors in the whole of this vast and wild country. Adding to their savage reputation was the fact that, unlike the Arverni and Aedui and other tribes closer to Gallia Provincia, the Belgae were far from the civilizing influence of Rome. It was said that they disdained the rich trappings of Rome so sought after by their southern brethren, claiming that Roman trade goods made a man soft.

But there was nothing disdainful in the demeanor of the Remi chieftains who came to meet with Caesar. They were great tall men, muscular and long-haired, dressed in the brilliant clothing and garish jewelry so beloved by all barbarians. But their fierce appearance was belied by the humbleness of their words. Speaking through Divitiacus, they told Caesar of their desire to become peaceful subjects of Rome. They had no stomach to test the strength of the legions, and for this decision they had already suffered much. The other Belgaic tribes were furious at their refusal to join the alliance. In retaliation they had mounted a siege against Bibrax, the Remi's main town. Caesar's legions were now the only force that could save the town from disaster.

If he would help them, their leaders declared, then they would join the legions in fighting against the confederation of their brethren. Even now, they told Caesar, an army of nearly three hundred thousand warriors was approaching, commanded by Galba, king of the Suessiones.

Caesar was highly practiced at maintaining a neutral expression, but his brown eyes glittered as the pleading speeches of the Remi nobles were translated for him. The quarrelsome nature of these people was their greatest foe, and he was precisely the man to take advantage of that weakness. Graciously he told the delegation that he would aid them, though not without concessions on their part to ensure against their changing their minds and deciding to join the tribal alliance after all. He demanded the children of the Remi chieftains as hostages, sent a contingent of archers and slingers to help the besieged town of Bibrax, and continued his march north.

The appearance of Roman troops coming to the aid of the Remi brought matters to an abrupt head. The Belgae abandoned their attack on Bibrax and sent messengers to Galba. The entire tribal force gathered and turned to face the Romans.

In times of war Druids accompanied the warriors of their tribe, and this occasion was no different. On the evening that the great army was assembling the last of its men, Veleda and Mau climbed to a hill to look out over the encampment.

It was the largest accumulation of people in one place that Veleda had ever seen. The encampment stretched for eight miles and was situated at the end of a broad marshy area. Two miles in front of the warriors, at the opposite end of the marsh, were the Romans. From their place atop the hill, Veleda and Mau had a view of both camps, and the striking differences between the two were all too obvious.

In the manner of all tribal armies the Belgae had brought their families along with them. Their gigantic camp was as colorful and disorganized as the tribes themselves. It bustled with life, as full of activity as a hive of bees. Horsemen galloped back and forth, veering out of the path of wagons and small herds of sheep and cattle being driven out to pasture beyond the confines of the camp. The smoke of thousands of cooking fires wreathed up to the sky and disappeared amidst the broken gray clouds. Shouts and laughter drifted in and out on the breeze, mingling with the sounds of chattering birds and the distant cries of hunting hawks. There was a peaceful, eager quality about the scene, lending it a deceptive appearance. It was far easier to believe that these tribes were gathering together for the midsummer festival, rather than the more serious purpose of massing for war.

By contrast, the encampment of the Romans was a strange place indeed. With the River Aisne behind them, they had constructed their camp on a hill facing north. While the Belgaic tribes were pouring haphazardly into their people's giant camp and being welcomed with joyous feasting by the ones already there, the Romans had been hard at work. They had dug a ditch both deep and wide, and had then built a rampart the height of two tall men all around it. Now they were busy digging more trenches, one extending from the front of the camp that faced the marsh, and another from the rear of the camp back to the river. At the end of each trench more legionaries were engaged in building what looked to Veleda to be small forts.

The day was thick with heat, especially near the marsh, and the Romans had stripped to their waists to perform their arduous work. Compared to the color and noise of the encampment that faced them, the Roman camp seemed drab and lusterless, almost lifeless. There was no singing or shouting, no clatter of racing horses and lowing cattle, only the shouts of officers as they directed the men at their tasks. In that aspect alone the Romans were not lifeless; they toiled at their work with a relentless eagerness, as if these ditches and ramparts were all that was important in their world.

Veleda watched them, fascinated and repulsed at once. It was the first time she had ever seen Roman legions and though she had thought herself prepared, the sight was far more disturbing than she had expected. Scouts had reported the Roman numbers days ago, and she knew that her people's warriors far exceeded the soldiers of these invading legions. She had been reassured by this knowledge, but that was before she had seen the Roman camp. Fewer in numbers they might be, but there was something deeply ominous about these small dark men. Their encampment was too perfectly ordered; their dedication to whatever task was set them too intent. They lacked fire, these Romans; their souls were not like the hot wild souls of Veleda's people.

"Look upon them," she said to Mau in a low voice. "They are as businesslike and without thought as a swarm of ants."

Mau narrowed his eyes. "Organized as ants, yes," he said. "But do not make the mistake of believing them thoughtless. They are disciplined, and that is a different thing entirely."

Veleda threw him a sidelong glance. "Go on, Mau. I know you are just bursting to say more."

Mau pawed the air in the direction of the Romans. His claws shot out, curved and gleaming, then hid themselves in the softness of his paw pads. "Those men are soldiers. Their business is fighting, not prancing about on their horses and drinking themselves into a stupor while they boast of their past exploits in battle. They are an army, and it will take an army to defeat them."

"We have an army." Veleda gestured at the Belgaic encampment. "An army several times the size of theirs."

"No," Mau said, his light voice as sharp as his claws. "You have a great many people gathered together, and while the men among those people may be warriors, they are not soldiers." His orange eyes flickered over the neatly organized Roman camp. "Now the Romans," he added, "are soldiers. If there is one thing you can say about them, it is that."

Veleda stared at him. "You sound as if you admire them."

"I respect their abilities, human girl"—he still called her that, though she was now a full-grown woman—"and so should you. Especially since your people do not."

"And that will be our undoing."

Veleda's voice had gone flat, her tone all the more emphatic because of its lack of inflection. She was no longer looking at Mau, but at the Romans. Heedless of her scrutiny they toiled on in the damp heat and broken sunlight. The hair at the back of her neck rose and cold-flesh pimpled her arms as she gazed on the distant legionaries. With such soulless dedication would they overcome every obstacle set before them—including the noble and impossibly brave warriors of the Belgaic confederation.

She finally looked back at Mau. "I must tell them."

If a cat could sigh, Mau did so then. "You can try. But it may be too soon. Use your gifts, human girl, to gaze at what lies ahead."

Veleda turned her eyes to the encampment of the tribes. Suddenly it looked different, for now she was staring at it with her inner sight. The noise and bustle had not changed; warriors still raced their horses, veering past wagon drivers and women driving cattle, all of whom still cursed at the errant horsemen. But that scene—so full of life and motion—was bathed in a dark red glow, and just below the distant shouts and laughter, there was the faint echo of another laughter that was all too familiar. Veleda went even colder as she heard that sound. She knew it did not come from any human throat.

The camp of the Romans drew her gaze back to it. It was so orderly, so perfect in its arrangement. The legionaries slept in small one- or two-man leather tents and row after row of them stretched out before her eyes, so neat and straight it made her dizzy to look at them. She blinked. The faint otherworldly laughter was still drifting on the wind, but no red glow bathed those small tents or the well-organized groups of soldiers going so industriously about their work.

Veleda could no longer bear to see those hordes of ant-like men dig and dig and dig. She closed her eyes, then opened them again to meet Mau's unblinking gaze. "We will not win when we go against them."

Veleda knew Mau as well as she knew herself, and while to another's eyes his face might show no expression, to her his face revealed much. He already knew the tribes would not see victory in the coming battle; perhaps he had always known.

The breeze was brisker now, bringing the scent of rain. The hawks had soared elsewhere and the birds had fallen silent. Veleda drew her green cloak tighter about her and turned away from the Roman encampment. Without comment, Mau paced alongside her as she set off down the hill. They walked for some moments before she spoke, and the words felt like stones in her throat. "This will be a hard thing for the chieftains to bear. Their blood flows hot and eager for war and they do not want to hear of defeat."

"Men never do," said Mau. "When the Hyskos invaded the Black Land with their chariots and their horses, which no one had ever seen before, Pharaoh and his generals did not wish to hear of defeat either. But defeat was crammed down their throats anyway."

Veleda frowned thoughtfully. Mau had taught her much about magic and how to use the gifts Bast had bestowed upon her, but he did not often speak of the past. She had learned to pay close attention to those times when he did. Even with her gifts she could not begin to imagine all the things this ageless being must have seen; there was much wisdom to be gained from all that he said.

"And you are saying that defeat will be crammed down our throats as well." Anger and despair stirred within her and she made no attempt to keep either from her voice. "Then has this all been for nothing? Has Bast brought me all this way to stand and watch my tribe and all our allies cut down by the legions?"

Mau flattened his ears in annoyance. "A foolish question, and not worthy of you, human girl. The people of the Black Land recovered from their defeat. They watched their conquerors and they learned. In time, they rose up under the leadership of another Pharaoh, and using chariots and horses as skillfully as the Hyskos themselves used them, they drove the invaders from the Black Land forever."

Veleda considered this. They had descended the hill and were approaching the outreaches of the vast encampment. The air was heavier now, humming with biting insects, another sure sign of approaching rain. "I think the people of your Black Land must have been very patient," she said. "But patience is not a quality my people are known for. Not the Eburones nor any other tribe in this land."

Mau's fur twitched as a few raindrops splattered off his back. He bounded off to the shelter of the tents and the wind carried his answer back to Veleda. "Then they will have to learn."

That night Veleda went before the kings and chieftains of the confederation. Ancamna and the Druids for all six tribes were there as well, and they listened to what she said with the same astonishment as did the kings and chieftains.

"You want us to *leave*?" Galba, king of the Suessiones, asked incredulously. "Lady, I have heard of your powers and I know that you are a great seer, but by the Oak and Ash, how can you ask such a thing of us?"

"The Romans are here just waiting for us to kill them," a chieftain shouted out. "With only the marsh and their puny trenches to protect them they will run before us like a flock of sheep fleeing from wolves."

"And we have three times as many warriors," another yelled. "But we could win against them if we had only one man to their every two, for we are the greatest fighters in the world!"

Roars of agreement resounded from all the freeborn men and women who were entitled to listen and take part in any council. The encampment echoed with their lust. Firelight limned the faces gathered all about Veleda, spreading scarlet fingers over their throats as if they already lay dead. She raised both arms in a fierce gesture for silence.

"There will be opportunities beyond counting to fight Romans," she shouted. "This is not a matter of bravery, but of omens. We will not win if we engage the Romans in this place. I beg you: pay heed to me. We can preserve our numbers for other battles, battles we can win."

Dumonorix stepped forward from his place beside Galba. His blue eyes were blazing, his cheeks darkly flushed in the glow of the torches. Of all those here the passion to go against the Romans burned brightest in the young Druid chieftain of the Aedui. The desire to shed Roman blood was like a pain within his souls, driven by the knowledge that an army of his own tribesmen, led by his own brother, awaited him along with his enemies on the other side of the marsh. Only through the cleansing power of the sword could he shed the stain of Divitiacus's actions from the honor of his people.

"I have seen no omens of misfortune," he said flatly. "Only signs of victory." He raised his voice so that it rang out clearly, like the calls of the hunting hawks Veleda had listened to that afternoon. "People of the Belgae, would you have these skulking stealers of men's freedom invade your lands as they did mine? Push them back now, so that they will never have the belly to come here again!''

The cheers and shouts erupted again, and this time Veleda did not seek to stop them. She looked at the torch lit faces ringing her in. People were mad with eagerness to do battle. As a woman of the tribes herself, she had seen this state all her life; indeed she had always been as caught up in it as anyone else. And because she had experienced that wild fierce joy, she well knew that once the madness had seized folk in its grasp, there was no swaying them from it.

''Lady,'' Galba said when the noise had subsided enough for him to be heard. He addressed Veleda with respect, but there was no yielding in his tone. ''By the gods, I hope that this one time you have not seen correctly. For in truth, the Romans have invaded our lands, a thing that you yourself once warned your own tribe of. To dismantle our camp and slink away would be an act of cowardice neither any other warrior nor I could live with. We would be leaving a piece of our own territory in possession of the legions! How could I face my kinsmen in the Otherworld after having ordered such a deed?''

Dumonorix broke in, ''I mean no dishonor to the outland Goddess under whose protection you are, Lady, but this Goddess is not of our land. She does not bide with our own Shining Ones.''

Veleda turned to him. ''We are facing a new enemy,'' she said quietly. ''This will not be like going into battle against the warriors of some other tribe who have raided our cattle. The outland Goddess understands that. Perhaps more than our own gods do.''

She looked beyond Dumonorix, to where Ancamna stood, flanked by the Druids of all five tribes. There had been much whispering between the Druids, but Ancamna herself had not spoken. She had only listened, wrapped in a silence no word of persuasion on either side of the argument had yet seemed to pierce. But ultimately, the final decision lay with her, not Galba, and everyone in the encampment knew it.

"You have not yet spoken, High Priestess," Veleda said, addressing her foster mother by her formal title. "What are your thoughts?"

Ancamna remained in her silence a few moments longer, patiently waiting until all the whispers and mutters had died away, until even the rustling movements of so many folk pressed together had ceased. Only the hiss and snap of the torches could be heard, when she finally stepped forward and spoke.

"We are the tribes of the Belgae," she said in a voice that carried to all present. "Our very name means proud. Never have we turned away from a foe who challenges us, and the Shining Ones would not look favorably on our abandoning that tradition, especially now, when these Romans have marched so arrogantly into the very lands that They themselves have blessed."

Triumph blazed over Dumonorix's face, lighting his handsome features as brightly as the flaring torches. Balling his hands into fists, he thrust both arms up to the sky. "Let the Romans beware," he bellowed. "What say you, Galba?"

Galba hurled himself forward. "I say: let the Romans pray to their gods. For we are coming to meet them. And by the Raven Goddess of Battle, we shall send them to whatever dark place it is that Romans go to when they die!"

Complete bedlam broke loose. Men and women shouted until their voices cracked. Swords and battle-axes were beaten against shields, and those holding them leaped into the cleared circle. When not another man or woman could possibly squeeze into the space, the leaping and clamor spread throughout the encampment. The very air shivered with the heat and fury of it. In their quiet orderly camp beside the marsh the Romans could not help but hear the belly-chilling sounds of a vast army bent upon their destruction.

Veleda looked upon the wild scene with wide unseeing eyes. Only when Ancamna touched her shoulder did she come back to herself. She looked at her foster-mother. Her last hope had been that the High Priestess would support her. But from the moment Ancamna had stepped into the circle she had known that this was no longer a possibility she could hope for.

Both women stood together, listening to the clamor of roaring voices and the crack of weapons clashing against shields. At length, Ancamna spoke. "It has happened before, you know," she said. "This contradiction of omens. Men will gather for battle and some Druids will see ill fortune, while others insist that the signs are favorable. Thank the gods, it doesn't happen often, for as you see, it is a difficult matter for all concerned."

Veleda gripped Ancamna's shoulders in her strong hands. "You are High Priestess, Mother's Sister," she said urgently, her voice nearly breaking with the intensity of the purpose that drove her. "You, they will listen to. You have the power to declare this a bad time for battle. Tell Galba you have changed your mind. Say that we must pack our wagons and depart—"

"I cannot." Ancamna frowned at her. "And you should know that. You are no longer a green girl, Veleda. You're a woman grown, and you are of the Eburones. Our honor rests upon our courage. What is worse: to counsel men to fight and die bravely, or tell them to cower away, back to their homes with tails between their legs, feeling in their souls that they are cowards?"

Veleda met her gaze unflinchingly. "I think it is better for us to learn new ways, so that we may live on to keep our freedom and fight at a time when we will win," she said with quiet stubbornness.

Ancamna's frown deepened. "You have spent twelve years learning the ancient traditions of the Brother and Sisterhood of the Oak,'' she said sternly. ''Are you now choosing to forsake those ways?''

''Oh, Mother's Sister,'' Veleda said despairingly. ''You must know that I am not. I am trying to protect us. All of us.''

The tumult of roaring voices and clattering weapons intensified. Servants were bringing out wine and cormu, a sure means of extending the battle celebration until dawn. Smoke from the flaring torches drifted over the leaping whirling figures, dropping a veil over them, as if they were already in the Otherworld, dancing and shouting for the rest of eternity. There were many familiar faces among them. Veleda caught glimpses of her father and brothers, their faces transfigured with the holy passion that was so necessary for those going into battle.

Ancamna stared at her kin, and in that moment, Veleda was certain that the High Priestess understood what would happen if battle was joined with the Romans in this place. ''A Druid's duty is to indeed protect the people.'' Ancamna's voice was so low Veleda had to lean forward to hear it over the noise. ''But foremost in that duty is to safeguard their souls and their hearts, to preserve what makes them so glorious a people.''

Veleda's hands were still resting upon Ancamna's shoulders and the older woman laid her own hands over them. ''Pray to the Great Mother Anu,'' she said quietly. ''And pray to your outland Goddess as well. Pray hard, Foster Daughter. For our need is great.''

Veleda shook her head. Her eyes burned with the unaccustomed sting of tears, and her heart was like a chunk of ice in her breast. ''Prayers will do no good,'' she said heavily. ''It is too late.''

13

WITHIN A DAY THE FIRST real steps towards confrontation began. Caesar left two of his legions in camp to defend it and deployed the remaining six legions in the usual battle formation of three long lines along the front slope of the hill Veleda and Mau had climbed to look out over his encampment.

Seeing these preparations, the Belgae encampment went into a flurry of answering activity. Galba brought his massive force of warriors up in battle lines as unruly as the Romans' lines were orderly. But once this was done, surprisingly, the tribes did not attack. Galba, for all his eagerness to shed Roman blood, was not a fool. He did not want to take his warriors through the marsh, with its treacherous footing and hidden bogs.

Neither did Caesar. The two armies eyed each other for most of the day, each waiting for the other to make the first move. When it became apparent that the Belgae were not going to attack, the Roman commander ordered his legions back into camp.

But the blood of the tribes was on fire, thirsting for blood with a thirst that only Roman blood could quench. In spite of Galba's wisdom in holding them back from the dangers of the marsh, they were not willing to wait very long. The next day a large number of warriors circled around the Romans' left flank in an attempt to cross the river and attack the legions from behind. Caesar, with his usual caution, had posted lookouts, and they quickly reported the barbarians' movements. The Roman commander responded swiftly. He sent all his cavalry and a force of infantry to the rear of the camp.

Along the opposite bank of the river, they caught the Belgae in the midst of fording the swift-moving current, burdened down by their weapons, shields, and armor. Savage fighting ensued. The warriors were at an enormous disadvantage. Their plan had gone horribly awry, but their bravery was unimpeded. Huge numbers fell beneath the hooves of the cavalry and the short stabbing swords of the infantry. The water swirled red with blood, but not the Roman blood the warriors had set out to spill.

Boldly those men who had survived the first attack attempted to cross the river over the bodies of their fallen comrades, but a shower of javelins from the infantry drove them back into the water. Still, despite the odds arrayed against them, there were men who made it through the bloody water. These were quickly surrounded by the cavalry and killed, as were the warriors who had been driven back into the river.

It was a painful and shocking defeat for a people unused to defeat. The fact that Veleda had predicted it made the situation even worse. It was useless now for folk to wish they had paid heed to the seer's words of warning. The heaps of dead sprawled in the graceless postures of death brought a new and sobering reality to the tribes. This was a disciplined and experienced foe they were facing, entrenched in a position that was well nigh impregnable. The ditches they had made mockery of had served their purpose all too well. The warriors could not use their favorite method of attack—a direct frontal charge—without piling up in a helpless mass as they tried to cross those deep trenches. In the face of such obstacles, their fury to do battle abated with the swiftness of the winds that gusted down off the hill.

The Bellovaci were the first to leave. "This was to be a battle fought swift and certain," their king complained to Galba. He was a massive man, knotty as a tree trunk, his face ravaged by grief. He had lost a brother and two sons in the fighting. "How can food and drink continue to be supplied to all of us if we stay here any longer?"

Galba's entreaties to him to stay, to keep the confederation together, went unheeded. The Aedui, ancestral enemies of the Bellovaci, were greatly emboldened by the Roman victory at the river. The army that had accompanied Caesar was far too close to the Bellovaci's homeland, and the king, as well as his warriors, was alarmed at what might befall those who had been left behind to care for crops and cattle. Family was there: kin who had not been allowed to come along on what was supposed to have been a great adventure. Now they were in danger.

It was time to return home, the king of the Bellovaci told Galba. And he ordered his army and all its followers to pack up and abandon this ill-favored place.

His decision was similar to a stick of kindling being pulled from a carefully arranged stack: the rest of the pile immediately fell apart. The kings of the other tribes swiftly prepared to follow his example. The best Galba could manage was to obtain the oaths of each king that he and his warriors would rush to the defense of whichever tribe was attacked first, and even that was accomplished only with the aid of the High Priestess and the eloquent pleas of Dumonorix.

Just before midnight on the day of that terrible defeat, the abandonment of the huge encampment began. To the Romans, watching from across the marsh, the departure of the tribes more closely resembled a rout than an orderly retreat. Noise and confusion shredded the night as people ran about dismantling tents, loading wagons and animals, and shouting at each other to hurry. Each man had wanted to be the first to wet his sword to the hilt in Roman blood. Now each man wanted to be the first to leave this place and get home.

No one dared give voice to it, but the reek of fear mingled with the dank air from the marsh. A new enemy had entered their land, an opponent who did not fight in the time-honored traditions of proper men. Caesar had done more than defeat the tribes with his tactics. He had created uncertainty among them, and that was perhaps the most dangerous weapon of all.

From the moment the first bodies had been carried back to camp, Veleda had remained conspicuously silent. She took no joy in having been proved right. The respect and awe she saw in people's eyes only made the pain worse. Now they came to her—Galba, and even Dumonorix—asking for her advice, and there was nothing she could say, no words of reassurance she could offer them. When she looked across the paths of her inner vision she saw only darkness and more darkness. The corpses of the dead, and the stunned looks on the faces of the living, ate at her like a canker. She had failed them. Bast had chosen her, had given her great gifts, and still, she had failed those she was meant to protect.

"You did not fail them," Mau said impatiently. "They chose not to listen. That was their choice. Not yours."

"It matters not whose choice it was." Veleda stared through the darkness at the chaotic scene before her. The moon had ripened three quarters of the way to her Mother aspect, and her silvery glow flowed down, aiding the illumination provided by the torches. The flaring torchlight was unsteady, swaying in the night breezes, revealing the bulky shapes of wagons in fits and starts, their wheels creaking over the sounds of shouts, lowing oxen, and whinnying horses. "I could not help them." She made a savage gesture. "It was my task to help them, to unite the tribes against Rome. I failed in what Lady Bast charged me to do.''

"Allow Lady Bast to decide that," Mau said in his blunt way.

Veleda looked at him, at his fiery eyes glowing in the cold silver light of the moon. "She has not spoken to me, Mau. I fear she is angry with me."

"Foolish human girl." There was an odd comfort in the cat's dry tone. "My Mistress is not angry with you. Nor will She ever be. You are angry with yourself."

Veleda continued to stare at him. "The blood is not done with spilling," she said in a low voice.

Mau met her eyes in silence. He did not disagree.

Ancamna's tall form came towards them, passing through flickering patterns of torchlight and moon shadows. There had been a subtle tension between she and her foster-daughter since the debacle. It was not an obvious thing, but to Veleda, who had always felt totally at ease with her mother's sister, the change was painful. Still, she was as responsible as Ancamna for the unease, and she could not help herself. Within her was the knowledge that the High Priestess could have prevented this. Ancamna knew it as well, and thus the strain between them remained.

"My wagon is almost ready." Ancamna's expression and voice were serene as ever; revealing no hint of the trouble that lay behind her dark eyes. "Will you ride with me, Foster Daughter?"

"If you wish it, Mother's Sister." Veleda's voice was as calm and formally polite as that of the High Priestess.

"I do." Ancamna stood silent, her gaze resting upon Mau. "None of it can be undone," she said suddenly. "Perhaps it was not meant to be." She gave a short hard sigh. "But if I could—"

"It does not matter." Even as she spoke the words, Veleda felt the truth in them. There was little purpose to be served in looking back. But dread weighed her down like the cruel laughter of Sekhmet. Her very bones were cold, warning her that what lay ahead would be no better than that which lay behind.

She saw her father hurry by, tugging several horses after him. By the grace of the Shining Ones, Raricus and his sons had miraculously survived the fighting, unscathed but for a few minor wounds. They were as uncomfortable with her as was Ancamna, for along with everyone else, they had ignored her warnings. As her family, they took great pride in Veleda's powers, but they took an equal pride in their prowess as warriors. Her private attempts to convince them had been no more successful than her public addressing of the council. They had been too excited to listen, boasting to her and each other of the Roman heads they would bring back at the day's end.

They had brought back defeat instead, and now they were ashamed and uneasy in the presence of the daughter and sister who had tried to protect them from it.

Ancamna had followed Veleda's gaze. "It is difficult for him," she said quietly. "His own daughter predicted this, and he did not pay heed. Words have never been easy for him. They come even harder now."

Veleda watched her father lead the horses on into the darkness. "It will do us no good to leave."

Her voice was so soft a person uninitiated in the mysteries would not have heard it. But Ancamna was High Priestess. She turned to face Veleda, her dark eyes glittering and intent. "You wanted us to leave," she reminded her. "You begged me to persuade Galba that we must."

Veleda did not look at her. "Death is on the wind," she whispered. "And now it will follow us. No matter where we go."

Julius Caesar stood in the doorway of his tent, watching and listening to the clamor in the darkness. The Roman camp was too far away for him to make out shapes, but through the reeds and grasses of the marsh he could see the sway of torches, their lights flickering like small orange beacons in the moonlight.

His thin mouth twisted into an expression of disgust. "They flee in as disorganized a fashion as they fight," he observed to the tribune beside him.

The man nodded his agreement. "Shall I give the order to break camp, Commander?" he asked. There was eagerness in his question. After yesterday's victory, he and his fellow officers could scarcely wait to consolidate their triumph by chasing down their disheartened adversaries.

"Not yet," said the governor. "There will be time for that."

The two guards who stood at either side of the commander's tent came to stiff attentiveness as a tall figure approached. Caesar gestured to them to let the man pass, and smiled in greeting. "Bid you good evening, Divitiacus, my friend," he said warmly.

"And to you, great commander," responded the Aeduian king. He was dressed in bright green bracae and a brilliant red cloak that seemed a direct imitation of the crimson cloak Caesar always wore on campaign. Torches mounted in tall holders stood outside the tent and lamps glowed from within. The light caught at the gold adornments that glittered all about the chieftain, at his throat and ears and on the brooches that affixed his cloak.

Divitiacus's strong white teeth gleamed in a wide smile as he joined the two Romans in staring across the marsh. "They are leaving," he said, an expression of even greater satisfaction lighting his handsome features. "The wisdom of your tactics and the bravery of your men have sent them scuttling like rabbits."

"Indeed." Caesar's tone was dry. "In spite of their great numbers they have no more sense of battle strategy than a flock of gulls. And they are just as noisy."

Divitiacus's grin widened. It was a rare pleasure to hear his tribe's ancient enemies—reputed warriors that they were—spoken of so disparagingly. "My only regret is that my own men had no opportunity to share in the victory," he declared. "But now that you have made a mockery of their boasting and driven them back to their lands, what are your plans, Governor?"

Caesar's brown eyes were flat and hard, rendering the smile he gave to the Aeduian king even more dangerous. "We will pursue them, of course. Destroying as many as we can."

It was not a statement made out of cruelty or a desire for more bloodshed, but another step in a carefully considered strategy. From the moment he had learned of the Belgaic tribes joining together in a confederation, Caesar had anticipated this opportunity. Here was the chance to add even more of these rich lands with their wealth of gold, furs, slaves, and timber to the Empire, and even more importantly, to the growth of his own power.

He saw a tinge of dismay cross Divitiacus's face. "Something troubles you, my friend?" he inquired. "Surely you care nothing for the fate of those who have long been your enemies."

"No, no," the king assured him. He paused. "But my brother will probably flee with them. He is young and foolish, Governor. He has been led astray by poor counsel."

Caesar exchanged glances with his tribune. "And who has given him this poor counsel?" He waved a hand, continuing on before Divitiacus could respond. "I suspect I know the answer to that already. Druids are responsible for this hostility to Rome, aren't they? Being a Druid yourself, you would know the truth of that, would you not?"

Divitiacus drew himself up in anger. "Have I not proven my friendship?"

"You have." This time Caesar's smile was genuine. "Many times. It is not you I question, but your brother, and the men of this order of Druids who have given him such poor counsel."

"Women are Druids, too, Caesar," Divitiacus, reminded

him. "Indeed, their abilities are often more powerful than those of any man. A woman is now High Priestess of the Eburones, one of the Belgaic tribes which came here to fight you."

"A woman!" Caesar let out a burst of laughter, the tribune joining in his mirth. "No wonder these tribes are so flighty and disorganized. Divitiacus, you are a man of sense. How can you accept women as a part of your sacred order? They are fragile creatures, my friend, meant for bearing children and running households under the protective guidance of their husbands. Why, they are nothing more than children themselves. Allow them too much freedom as you Gauls have done, and you see the result. Women probably took your brother in with their bad advice, and he the greater fool for listening to them."

Divitiacus sighed inwardly. He and the Roman governor had had these discussions about women before. As much as Divitiacus admired Caesar, on this subject they disagreed. But that was secondary to the matter of his brother. "My brother has not acted wisely," he said carefully. "But I would hope that out of friendship for me. . . ."

Caesar raised his hand in a gesture both regal and magnanimous. "I will give orders that your brother be captured alive, Divitiacus. My word upon it."

Divitiacus relaxed. He was furious with Dumonorix for his treachery, but blood was blood. He could no more stand by while his younger brother was slain than he could have acceded to the governors' request that Dumonorix be arrested. He had done his best to see to his brother's welfare.

Let those who were with him be killed or captured as slaves, each one as the gods willed.

At dawn Caesar mustered his cavalry and three legions and sent them in pursuit of the Belgae. The foot soldiers marched quickly. Their blood was already heated by their earlier victory, and the fact that their opponents were now fleeing aroused them even more. As swift as the infantry was, the cavalry was even swifter. Their horses overtook the massive train of lumbering ox-drawn wagons in a very little time. And the carnage began.

What had started as a hurried departure for home now became a rout indeed. The Belgae were no more prepared for such tactics than the Helvetti had been. Making war was a serious business, but it was a time for celebration as well. Everyone traveled in great unwieldy caravans of family and servants when a tribe went off to fight. They almost always returned safely; there was an unspoken honor in not attacking wagons crammed with those who had come to cheer their warriors on in battle.

Caesar, however, observed no such distinctions.

As befitted her position as High Priestess, Ancamna's wagon had been among the leaders in the ragged line of hurrying Belgae. A number of high-ranking Druids rode with her, including Veleda and, of course, Mau. Veleda had been on edge all morning, and though Mau would not speak to her in the presence of others, she saw the tension in him as well. Suddenly the cat stood up and glared back in the direction they had come. A deep growl rumbled in his chest and his tail fluffed to twice its normal size.

Veleda followed Mau's gaze. The disorganized procession was strung out in several long lines of wagons, herds of cattle, and mounted horsemen. No one else seemed aware of any danger, not even the other Druids. But the danger was there. Veleda's blood cried out with it.

Ancamna saw her face. "What is it?" she began. Then she, too, felt it.

A moment later, the Druids in their wagon and others leaped up and began shouting out their warnings.

Before the first wave of cavalry broke into the valley, Veleda was already on her feet. "We must get the High Priestess away from here, to a place of safety!" she yelled to the mounted riders around them.

"No." Ancamna, too, was on her feet, slamming her staff down to help her rise. "It is my duty to stay. A High Priestess does not desert her people."

"Mother's Sister," Veleda cried in exasperation and terror. "How can you help them if you are dead?" All anger at her foster-mother had vanished at the first sound of horses. Before her eyes a black mist tinged with red swirled about Ancamna. The unmistakable precursor of death.

No, Veleda screamed in her mind. *Not her!* She was nearly frantic with the need to save Ancamna, to prevent the fate she saw reaching out its black fingers toward her from taking hold.

Ancamna's dark eyes blazed into Veleda's, filled with a deep and inexorable knowledge. Whatever words of persuasion Veleda wanted to say died in her throat. The High Priestess knew what awaited her, and it did not alter her determination in the least. The enemy cavalry was closing rapidly, the riders bursting into a chorus of battle cries as they neared their prey.

"If it is my place to leave this world for the other, then so be it," Ancamna shouted above the hoof beats and shouts of the Romans. "But I shall not flee while those in my charge stand and die."

As the inexorable thunder of nearing hoofbeats pounded around people's ears, men and women alike seized weapons and leapt from the wagons. Those who were already mounted raced out to meet the enemy. It was a brave effort but one that was doomed from the start. The Romans thundered in amongst the wagons and began slashing at the defenders. Screams rose on the hot air, torn from human and animal throats both. Blood gouted out onto the grass, spreading in ever-widening pools as the legions of foot soldiers converged on the caravan and surrounded it.

The tribes had left their camp in no organized fashion, and as a result, they could not draw together now to defend themselves in any sort of cohesive way. Mounted warriors were separated from one another, fighting alone, until they became trapped amidst Roman cavalry and cut down. The men and women struggling to defend themselves on foot suffered the same fate. The valley in which the wagons had been overtaken became a scene of chaos and blood and hapless courage. Children and the old were slain indiscriminately alongside those battling to defend them. Bodies piled up upon bodies, their blood-soaked arms and legs tangled up with the limbs of fallen horses and oxen. And still, the killing continued.

The massive train broke apart into small groups, as those who had survived the first wave of slaughter desperately tried to escape the remorseless swords and javelins of the legions. Spurred on by bloodlust and the sight of the fleeing tribes, the Romans gave eager chase. Caesar's orders, passed on to his officers, had been to slay every man, woman, and child who could be found, and the legionaries carried out this command to its fullest degree. It had been midmorning when the Romans came galloping down upon the Belgae. All through the remainder of that long summer day, the pursuit and slaughter continued.

The Keltoi trained with weapons from the time they were old enough to hold a sword. As a result, most Druids knew how to fight, despite the fact that they were sacred and therefore immune from battle. There was no greater crime than to kill a Druid, a knowledge lost upon the Romans. Indeed, their orders were to single out Druids in particular for destruction. This was difficult to do in all the confusion, but nevertheless, many of the Brotherhood and Sisterhood of the Oak began their journey to the Otherworld under the relentless onslaught of the legions.

A scarlet rage enfolded Veleda. From the moment it became clear that there would be no escaping this attack, she allowed the battle fever to sweep over her, embracing it gladly. She fought with savage abandon, as did every other person old enough to wield a blade, regardless of whether or not he or she wore the robes of holiness.

Ancamna was by her side, a longsword in one powerful

hand, her staff in the other, but in the clamor and confusion, Veleda soon lost sight of her. Too late, she became aware of this. Screaming out the High Priestess's name, swinging and slashing with her sword, she desperately tried to find the tall figure of her foster-mother. It was hopeless. All her straining eyes could make out were a sea of Romans, most of them far shorter than she, their faces masked by their peculiar helmets. Among the obstacles of the haphazardly placed wagons, the legions could not form their phalanx, but they were no less deadly for all that. They were slaughtering everyone they could reach.

Veleda's sandaled feet trod on the bodies of her fallen people. The flesh was wet with blood and still warm. Some moved in agony, not quite dead, hands clutching up at her, almost tripping her, rendering her vulnerable to the legionaries' merciless attack. Ancamna must surely be among these piles of quivering corpses, her three souls already flying to the Otherworld.

Veleda, too, might have died in this once quiet valley, her lifeless form tumbling among the bodies of so many others, but a quiet piercing voice saved her.

Leave this place, Daughter. You must not pass from the world. Not yet.

The voice belonged to Bast. The Goddess's words sliced through the haze of battle, banishing the fever in Veleda's brain. Directly in front of her she suddenly saw Mau. The cat waited to make certain he had her attention, and then set off, slipping unconcernedly through the fierce desperate battle.

In blind doggedness Veleda followed his sleek shape, darting past the whistle of javelins and the looming bodies of rearing cavalry horses. Everywhere around her, people were falling, screaming and cursing in the final throes of resistance and end of life. At any instant it seemed that a sword or javelin must pierce her body as the bodies of others were being pierced, but miraculously, this did not happen.

All at once it grew quiet. They had reached the forest that fringed the valley. Safety enfolded Veleda, but it was a false sensation, one filled with pain. There was no joy in being safe when so many others were not. She became aware of a heavy weight burdening her arm and realized that she still carried the sword she had seized from the wagon when the Romans came. Its long blade was stained and crusted with fresh blood. She stared at it and felt the fires returning to her brain.

"I must go back." Her teeth bared themselves in a snarl of rage. "My father and brothers are there. My foster-mother is there. I must stand with them—"

Without seeming to move, Mau was suddenly in front of her. "You will not," he said flatly. "My Mistress has saved you. And besides, what purpose would it serve for you to die?"

Veleda's hands clenched on the sweat-slick hilt of the sword. "Honor," she gritted out. "The honor of standing with my own."

"And falling with them." Mau was motionless save for the irritated twitching of the very tip of his tail. "Come back to yourself, human girl. You have other work to do than to go off and die. Those who survive this day will have greater need of you than ever."

Veleda stared into the cat's wide unblinking eyes. His pupils were black against the orange irises, two thin vertical lines bisecting each glowing ball of bright flame. His whiskers stiffened as he met the human's gaze, and Veleda felt the fire in her souls being drawn out of her, merging into the fire-bright eyes of Mau, leaving her own mind clear and cool.

"Yes," she said, and wearily let the bloody sword drop to the grass. She looked out through the trees. Now and then the sounds of battle were borne to her on an errant breeze, but they seemed to be fading. Perhaps because everyone was already dead. "Do you think anyone else got away?" she asked in a low voice.

"I do," said Mau. "And the Romans will be pursuing whoever they did not yet kill. You must find as many as you can and lead them to safety."

"Safety." The word was bitter as gall in Veleda's mouth. She laughed harshly. "Never will there be safety again. For any of us."

14

FOR CAESAR IT HAD BEEN AN-
other good day. The vast and
sprawling assembly of Belgaic
tribes was broken; the demoralized
survivors fleeing in terror from his
pursuing legions. Now was the time
to strike again, and hard. He ordered
camp to be broken and led his
troops on a rapid march through the river valley, his destination: the fortress capitals of each of the tribes he had
just defeated.

He reached the *oppidum* of Galba, king of the Suessiones, first. This was a large and thriving town, strategi-
cally located on a promontory overlooking the river. Galba
was not there; he was thought to have fallen in the fighting,
though he had wisely left his capital well defended. By the
time Caesar arrived, the town's numbers had swelled even
more as those who had escaped the slaughter took refuge
within its walls.

The Romans' first attempt to break into the fortress
failed, and the Suessiones' courage, so badly damaged by
one defeat on top of another, began to return. They jeered
the soldiers from the massive walls of the *oppidum*, vying
to see who could call down the worst imprecations and
curses upon the heads of their enemies.

The Romans paid little attention. Under the orders of
their commander they prepared for an extended siege. They
began filling in the giant protective ditch that lay in front
of the town. The townspeople watched them work, still call-

185

ing out their mockery. But when the soldiers swiftly built
and mounted a tall pair of wooden towers against the walls
of the fortress, their jeers faded into amazed silence, and
then to downright fear. Far too vivid were the tales the
survivors had brought back with them of Roman savagery.
Without Galba to strengthen their resolve, it seemed far
wiser to follow another course of action.

They sent envoys out of the *oppidum* to negotiate a surrender.

Caesar demanded that the Suessiones give up their weapons. He took six hundred hostages, stationed a garrison in
the town, and headed west, crossing another river to enter
the territory of the Bellovaci. The tribal capital was an *op-
iddum* called Bratuspantium, large, but not so well defended as the *oppidum* of the Suessiones. Caesar ordered
camp set up on the heights overlooking the fortress town,
a strategic move that, combined with the terrible stories
being carried by fleeing refugees, ate away at the bravery
of the people inside the fortress.

The surrender of Bratuspantium's inhabitants was even
more rapid than that of the Suessiones had been. Caesar
again demanded weapons and hostages, then took his legions north against the tribe of the Ambiani, who quickly
surrendered their capital.

But while the once-proud confederation of Belgaic tribes
seemed to be wilting under the furious advance of a smaller
but far more disciplined army, the shattered remnants were
drawing together once again. The territory of the Nervii was
next in Caesar's line of march, and it was here that Veleda
fled to, here that she tried to reawaken the flames of battle
in the disheartened tribes.

In the absence of the High Priestess and so many other
high-ranking Druids, the task had fallen to her. People
looked to her now, not only because they remembered the
truth of her warnings but also because she exuded a quiet
and fierce determination that they desperately needed. Ancamna herself was not dead, as Veleda had feared. Her fate

was worse than mere death: she had been taken captive. The fact that she had not been killed outright was a clear indication that the Romans knew of her status and were reserving her for some special fate. Dumonorix had been captured as well, and brought back to Divitiacus, his traitor brother, in chains.

Perhaps they would both be sent to Rome, to die in the hideous games so beloved by the soft people of that city, who sat and watched in avid delight as brave men and women spilled their lifeblood out onto the sands. Veleda was heart-torn at what could be waiting for her foster mother, but if that was to be Ancamna's path—as well as Dumonorix's—there was nothing she could do to prevent it. Her responsibility lay with those who were still free.

And there were others besides Ancamna to grieve for. So many had embarked on the journey to the Otherworld. All of Veleda's brothers were dead. Her father, though he had managed to make his way to safety, had been gravely wounded and died soon after. Garkol, the warrior who was the first one she had saved from the plague, had died in the ill-fated attempt to cross the river and attack the Roman camp. His father Brucettus had fallen when the Roman cavalry swept down upon the train of wagons.

All had died the kind of death of which warriors dreamed, acquitting themselves bravely on the field of battle. They had fallen covered in honor and glory, and they had earned their places in the Otherworld. Surely they were there now, feasting and hunting and enjoying themselves. Veleda wanted to be happy for them, for she knew that they themselves were happy. But it was hard. She yearned for her kin now that they were gone, and the pain of her yearning was sharpened by regret. The long years of her training had put distance between she and her father and brothers. Now, as long as she remained in this world, that distance could never be bridged. It would fall to her to tell her mother that the bodies could not even be recovered for the burial that was due those of noble status. Raricus and his sons would never be laid to rest covered in the honor and riches they so greatly deserved.

But in truth, there was no time to devote to grief—Caesar and his remaining legions were rapidly advancing. They had been marching northeast for two days, heading steadily in this direction. A battle loomed in the fates of the Nervii and those who had taken refuge with them. It had to be planned for.

The Nervii were a fierce people, highly respected for their ferocity in war. Their claim that they never ran from a fight was no idle boast; they had proven it time and again. Their assertion that they never traded for Roman wine or other luxury goods for fear that such things would dilute their courage and make them soft was not quite so accurate. It was true that they looked with contempt on the southern tribes and their eager contacts with Rome, but there were many among the Nervii who nevertheless enjoyed their jugs of Roman wine.

Still, regardless of any ambivalence toward Roman goods, the Nervii had been quick to offer shelter to what remained of the confederation. Even more important, they were willing to go into battle against the legions again. Indeed, the very idea filled them with fierce delight.

"*We* will not run," the Nervii king told Veleda grimly. "Nor will we surrender like the weaklings of them tribes who offered themselves as slaves when these Romans came to their *oppida*. Pah, they are all cowards. It shames me to remember that they belong to the tribes of Belgae."

Veleda looked at him sternly. "Take care, my lord. Mistakes enough have been made as it is. One of them was underestimating our foes. We must not do that again."

The king was a broad man, and blunt spoken, at times reminding Veleda piercingly of her father. This was one of those times, as he said, "Meaning no disrespect, Lady, but what do you know of battle strategy?"

"I am the daughter of a great warrior." Veleda's tone was calm and even, betraying no hint of pain or anger. "I saw what happened when our army tried to attack the Roman camp, and I fought with my own hands to protect our people when the Romans attacked the wagons. I know enough," she said, "to tell you that we must plan carefully, using our brains as well as our strength. And we must fight together, as our enemies do."

The king laughed, teeth flashing through his beard. "You are a warrior, indeed, Lady. And a Druid. By my honor, it's a potent combination." His face sobered, and he regarded her with keen serious eyes. "I know that you foresaw the evil fate those accursed Romans visited upon the confederation. I know you tried to warn Galba and the others that going into battle was ill-omened. Tell me, Lady, what do you see now?"

Veleda stared past him. She and the king stood on the high thick walls that sheltered his fortress. The town behind them fairly sang with activity as people went about their daily activities amid the other duties of preparing for war. Below them warriors were gathering in ever increasing numbers. They pushed in good-natured competitiveness as they passed through the gates of the *oppidum*, seeking out smiths to shoe their horses and armorers to put new edges on their weapons. Entering with them were freeborn farmers and their families, driving their stock before them.

It was a familiar sight, one Veleda had seen among her own people many times. She knew that throughout the country of the Nervii similar scenes were being enacted: warriors preparing themselves while common folk sought out the safety of the nearest *oppidum*.

"Your country is beautiful, lord," she said softly. "It makes me think of my own."

"Yes, yes," the king said impatiently. "But what of my question. What have you seen?"

Veleda turned to face him. "Nothing," she said honestly. "Neither for good or ill. Not as yet. But whether or not I see the omens does not change the fact that we must be prepared."

The king was a practical man. He listened and nodded. "We will be," he said in his blunt way. "You need have no fears of that."

He was as good as his word. Both he and his councilors took the matter of strategy seriously. He called an immediate meeting of those most seasoned in the arts of war, asking Veleda and any other surviving Druids to attend so they could listen and render advice from the unseen realms.

Many were the ideas for strategy that were thrown out. But it was Veleda who described a tactic so simple its beauty outshone any other battle plan proposed thus far.

"Wait until they start to set up their camp," she said with quiet intensity, "and then fall on them with all the force we can muster. Romans love organization. They devote themselves to it as we Druids worship the gods. They will be so occupied with digging their trenches and putting up their tents in neat straight rows that it will be easy to catch them off guard."

Her eyes blazed as she spoke. The everpresent cat that everyone whispered was a magical link to the outland Goddess who had given Veleda her powers sat beside her, his eyes as bright and fierce as hers. The men and women gathered in the council looked into those eyes, and it seemed to them that the blazing orbs of both woman and cat reflected the coming battle in their depths. They could see the Romans taken unaware, their orderly legions in disarray, the Nervii warriors and their allies visiting death upon them as savagely as they had visited death upon so many others. It was a glorious sight.

"Yes," said one of the Druids softly. Veleda had come to know him on the trek to meet Caesar's army. He belonged to the Atrebates tribe and, as was the custom with many Druids, he had been married with several children. His entire family had been slaughtered when the cavalry overtook the wagons. "The gods will favor such a plan," the man went on in his soft voice. "My bones tell me that the omens are good."

The Nervii king looked at Veleda, and his eyes shone with an implacable joy. "It shall be done as the seer of the Eburones describes. And Lady, may our gods and the outland Goddess who protects you look generously upon this venture."

On the afternoon of the third day of marching, the legions came to a wide shallow river, and Caesar's scouts reported back to him.

"The barbarians have taken up a position in the woods on the river's northern bank," the leader of the scouts said. "If you can call it that." There was barely concealed contempt in his tone. "They're behaving in as wild and disorganized a fashion as any other tribe we have seen."

Caesar nodded. It was a situation he was well familiar with by now. "They seem to have little capacity for learning from their mistakes, do they?" he remarked conversationally to his aides. "Send the surveyors out with patrols to protect them," he ordered. "We'll make camp as soon as they have picked the best spot."

The surveyors' task was easy. A hill overlooking the near side of the river was the natural choice. As soon as Caesar approved the place the main body of his force set about their accustomed work. Busily they began constructing the network of ramparts and ditches that would protect them from attack.

From the shelter of the woods Veleda stood in a circle with the other Druids, watching the Romans at their work. A wave of hatred swept over her. Her hands turned into fists at her sides, and a veil dripping with the blood of the slain dropped down before her eyes, obscuring her vision. The depth of what she was feeling shocked her. Hatred so intense was not useful; it interfered with the clearness of her power as a seer. She closed her eyes, and with an effort, called upon her inner disciplines to bring her calm and cool the heat in her souls.

She opened her eyes, to hear someone saying, "The order has been given for our cavalry. Look you, they're already drawing the Roman cavalry out.''

Peering out through the trees, Veleda saw a sight that swelled her heart with pride and loss. A narrow plain lay on the far bank of the river, and there the tribesmen were riding as only they could ride, each man melding with his horse and the maneuvers of which he was a part, with a fluidity that made the Roman cavalrymen appear stiff and utterly out of harmony with the mounts on whose backs they sat. Raricus had been a horseman without peer. He had passed his love of horses and riding on to all of his children, including Veleda. If he were here now, he would be clinging to his favorite stallion's back, his booming laughter trailing behind him as he skirmished with his enemies.

"The Romans are getting the worst of it," another Druid observed with satisfaction.

Veleda smiled to see this, though her smile was a cold and dreadful thing. "It seems they are discovering that riding down upon old people and children in wagons is a far different state of affairs than meeting mounted warriors who are prepared," she said.

But the main body of Romans seemed unconcerned with what was happening on the far bank of the river. They had grown even more occupied with laying out their camp and building their fortifications and were paying little attention to anything else.

It was then that the enemy came.

The entire Nervii army burst out of the woods and raced across the narrow plain. There were thousands and thousands of them, coming in wave upon wave of color and rage. Screaming their war cries they swept the astonished Roman cavalry in front of them and leaped into the river. They swarmed across the shallow barrier of water, heading straight for the equally astonished legions.

Chaos ensued. Frantically the trumpeters sounded the call to battle, as men rushed to seize swords, helmets and shields and get into fighting formation. But there was no time. Within moments thousands of warriors had forded the river, surged up the hill, and hurled themselves into the Roman camp. They attacked so swiftly that their enemies had no chance to find their units or even take off their shield covers. Caught off guard, demoralized as they had so often demoralized the tribes, the Roman troops found themselves scattered haphazardly across a mile-long front, each facing in a different direction, and fighting for their very lives.

At the first blare of the trumpets Caesar tore out of his tent, to be confronted by the horrifying sight that had already engulfed his legions. Instantly he saw that here was a crisis capable of destroying his entire army, and he was as unprepared for it as his men. He snatched a shield from a soldier in the rear ranks and headed for the front ranks.

"Hold fast, men!" he roared out as he ran. "Keep up your nerve! Remember our traditions of bravery. Live up to them, men. Live up to them!"

His voice rose above the smashing weapons, screams, and battle cries. But all about him his soldiers were falling to the ground slashed nearly to ribbons by the vengeful swords and axes of the maddened Nervii. Caesar ran from one cohort to the next, calling each of his centurions by name, and shouting encouragement to his beleaguered troops. His presence heartened them, for he was truly fearless in the face of death. Yet even his breathtaking courage did not seem to be enough to save the legions from a massacre.

Brave as Caesar and his men were, the Romans were suffering heavy losses. One after another, the centurions, each commanding a century of one hundred men, were cut down. The Twelfth Legion had become entirely surrounded, and still the warriors swarmed forward. The pending defeat that hung like a stench in the nostrils of the Romans was a sweet smell for the Nervii, for it carried the heady scent of victory. Not yet had they known victory in their clashes with the Romans, but on this day it seemed that the tide was finally turning in their favor. They closed in with ever-increasing ferocity, hungry for the triumph so clearly within their grasp.

His voice cracking with the strain of constant shouting, Caesar roared out orders for the legions to advance and open their ranks. It was a maneuver laden with risk, but the only way his men could use their swords more effectively. And slowly, it began to work.

On the left flank, by some miracle of the gods, the men of the Eleventh and Tenth had been managing to hold the attacking warriors at bay. All at once something gave way, and with the suddenness that often happens in battle, the impetus changed. Now it was the soldiers of the Eleventh and Tenth who were driving forward. They pushed the Nervii down the hill, drove them across the river and fought their way up the hill on the opposite bank.

From their place in the woods, Veleda and the other Druids stood motionless. Not one of them had spoken since the battle began. Even when it looked as if the army of invaders would finally meet with the destruction they so richly deserved the Druids kept silent. Fate was always capricious, and the omens had not presented themselves clearly to any of them, even Veleda.

When the two legions turned on their attackers and pushed them back across the river, the group of Druids froze into a stillness that quivered with tension. To their eyes the battlefield was a scene of utter confusion. Each army was now fighting on both sides of the river. Men were struggling against each other in life-and-death clashes, while horses, many of them riderless, reared and plunged, or fell kicking to the bloody ground. Piles of corpses lay everywhere. Their numbers were mounting steadily, these twisted and tangled stacks of the dead rising so high they interfered with the fighting of those who still lived.

Veleda felt the brush of soft fur against her leg. Mau had appeared beside her. He stared up at her, and she could feel him pulling at her with his eyes. Together they slipped away to the far side of the trees, as far from the other Druids as they could, though it mattered little: the Druids were too intent on what was happening beyond them to notice anything else.

"This will not end well," Mau said quietly. "Can you not feel it?"

Veleda listened to the clamor of fighting and dying men. "I'm beginning to." She spoke with reluctance. It was difficult to concede even that much. The day had started so well; there was so much bound up in this battle—not the least of which was the heavy burden she bore as its strategist—that to admit anything dire was more than she wanted to do. Not while there was still hope.

But there had never been any hiding from Mau. "Set aside your pride, human girl," he said impatiently. "There is too much at stake. The Romans are going to reach the top of the other hill, and when they do, they'll overrun the Nervii camp. You must be away before that happens."

Veleda's jaw tightened. "You ask me to leave? And me responsible for the way this battle has been fought."

Mau's tail lashed against his flanks. "More than one battle is being fought this day," he hissed. "Open yourself. Look beyond the obvious and see what you should have seen already."

His words jarred something loose in Veleda. He was right; she had been so concentrated on watching the seen that she had shut out what was far more important: the unseen. "Bast is here," she breathed.

Mau looked at her. "And so is Sekhmet."

"Yes." Briefly Veleda closed her eyes. Now it swept through her, the force of Their struggle buffeting her as though she stood in the vortex of a storm. "Bast is trying to protect us," she exclaimed softly. "She is trying to drive Sekhmet away."

Disgust twisted her insides. She could see the dark Goddess before her inner eye, glutted on blood, suffused with it, the fangs in Her great lioness mouth stained and dripping red. Her laughter was alive, writhing and swirling about the battlefield, drawing in ever more blood for Her to feast upon. She was strong. So terribly strong.

"My Mistress is also strong." Mau's light voice bristled like the fur that rose along his back. "And yet Sekhmet has two advantages that She does not. One is the discipline of the Roman troops. The other is Julius Caesar. With such advantages and the amount of blood spilled here today, Sekhmet is drunk with power. She will seek to add you to the army of dead who feed Her thirst, and Lady Bast is too occupied in fighting to protect you properly. Take out the rods my Mistress gave to you."

At that moment a great roar went up from the Roman soldiers. The last two of Caesar's legions had been marching in the rear, far beyond the baggage train. Just now appearing on the ridge behind the battlefield, they stared in horror at the sight of their desperately fighting comrades, then broke into a dead run, rushing forward to attack the Nervii from a different direction.

"Hurry!" Mau's voice sounded startlingly like the yowl of a mortal cat.

Veleda tore open the pouch she always wore at her belt. The rods came alive in her hands as she pulled them out, warm with the power they always took on the moment she touched them. She glanced about her, her senses alert, searching for the first glimpse or smell of Sekhmet's demons.

But Mau, shoving his body against hers to get her moving, said, "No, Her creatures will not appear this day. Why should they?"

Veleda understood. Sekhmet did not intend using Her minions to slay Veleda; there was no reason. Not with so many Romans here to do Her bidding. They would boil up over the hill, enraged by the near massacre, and bolstered by the newly arrived legions. Determined on slaughtering everyone in their path, they would see Veleda as simply one more target to be cut down.

Mau's sharp voice broke in on her thoughts. "Hold the rods as I tell you. Then focus your powers and recite the words after me. A spell will form that will protect you from the sight of the Romans."

Veleda hesitated. "Will the power in the rods protect others?"

The cat's tail lashed more furiously than ever. Veleda could read Mau's expression as easily as he could read hers and his frustration was evident. In truth, he cared nothing for the fate of those in the Nervii camp; his concern lay with her and her alone. But he also knew that to Veleda, the fate of her people was as important—perhaps more important—than her own. The two were inextricably linked.

He made a growling sound deep in his throat. "If that is the only way I can get you away from here, then, yes, the rods can protect others. Now *will* you come?"

The camp of the Nervii was as disorganized as any other tribal camp in times of war. People rushed back and forth, arguing over the status of the battle. Some were throwing their belongings together in preparation for fleeing, while others insisted that they stand fast, that the Goddess of Battle had already granted them victory.

Veleda burst in on this scene of arguing and confusion. "Come to me," she roared above the clamor. "The Romans will soon charge over the hill and slay everyone they see. Gather around me so that I may keep you safe!"

Her words only seemed to create more confusion. Handfuls of people ran to her, demanding to know what she meant. Others came, too, but only to insist that she was wrong. Still others took her warning as proof that they should flee, and ran from the camp, desperate to reach farmsteads and family who had been left behind, hoping to save whoever and whatever they could from the legions that would now advance over their lands like some terrible plague.

"No," Veleda cried as she saw the scattered clusters of Nervii run past. "They will only find you——" She quickly broke off her plea. Seeking to call them back was useless; she could only save those who were willing to stay with her.

She thrust the rods up over her head. Mau was close beside her, waiting to give her the spell. The words he recited were soundless, resounding only in her head, but she spoke each one aloud as she heard it. The spell could only be given in the tongue of the Black Land; therefore, the words were in a tongue that would have been incomprehensible to any person alert enough to listen. But no one did listen; they were all too busy shouting out their own questions and concerns. Even when the cloud billowed up, seeming to appear from nowhere and everywhere at once, no one noticed it, except for Veleda and Mau.

It enveloped everyone who stood near the Druid and her feline companion. It swirled and shifted, dense as a fog in late Seed-Fall, and yet as transparent as mist burning off a river in the sun. Perhaps that was why people did not see it—or perhaps they did not see it because something greater claimed their attention.

The first wave of Romans had hurled themselves over the ridge of the hill.

These were the men of the Tenth, one of the legions taken off guard in the Nervii's attack. They had still not had time to put on their helmets and their faces were clearly visible in the slanting afternoon light. Expressions of fury and hate dominated their dark features. There would be no mercy for any living creature unfortunate enough to be caught in their path.

"Stay near to me." Veleda's voice was quiet in the din of charging legionaries, yet every man and woman who had gathered about her, whether by accident or design, could hear each word she spoke. "They cannot see you so long as you stay near to me. Do not move."

And it was as she said. The soldiers swept by, swords

and javelins cleaving the air, yet not one person who stood in the great circle that had gathered about Veleda was touched. They could see through this cloak of invisibility that she had called up to shelter them. Indeed, they could see through it all too well. Those who were not within that magical radius were cut down, not without fierce fighting on their own part, but cut down nonetheless. The tide of the battle had turned in favor of the Romans, and all who were still alive, both legionary and warrior, could feel it.

"Come," Veleda said to the people around her.

Grief engulfed her as profoundly as the spell of protection. This day would see another tragedy for the tribes; the air itself sang with it. Bast and Sekhmet still fought, but Veleda did not need Mau to tell her what she had already realized. Blood was blood. Whether it flowed from Roman bodies or Nervii, it was all the same to Sekhmet; it still fed Her, and gave Her strength. There was nothing more Veleda could do now except try to save whomever it was in her power to save.

She began to walk through the remnants of the camp, heading for the deep woods where the Druids had stood to watch the battle. "Come," she called out again. "Follow along with me, and you will not be harmed."

She led those with her past squadron after squadron of legionaries. The fury of the Romans had not abated. If anything it was greater. They had expected to find more barbarians in the enemy camp than they had, and while many lay dead beneath their sandals, the thirst for blood burned hot as ever. The Tenth's commander was a seasoned soldier called Titus Labienus. Satisfied that the Nervii camp was destroyed, knowing that the heights of both hills were now in command of the legions, he directed his men to join in the inflicting of a now-inevitable defeat upon the tribe that had dared attack them.

Veleda, Mau, and those under the spell's protection had reached the safety of the trees. They looked down at the plain between the hills, watching as their warriors were steadily squeezed in and then completely surrounded by the legions. The Nervii and their allies fought with the fearless courage of the doomed. They knew they had lost. Their great gamble had not been successful. Now they could only end this battle with as much joyous bravery as they had begun it.

The heaps of dead mounted, but most of the bodies were tribesmen now, and not Roman. The surviving warriors showed no dismay; indeed they even stood on the piles of corpses, the better to throw their spears. Their courage was as enormous as it was futile. The legionaries, fully disciplined once more, gradually overpowered them. The fighting turned to butchery, and the Nervii fell by the thousands.

Even Caesar had to admire the bravery of these ragged barbarians. He was still stunned by what had almost happened here. Self-honesty was one of the qualities he prided himself on, and he could not deny the obvious. The Nervii had taken his army by surprise. Only his quick action had saved this day from utter disaster. The fighting had occupied no more than a turn of the hourglass, but it had been a desperate turn, and humiliating: Caesar's first brush with defeat. The memory of this afternoon must be wiped out in the only way possible, by annihilating the source of the humiliation.

When the killing finally ended and stacks and stacks of corpses lay cooling on the battlefield, those who had not escaped with Veleda came to the Romans to offer their surrender. Sixty thousand warriors had embarked on the strategy to destroy his army and of that number only five hundred were said to have survived. The Nervii tribe, Caesar's commanders reported to him with satisfaction, had been virtually annihilated.

This was not quite the truth, although the Romans were not to learn of it for some time.

15

THE LONG BLOODY SUMMER was drawing to a close and with it the fighting season. But bolstered by the triumph over the Nervii and desiring one more victory, Caesar marched against another Belgaic tribe. Turning northward he led his troops to the *oppidum* of the Aduatuci. Captured warriors had told Divitiacus that the Aduatuci had sent an army to aid the Nervii. However, when the battle turned against them, the Aduatuci had swiftly deserted their allies, riding to the safety of their largest and most fortified stronghold.

When Caesar arrived at the *oppidum* his chief engineers immediately set about the task of building an enormous siege tower to breach the stone walls that protected the fortress. The Aduatuci had heard terrifying stories of these miraculous devices that the Romans could construct out of whatever materials were available. Plainly such feats could not be accomplished without the intervention of the gods, and this, coupled with the knowledge that the fierce Nervii had been vanquished, convinced their king and his chieftains that surrender was the only option. At least for now.

But Julius Caesar was not a trusting man. He ordered his legions to spend the night in their camp outside the massive walls of the *oppidum*. Thus, when the expected attack came, he was prepared. Shortly after midnight, the Aduatuci burst out of their fortress, to be met with a shower of arrows, javelins, and stones from well-positioned legionaries. The battle was short. Four thousand warriors were killed and the rest driven back into the town, although the refuge they found there was to be equally short. At first light, the Romans used a battering ram to smash open the gates, and took everyone inside prisoner.

Such treachery had to be dealt with firmly. Caesar had over fifty thousand tribespeople rounded up and then sold them to the slave dealers who shrewdly followed after his army wherever it went. Such auctions—although this one was larger than usual—had become commonplace on his campaigns. Selling his former foes into slavery not only provided a major source of income for himself and his officers, but also kept Caesar's name and exploits before the capricious eye of the Roman public.

The slave dealers immediately set off on the journey back to Rome, eager to make their profits in a market where foreign captives were always in demand. They marched their human merchandise in long lines, chained at the neck and wrists, attended by hard-faced drivers armed with whips and squadrons of soldiers sent by Caesar to protect the dealers from attack. These winding processions of shackled men and women were a blight upon the land. Awkward under the unaccustomed burden of chains, the Aduatuci stumbled through the country they had once walked as free people, and on into the territory of the Nervii.

The Nervii lands were not as deserted as the Romans thought. The people Veleda had saved had not been the only ones to survive. There were others who had escaped the carnage of the battle beside the river. Now they were slipping back to their homes, grateful that they had homes to return to, grateful that the legions had marched through their lands without ravaging them. More importantly, they were still free. And those who were still free watched those who were not pass by, helpless to do anything but stare, while rage smoldered within them like a slow fire.

Veleda, too, saw the slave processions. She and Mau had

started the journey back to the land of the Eburones. Word of the magic she had worked to save so many had spread among the survivors. She would have been welcome to hospitality anywhere among the remaining Nervii. But she could not accept it, any more than she could accept the gratitude of those she had saved. The great strategy had failed, and so had she.

She watched the lines of her chained people, heard the whips and harsh voices of their captors, and one question slashed into her thoughts with sharp fangs. *How many more failures lay in store?*

Smiling at Divitiacus, Caesar sat back in his chair, gesturing for his body slave to pour out two more goblets of wine.

The commander was in an expansive mood. Autumn was descending over the dense forests of the Belgae's remote land. A garrison had been set up and the legions were settling into their billets for the coming winter. This campaign had been highly successful and he was well pleased with himself and his men. Even the near disaster with the Nervii had instead become a great victory. In two seasons of campaigning he had defeated every tribe to come against him, and in so doing, he had firmly established his reputation among the barbarians.

Chieftains from as far away as Germany were now sending word that they wished to offer oaths of submission to this dreaded Roman. But so confident was Caesar that he in turn sent word back for them to wait until the following summer. He did not want to linger in Belgae territory any longer than necessary. It was time to return to Illyricum, where he could be closer to the happenings in Rome.

Caesar's dispatch announcing his final victories of the year was already on its way to the Senate. It would be followed by a great spectacle of slaves and plunder entering into the capital. Such enormous deeds on behalf of the empire would oblige the Senate to decree sacrifices to the gods, as well as festivals and public holidays. All in honor of the man who was being called "the Conqueror of Gaul."

But there was one piece of business that must be attended to before he left.

"So, my friend." The general took a sip of wine. "It is time I spoke with this woman who you tell me is regarded so highly." He chuckled a little as he spoke. Divitiacus had come to him on the day the cavalry attacked the broken and fleeing confederation. A powerful captive had been taken, the Aeduian king had said. The High Priestess of the Belgaic tribes herself. Caesar chuckled again. Only among barbarians would the notion that a woman could be so influential receive any credence.

Divitiacus did not join in his humor. "She is regarded so for good reason," he said gravely. "To be named High Priestess of all the tribes of the Belgae is a great thing."

"Of course." The Roman general's reply was tactful, if somewhat distracted. "However, the real question is how she may be of use to me." He studied his companion thoughtfully. "You say her word carries a good deal of weight among these people?"

"It does, Caesar." Divitiacus leaned forward, his handsome features intent. "Among every tribe in this land Druids are more important even than kings. They are the holders of our wisdom and our history. The arts of divination are theirs. They are the masters and mistresses of healing and music. And she who is named High Priestess is the most important of all. Our women are very different from the women of Rome, Caesar."

The general snorted. "Women are women, my friend. No matter what land they come from."

"No, Caesar." The king's voice held a note that caught the Roman's attention, reminding Caesar that ally though he was, Divitiacus, too, was a Druid. "Women are sacred in our country, and for good reason. Magic lives in women, inhabiting their souls and hearts in ways that no man can ever understand, much less possess. It gives them access to the highest of wisdom, to knowledge straight from the gods themselves. We as men can never hope to attain the gifts women are born with.''

Caesar downed the remainder of his wine and set the goblet back on the carved table with a sharp snap. "Let us see how wise this particular woman is," he said dryly. "I will have her brought to me, and I will offer her a simple choice. She can order these Belgaic tribes who revere her to swear complete allegiance to Rome and give me their oaths that they will offer no more resistance. Or she can die. If she truly possesses the wisdom you say she does, then she will make the right choice."

Within a short time, the High Priestess, chained and shackled as all captives were, was standing before Julius Caesar and the king of the Aedui. Caesar looked her up and down with ill-concealed scorn. This priestess who Divitiacus described with such respect was, to Roman eyes, quite unimpressive. She was unwomanly, as were most of the females he had seen in this land: unnaturally tall and muscular. Indeed, despite the considerable amount of gray in her mane of tangled matted hair, her muscles were as large as those of many men. He noticed, to his surprise, that she was crippled. Her manacled hands were gripping a beautifully carved wooden staff upon which she leaned for support.

Caesar glanced at Divitiacus. "You'll need to translate. I doubt she speaks any civilized tongue."

"There is no need for that," Ancamna said in rough but passable Latin. "I understand you well enough."

Astonished, Caesar looked at her more closely. "So you are what they call a High Priestess," he finally said.

"I am."

He continued to study her, making no attempt to conceal his profound disapproval. "You are a woman," he said unnecessarily.

There was more than a little amusement in her tone. "I am."

The Roman's thin lips grew even thinner. "Divitiacus

has told me of your position. For a woman to be invested
with such power is against the natural order.''

"And what do you," Ancamna asked, "know of the natural order?''

He leaned forward, his brown eyes narrowing on hers.
"I know this, woman: that we have defeated your people
everywhere and every time we have clashed in arms. I
know that we have killed you in the thousands, and those
who have not died are running for their lives, or else being
taken to Rome in chains to be sold in the slave markets.
Now if it were not against the natural order for the women
of your race to take on leadership that should be reserved
for men, why have you suffered such terrible defeats?''

Ancamna's gaze met that of Caesar. Her eyes were as
brown as his, yet hers were filled with depths and shadows
that his did not, and never would, contain. "Can defeat not
become the path to victory?'' she inquired as casually as if
she were asking for a goblet of wine.

"Not for your kind,'' Caesar told her, clipping off each
word. "For all their size and courage, the warriors of your
land are like children. They do not know how to fight. Not
when it counts.''

Ancamna did not reply. She smiled.

Baffled, Caesar stared at her. "You find my telling you
that your armies cannot stand against us amusing?'' he demanded.

She continued to smile. "You Romans see everything in
straight lines. But it is not so simple as that. The world is
a circle within circles, and all that happens upon her goes
back to the beginning.''

"Well, here is something that is very simple.'' Caesar
disliked the obtuseness of religion, and this woman spoke
as irritatingly as any priest. Watching her, he summoned a
smile of his own. "I have ordered your execution.''

He paused, studying her carefully, searching for some
sign of dismay or fear. Caesar was a seasoned reader of
men, able to detect such emotions even when those feeling

them tried to hide it. But this tall crippled woman leaning on her carved staff confounded him. She seemed honestly unconcerned at the sentence of death he had just pronounced upon her.

He decided to continue as if she had reacted as he had expected. "However," he said, "you may avert my decree, if you comply with certain conditions."

Ancamna laughed. "One cannot place conditions on death, Caesar. Or on life."

"I can." The Roman's voice was calm, the way it was when he was intensely angry. "And I have. You will die, woman. I know your people set great store on an honorable death. But your death will be very public and very shameful. Is that what you want, for the tribes who put you in your high position to see their High Priestess shamed?"

She regarded him with a calm that was equal to his, and yet far different. For Caesar's calm was outward, concealing the turbulent emotions that lay beneath. Ancamna's calm was inward, and it concealed nothing. "What I want is of no consequence," she said. "What will happen is in the hands of Anu, our Great Mother."

Caesar turned to Divitiacus who had been standing, silent and troubled, throughout this exchange. "Talk to her, my friend," he said curtly. "Perhaps you can find words of reason that will penetrate her woman's foolishness."

"Lady." Divitiacus made a mighty effort to keep his voice even; Caesar might not understand them, but his keen ears would be more than able to detect any sign of the profound unease that gripped the Aeduian king. "Pay heed to me, I beg you. All he asks is that you counsel the tribes of Belgae to accept Rome's presence within their lands and cease fighting against it."

Ancamna stared at him until Divitiacus could no longer meet her eyes. "All?" she asked, when he had dropped his gaze.

"It is a small enough thing," he muttered uneasily.

Divitiacus was not ready to give up. As a Druid, he thus

far stood alone in his support of Rome. Dumonorix was as
obstinate and savage in his determination to resist Rome as
ever. Caesar had ordered him sent back to Aedui territory
under close guard, a decision that Divitiacus could not argue with, given his brother's behavior.

However, if he could convince the powerful High Priestess of the fierce Belgaic tribes to stand with him, it might
convince Dumonorix to do the same. It would be an enormous accomplishment, one that would increase his favor
with Caesar, as well as with his tribe and all others. But
beyond that there was the horror of what the Roman commander threatened to do to Ancamna. Divitiacus was still
a Druid, the ties of the oak still bound him, and to slay a
High Priestess was sacrilege, the most profound sacrilege
of all.

"The legions have already destroyed the confederation
you formed to keep them out of your lands," he said with
as much firm persuasion as he could muster. "You would
be doing nothing more than helping them to accept the
inevitable."

Ancamna's eyes fixed on his, dragging Divitiacus's gaze
up to meet hers as if a cord bound them. "King of the
Aedui, who is also a Druid," she intoned in the low expressionless tone that both knew was the voice of power.
"With such counsel, you betray your oaths as a king and
as a Druid. The foul words that spew from your tongue put
your souls at risk of being exiled beyond the Ninth Wave
for all time. Is the enjoyment of following at this Roman's
heels worth such a fate?"

Divitiacus repressed a shudder. The curse of the Ninth
Wave was not a thing to be taken lightly, even by a king.
"I do what I believe to be right," he said sharply.

"No," said the High Priestess in that same quiet terrible
voice. "You do what is best for yourself, and no other. But
it is not yet too late, my Brother of the Oak. Turn from
this path you have set your feet upon and come back to the
ways of rightness. Save yourself. While you can."

Divitiacus felt as if a great wind were tearing through him. He knew that Caesar was watching him, the general's sharp eyes assessing the king's expression, judging from it as to what was passing between he and the High Priestess. For an instant he teetered on the brink of a great chasm, able to go forward or backward at his own choice. Then the moment passed. "It is you, Lady, who must worry about saving yourself," he heard himself say. "For it is you, not I, who stand here in chains."

She shook her head. "I am already safe. The Shining Ones know I have lived my life in this world in accordance with their wishes. When the time comes for me to leave, Anu will take me to Her breast and I will be welcomed into the Otherworld. But you, Divitiacus, you are not safe, and never will you be. Do you think my death will be the end of it?"

Divitiacus could not answer her. Abruptly he swung back to Caesar. "I regret, General, that nothing I can say will move her."

Caesar sighed. By Jupiter, the creature was stubborn. And foolish, as all women were. He had hoped Divitiacus would be able to persuade her to support Rome, but she was as lacking in good sense as all members of her sex. He took little pleasure in ordering the death of an aging woman, Druid or no. But she would be worth little in the slave markets and sending her to the arena where she would be killed anyway would accomplish nothing other than providing enjoyment for the citizens of Rome. She would serve a far more useful purpose if she were executed in her own land, before her own people. Word of her death would spread rapidly, demoralizing the tribes still further.

"So be it," he said to the king. "There is nothing more to be said. Your execution will be carried out tomorrow," he told Ancamna. "If you reconsider and show yourself willing to listen to reason, I, too, will be reasonable. I will rescind the decree I have issued against you."

Ancamna favored him with that maddening smile. "The

circles continue to form, General of Rome," she said. "And the ending of one will be but the beginning of another."

She was impossible. Beyond the comprehension of civilized men, as all the men and women of this strange land who called themselves Druids were. Divitiacus was the one exception. Thank the gods the king of the Aedui did not have eyes like this woman. Fathomless eyes, deep and dark, drawing him in and confusing him with their secrets. Caesar was discovering that he did not want to look into that dark gaze for very long, though of course he would never admit it; not even if all the gold in this rich land were offered to him by the gods themselves. He gestured for the guards to remove the captive from his tent.

Soon Ancamna was back in the small tent where she was being kept alone, the only concession to her rank. She stood in her shackles, straight and tall despite the handicap of her weakened leg. Her eyes took on a distant expression, looking far beyond the Roman camp. Her vision carried her, flying over forests and hills and rivers, enabling her to see the things they had not seen before.

Yes, she said to herself. *It all fits together now, and it always has.* She rejoiced at her part in it. She thanked Anu and all the Shining Ones, even Veleda's outland Goddess, for allowing her this role in what lay ahead.

"Come to me, Foster-Daughter," she whispered. "Come and see my death, so that you may be reborn."

Veleda had returned to the lands of her people. It was a somber return, dark with grief and the silences left by the many who would never return. Those who waited for the vanished had to be told, among them Veleda's own mother. From her daughter, Bormana learned that her husband and sons were gone, and her sister was a captive of the Romans. Bormana was a strong woman, but this was difficult news to bear. She thanked Veleda for bringing her this news and praised the gods for having spared her daughter, doing all of this with a formality that spoke eloquently of the depth of her pain. Then she withdrew into herself to grieve.

Veleda herself had slept little since the confederation's first ill-fated battle at the marsh. Whenever she tried, even with Mau curled up purring by her side, the scenes of the blood-soaked summer unfolded again and again, haunting her until she rose from her sleeping place, knowing that rest was futile.

Today, though, exhaustion finally won out. Or perhaps something else caused her to spread her mantle beneath a solitary oak and stretch out in its shade. It was midday, and Lugh the sun god stood high in the heavens, glaring down at the earth below. The air was hot and still, humming with heat and humidity and the high bright songs of the insects of high summer. The insects were the only ones with energy enough to speak; all other creatures lay in resting places similar to Veleda's, waiting for the day to cool.

On such a day, even one who was heart-wounded could find it in her to sleep. Veleda slowly relaxed, lulled by the insects and the relentless heat into a light doze that deepened gradually into sleep. It was a sweet sleep. Ancamna came to her in it.

Her foster-mother was smiling, looking at her with love and pride in those familiar well-loved eyes that were so deep and dark and filled with wisdom.

Mother's Sister! Veleda ran to her. Ancamna was there, and yet she felt insubstantial in Veleda's arms, as if she were no longer a part of the world. Was it the dreaming, or did her shadowy feel portend something else? Veleda was a seer; she knew what it meant. And she did not want to know. She sought to hold Ancamna closer. *Praises to Anu, they have not killed you!*

Not yet, my beloved child, Ancamna replied gently. *But they will.*

Behind the High Priestess a vast figure loomed up. The

gentle tinkling of the music Veleda had once heard in the temple of Bast wafted around her and the deep wondrous voice thrummed all through her being.

She understands her purpose, My daughter. She embraces it, as she embraces you. Go to her. Go. . . .

Veleda jerked awake. Everything about her was the same. The sun still blazed, running long gold fingers through the oak leaves. The heat still lay on the land, heavy as an untanned bearskin, and the insects still sang. But one thing was different: Mau sat in front of her, watching her with his usual intent stare.

She sat up, brushing the hair out of her eyes. "I have dreamed, Mau. We must go to the Roman encampment. I must be there for my foster-mother, when they—when she leaves upon her journey to the Otherworld." She half expected Mau to argue, to try to dissuade her. Placing herself so near the Romans, who had seemingly declared a personal war against Druids, was highly dangerous, and he *was* charged to protect her, after all.

But Mau merely rose, stretched himself, and said, "We had better leave, then. There is very little time left for her in the houses of the living."

As Veleda prepared for her departure her soul-friend Sattia came to see her. Sattia had never married; no man could hold her interest for that long, she declared. She was a warrior-woman now, tall and powerful and utterly dedicated to the arts of war. She had not gone along on the ill-fated expedition of the summer; her task had been to remain behind as one of the few but highly important warriors delegated to protect those who had also stayed home. Sattia had been ill-pleased at missing what promised to be a magnificent battle, but as it turned out, the Shining Ones had been shielding her, saving her perhaps, for some other purpose.

Sattia was not so sanguine about what Veleda planned as Mau had been. "You cannot do this!" she cried. "Your wits have been snatched up by a dark spirit if you think you can walk into a Roman camp and be safe. The Romans are hunting Druids. They hate our holy ones. Veleda, you cannot take the risk!''

''I must,'' Veleda answered simply. ''I have to go to Ancamna. It is part of the pattern.''

''What pattern? For you to be killed, as well? Has your mother not lost enough of her kin as it is?''

Veleda laid her hands on Sattia's shoulders. The muscles felt strong under her fingers, tense with anger and worry. ''I will not be killed, soul-friend,'' she said patiently. ''The pattern does not include that for me. And I will not be the only one to go there.'' Her voice hardened, her eyes taking on a distant glitter. ''The Romans will want an audience for what they plan to do.''

''And what is that?'' Sattia's expression changed as she asked this. She knew Veleda well; they had been so close for so long that she often forgot who and what her soul-friend was. But at moments like this, when Veleda's eyes took on that far-off look and her voice deepened with inexorable knowledge, Sattia remembered.

Veleda's gaze turned back to her. ''That I cannot yet see,'' she said. ''But this much I know: we will lose our High Priestess, and I must be there when it happens.''

Sattia sighed. ''Then I will go with you. Not again will I stay behind.''

As it turned out, Sattia, Veleda, and of course, Mau did not travel alone to where Caesar had set up his encampment in the territory of the Aduatuci. Bormana, straight as a young oak, and stark in her grief, went, too, determined to witness the fate of her sister. Along with them went all the Eburones who could afford to leave their flocks and fields. The Eburone lands had not been formally conquered; their home lay further north than Caesar had cared to go this late in the season. And in any case, such a step was hardly necessary. Great had been the army the Eburones had assembled to do battle with Rome, and greater still had been its losses. In truth, though Veleda's homeland looked serene and untouched, it lay as prostrate under the oxhide sandal of Rome as the rest of the Belgaic tribes.

With Veleda's seeing of their High Priestess's fate, the Eburones were bound to go where she was. But they were not the only ones. A day after Veleda dreamt of Ancamna, Julius Caesar sent out messengers: swift horsemen who rode from one *oppidum* to the next, bearing word that a public execution was planned. The messengers did not say who was to be executed. Their commander had planned it this way, guessing that the not knowing would not only draw the tribes in, but keep them off guard as well.

It was an astute strategy, if a dangerous one. Sullen and worried, the people of the Belgae gathered in great numbers to see what the Romans intended. They were defeated, these fierce tribes of Belgae, but they were not cowed. Freedom flowed deep in their blood. Caesar and his legions had wreaked havoc on their tribal psyche; he had slain thousands of their warriors and taken entire tribes into slavery, yet the desire to be free was not dead. They would have to bide their time and wait for the right moment, something their impulsive natures were not accustomed to. But they had little choice. The Druids were counseling patience now, and even the most impatient of the people could see the wisdom in such advice.

The Roman encampment lay outside the conquered fortress of the Aduatuci. To see that *oppidum* ruined and humbled was like a spear thrust to the vitals. The Eburones stood in silence, grieving over that sight for some time. Only when Mau pushed against Veleda, prompting her to speak softly to her people, did they move on, joining their brethren, those who had already arrived and were continuing to arrive.

Veleda blended in amongst the crowds. As a precaution, she had wisely removed all signs of her craft, although it quickly became apparent that the heavily armed soldiers were more concerned with keeping order over the people in general than with singling out individual Druids. And there were other Druids present besides herself. They were not bound to Ancamna by ties of love and kinship as Veleda was, but they had come for the same purpose. They, too, had powers. They knew for whom Caesar's order of execution was meant.

On the second day after the Eburones had arrived, the sentence upon Ancamna was carried out. For the doing of such a deed Veleda would have expected a dawn as overcast and sullen as the mood of the people. Yet the coming of first light was attended by unseasonable warmth, a sky as blue as a newborn's eyes, and a sunrise that painted that sky with burning swaths of purple and rose.

Bormana's eyes also burned as she looked at the sunrise. "It seems," she said bitterly to her daughter, "that even the forces of earth and sky favor the Romans, to give them such a beautiful day as this to murder my sister."

"No, Mother." Veleda realized the truth as she spoke. "I thought so too, at first. But now I see the meaning of it. This day has nothing to do with the Romans. Its beauty is a gift. For Ancamna, and Ancamna alone."

The legionaries were already busy. Earlier they had constructed a platform, and now they were building something else. The tribes stared in bewilderment at the unfamiliar structure rising up into the bright sky: two broad pieces of wood nailed crosswise to each other. They muttered to each other, speculating as to its meaning. They glanced at Veleda and the other Druids among them, waiting for them to explain the thing's purpose.

But Veleda said nothing. A terrible coldness had sunk into her at the sight of those two pieces of wood. She was scarcely aware of Mau slipping through the legs of the bystanders to come up beside her. He, too, stared at the structure, and there was no doubt that he alone knew what it meant. He crouched next to Veleda, his ears flattened, a low growl rumbling in his chest.

The legionaries had finished their task. They drew aside and came to stiff attention, their fists raised in the Roman salute. The crowd shifted restlessly. Squadrons of soldiers were positioned all about them, alert to any sign of rebellion. Another squadron approached, escorting a group of officers. From the center of the group a lone man wrapped in a crimson cloak detached himself and mounted the platform.

Julius Caesar.

Veleda stared at him. So this was the man responsible for the many triumphs in the lands of the Belgae. Hatred vied with the coldness in her vitals. She wanted to blast him out of the world of the living, to call upon Bast and all the Shining Ones of her tribe to wither him where he stood. But she could not. Power was in this man's thin-lipped handsome face. A path had been set for him, and it did not include being torn apart by magic. At least, not on this day.

"People of the Belgae," Caesar shouted. "You chose to set yourself against Rome, and now you see the results. But Rome holds no anger toward you. We know you were drawn into this ill-conceived aggression by bad counsel. As Rome's representative I will be merciful. I will only punish the one who led your kings and chieftains into this madness. Even to her, I offered mercy, if she would but turn the influence she holds over you tribes to the common sense of working with Rome, rather than against us. But she refused. She has chosen death, and so will she receive her choice."

More soldiers had appeared. Their attention caught by Caesar, few people noticed them. But Veleda did. Or rather who was between them. She had to call upon all the strength of her training to choke back the cry that rose to her throat. Bormana followed her gaze. Not having Druidic discipline, she made a low sound composed of anger and grief. Her voice alerted Sattia, as well as others. The cry that Veleda had held back was wrenched from the throats of the Eburones she stood among and the distress spread quickly to the entire throng of watchers.

Ancamna had been allowed to keep her staff, a concession to her age. Balancing her weight upon it she walked as proudly as ever, despite the shackles that bound her. She dwarfed the soldiers who led her, both in dignity and in height. Her wise dark eyes flew unhesitatingly to where Veleda and Bormana stood, seemingly lost in this assemblage of similarly tall grave-faced people. She smiled at them, and both Bormana and Sattia cursed the Romans loud enough for others to hear.

Bormana was not the only one to curse. The legionaries stationed all about the great crowd tensed uneasily, their alertness heightened still more. Many exchanged glances, imperceptibly shaking their heads. In spite of their immense loyalty to Caesar, few felt happy about this very public execution he had ordered. The conquered tribes had no weapons; they had all been confiscated, and any person coming here had been carefully searched to make certain no hidden swords or daggers were smuggled in. But soldiers, including Roman ones, were often more religious than their generals. To the legionaries, killing the High Priestess of these barbarians before their eyes seemed an act calculated to draw ill fortune.

If the men charged with carrying out the actual execution felt the same as their comrades, they did not show it. Swiftly they lowered the wooden structure, removed Ancamna's chains, and stretched her upon it. They fastened her to the wood with nails through her hands and feet, and as the cruel sound of iron driving into flesh was heard, the agonized mutters of the people gathered helplessly to see her die grew louder.

He wants to give her a death without honor. Mau's voice pierced the haze of rage and pain enfolding Veleda. *This is the way they execute criminals in Rome.*

Finished with their task, the legionaries levered the planks with their bleeding burden back up in the air. Caesar had watched all this, his attractive features expressionless. Now he stepped forward, his brown eyes sweeping out over these unwilling subjects of Rome. "People of Belgae," he said. "I will still be merciful. In Rome, this woman would be left to slowly die under the hot sun of our land. But I will be merciful. I will give her a quicker death than she would otherwise receive."

He nodded to one of the legionaries. The man approached Ancamna, a javelin held ready. Caesar's voice rose to a roar. "Behold! Thus die the enemies of Rome!"

The javelin thrust home, withdrawing to be followed by a gush of blood.

Ancamna's dying eyes looked out over her people. Death was reaching out for her with swift certain hands but the light in her dark eyes was still strong. "Hear me, my people," she cried. There was no pain in her voice, only power, thrumming so loudly it seemed astonishing that the Romans could not feel it. "Brothers and Sisters of the Oak, I name my successor without speaking her name, lest my fate be hers. I counsel you to accept my choice. The one I name is our only chance for freedom. Pay heed to her. She has healed our people once with the aid of the outland Goddess, and she will do so again."

The Eburones knew the person she meant. Their eyes flashed to Veleda.

But Veleda was not looking at any of them. She was staring at her foster-mother, her eyes going past the physical body, its limbs twisted into the grotesque unnatural position the Romans had forced it into. She saw past the blood and the pain, into Ancamna's eyes. And in those dark eyes she saw Mother Anu, reaching out to draw her daughter home. Leaving Veleda in the halls of the living, her feet set on a path that now seemed lonelier than ever.

A silken paw tapped gently at her leg. A familiar voice danced lightly inside her head. *My Mistress watches over you, human girl,* Mau said. *And so do I.*

High Priestess

16

HORI HATED THIS LAND. HE was sitting as close to the fire as he could without igniting himself, his woolen cloak was pulled up around him as tight as he could wrap it, and still he was chilled to the bone. But that was hardly surprising. How could one ever be warm in a country where even when the sun did emerge, it lacked the life-giving heat of the Black Land?

He sighed, his fingers going automatically to the amulet of Bast that he wore about his neck. His mother, a priestess of the Goddess, had given him the amulet before he left to follow the legions as an auxiliary archer, and in all these weary seasons he had not removed it. There could be no doubt that it had kept him from harm. Lady Bast was a great and powerful protector of children and Hori's mother had offered up many prayers for the safety of her son. Adult he may be, she had informed him with her usual crispness, but he was still her boy and would always be so.

She had not approved of his enlisting with the legions, but like most sons his age, Hori had disregarded her opinion. He was young and eager for adventure, his blood burning to see the world that lay beyond the borders of the Two Lands: the rich Black Land of the Nile and the barren Red Land of the desert. Once, in the days of Kemet's greatness that were long past, he could have satisfied his restlessness by joining Pharaoh's army. In such a way had many a man of good but not royal birth risen high and made himself a great career.

But Egypt, the Greek name by which Kemet had come to be more commonly known, had long been under the rule of Alexander the Great's descendants. Her own days of empire and glory were as distant as the dust from the Pharaoh's tombs. Nowadays young men went into Rome's armies if they wanted to fight and see the world.

Hori glanced up as another of his comrades approached. Seti was a good-natured sort, fond of food and drink, and skilled with a bow and arrow, though he was well content to follow, rather than lead. He lacked Hori's restlessness, yet even his good nature was beginning to show signs of strain as winter drew in about this hostile and magic-haunted land.

"Remember when all of us talked about snow?" Seti asked, his round face glum. "One of the centurions just told me we're probably going to get our first look at some by tomorrow."

Hori threw several more sticks on the fire. Snow. The mysterious white substance that none of the Egyptians had ever seen had sounded mysterious and fascinating when they speculated about it under the cloudless blue sky and blazing sun of home. But not here, under the cold and rain or the relentless gray clouds that obscured the sky for days on end. They had tried praying to Ra, the God Whose eye was the sun itself, asking Him to bring His burning smile to this dark tree-filled country. But Ra belonged to Kemet. Obviously He had no power here.

"I suppose it will grow even colder then." Hori watched the sticks catch, flaming up and sending out a flare of heat that was all too thin.

Seti regarded him with horror. "How much colder can it get? The air already freezes my blood like the breath of Set."

"So far we've only had rain. In order for it to snow, I would guess the air has to be colder still."

Seti muttered an oath. He touched the amulet of his personal protector, Sobek the crocodile God, that hung about his neck. But there were no crocodiles in the many rivers and lakes they had seen while campaigning with Julius Caesar or his legates. Such creatures would not live long in the frigid waters of this land. Other gods held sway here, and they were not friendly to intruders. All the men from the Black Land felt that deep in their bones.

Seti hitched himself nearer to the fire. His black eyes darted past Hori, nervously taking stock of what lay beyond the Roman garrison. Trees. An endless number of them, one dark stretch of forest blending into another, until the whole world seemed black with them.

"Sacred Eye of Horus," the normally cheerful Egyptian said to his comrade. He was whispering, as if he feared the trees would overhear him and be displeased. "Never in any dream could I imagine so many trees in one place. It's not natural. Not for Romans, and not for we who come from Kemet. In our countries the sun is strong. Ra rules there— yes, even in Rome, though the Romans are too stupid to know it. A man can look out and *see*. His eyes are not blocked by"—he waved an arm at the looming forest— "all that."

"You're homesick," Hori said reassuringly. "You need some good bread and beer from one of the market stalls in Memphis. That would lighten up those dark thoughts of yours."

In truth, he understood Seti's feelings all too well, but he could not afford the luxury of expressing his own unease. When the leader of their auxiliary troop had been killed in the great battle with the Nervii, the centurion who commanded them had appointed Hori in his place. It was a popular decision. Hori was well liked by his comrades, and he himself was eager to lead. But he had quickly learned the lonely lesson that a leader must, of necessity, put space between he and those he led.

"No, Hori." Seti's voice was insistent. "Bread and beer

have nothing to do with this. We should not be here. The land does not want us.''

Hori smiled grimly. "Neither do the people. But when has Rome ever paid heed to the wishes of people or land when she's in a mood to conquer?''

Seti's shiver had little to do with the cold. "The Romans don't understand. This land is filled with magic. It peeks out at us from every tree and stream. It mocks us in the rain and wind. These Romans we fight with can neither see nor hear it. They don't carry the knowledge of magic within them the way we do.''

"Perhaps not," said Hori. "But Rome still rules the world. And Rome will rule over this land, too, soon enough.''

"Well, Caesar has not been having an easy time of it with"—Seti stumbled over the names—"the Menapii and the Morini tribes. They leap out to attack his legions, and then disappear into the worst parts of their country. The land protects them.''

To this Hori had to nod in sober agreement. Caesar's victories of the summer had created an uneasy peace that was proving to be easily disturbed. The powerful Venetii, a tribe known for their seafaring abilities, had risen up in anger over the governor's holding of hostages. Caesar had crushed the rebellion with ruthless determination, but not without terrible battles in the meantime. Other tribes were issuing challenges as well, so many that Caesar had found it necessary to send his legates Crassus, Sabinus and Labienus to deal with them.

The commander himself had his hands full with the Menapii and Morini. Their belligerent refusal to surrender had convinced Caesar to alter his plans to leave the north and mount an autumn campaign against the two tribes instead. But the northeastern country of the Menapii and Morini was a coastal land of marshes and forests, a land from which warriors who knew its every hiding place could strike out and then fade back into safety. Such tactics had not been used against the legions before, and so far, they appeared to be working.

"They say that the success those tribes are having against Caesar is the doing of the new High Priestess," Hori said reflectively. "I've been learning the native tongue and I've heard that she traveled to the Menapii and Morini and bid them fight as they have done."

Seti's eyes widened. "Have you heard anyone speak her name? Caesar himself would pay you a fortune in gold if you brought that knowledge to him."

"Of course not." Hori shook his head and grinned. "No one would be that foolish. Everyone calls these people barbarians and mocks them for their uncivilized ways. But I tell you, Seti, they are far wiser than our commanders give them credit for."

"Well," Seti growled in disgust, "I would just as soon they all be stupid as a field of Nile mud. And I wish they would tell you how to find this priestess of theirs. The sooner they are all conquered the sooner we can go home."

Veleda watched Amborix pace back and forth among the trees, considering what she had told him. She had spoken to many kings since Rome invaded her land, and whatever awe she might have felt in the beginning had long since passed into familiarity.

But Amborix was king of the Eburones, and her father had known him well. Raricus had always spoken highly of the king and Veleda had come to share his opinion. Amborix was a wise man who had aged into a skillful leader of his people. Even more important, he was able to maintain a disciplined hold over his warriors, a quality Veleda valued above all else.

Amborix paused in his pacing and turned to look at her. "You have truly seen that this will succeed, Lady?"

"I have, lord. In splitting up their legions for the winter the Romans have made themselves vulnerable. It is an opportunity that will not come again."

Veleda's tone was calm, but Amborix apparently felt the need to explain his question further. "I know the strength of your powers, Lady," he said, "and I mean no offense by asking. But I am a king and above all things I must see to the welfare of my people. The gods have laid this duty upon me. I cannot knowingly lead my warriors into a battle they will lose. Too many have gone to the Otherworld already."

"Your concern does you credit," Veleda said sincerely. "You speak as a king should, and I honor you for it."

Amborix sighed. "Then forgive me for speaking plainer still. But you yourself told me the strategy the Nervii used against the Romans was your idea. What signs have you been given that if we do this thing you counsel, it will not end in the same way for us as it did for the Nervii?"

Amborix was a man of integrity. His question, though hard, was honestly meant. Concern for the Eburones lay at its heart. Veleda could respond in no less of a vein.

"I cannot give you the answer you are seeking, lord," she said honestly. "I have been shown that this will work, and like a pebble tossed into still water, it will create ripples. Our success will embolden other tribes to take the same path. But"—she paused, staring sadly into the king's eyes—"you want me to tell you that our people will be safe. That I cannot do. I can see only so far, and no farther. Nothing in the world of the living is without risk. You must decide if you want to take that risk."

The king was silent for a moment. "It is a heavy thing you ask of me, Lady," he said at last. "For the risk is not mine alone. The fate of our tribe could be at stake."

"That is so," Veleda said quietly. "And yet, what will our fate be if we do not attempt this? None of us can have illusions about what Rome intends for this land any longer."

She took a step closer to the king. Her voice was still quiet, but there was a deep note of power in that controlled tone. It thrummed throughout the deserted glade where they had come to talk, freezing Amborix in place. "Two years have passed since they murdered my mother's sister, and in that time the arrogance of the invaders has only grown. Now they tell you—not ask, as one equal does to another, but tell you—that we must feed and shelter their soldiers through the winter. Eight legions have they split up amongst us, and this in a season when the grain harvest has been poor.

"The small amount of grain from our fields, and the meat of the beasts we sacrifice at Samhain, will not go into the mouths of our people. No, the Romans will stuff their greedy maws with food that should nourish our hungry children and old ones. What will they demand of us next? That we willingly send our young men and women to Rome as slaves?"

Amborix's face had grown tight, his massive body tensing as he listened. He gave Veleda a piercing glance of admiration. "You see far, High Priestess, and well do I know it. You warned the confederation not to fight that first battle, but we did not listen. The Menapii and Morini have listened to you, and Caesar has been unable to conquer them." Abruptly he made up his mind. "I shall do as you suggest."

For an instant Veleda was reminded of the Nervii king, but the moment quickly passed. Amborix did not laugh, grinning with hungry eagerness for battle, as that ruler had. The face of the Eburonian king was grave, deep lines of anger and worry etched within his sun dark skin. "Blood-debts are owed," he said. "It is past time for payment."

A day later Amborix went to speak with the Roman commanders, who had set up their winter quarters at an *oppidum* called Atuatuca, well within Eburone territory. Julius Caesar was not among the officers the king traveled to see. The famous general had gone back to the friendly territory of the Aedui for the winter. Whispers abounded that he had retreated because he was all too aware of the tension his

campaigns had created throughout the Belgae lands and was
content to let his legates deal with whatever problems might
arise during his absence.

Amborix did not care either way, although the High
Priestess had told him Caesar's absence was one of the
reasons their plan would succeed. The outland Goddess had
much to do with the Roman's decision, Veleda had said
with an enigmatic smile, and Amborix did not question her.
He was no Druid, but he could recognize the odor of magic
when it wafted about him. There was no point in wanting
to know more.

Instead, he concentrated on the part he must play before
these Romans. Arrogant the invaders may be, but they were
not stupid. The success of the plan hinged on him now. He
must be convincing.

The Romans had taken over the *oppidum* with the same
thoroughness with which they seemed to do everything. A
full legion and a half were to be quartered here for the
winter and the people who had once lived in Atuatuca had
been banished to accommodate the invaders. Even so, there
was still an overflow of men. Winter quarters were being
constructed outside the fortress's walls to contain them, and
the look of the town had changed dramatically. Neat lines
of wooden huts were busily going up, filling the air with
the sounds of hammering and sawing. Here and there small
groups of soldiers stood or sat around crackling fires. Amborix smiled to see them. *Riuros*, the Cold-Time, had not
even arrived yet, and already these men looked miserable.

The Eburonian leader was admitted to the presence of
the commanders with little delay. Subjugated his people
may be, but Amborix was still a king and therefore deserv-
ing of a certain amount of respect. An orderly conducted
him to what had once been a noble's hall, now completely
transformed by Roman trappings: couches, heated braziers,
and thick rugs. Politely the orderly offered him mulled
wine, which Amborix eagerly accepted. He emptied his first
goblet in a few swallows and was pouring a second when

Titurius Sabinus and Aurunculeius Cotta, the two leg
Caesar had left in charge, joined him.

They greeted Amborix with courtesy, but the king was
not deceived. He saw the wariness and contempt behind
their eyes, and he set himself to overcome the one and
ignore the other.

"A good day to you, commanders," he shouted with the
effusiveness he knew they expected of "barbarians." He
waved an arm about him. "I see that you have made yourselves comfortable."

There was heavy irony beneath his cheerfulness, but the
Romans did not seem to notice. "It will do, lord," Sabinus
said, giving Amborix the title, if not the respect. "For the
coming winter at any rate."

"Hmm." It was artfully done, containing just the right
amount of hesitation to catch the legates' attention.

Cotta frowned. "Is something wrong, lord?" he inquired.

Amborix cleared his throat. "Commanders," he said,
when he saw that they were beginning to fidget. "It concerns me to speak of this, but I feel that I must. My duty
as leader of my people demands it."

"Demands what?" The Eburonian had fallen silent once
more, and Cotta had little patience with him. "Speak
plainly, lord, I beg you."

"Very well." Amborix dropped a pause into the air with
delicate skill. "I regret having to speak these words, but I
fear that your men may not be safe here."

The silence now belonged to the Romans.

"And why is that?" Sabinus asked. His tone was very
cold.

Amborix raised his hands, palms up, a gesture eloquent
of helplessness. *These are matters beyond my control*, his
hands seemed to say, and his carefully thought out speech
confirmed it. "Commanders," he said. "I have accepted
the fact that you are here, and I have counseled my people
to do the same. But there are those who will not listen to

my wisdom. They are young and foolish, and they have convinced men who should know better to go along with them. They mean to attack you in this camp. I tried to dissuade them from it, but they would not heed me. I have been left no choice but to come here and warn you."

The two legates exchanged glances. "A man always has choices when it comes to fighting," Cotta said harshly. "Especially a king. Why have you chosen to protect us over your own people?"

The Roman had small, light-brown eyes; Amborix stared straight into the other man's gaze. "I am choosing to protect my tribe, good commander." He allowed a small amount of honest anger to creep into his voice. "A king must think of all his people, not just part. What sort of leader would I be if I allowed this to happen? The fury of Rome would fall upon the Eburones and we would all be destroyed. In looking after your interests, I am looking after our own."

It was a good answer. It was the only answer they would believe. The High Priestess had known that, just as she had known the question would be asked.

"Excuse us a moment, lord," Cotta said, and he and Sabinus drew off to one side to confer.

Amborix poured himself another goblet of wine. Murderers utterly lacking in honor these Romans may be, he reflected, as the sweet hot liquid bathed his throat, but they made wine fit for the gods. Surreptitiously he watched the legates from the corner of his eye. They had turned their backs to him and their voices were too low for him to make out the words, but he did not need to hear them to know what they were saying. These quarters they were setting up in the fortress they had seized from its rightful owners were at the easternmost tip of their progress into this land. Any sensible man could see that they were exposed to attack in this place. Amborix had only to play upon the fears that already hovered beneath the surface.

The legates finished their talk and strode back to him.

Both their faces wore carefully neutral expressions. "So be it, lord," Cotta said. "You have brought us this information, and we thank you for it. But will you carry it even further, by giving these ones who preach such dangerous tactics into our hands?"

Amborix was prepared for this. "Ah." He raised his hands again. "If only I could do as you ask, Commanders. It would simplify matters for us all, would it not? However, my tribe is sorely divided. I have spoken in council and warned against attacking your camp, and because of my disfavor, the faction in favor of doing you harm has gone into hiding. As you have well seen," he added with a sigh, "we are a people who can never agree on anything for very long. Including whether to go into battle."

The two Romans did not notice the slight tensing of the muscles in the king's jaw as he said this. They were nodding to each other, in both agreement and barely veiled contempt. "Then what do you propose?" Sabinus demanded. "That we sit here and wait for the fools among you to attack us?"

"Why, no," the Eburonian protested. "I wish to protect my tribe and earn your goodwill at the same time. I can take you to a camp that is much safer, where you will not be as exposed as you are here."

The legates looked at each other again. "And what surety do we have that we and our men will arrive there safely?" asked Sabinus.

It was an insulting question, an inquiry that cast aspersions on the honor of the one making the offer. Amborix allowed himself the luxury of showing anger. "I am the king of the Eburones," he said stiffly. "And as king, I give you my guarantee that I and my warriors will guide you in safe passage to this new camp."

He waited while the Romans pondered his offer. Their uneasiness was apparent. They did not like this land or its people; that was also apparent. Inwardly the king seethed. Why had they come all this way to conquer and destroy, when they so clearly wanted to be somewhere else?

"How far is this camp?" Cotta asked tersely.

"A fair distance. Some eighty leagues. And the way is difficult for those not used to this country. That is why I offer myself and those faithful to me as your guides."

He waited again. The two men stared deeply into his face as if they were seeking to divine his true intentions. But they were Romans, not Druids. They had no powers to help them see what lay behind the surface. It was fortunate for him that they could not.

At last, Cotta spoke. "Very well, lord," he said. "We will accept your proposal of safe passage."

He did not sound as if he were utterly convinced that he and Sabinus were making the right decision.

Amborix was not about to tell him that they were not.

It was just before first light when Hori went out to relieve himself. He did not go far. The Eburones had no weapons and had submitted to Rome, but as far as Hori was concerned there was still reason for caution. Shivering in the damp cold, he stared about him warily as he fixed his linen tunic and pulled the woolen cloak tight. The massive trees, darker than ever in the gloomy predawn, loomed all about him. He could feel them watching him, just as Seti claimed they did, yet to Hori their scrutiny did not seem malevolent.

Although it should, he thought to himself, *for had he not come here to fight alongside enemies of this land?*

A sudden movement flickered among the trees. Hori's every muscle went stiff, his hand going automatically to the shortsword at his belt. His eyes darted through the woods, searching for a human shape. But what slipped out from behind a particularly massive tree was not human.

It was a cat.

Hori stared in disbelief. As swiftly as his hand had gone to his sword it now went to the amulet of Bast about his neck. There was magic here. He should have sensed it before, in the stillness of the trees, in the sudden urge that had driven him out to relieve himself far earlier than he usually did.

The cat moved closer, gliding with fluid grace in the nature of its kind. Yet Hori knew in his bones that this creature was as far from an ordinary cat as a beerseller's stall was from the tomb of a Pharaoh. The animal had eyes of a huge brilliant orange and they watched him with unrelenting intensity. Hori saw shapes in those great eyes, shifting shadows that drew him to move closer.

He lost track of how long they stood there: an Egyptian, and this cat that was so much more than a cat. He was utterly caught up in the pictures that flowed deep within that orange gaze. He saw himself. He saw his men. All of them were caught up in swirling patterns that were interspersed with the figures of other men.

A woman's face suddenly appeared in the cat's magical eyes. She was neither Roman nor Egyptian; her features clearly marked her as one of the people of this land. Her eyes were large and green and they were as filled with magic as the cat's. Abruptly the woman's face was gone. As the image vanished, Hori heard a deep ringing voice that seemed to come from beyond him and within him at once.

The cat will lead you to safety when the time comes. Pay heed to him.

Hori staggered, falling back from the hold of the cat's eyes as if he had been struck. He discovered that he was still gripping the amulet of Bast. Indeed, his fingers were wrapped so tightly about the small figure that deep grooves had carved themselves in his flesh. The Goddess had spoken to him. Here in this remote land, so far from the heat and sand and the rich black land that was a gift of the Great River Nile, Lady Bast had sought him out. She had sent a sacred messenger, and offered him protection.

But from what?

He looked down, hoping the cat could tell him.

But it was gone.

17

THE BEGINNINGS OF THE WIN-
ter quarters at Atuatuca were
quickly abandoned. Having made
up their minds to go along with
Amborix's plan, Cotta and Sabinus
wasted no time in issuing marching
orders.

Hori returned to the fortress to
hear the trumpets blaring out the familiar notes for wake-
up. Centurions were already hurrying about calling out
commands. Frowning, Hori stared about him, then made
his way swiftly toward the place in camp assigned to the
auxiliary troops: the Nubian spearmen, Cretan and Egyptian
archers, even warriors from other tribes that had already
submitted to Rome.

"Hori, there you are," a voice bellowed out. Quintus
Cillius, the centurion in charge of the Egyptian archers
shoved his way past half a dozen cattle being moved along
to join the larger herd. "You picked a fine time to take a
leak. We have orders to move camp. We march out this
morning."

"So I see." It was not the place of an auxiliary archer
to question orders, whether they came from a centurion or
any other Roman officer. But Hori was puzzled and disturbed by these particular orders, and his tone made that
clear.

Quintus Cillius was not offended. He was a squat, powerful man, the grizzled survivor of many a long campaign,
and he liked Hori and the skill of the Egyptian archers in

general. "By the hymens of the Vestal Virgins," he burst out. "It makes no sense to me either. Here we are, getting settled into a perfectly good winter camp, and the legates decide we have to up and go somewhere else. But there's nothing we can do about it, lad. They give the commands and we obey them. Now go and see to it that your men are ready."

Hori obeyed. But uneasiness sat on him as heavily as the dank weather. He had received an omen, yet how could he share it with those who had the authority to do anything about it? He had not understood what he had seen well enough to explain it to Romans, and even if he had, they would be unlikely to give credence to any warning from an Egyptian Goddess. They had their own gods and omens, and they paid little heed to anyone else's.

It had begun to rain, a steady downpour that promised to continue all day. Already miserable, the Egyptians went about their tasks stoically, wearing the resigned expressions of men who knew they would be marching with wet feet for many hours.

As the columns formed for the march, Hori gathered his eighty men about him. Quickly, his voice low, he described what he had seen in the woods outside the town. The faces of his comrades grew tense as they listened; unlike Romans, they would need no convincing that this was a true omen.

"I knew it," Seti exclaimed. "I told you the land doesn't want us here. And now our own Lady Bast, Mistress of Magic, has sent us a warning."

"Well, what are we supposed to do about it?" snapped a slender man called Ahotep. "We can hardly refuse to march, or even worse, desert our places. The punishment we'd get from our commanders would be little better than if the barbarians caught us."

Hori gestured for silence before anyone else could speak. "No one has said anything about deserting or refusing orders," he told his men firmly. "And yet we must be prepared."

"For what?" asked Ahotep.

Hori frowned, his gaze swerving to the impenetrable woods, now dripping with rain. "I don't know," he said truthfully. "But whatever lies ahead for us, remember this. The cat will lead us to safety."

Concealed in the woods, the warriors of the Eburones waited with uncharacteristic patience. In times past, their strategy would have been considerably different, but these were new times, calling for new measures, and so they waited.

All the Druids of the tribe, including the High Priestess, stood with them, which helped the warriors maintain their vigil. But the Romans were at last drawing near to the place of ambush, and the closer they drew the more difficult it became for the Eburones to remain quiet and hidden. Long and long had they waited to repay blood with blood, and now the moment was finally approaching. They could scarcely contain themselves. Hands tightened on weapons that had been carefully hidden when Caesar ordered all swords, javelins, and battle-axes to be surrendered. The breathing of the warriors had been slow and even, but now it grew quick and hard.

Veleda sensed this. Silent as a wraith of smoke, she moved among the massed warriors, whispering to one, touching another on the arm. "Remember your oaths." Her voice was like the murmur of wind through leaves. "Wait for the moment. It will come in the rightness of time, and when it does the Shining Ones will bring us victory."

There were women among the warriors, as girded for battle as the men. One of them was Sattia, but unlike so many others she showed no restlessness. Utterly composed, she stood in her place, holding the great sword that had to be wielded with two hands and which many a Roman could not have wielded at all. But when Veleda laid a hand on her soul-friend's arm, the tension that lay quivering beneath Sattia's composure leaped out at her like a blow.

Sattia turned her dark eyes to Veleda. Fire blazed in them, and hatred. The lust to kill was raging through her veins, but still she stood calm. "I am prepared," she whispered to the High Priestess who was also her friend. "I will not move until you tell me to."

New sounds suddenly began drifting through the steady patter of falling rain. The hoofbeats of horses, the rattle and clink of bridle bits, weapons, and armor. The Romans were approaching.

The first of them appeared through the trees. As always, the cavalry was in front, with the two legates, Cotta and Sabinus, riding in the lead. Amborix rode beside them, accompanied by a number of warriors who had fanned out through the trees to act both as guards and guides. The horses clattered toward the Eburones' hiding place, carrying their heads low in the rain. After the cavalry came the main body of the force: nine thousand men, column after column of them, marching in the close-ordered ranks the Romans were famous for. Far behind the columns, heard but as yet unseen, were the baggage train and the herds of beasts kept to feed the legions.

The distant lowing of cattle wove in and out through the monotonous rain. There was comfort in the sound. Veleda could almost imagine herself lying in bed in her father's hall of an early morning in Seed-Fall, listening to her family's herds being driven out to pasture. She fastened her gaze on Amborix.

The king appeared completely at ease. He was smiling as he rode, gesturing cheerfully as he talked to the legates. By contrast, the two commanders were solemn-faced, almost grim. Even from her place in the trees, Veleda could see their eyes darting back and forth in an unceasing search for enemies.

But they were not Eburones. The land hid her secrets from them, concealed the dangers that lay within her deep folds. Even with the losses they had sustained in earlier battles, Veleda's tribe remained large. Throughout these woods thousands of warriors lay hidden, and they had the advantages of both position and surprise.

Amborix's eyes flickered. There was no break in his cheerful talking, but his gaze was searching for Veleda. He was fast approaching the place of ambush. All he needed was the sign from the High Priestess that the attack could begin.

Veleda closed her eyes. Within her the world shrank to a single pulsating thread of awareness. Tighter and tighter the shining thread wound itself, until there was nothing but that tension filling the inner places of power behind her eyes. Abruptly the thread snapped, spiraling outward in a dazzling burst of color and flame. Her eyes still closed, Veleda let out an ululating shriek: the battle cry of the Eburones.

So swiftly that it seemed to happen at the same instant, Amborix's face changed from cheerfulness to rage. With a bellowing roar he whipped out the sword that had been concealed in his heavy cloak and struck off the head of Cotta, who had been riding next to him. A spray of blood fountained up from the legate's neck. Even as the headless body jerked and toppled from the frightened horse's back, the warriors who had been acting as guides turned on the astonished Romans. Swordblades flashed in the rain. Battle howls echoed the king's, and officers were cut down before they had time to realize their lives had ended.

Yanking out his sword Sabinus began shouting out commands. But it was too late. The rain-drenched woods seemed to come alive as thousands of warriors came streaming out of the trees to fall upon the columns of soldiers.

Legionaries marched heavily laden. They each carried bundles attached to their javelins containing spare clothing, food rations, and utensils. Every man also carried rope, short stakes, a wicker basket for carrying dirt, a shovel, lengths of chain, hooks, and a saw. All of it added up to a good deal of weight that was always discarded when it came time to fight. On this day, however, there was no time for the men to throw off the cumbersome packs before the enemy force was upon them.

The outcry was deafening. The quiet woods, accustomed only to the steady music of falling rain, erupted with the rage of a subjugated people bursting free. Warriors charged at the Romans from every side, wielding weapons they should not have had. Frantically the remaining officers tried to organize their cohorts, but the place of ambush had been chosen well. The forest was deep and thick here, the road that led through it narrow. In such a spot the cavalry had no room to maneuver, the infantry no space in which to form a bulwark against their attackers.

There could be only one result: a massacre.

Veleda's eyes had opened at the moment Amborix let out his war cry. She was alone in the trees. The other Druids had spread out through the woods, raising their arms in prayers that would strengthen the fighters. Veleda, too, moved closer.

The dark woods, made even darker by the rain-drenched day, were a mass of struggling screaming men and horses. Somehow, Veleda caught a glimpse of Sattia. The warrior-woman's arms were red to the elbows, drenched in Roman blood, as she slew and slew. Her face was exultant, and the expression on it drew Veleda forward in fierce longing.

Oh, how she yearned to join Sattia and the others! To seize a sword and wield it, driving it down again and again, plunging the blade into one Roman after another, until her arms ached.

There were her enemies before her, screaming and dying, unable to believe, even in their last moments, that this was happening at all. It was with enormous effort that she held herself back from rushing in to help them on their way to death. As High Priestess she could not take part in battle unless the circumstances were dire, as when the Romans had attacked the fleeing confederation. She reminded herself that she was the one who had brought this victory about, that it was through her working that these Romans were dying. But somehow that did not satisfy the visceral urge to slay through strength and muscle, rather than through the more powerful but less physically satisfying means of magic.

The killing went on and on. Taken off guard, trapped in an indefensible position, the Romans nevertheless fought bravely. But as more and more fell under the wrath of the blood-maddened Eburones, the outcome became all-too-clear to those who still lived. Every legionary had heard terrifying stories of the fate that befell any Roman unfortunate enough to be taken captive by barbarians. They were tortured to death in hideous ways, sacrificed to dark gods, crammed into tall wicker structures and set on fire to be burned alive. Anything was better than such a death, even the taking of one's own life.

And as the warriors swarmed over the legion and a half of Romans, that was what many of the men began to do. Turning their swords on themselves, they committed suicide in droves, falling to a ground softened by a cushion of leaves and mud and blood to lie beside those who had already died at hands other than their own. Sabinus himself, seeing at last that there was no way to escape this horror that his and Cotta's decision had wrought, was one of them.

Eventually a silence fell that was deafening after the clamor of battle. The last of the legionaries had been killed, either by the Eburones or by his own hand. Amborix raised his sword and let out a mighty yell of triumph. Immediately the warriors took up his roar. The quiet woods, wrapped in their mantle of early winter, rang with the joy of the victorious.

Amborix left off his shouting and sprang forward to where Veleda stood. He raised his sword, the blade still dripping with blood, to her. "High Priestess," he said when the shouting had stilled. "High Priestess." His voice was filled with reverence. "You have given us this day."

Everyone else crowded forward, Sattia in the very front, all of them raising their swords to Veleda. She had never been looked at in such a way.

It humbled her. It made her glow with fierce joy that her powers had at last brought about a victory.

And it made her afraid.

The men from Kemet, along with the other auxiliary troops, had been marching far back in the column, just ahead of the baggage train. All of them, including Hori, had fallen into the familiar pattern any infantryman adopted when marching through this inhospitable country: head down, mind blank, as he slogged through the mud and rain.

But as the road they followed narrowed into little more than a forest track, winding through woods that grew darker and denser with every passing moment, Hori shook off the self-protective mantle of endless campaigning. He stared about him uneasily. Suddenly he could see the cat's brilliant eyes gleaming at him in his mind's eye. The images he had seen in the orange depths swirled before him, and his sense of foreboding grew.

"I have a bad feeling about this place we are entering," he murmured to Seti, who was marching closest to him.

The round-faced Egyptian lifted his eyes and sighed. "How is it any different than the rest of the gods-forsaken land we've been struggling through?" he asked testily.

"No." Hori's voice was tense. "Something is going to happen. I can feel it, waiting for us." His gaze searched the dripping trees. He wanted to turn and flee, and at the same time, he felt pressed to go forward. Then he saw it. Just ahead of him the cat was perched on the lowest branch of an overhanging tree, looking down at him.

Hori slowed his pace, nudging Seti. "Look there," he whispered.

The other man paused, his eyes widening as he saw the cat.

"Start passing word to the others." Hori kept his voice

low. "We must be prepared to follow him."

Like a breeze rippling over a stream, the news moved swiftly through the ranks of the men from Kemet. No sooner had the last of them been told of the cat's presence than the first sounds of battle rang out from far up the column. The cat leaped from the tree, his orange eyes fixed on Hori.

"Quickly!" Hori gestured to his comrades, and at that moment, the world around them went mad.

But it was a madness that did not touch the Egyptians. The magic of Bast Herself must have been protecting Hori and the others, for the cat led them far away from the sounds of fighting and dying. The thick woods shook with the fury of rampaging warriors, but it seemed as if a spell had enfolded the company of archers, shielding them from the eyes of the Eburones. They passed in safety from the horror of the ambush.

Doing so was far more difficult than any of them had imagined. For Hori, who was in command, it was the hardest of all. True, the cat was a messenger from Bast enabling him to save himself and his men, but what of all those left behind? He had fought beside these Romans, suffered with them through the inhospitable weather and grueling marches. He had accepted many as friends, just as he had accepted the slight distance that would always remain between full legionaries and auxiliary soldiers.

Yet, in the back of his mind, he had hoped he might be able to save some of his Roman comrades. It was a vain hope, dying as swiftly as his centurion Quintus Cillius had died. A huge warrior had leaped out and decapitated the burly Roman with a single blow, at the same instant Hori called out to his men.

Now, he and the other men of the Black Land could only follow the sleek shape of Bast's messenger through this alien landscape of looming trees. They had no idea where the cat was leading them. All they knew was that it was away from death.

For the moment.

18

IN AND AROUND THE GREAT hall of Amborix, the celebrations went on through the night. Nine thousand Romans lay dead, their bodies scattered throughout the woods and their heads taken as battle trophies. It was the greatest victory the tribes had achieved over the invaders, and their new High Priestess had brought it to them.

Veleda sat in a place of honor, the same seat Ancamna had once occupied. For the first time since her foster-mother had been murdered, she felt the rightness of being in the High Priestess's place. The full blood-price had yet to be paid; perhaps it could never be paid. But this day had been a start.

When the warriors boasting of their prowess and the accolades to Veleda's powers had become lost in waves of general drunkenness, Mau appeared beside her. He sat down, curling his tail about his paws, gazing enigmatically at the riotous celebrants.

"They used to feast like this in the Black Land," he observed. "At the court in Thebes, in the days of the old Pharaohs, people would wear cones of perfumed fat on their heads. A peculiar habit, I know, but they claimed the fat cooled them off as it melted. Of course, with this weather, you don't need to resort to such practices."

Veleda put down her cup of honey-sweetened cormu.

"Where have you been? I thought you would be near me on this day of all days."

"I was not far."

Veleda waited for him to say more. When he did not, she stared at him. "And where was 'not far?' " she asked.

The cat's huge eyes met hers. "Do not forget your purpose, human girl."

The admonishment in his voice stung her. "That is a thing I never forget," she shot back at him. "How can I, when it rules my life? Do I not have the right to be glad after the victory I gave my people?"

"The battle was a success," Mau agreed. "But your thoughts are as red as the blood of the Romans that was spilled today. You were thinking of blood-price then, and you are thinking of blood-price now. Your foster-mother is gone, and no amount of Roman heads will bring her back. There are greater matters at stake here."

Veleda glared at him. "It is difficult," she said through gritted teeth, "not to dislike you intensely when you speak as you do now."

"I speak the truth." Mau lifted a front paw and gave it a few negligent licks. "And you are well aware of it. That is why you are a seer. Put aside your desire for vengeance, and tell me what you see."

Veleda was still angry. But he was right, and she knew it. She closed her eyes. Bast had been with her this day; she had felt the warmth of the Goddess flow over her, steadying and surrounding her. Sekhmet had been there as well. The Latter would have preferred that Eburones blood be spilled, since She had allied Herself with the Romans, but in the end, blood was blood. Even She was satisfied.

Visions swirled past her inner sight: bright and savage, glowing with bravery and fury and death. Veleda felt the presence of both Goddesses again. She opened her eyes, returning sharply from where she had been. Around her the people were still singing and drinking and eating, although many had fallen asleep where they sat, or stumbled off to find their beds. No one was taking notice of the High Priestess any longer, or of the cat sitting beside her.

"There is uncertainty, Mau."

Before Amborix and her tribe—even before family and friends—Veleda could show neither anger nor frustration. Too many depended on her wisdom, on the unshakable calm a High Priestess, who was responsible for judging the disputes of people's lives as well as overseeing all religious matters, must always display. Ancamna had managed it admirably. But then Ancamna had come to her position in the fullness of age. She had grown into it, not had this awesome responsibility thrust upon her the way Veleda had. Thank the Shining Ones for Mau, to whom she could reveal her doubts and fears! How had her foster mother managed without such a confidante? Veleda sighed. Perhaps she had not needed one.

"There is uncertainty," she repeated, making no attempt to keep the exhaustion from her voice. "I see glory and I see despair, and they both whirl about in my head until I feel as if I see nothing. Why must that be?"

"There is always uncertainty," said Mau. "You told that to Amborix yourself."

Abruptly Veleda drained her cup. The honeyed mead tasted bitter in her mouth. "Amborix has put his faith in me, along with the welfare of our people. He will follow whatever advice I give him."

"Then give it."

"Even if it leads to defeat?" Veleda slammed the cup down. "Have not enough souls gone to the Otherworld to satisfy Sekhmet's thirst? Why can Bast not be clear with me? She is a *Goddess*, Mau. For once, let Her tell me what lies ahead!"

Mau watched her, clothed in a serenity both feline and magical. "She would if She could, human girl. Don't you know that by now?"

"I do," Veleda said. "And it comforts me little to know it. It requires no divine art to see that the next logical move is for us to attack the winter camp the Romans thought they were being taken to. Amborix will ask me what the omens say, but what he expects is that we will win again.''

"There are other ways of winning besides hacking your enemy's head off with a sword," Mau said dryly. "A great victory was gained today, the first to be won against the Romans. And your tribe was responsible for it. Even if the next outcome is not what you would wish, the memory of this day will remain. Other tribes will be emboldened by what the Eburones have accomplished. They will follow your lead, and soon, another confederation will form.''

"And what of the first one?" The look Veleda gave the cat was angry, but it was an anger directed more at herself, than at him. "That confederation came together at my urging. I hoped it would be enough. It wasn't.''

Mau slitted his eyes. "Hopefully, the next alliance of tribes will have more discipline.''

Veleda said nothing. She, too, had seen what Mau spoke of. But she had seen more deaths as well. True, they were honorable deaths, and the ones dying would welcome the opportunity to enter the Otherworld as noble warriors. But for Veleda it was not so easy. It was through her words, and her advice, that so many were giving up their lives. At the moment it was difficult to know if all of it justified the goal.

Caesar was in a rage. Divitiacus had never seen him this way, and it was a sobering sight to behold. Along with a collection of high-ranking officers, the Aeduian king watched in silence, as the governor strode up and down the hall he had commandeered for his winter quarters. The familiar red woolen cloak snapped with each stride, and the Roman's hands clenched and unclenched, the knuckles white as his fingers pressed into the palms.

Without warning Caesar wheeled about, fixing Divitiacus with his dark gaze. "Did you hear any rumors that this might happen?" he demanded.

"Commander!" Divitiacus stared squarely into the Roman's eyes. "I have proven my loyalty time and again. You impugn my honor by such a question."

Caesar did not back down. "Nevertheless, it must be asked. You may have thrown your lot in with that of Rome, but you are still a Gaul."

"No, Commander, I am not."

Divitiacus was truly angry now. The Roman officers were watching him with cold hostile eyes. Most of them, including Caesar himself, had shared his hospitality, eaten and drunk with him, called him friend. Now they stood apart, glowering at him as though he was indistinguishable from the fools that had committed this madness.

"I am Aedui," he went on. "It is Rome who has given the name 'Gaul' to all the people in these lands, as though we were one tribe. But we are a gathering of different tribes, not the single people you would believe us to be. The tribe that destroyed your legions has long been an enemy of the Aedui."

Caesar watched him a moment, then turned away. "A legion and a half," he whispered. "Nine thousand men. All of them beheaded. And among them, my friends Titurius Sabinus and Aurunculeius Cotta." He spun back to Divitiacus. "And your brother sits in his hall celebrating!"

"My brother," Divitiacus said evenly, "is a hostage of Rome. He has never made secret where his sympathies lie. Just as I have never hidden my own."

Caesar sighed. "That is so," he said, and with those words the tension in the room subtly began to ease.

The commander's sharp gaze went to the officers. He was all business again, his attention utterly focused on the tasks at hand. "Troops must be gathered from the winter quarters throughout Gaul without delay," he said briskly. "This morning a slave arrived with a message from Quintus Cicero. The Eburones have begun a siege of the other winter camp in their territory and other tribes in the area are flocking to join them. We must save Cicero and his legion. This fire must be stamped out before it becomes a conflagration that sweeps away any more of our men."

He looked piercingly at Divitiacus. "You and your warriors will join us."

It was a statement, not a question, but Divitiacus did not take offense. "There were Aedui among the auxiliary troops of the destroyed legions," he pointed out grimly. "Of course we will join you. Our oaths demand it."

Caesar nodded. "Well, I will swear an oath of my own." His blazing eyes fixed each of the men in turn. "I will cut not a hair of my head or my beard until the murders have been avenged and the leaders of these crimes stand in chains before me."

The legion of Quintus Cicero huddled in its winter camp in the territory of the Eburones, terrified at the skill of the barbarians besieging them. They had been trapped for more than a week, surrounded by thousands of warriors from the Eburones as well as six other Belgaic tribes—including a large number of Nervii, whose annihilation Caesar had boasted of in his dispatches to Rome.

The barbarians had appeared like a swarm of demons from out of the spirit-haunted woods. But they did not behave like barbarians. To the astonishment of the Romans, they began to build siege equipment equal to anything constructed by the legions. Under the increasingly apprehensive eyes of Cicero and his men, ditches were dug, ramparts built, even moveable towers put up. Their surprise and apprehension soon turned to a struggle to stay alive. The tribes had not only learned Roman siegework; they had learned Roman dedication to a single goal.

These warriors who had gathered around the legion like wolves around a snowbound herd of deer were not capricious. They did not hurl themselves at the enemy in savage bursts of fury that ended just as suddenly in retreat. They set about the grim business of besieging the trapped Romans with a studied ferocity that showed no signs of breaking. For the men in the winter camp, the situation soon grew desperate. Adopting even more techniques from their battles with the legions, the warriors repeatedly managed to set fire to the encampment with heated sling stones and well-aimed fire arrows. Only by the grace of mighty Jupiter were the flames extinguished before they could do too much damage.

Quintus Cicero made many unsuccessful attempts to smuggle messengers past the blockade before a slave finally slipped off through woods lightened by a first dusting of snow, on his way to Caesar. Now the men left behind could only wait. And pray that help would come in time.

Fear sat on the Roman camp, croaking over the trapped legion like the great black ravens that perched in the trees, waiting to pick over the bones of the dead. Men went about their duties stoically, only their pale, drawn faces revealing the dread each of them felt. By now, they all knew about the destroyed legion, and the fact that many of their ambushed comrades had chosen suicide over falling into the hands of the Eburones. Huddled around fires and in wooden huts, they discussed when and if the same course of action would become necessary.

Hori, however, was not one of those who took part in such discussions. He was unafraid. The cat had led him and his men safely to this camp. Surely Bast's messenger would not see to it that they were spared in one place, only to bring them to death in another. Hori had not seen the cat since he arrived here, but this did not trouble him. His *ka*, his inner soul, knew they would all be saved.

There had been many questions directed at he and his men as to how they had survived the massacre, but for the most part the Egyptians were treated with respect. Their bravery and skill had been proven in other battles, and if they had managed to escape this battle unscathed, more power to them. This was the prevailing attitude, not only among officers but among the rank and file as well. Matters were too desperate for anyone to feel otherwise.

In contrast to his fellows who looked out at the gathered warriors no more than they had to, Hori spent much time staring out at the tribal force. There were women among them, both as warriors and as Druids. And there was one woman in particular who directed many of the siege activities. Most of the time she was too far away for Hori to see her face, but she wore the robes of a Druid, and all the warriors, no matter what tribe they belonged to, clearly deferred to her. On the eighth day of the siege, however, she had drawn close enough for him to catch a glimpse of her features.

His entire body had stiffened, and he had stared and stared, long after she moved back into the trees. He had seen the shifting image of that very same face reflected back to him in the brilliant orange eyes of Lady Bast's cat. There was magic here indeed. But it was a troubling magic, hinting at things he did not understand. He no longer feared death; he feared the purpose for which he had been spared.

There was little time for him to ponder it, though. A day after seeing the woman, Caesar arrived with two legions to relieve Quintus Cicero and his battered legions from the siege.

The danger was over, yet the rejoicing among the men was strangely muted. After so many seasons of fighting and watching comrades die, Caesar's troops were at last losing morale. The men were tired of battle, tired of shivering in the cold of this inhospitable country. They wanted to go home.

Caesar went among them, speaking words of encouragement and cheer. For the first time in the four years since he had brought an army into Gaul, he decided to stay with his men, rather than returning to Rome as was his wont. In a further effort to bolster flagging spirits, he summoned Hori and his company before him to congratulate them on having survived the barbarian ambush.

It was an enormous honor to be called before Caesar himself. Many legionaries went through their entire enlistment without ever having personal words with the commander of the army. For mere auxiliary soldiers, it was an undreamed-of tribute. Eagerly the Egyptians bathed and shaved and prepared themselves to look their best, chattering to each other all the while about the upcoming meeting.

Only Hori went about his ablutions in silence, his eyes so distant he scarcely seemed to realize where he was. Finally sharp-eyed Ahotep took note of his leader's peculiar mood. "What ails you?" he demanded. "Of all of us you should be the most joyful. You were the one who Lady Bast's messenger sought out to save. The rest of us were merely fortunate enough to be with you."

Hori turned to him with sudden intensity. "But *why* were we saved, Ahotep? That is what I keep asking myself."

Ahotep shrugged. He was a practical man, not overly given to reflection. "Cats have always protected us from demons," he said with matter-of-fact certainty. "From the beginning of time it has been so. And what greater demons are there than the barbarians who haunt these woods like spirits of the night?"

"No." Hori answered him with the same certainty. "The people of these tribes are not demons. There are many things I do not know, but this I understand. These people are not demons. They are fighting for their country. As our ancestors once fought to regain the Black Land from the Hyskos invaders in the days of the Pharaohs."

Ahotep stared at him in amazement. Hori had never spoken this way before. Hori himself was surprised at what he had said. Yet he did not regret the words. There was truth in them. Behind his eyes he saw the face of the woman again. He turned away from Ahotep and said nothing more.

19

"AGAIN, THEY DID NOT LIS-
ten!"

Alone with only Mau to hear her, it was a luxury for Veleda to raise her voice. Even so, it was not enough. She wanted to howl her rage to the skies, to pound her fists in frustration, to call down curses on the heads of her own people.

"Why will they not learn? *Why* are they such fools?" Shaking with anger, she pressed both hands against the rough unyielding bark of a sacred oak.

Mau yawned, stretching his lips back to reveal long gleaming fangs. "How should I know?" he asked mildly. "They are your people."

Veleda glared at him. A scathing reply sprang to her lips, but went unsaid. It was not Mau she was angry at, after all. The Eburones, the Nervii, and the other Belgaic tribes who had come to help them were responsible for this latest defeat; no one else. Except for their High Priestess, of course, who had not been able to summon the power necessary to make them do what they needed to in order to win.

Use the Roman's own methods against them, she had counseled Amborix and the council of chieftains. We have seen how they build their towers, she said; let us do the same. And in that, the people had listened to her. They did not have the proper tools for the work, but this did not stop them. They used their swords to cut the sods and removed the piles of dirt with their hands and their cloaks. As implacably as the siege equipment rose before the startled eyes of the legionaries trapped inside the camp, so did the fear. The dread the Romans felt as they watched their own strategies used against them stank on the air, and Veleda drank it in as if it were the sweetest wine.

But when scouts reported that Caesar was approaching with two legions, the sense of organization she had tried so hard to instill within her impulsive people began to fall apart. Soon it was gone entirely. The warriors abandoned their disciplined siege and raced away in droves to confront the enemy in its camp a few leagues distant. The combined efforts of the High Priestess and Amborix could not hold them back. Their blood was aflame with the earlier destruction of the legion commanded by Cotta and Sabinus, and the lure of adding two more legions, plus Caesar himself, to the tally of heads taken was too great to resist.

The Roman commander resorted to a familiar strategy, one that fooled the overeager warriors once again. Ordering his troops to retreat behind their barricades and pretend they were afraid, he waited for the mob of impatient tribesmen to struggle up the steep slope that fronted his camp. When they did, the infantry burst out at them, followed by a surge of cavalry. Taken by surprise, the Belgae panicked and ran, just as they had in a score of other battles. Amborix faded away into the woods to escape capture, as did Veleda—but not before she stood and watched the waves of retreating warriors. The sight of bright-patterned cloaks weaving through the trees in a flurry of red and green and blue and yellow had been a scene that was all too familiar, and utterly infuriating.

"We could have had another victory," she said fiercely. "An even greater one than before. We could have destroyed two more legions. Caesar himself might have fallen before us. The Romans are in poor heart. Their taste for battle has left them. We may never have a chance like this again." She pressed her hand against the ancient tree, fighting the urge to smash her fist against the oak's sacred body. "And now we have lost it."

Mau watched a brown wren alight on a nearby branch, his orange eyes narrowed and intent. "They listened to you for a while, though," he said, turning his gaze back to Veleda. "They are closer than they were, your people. They are learning what they must do to win. But they are not quite ready."

Veleda flung herself away from the oak. "How many times have I heard that!" she shouted. "When will they be ready?"

The cat stared at her for a long moment, and then looked away, back at the wren on its branch. "Soon," he said. "Soon."

The small brown bird chattered at him and flew away. Frowning thoughtfully, Veleda watched. All birds were omens, carrying portents of good or ill depending on the numbers one saw them in, and the kind of bird they were. Wrens were carriers of good luck, but a single wren meant only a small amount of luck. Her people, she thought with a sigh, needed a whole flock and more.

Caesar's vengeance was a grim and terrible thing. In destroying his two legates and their men, and in nearly succeeding with their siege of Quintus Cicero, the Eburones had struck at the very heart of his accomplishments in Gaul. Victories were necessary, and they had to come quickly, not only to satisfy Caesar's own thirst for revenge, but to also raise the disheartened spirits of his legions. A major show of strength had to be made in order to subdue these troublesome Belgae once and for all.

The Roman commander's hair and beard grew until he began to resemble one of the warriors he fought against. In spite of the winter snows he relentlessly pursued the Belgaic tribes, hunting down the Eburones with particular dedication. They fought back, often hunting him as he hunted them, determined to make further inroads on the rebellion that had started with the massacre of well over a legion of soldiers.

Amborix's treachery had been well documented by now, and there were even more disturbing tales that he had been led into this betrayal by the mysterious High Priestess who had replaced Ancamna. Caesar wanted them both.

To his immense frustration they eluded him in battle after battle, but others were not so lucky. Labienus, one of Caesar's most competent legates, persisted in his pursuit of the Treveri, and after an especially bloody engagement, he cornered their leader, a chieftain called Indutiomarus, in a relatively open patch of Treveri territory. A delighted Caesar sent cavalry in to hunt him down. The chieftain tried to escape across a river, but was caught. In a gesture to the ways of their opponents, the triumphant horsemen returned to camp and their waiting commander with the dripping head of Indutiomarus.

Word of what happened soon reached the Eburones in the secret places where they had taken refuge from the constant hunting. Their hatred of the Romans had grown to a passion as unrelenting as the Romans' pursuit. They had good reason. Caesar's desire for revenge included more than slaying as many people as he could find. He had ordered the Eburones' lands laid waste and their animals slaughtered. Throughout the country precious fields whose breasts would have nurtured the next season's crops flared up in flames, while the bellows and cries of cattle and sheep shredded the air. Precious stores of grain were carted off to feed the legions, and grim-faced soldiers put entire farmsteads and towns to the torch.

The once beautiful country of the wealthy and powerful Eburones wept beneath a pale winter sky. Smoke from the burning twisted up into the air, blackening the days and leaving a bitter stench in the air. Ash drifted over the land, dirtying the fresh-fallen snow and wreathing the trees with bitter reminders of lost homes. Even in their remote hiding places the people smelled the destruction and wept along with their land.

But they also burned. A price would be exacted for this desecration of Mother Anu's earth. If Caesar thought to demoralize them by such wanton acts, then he knew nothing about Eburones courage and will. Those who were unable to fight had slipped away with whatever food they could carry and animals they could herd. Winter would be hard, but these were people who knew how to survive in their own land. Not only would they survive, they assured each other, but they would fight as well.

"The problem with your people," Mau said irritably to Veleda, "is that they are far too eager to die."

Another skirmish, one in an endless line of them, had just taken place. Many had been killed, but Sattia had led the surviving warriors back to camp, all of them boasting of victory and brandishing the severed heads of Roman legionaries.

"Look at them," Mau continued. "Crowing over an engagement they had no need to fight in the first place. The Romans had greater numbers and better ground. It would have been safer and wiser to wait for a time when your warriors, and not the Romans, had the advantage."

Veleda sighed. They had had this conversation before. "The omens were favorable to fight today," she said. "It would have been difficult for me to hold them back. With the death of Indutiomarus and the destruction of their homes, they needed this battle."

Mau let out a hiss. "They did not need to die," he snapped. "There is not an inexhaustible supply of warriors among your people, you know."

"Neither is there an inexhaustible supply of Romans," Veleda retorted. "The Eburones must fight. It is in our blood. We live for it. You may as well ask a warrior to stop breathing as to turn away from a battle when the omens are good."

Mau sat and looked at her for a moment. "It may be in

their blood to fight," he said at last. "But it is also in their blood to die. That is what gives Romans the advantage. *They* do not want to die, and because they do not, they fight well—better than your warriors." He saw Veleda bristle, but continued undeterred. "They do not take unnecessary risks, they do not throw themselves into foolhardy situations, and therefore, they survive. Their goal is to keep on living. The goal of your people is to die."

The words, so bluntly spoken, took Veleda aback. Images of the dead suddenly filled her mind, thousands and thousands of them. Her memories were soaked with blood. A river of the life fluid of her people flowed past her inner eye, rich with those who had fallen and hungry for those who had not.

All at once a new image burst into her mind. There was no warning of it. Suddenly it was just there. The force of it doubled her over, causing her to cry out. Black spots danced before her eyes, and when they cleared she slowly became aware of hands gripping her arms. Sattia and the party of warriors had rushed to her side. Someone had told Bormana, and she was hurrying toward her daughter. But well ahead of her strode every Druid in the encampment, drawn by their own inner knowledge to their High Priestess.

Axiounis—the elderly lawgiver who had challenged Veleda's first vision so long ago—spoke first. "High Priestess," he said tersely. "What have you seen?"

Supported by Sattia and Bormana, Veleda straightened up. Beyond the knot of people gathered around her she saw Mau. He couched as if about to spring, his orange eyes fixed unswervingly on her face.

Veleda trembled, and once the trembling had begun, she could not seem to stop it. "They are marching toward the *nemeton*," she whispered. "They mean to burn it down, along with every sacred grove in our land."

There was an appalled silence. Veleda blinked to clear her vision. A fog hovered around the edges of her vision, dark and streaked with red. She heard a sound she had not heard in months: the harsh discordance of Sekhmet's laughter. It was distant, but drawing closer. Just as the Romans were.

"What has happened here?" Amborix pushed his way through the people crowded about Veleda. He saw their faces and his own grew grave.

"The sight has come to the High Priestess again," Axiounis told him. "And it is an ill one. The Romans will seek to destroy our sacred places."

Amborix stiffened. "Then they must be stopped," he said harshly. He stared at Veleda with blazing eyes. "Where do we fight first?"

Veleda went inside herself. The stabbing sharpness of the images had faded, but now she was conscious of a curious detachment. She swayed again, though she was not aware it, nor of the hands that reached out to steady her. Thoughts clattered about in her head, and grim purpose. Abruptly she shook herself, her body jerking with such strength that she freed herself of Sattia and Bormana's support.

"Caesar wants to destroy the Nemeton of the Circles first," she said. "But they must find it first. They do not know where it is, or even what to look for." Her teeth bared themselves in a snarl. "Divitiacus is helping them."

Amborix, too, bared his teeth, their whiteness shining through his heavy mustaches. "Then we must go there and prepare for them." He thought a moment. "I will ask our allies to delay the Romans' progress as much as they can."

The Eburones set off immediately for the Nemeton of the Circles. It was in this great roofless sanctuary that Veleda as a young girl had brought an empty wicker cage to Ancamna, and tried to explain why she had freed the cat so essential for the ritual meant to drive away the plague. Now she was returning there, driven by the need to save this sacred place with its power that had protected her people from the beginnings of memory.

That power reached out to her as she and her people entered the deep forest that surrounded the nemeton. The talking ceased as they reached the trees carved into intricate representations of the Shining Ones, symbolic images that were heavy with magic. Even young children fell into a reverent silence, gazing about them with wide eyes at Great Mother Anu, Dagda, the Father of the Gods, and all the other Shining Ones. They and their parents could go no further than these holy images. Unless it was decreed otherwise, only Druids were permitted to pass through the nine sacred pathways that led to the inner grove.

The strength of the place grew stronger and stronger, curling about Veleda as she dismounted from her horse and led the Druids of her tribe into one of the pathways that led to the inner grove. They walked in silence, each of them wrapped in his or her separate thoughts. The Nemeton of the Circles took its name from the circularity that was at the heart of its power. Spirals were everywhere, carved into branches and trunks; even the nine paths wound through the trees in one spiral pattern after another, until they all merged in the wide grassy space of the consecrated center.

When they all stood together, Veleda looked about her. "We will hold the ceremony of the coals," she said decisively. "The omens will tell us how we can best defend our sanctuary. I name Amborix as the one to bring me the sacred entrails."

She had called a ritual of extreme significance, and one that was a highly ordered event. A person of distinction was always chosen to walk across the burning fire bed, carrying the entrails of the sacrificed bull to the High Priestess and her retinue. Amborix was the obvious selection, and no one questioned the honor that had been bestowed upon him.

Axiounis nodded. "It shall be carried out tonight."

Labienus's idea was inspired, Caesar thought. To a civilized man like a Roman, trees were trees, but to these barbarians they were as sacred as an image of Isis or Jupiter. Turning their sacred groves to ashes would strike at the innermost heart of these rebels, wounding them more terribly than any sword.

He reined in his stallion and gestured to one of his officers. "Bring Divitiacus to me," he ordered.

He waited impatiently for the Aeduian king to canter up to him. It had snowed again and the hooves of Divitiacus's horse threw up clods of icy mud as he approached. They would have to make camp soon: another long miserable night when his men would shiver in their leather tents while they waited for morning.

"How far are we from this place you told me of?" he asked without preamble when Divitiacus pulled up. "The men are tired."

The king nodded in understanding. "And so they should be. This is not the season for traveling, much less making war."

"That," said Caesar, "is precisely why we are doing it. Answer my question."

"The *nemeton* is not far." Divitiacus gazed out over the bleak landscape. "We should reach it tomorrow. I would suggest an early camp, so your legions can rest tonight and be prepared to fight."

Caesar regarded him, thoughtful and skeptical at once. "And how are you so certain of this?" he inquired. "These are not your lands."

The Aeduian looked at him. "I am a Druid, Caesar," he said quietly. "We always know where to find our holy places, no matter what country they may lie in."

He said nothing more, and in a move highly uncharacteristic of his dealings with the Roman commander, he jerked his mount's head around and rode back to his place in line.

There was evil following the king of the Aedui. It was accompanying them all, but it had singled out him in particular. And Divitiacus knew why. He was leading the Romans to a holy place, a sanctuary consecrated to the gods.

Caesar had assured him he meant the *nemeton* no harm, that it was Amborix and the High Priestess he was after. Divitiacus knew this was a lie. All Druids, even one who had fallen as far from his dignity as he had, could always recognize an untruth. Yet despite his knowledge he continued on with this terrible thing, this sacrilege. Matters had gone on too far; his fate was inextricably wound up with that of Rome, and there was no turning back.

First the unholy murder of a High Priestess, and now the coming destruction of the sacred groves. Despite the cold, sweat broke out on Divitiacus's face. Shaping his hand into the sign against evil, he murmured spells of protection under his breath. He had been whispering them for days.

He knew they would do him no good.

At nightfall, just as they had done almost twenty years ago, the Eburones crowded into the consecrated clearing for the ceremony. Many of the faces present on that long-ago night, when another danger had menaced the people, were now gone. Standing alone by the altar, the weight of the sacred white bull hide heavy upon her shoulders, Veleda took note of the losses. She could not help it. So many in the Otherworld, and yet those who remained were still willing to fight on. She looked out over them and understood deep in her bones what she could not have truly understood as a girl, how closely the danger then and the dangers now were intertwined.

The clouds that had blanketed the sky all day had cleared, turning the night frigid. Above the leaf-stripped crowns of the great trees stars burned in an icy clarity. Frost mantled the ancient branches and the snow-covered ground, crunching with each footstep as people trudged through the hard layer to gather in the clearing.

Torches burned clear and pale in the cold air, lighting the nine pathways and flat inner space of the grove, throwing shadows off the mystical representations carved into the trees. At sunset a bonfire had been kindled in the center of the spiral design. Now it had burned down to a bed of shimmering coals. Druids were gathered about it, their ceremonial robes as white as the breath that steamed out of their mouths. Amborix stood with them, garbed in his finest garments and richest jewelry. His eyes were distant, as if he was unaware of where he stood. Heedless of the cold, he stood barefoot, his feet planted firmly in the snow.

Veleda watched sadly as with great honor the sacrifice was brought along the widest pathway. It was a red and white bullock, his winter coat heavy and thick, his nostrils streaming spumes of frost. She did not want to kill this animal. During all her duties as seer and priestess she had performed sacrifices only when absolutely necessary, and given her power to communicate with animals, they had not been necessary very often. She was usually able to glean the information she required from them as she had with the goat in the early days of her training.

But this night was different. The Ceremony of the Coals called for a death, and much as she would have preferred that it be otherwise, it was her task to mete out that death. She laid a gentle hand on the bullock's head as the Druid leading the animal halted him at the altar. The tribe had fallen silent at the moment she touched the sacrifice, and only the sound of so many people breathing could be heard, as she gazed deeply into the bullock's big mild eyes.

Time stretched. Some of the younger children began to fidget, and still the High Priestess and the bullock stood motionless, locked within their silent communion. Then, with a smooth motion, Veleda lifted the knife of sacrifice, its thin curved blade glinting as sharp and silver as the frost.

It was quickly done. The bullock was dead before he realized his life had ended. The blood from his severed throat gushed out into the silver bowl held by one of the Druids. The beast stood stolidly on his feet, and then, slowly, so slowly, his knees collapsed and he toppled onto his side. People sighed in relief and approval. It was always a good omen if the sacrifice went willingly to his death, and a terrible portent if he did not. They leaned forward, staring intently as Druids gathered about the carcass, their knives as swift as the bullock's collapse had been slow.

Veleda's voice rang out. "Let the honored one approach."

Amborix came forward, his bare feet moving with measured strides over the frozen ground. Reverently he accepted what was handed to him: the steaming pile of the bullock's entrails. Holding them in his hands, he turned and walked back to the heart of what had been a blazing bonfire.

A great quiet descended over the Eburones. Before there had been the soft noise of breathing; now it seemed as if even that had ceased, as Amborix set one foot deep into the smoldering bed of coals. He followed it with the other, then slowly began to cross over the bright embers. The fire's heart was still murderously hot. Small flames popped up as he walked, some flaring directly about his bare feet. Blood dripped from the pile of entrails he carried, sending up more hisses of flame, but Amborix appeared oblivious. If he felt any pain at all, he did not show it.

Three times he walked over the coals, moving in that same stately rhythm. After the third pass, he proceeded to Veleda, who still stood before the altar. He held the entrails out to her. She accepted them gravely and laid them down on the flat carved stone. Amborix turned back to face the people. He lifted first one foot, and then the other, showing his soles, their flesh reddened but without a trace of burning.

"I am unharmed," he said.

A burst of acclamation broke out. The tension that had held the tribe in its grip was broken. Just as it was important for the sacrifice to die easily, so was it significant that the person chosen to walk over the coals do so with ease. Everyone knew that the Druids coated the soles of the chosen one with special ointments meant to protect the tender flesh from burns, but they also knew that ointments meant nothing if the gods were not favorably disposed. If the person escaped unharmed from the fire, the omens were good. But if he suffered harm, it was a terrible portent, a sign of the greatest ill luck for both person and tribe.

Veleda let them celebrate Amborix's success for a few moments, and then she spoke. "Do not forget, my people," she warned. "The ceremony is not yet finished."

Her words had the desired effect. People instantly fell silent again, and the air of tension returned. Veleda stared down at the entrails spread out before her. In spite of the cold, slight tendrils of steam were still drifting upward from the pile of pale innards streaked with blood. Reading the intestines of a sacrifice was an art. To one uninitiated in the mysteries, this heap of organs was simply that: raw flesh, soon to decompose now that it had left the warmth of the body that had housed it. But to Veleda the bullock's entrails told stories. They spoke to her, as the soul of the bullock had, and in the winding twisted guts, she saw the future.

It struck her like a blow.

She stepped back from the altar and raised her hands. "The omens are favorable," she said, pitching her voice so that it would carry to the outer edges of the *nemeton*, where those who had not been able to squeeze into the grove had gathered. "The Romans will arrive tomorrow, thinking to surprise us. Divitiacus, who has fallen from his dignity in betraying his oaths, will tell them we are unprepared, for indeed, he will believe that we are. They will try to set fire to our holy trees, seeking to herd us inside our *nemeton* like the cattle driven through the fires at Samhain. They will fail. And I, as your High Priestess, will stand beside our warriors, fighting to defend this holy place"

Exultation rose to the remote star lit skies when she had finished. The other Druids of the Eburones smiled and embraced Veleda, praising her. As the noise grew louder and louder, some of them left her, in order to cut up the holy remains of the bullock. His flesh would promptly be roasted and distributed to the people, although with so many each person would receive little more than a mouthful. However, the amount was unimportant; to eat of the sacrifice's flesh in any amount would further strengthen these good omens.

Soon Veleda stood alone, as she had at the beginning of the ceremony. Inwardly she thanked Bast and all the Shining Ones for helping her to keep her voice so strong and even when she delivered her reading of the entrails.

She had not spoken of the other thing she had seen, and she did not intend to.

But deep in the night, when everyone slept, Veleda lay in her furs, her eyes open, staring into the dark outlines of the holy grove. Mau had slipped away before the start of the ceremony. Now he returned as silently as he had left. He had been hunting, and he smelled of night and darkness and death. He set to work washing himself, his tongue rasping away every trace of blood before he stepped delicately onto the furs. Tucking his paws underneath him, he crouched before Veleda's face, half-closing his eyes as he looked at her, the beginnings of a purr rumbling in his chest.

Veleda's voice was very soft. "Do you think I should stand with our warriors to defend this place?" she asked, knowing there was no need to explain what had taken place during the ceremony.

Mau's whiskered face, so familiar to her now in all its nuances of expression, was solemn. "I think you should do as your will bids you." He paused. "Whatever that may be."

It was an answer, though not the answer she would have liked. The words were as oblique and indirect as the cat himself.

"It is not my will that drives me," she told him abruptly. "But my oaths. As a Druid, a High Priestess, and most of all, as an Eburone."

Mau was silent for so long that, but for his purring, she

would have thought him asleep. Then he spoke, and there was an odd blend of affection and impatience in his tone.

"Where humans are concerned," he said, "the two are often one and the same."

20

AMONG THE KELTOI TRIBES days were counted in the length of one sunset to another. To Veleda the day that had begun with the bullock's death at sunset was the longest she had ever known. The Romans were driven by vengeance, she and her people by religious devotion. Two such powerful emotions could not but collide with terrible force.

Veleda fought with the warriors, as she had said she would, but she did not defend the *nemeton* with a sword. Her weapons were far more powerful. From the time dawn tinted the massive snow-dappled oaks until night spread its frosty mantle over the sacred grove once more she stood motionless, her eyes closed and her arms raised to the sky. Her lips moved, though if she spoke any spell aloud, no one could hear it. Yet there were forces beyond human ears that heard.

The skies darkened, and as warriors and legionaries clashed, it began to sleet. A torrent of freezing rain and heavy wet snow poured down, drenching the combatants and, even more significantly, dousing the fires the Romans repeatedly tried to kindle. Caesar's plan had been to surprise the Eburones, engage them in battle, force as many as possible into the center of the *nemeton*, and then set the trees at the outer edges afire. It was a worthy strategy, but under the relentless onslaught from the heavens, it was doomed to fail.

Uncounted legionaries lost their lives to the *clads*, the longswords of enraged warriors, as they squatted, trying desperately to kindle water-soaked branches into flame. Sometimes a fire would spring briefly to life, only to sputter feebly and hiss into smoke as the sleet and snow suddenly seemed to intensify in that precise spot.

Late in the day an enraged Caesar called Divitiacus to him. The Roman commander was as furious with himself as he was with the Aeduian king. He had little faith in Druid magic, but since this was a Druid place, he had been willing to trust in his ally's assurance that he could influence the outcome.

"You said your powers would enable us to creep up on them unawares," he snapped. His voice was cold as the sleet, his clipped words betraying his anger more than shouting would have done. "What has become of your Druid magic?"

Divitiacus's handsome features were distraught. His blue eyes held a wild expression. "There is one here who is more powerful than I," he cried. "Caesar, I gave you bad counsel in leading you here. This is a holy place—"

Caesar's brown eyes sharpened. "The High Priestess then," he hissed, cutting the other off. "Where is she? Tell me. I order it."

"She is—" Divitiacus choked, feeling as if a hand had suddenly closed about his throat. An image flashed across his Druid's vision: two Goddesses, both possessing the heads of great cats, snarling at each other, Their huge fangs bared. He choked again, and all at once the pressure shutting off his breath was gone. "She is within the grove," he blurted out. "You cannot mistake her. She stands by the stone altar, wearing the white robes of ceremony."

He regretted the words the instant they left his mouth, but it was too late to call them back. Laughter beat against his ears as Caesar left him, calling out for his officers as he went, dispatching orders in his field commander's voice as swiftly as the driving sleet. Divitiacus swung around, searching for the source of the laughter.

It was a useless effort. He knew already that he would not find it.

Veleda was amazed that she was not tired. The magic had buoyed her, but even magic had its limits. Night had passed into night, and still she stood with her arms raised, calling down the elements. It seemed as though she had been this way forever. Around her the sounds of battle raged, but in her entranced state, the clamor was distant, reaching her as if she were wrapped in layers of fog. Time had frozen, leaving her alone with her magic.

Gradually, though, the knowledge grew in her that she was indeed alone. The noises of fighting were gone, replaced by a deep and utter stillness. The odors of blood and smoke no longer hung on the air; now there was only a lingering sweetness as if from distant flowers.

Veleda began to pull herself back from the spell's hold upon her. She did so very slowly; such things could not be hurried, and she had been within the hold of magic for a long time. Awareness returned to her arms, rushing along the nerve endings like tingling fire. Her eyelids were no longer weighted down by the magic she had called up; they strained to open, to see what lay around her. She lowered her arms and opened her eyes.

Light, glimmering and dancing in a host of unknowable colors, met her gaze. An enormous moon shone down as brightly as the sun. The trees that surrounded her were not the familiar oaks of the *nemeton*. She stared at their graceful soaring shapes, and knew she had entered the Otherworld.

So she had died, then. But how had it come about? She had no memory of being attacked, no sharp thrust of pain to tell her that her life had ended.

Perhaps she had been brought here, as Mau had brought

her that first time, to speak with Bast. But when she looked about, the cat was nowhere to be seen. She strained her eyes peering into the bright woods, yet no sleek dark shape slipped out of the bushes to greet her. His absence left her heart-sore. He had been with her so long, his dry wisdom and even drier wit a source of comfort that had become as natural and expected as waking up each morning.

But Veleda would not wake up again in the realms of the living, and Mau was gone. She was indeed dead.

She entered the woods. There was nothing else for her to do. Aimlessly she wandered through the trees. Time did not move in this world as it did in the other, and she soon lost all sense of how long she had been walking. The going was easy. There were myriad paths winding through the forest, trails forged by the animals of the Otherworld, who could be hunted and killed by the warriors who had won entrance here, only to spring back to life as soon as they had been felled.

Veleda was numb, strangely disconnected from where she was and what had happened to bring her here. But the forest of the Otherworld did not match the deep silence she felt within her. Hundreds of brilliantly hued birds flitted through the stately trees, singing until the very air vibrated with their music. Groups of deer trod along the paths, gazing at her with mild friendly eyes as they passed. A fox stared at her with bright black eyes and a bear and her two cubs lumbered off through the trees. In the distance wolves howled to each other, their voices blending with the liquid melodies of the birds.

At last she came to a small glade. She paused, and as she did so, a figure stepped out of the trees. It was a human figure, tall and golden, gleaming so wondrously that Veleda at first thought one of the Shining Ones had come to her.

Then she recognized him. She stared, and felt the numbness leave her. "Dumonorix," she whispered.

"Yes." The chieftain smiled at her. "I bid you welcome, High Priestess. I, too, have left the realms of the living."

Veleda gazed upon him in anger and pity. "Divitiacus had a hand in it, didn't he?"

"Ah, my poor foolish brother." Dumonorix's smile was deep and sad and filled with knowledge. "He took a hand in my death from the first moment he welcomed Caesar into our lands. Look and see how it happened."

He waved a hand. The glimmering colors dissolved into the familiar greens and browns of the world of the living. The vast reaches of the ocean undulated before Veleda's gaze, the gray waves stretching out to merge with a gray sky until it became difficult to see where wind-tossed water ended and sky began. A group of men were gathered on the rocky strand. There stood Dumonorix, as he had been in life, surrounded by a cordon of soldiers. Caesar faced him, and alongside the Roman leader stood Divitiacus. The king shifted restlessly from foot to foot, doggedly refusing to meet his younger brother's eyes.

"I would stay here," Dumonorix said to Casear. "I have no wish to leave my country and watch you crush the freedom of the tribes in Albion."

Caesar smiled thinly. "And why should your wishes be taken into account? You are a hostage. It is up to me to determine what shall be done with you. I have decided that you will accompany me. You are far too volatile an influence among the people of your own tribe—not to mention those of other tribes—to be left here, where you would be able to cause further trouble." He turned to the officers who stood behind him. "When this accursed weather clears, we will be able to cross the channel to Albion. Until then, see to it that he is guarded well."

"And they guarded me indeed." Dumonorix's voice hovered about Veleda. "I prayed to Tarinis to send his thunder down upon our heads and to Lugh to withhold the healing warmth of the sun, but perhaps the Roman gods were stronger than our own, for the weather cleared, as Caesar had hoped it would. However, when the time for departure drew nigh my guards grew lax with all the preparations that needed to be made. I escaped, along with the warriors of my retinue. Look again.''

Under a bright sun a cluster of men on horseback thundered along a ridge overlooking the sea. Their colorful cloaks billowed behind them. The man in the lead was mounted on a bright chestnut mare. His long yellow hair swept back over his shoulders in a shower of gold. Dumonorix. He and the men of his retinue were lashing their horses, urging them to greater speed. There was good reason for urgency. An entire squadron of Roman cavalry was galloping in pursuit, and they were closing rapidly.

Veleda stared at the scene, willing the Aedui to escape, even though she knew they had not. And inevitably, with heartbreaking speed, the Romans overtook their targets and closed in around them. Fighting broke out, swift and fierce. One by one the warriors were slain; Dumonorix was the only hostage Caesar wanted brought back alive. When he alone remained, the cavalrymen shouted at him to surrender. Dumonorix responded with a roar that was part laughter and part battle cry.

Sweeping about him with his sword, pulling his foaming mare into a rear, he screamed out in a voice that pierced to the Otherworld and beyond: ''Never, never will I surrender! Kill me, Roman offal, before I kill you. For I am a free man of a free nation, and that is how I will die!''

He brought the mare down and sent her charging into the cavalrymen. The Romans did not want to slay their valuable hostage, but the savagery of Dumonorix's attack left them no choice. Within moments, the animal plunged away, her saddle pad empty.

''It was a good death,'' Dumonorix said to Veleda as the scene faded. ''I was proud to die so.''

''Indeed,'' Veleda answered sadly. ''But your loss will be felt by those who remain in the living world. Men of your bravery are needed.''

''Men of bravery are always needed, and they will always die.'' Dumonorix's voice was serene. ''It is the same with women. You also died a good death. But the world of the living is not through with you yet, as it is with me."

Veleda looked at him. "What do you mean?"

"That you must discover for yourself." Dumonorix smiled at her. "I wish you could stay in this glorious place, for you have earned it. I wish we could hunt and feast, perhaps even make love together; I had thought about us doing that in life, you know. But I must go one way"—he gestured to the verdant woods—"and you must go another. Take care on your journey, Veleda, and return quickly. I will be eager to see you again."

"Wait," Veleda called after him. But the tall gleaming figure flowed away from her like mist rising through a thick grove of ash trees, vanishing into the singing forest.

"Well, you got here at last," a familiar voice said. "It certainly took you long enough."

Veleda swung around. "Mau!" The sight of him, long and sleek, tail curled about his paws, enigmatic eyes gazing up at her, made her want to grab him up and hug him as though he were a mortal cat, and not a creature of magic. She might have done it anyway, but for his next words.

"Come along," he said. "It's time to speak with Her."

There was no need to ask whom he meant. But as she fell into step beside him Veleda stooped briefly and stroked the thick silky fur of the cat's back. His tail went up, and just as quick as her caress had been, he arched his back in pleasure.

"I thought you were gone," she told him. "That I would not see you again."

He paced along beside her. "Do not mistake my being here," he said after a moment. "This is not like the other time. You are indeed dead, as you first thought."

"How did it happen?" Veleda was not surprised, and she felt no grief, only the need to know how her life had ended. "I must have died bravely, or I would not be here."

Mau's whiskers stiffened. "There you go again," he snapped. "Prattling on about dying as though it were a holy act. Death is death, human girl. Have you not learned that yet? Even now, with you being dead yourself?''

"You have not answered me," Veleda pointed out.

"Divitiacus told Caesar where to find you," Mau said without preamble. "He sent his archers into the *nemeton* with legionaries to defend them, and one of the archers succeeded in putting an arrow into your throat." He bared his teeth. "They were men from Kemet, those archers. Our bowmen have always been highly skilled."

"Ah." Veleda said nothing more for a time. "You knew this awaited me, didn't you?" she finally asked.

"I knew," Mau replied curtly. "But I could not protect you from it. Nor was I supposed to."

Veleda looked at him for a time, and then nodded. Suddenly she became aware of a lightness at her waist. She touched the belt of her tunic. The magical wands that had hung there for so long were gone.

Mau followed her gaze. "They were torn loose when you fell, and they got buried in the snow and mud and blood. It does not matter. You will not need them again."

They went on in silence. The mountaintop where Bast's temple sat loomed before them, and they began to climb, following the winding path Veleda had taken with the cat once before. As they drew closer, Veleda's pace unconsciously slowed and quickened, slowed and then quickened again. She yearned to see the Cat-headed Goddess, and at the same time she wanted to flee back into the safety of the singing woods. Dead though her physical self might be, her emotions had come roaring back into life. She was racked with grief; not for herself, but for her people. She had failed after all in the great task Bast had set her.

The pink stones of the temple rose up, dazzling her eyes, and she stopped. "Was the *nemeton* saved at least?" she asked Mau.

He shoved against her with his head to get her to continue. "It was," he told her. "Your calling down that foul weather succeeded. The Romans could get no fires going, and they were losing so many men that Caesar finally called off the act. He was,'' the cat said with satisfaction, ''very angry.''

They went into the temple courtyard, passing through the vast array of purring cats and into the inner recesses of the temple itself. The Goddess's presence drew Veleda forward, enfolding her in a warmth as soft as Mau's fur. There was no need for him to guide her through the wide torchlit halls laden with the sweet odor of incense; she found the way herself.

Gentle music drifted out to greet her: low singing voices mingling with the harmony of tinkling bells and the strumming of a harp. They came to the doors of the inner sanctuary, ablaze with gold and silver and the brilliance of gems. Inside Bast was waiting for them upon Her throne of gold. Veleda halted in wonderment. Gilded in dancing light, draped in Her gossamer linen that glowed of silver and gold, the Cat-Goddess was as glorious as she remembered. But She was not alone.

With Her was another Goddess. She stood beside the throne, a shimmering presence as vast as Bast Herself, though not a solid figure as the Cat-Goddess was. The face and form of a woman hovered within the light that surrounded Her. Radiant, She looked out at Veleda, and even as the human woman stared, the Goddess changed and changed and changed. One moment She was a young girl with budding breasts and newness in Her eyes. Then She was a grown woman, Her breasts rich with milk, and Her stomach rounded with new life. At last, She was a crone, Her breasts flat and withered, Her lined face deep with wisdom. Each incarnation was clothed in its own beauty, and together they created a presence that defined life itself.

She was Anu, the Great Mother-Goddess.

We welcome you, My daughter. Bast's deep rich voice vibrated throughout Veleda's being. *Our blessings be upon you.*

"No, Lady." Veleda's voice was ragged with pain. Suddenly she could not meet those shining gazes, could not tolerate the all-encompassing acceptance that emanated from both Goddesses. "I deserve neither Your welcome nor Your blessing. The Romans occupy our lands and the tribes will not unify to fight them. The gifts you gave me have been wasted. I have not done as you asked."

Not yet, the Cat-Goddess said with a vast calm.

"My chance is over!" Veleda cried. "An arrow took me from the land of the living. How can I help my people now?" Unwillingly she thought of Sekhmet. She did not want to say it aloud, but there could be no doubt that the Lion-Headed Goddess had grown in strength, just as She had boasted She would. Indeed, She was stronger than Her great and wise Sister, stronger perhaps, than even Bast and Anu together.

Sekhmet is a Goddess of death. Bast had seen Veleda's thoughts as clearly as though she had spoken them aloud. *She thirsts for blood, but She draws Her power from death. In that, the beliefs of your own people aid Her. Even you, My daughter, have helped Her in this.*

"That," Mau broke in, "is what I've been trying to tell her. But she would not listen, and so, here we are."

The Goddess nodded Her shining cat's head gravely. *I am a Goddess of life. All that lives is sacred to Me. To Sekhmet it is death that is sacred. As sisters, We are two halves of the same circle. Yet, as long as you and your tribes celebrate death, rushing into it with eager arms, She will always be the stronger. I did not foresee this love your folk bear toward death would be so great. My Sister did not see it either. But She was quick to take advantage of it, and now She blends with new ways and new gods, growing stronger, while We, the Old Ones, grow weaker.*

"Then it is over." Veleda was washed in a terrible sadness. "The tribes of Belgae had begun to band together again. If I had lived, perhaps I could have persuaded even more tribes to stand with us. But even so, their beliefs about death would not have changed. They are a part of us, Lady. As Druids, we teach the people that death is but a means of being reborn in the Otherworld. And look''—she waved an arm about her—''we are not wrong. The world that awaits us is beautiful indeed.''

The beauty of the living world is greater still. The voice of Anu thrummed throughout every corner of the sanctuary. *One should not be in such a hurry to leave it.*

The pattern must be broken, Bast said. *Your people feed Sekhmet with their blood and with their deaths. It is a deadly circle, and She is at the heart of it.*

''But how?'' Veleda had the eerie sense that neither Goddess understood that she was dead, though of course they had to understand it, she told herself. They were Goddesses. ''Will You choose another to take my place?'' she asked.

My child, the Great Mother-Goddess said with an ever-reaching gentleness. *Bast chose you long ago. And now I choose you as well. We will not choose another.*

But now you must choose. The voice of Bast enfolded Veleda like arms as she spoke. *There is a way for you to return to the realms of life, if you are willing.*

''I am willing,'' Veleda said instantly. Her thoughts raced. To go back. To have another opportunity to drive out the invaders and restore her people's freedom. It was a chance she could not have dreamed of.

Speak not with such haste, Bast cautioned. *There is a price to be paid for a return such as We offer you.*

Veleda found herself thinking of Ancamna. Surely her foster-mother was here in the Otherworld, happy in this place of eternal beauty. A woman of such courage and wisdom could be nowhere else. If only she could see her. But she knew what Ancamna would say if she were in her place. She smiled. ''There is always a price, Lady. Tell me what it is. I will pay it, and gladly.''

Bast regarded her gravely with Her enormous green eyes. *You must forsake the oath of chastity you swore when you became High Priestess. Such vows have no place in My worship, or in that of Anu, though your people believe differently. We represent life.*

And death, said Anu's great voice. *Mortal lives are passing short, and yours will be shorter still. It cannot be more than that.*

The Mother-Goddess smiled at Veleda. Her ever-changing face was translucent in the shimmering silver mists that surrounded Her. *There are times, My child, when the fates of mortals and gods converge. Go on with your task of seeking to unify the people. In returning from the Otherworld, you will be listened to as never before, and that is necessary. For there is an opportunity here, a moment in which time may be altered and history changed. Caesar is the force behind the invasion of My holy Self, and he is in Rome, struggling to hold onto the power he has built on the blood of My children.*

The sons and daughters to whom I give life are stubborn. Yet, if they can finally learn to control their impulsiveness, they may indeed triumph over the Romans. But time is fleeting and the opportunities it presents rare. Only one chance will you have to call the tribes together, and We can no longer depend upon its success. We must lay a new task upon you, the most ancient and blessed of all the gifts We have given to women. You must bear a child.

Veleda stared in wonderment. She could not remember the last time she had given thought to children. From the time the plague struck and Mau had led her to Bast in this temple of pink stone, she had carried burdens that left no room for thinking of the joys and weight of motherhood, much less mourning their loss. To have the idea presented to her now, under such circumstances, was so completely unexpected she was not sure what to think about it.

"Why would You have me do this, Lady?" she asked in bewilderment.

Because We are afraid. Though She had not moved from Her glittering throne, Bast seemed to have drawn closer.

The enormous cat face filled Veleda's vision. Unknowable wisdom shone there, and unknowable sadness. *Yes, My Daughter, even Goddesses may know fear. We fear being forgotten, having those who once revered Us turn away from Our altars in favor of new gods. In such ways does a Goddess die.*

"But how will my giving birth to a child help You?"

Your people are brave. There are none braver. But if in the end, Roman discipline proves stronger than bravery, you, Our chosen one, will live on. And as you live, so shall We. The child you bear will be Our daughter as well as yours. She will come into the world knowing Us, and so shall the daughters who come after her. Through them will the ancient wisdom be able to continue. If men forget Us, if Our temples are deserted, left to fall into dust and ruin, as must eventually happen with all things in the fullness of time, there will still be women who remember, who hold Us sacred in their hearts. Thus will We go on.

It was a desolation of spirit to hear such words, and Veleda cried out with the pain of it. "But how can one daughter console You for the loss of Your worship?"

Serene in Her wisdom, grieving in Her knowledge, Bast answered her. *While one mortal heart beats to Our ancient rhythms, then will We continue.*

And in time, Anu added in Her thrumming voice, *though it be a time far beyond your reckoning, We will return.*

Veleda looked long into the countenances of the two Goddesses. "I will raise her as one who venerates You always," she promised. "May the skies fall if I break faith with this oath I give You."

From the corner of her eye she saw Mau shift restlessly, and then Anu spoke. Her voice was like a whisper in Veleda's ears, and at the same time it seemed to resonate through each thread that tied together her souls. *No, child,* She said. *It is not your fate to raise this babe. Daughter of your body she will be, but mother to her you may not be. Even Our powers are not enough to send you back to live out your life, as you might have done if the Romans had not come. When this babe is safely born, then will your task be done, and you will be called away from the land of the living, this time for all of eternity.*

Or you may stay here, added Bast. *Do not fear Our anger if that is what you wish. You have more than earned the right to enjoy the pleasures of the Otherworld, and We will not blame you. The choice is yours to make. If you return, it must be done of your own will, for what We ask of you is a hard thing, indeed. Sekhmet will learn of this new plan, and She will do all She can to prevent it. You must ever be on your guard that My Dark Sister does not succeed.*

Veleda stood silent. Around her the faint music still played, but so softly it was like the sounds one hears when drifting over the edge of sleep. Mau was watching her. He had changed, as he had the first time she had come to Bast's temple. His coat was the color of power: a deep shimmering brown burning between silver and gold. His brilliant orange eyes were as sad as Bast's.

"Have you always known it was going to come to this?" she asked quietly, meaning her question for him as well as the two Goddesses.

Anu answered. *Not even the Shining Ones can always know the time when or how a mortal's days will end,* She said in Her vast gentle voice. *In the matter of life and death, you give Us great power. You understand so little yourselves that you hope We are able to control what you cannot. But even the wisest among you understand less than you know. We can alter your fate, child, but We cannot change it. Bast and I have done the best We can with what has been given Us. As must you.*

Veleda was silent again. If she went back the people would regard it as a wondrous sign. They would flock to her, just as Anu had said. Perhaps they would coalesce into a force as solid as Caesar's legions and succeed in driving the Romans out at last. It was a glorious chance, and, as Anu had said, it would not come again. But would she herself be able to stay long enough in the world to see it?

Her body would ripen with new life; she would feel her daughter growing inside her. Finally she would know for herself the tearing, sweat-soaked, and yet wonderful pain of childbirth. And when it was over, she would have to leave that new life she had brought into the world, leave her babe to be nursed at breasts other than her own, raised by hands that would never be her true mother's. To this daughter, her mother would not even be a memory.

She could be spared all that if she stayed in the Otherworld. She could have peace. Peace. The thought of it beckoned to her, as tantalizing as spring-cooled mead on a summer's day. But how could it ever be anything more than an illusory contentment, if she rested here knowing that she had not done all she could in the realms of the living?

"I will go back," she said. She looked steadily into those divine countenances that most from the realms of the living would have turned from in awe. "This is my choice, and I make it freely, of my own will."

The Goddesses watched her gravely. *You are Our true Daughter,* Bast said in Her rich voice. *Our blessings will follow you in the days that lie ahead.* She raised her hands.

Anu, in her constantly shifting forms, did the same. *Return, then.* The Mother-Goddess's words swirled about Veleda. *We will be waiting for you when your task is done.*

The same gentle mist that had carried Veleda back to the realms of the living so long ago swirled up. Tinted with silver it enfolded her, lifting her up and sweeping her out of the sanctuary.

As a young and frightened girl she had lost track of all thought and sensation when this had happened before, but not now. She looked down through the blanket of mist, seeing the temple's glowing halls flow past her. The cats gathered in the courtyard watched her sweep by in a cloud of silver, miaowing as if in farewell. The mist carried her faster now, lifting her as if she were a feather caught in the wind, high over the mountain and its shining path, higher than the enormous moon hanging overhead, and into a sky black and dense with stars.

In the space between worlds Veleda drifted. It was a peaceful sensation, and a surprisingly crowded one. There were voices all about her, some murmuring, others laughing, still others weeping. All of them were bound past her, on their way to the Otherworld. Suddenly one of those voices touched her, the sound of it so familiar that she cried out in recognition.

"Sattia!"

Her soul-friend appeared out of the star-silvered darkness, tossing her unruly shock of black hair in the familiar gesture Veleda had seen her use all her life.

"Oh, Sattia," she whispered. "You, too."

Floating in the black sky, they embraced. Sattia felt warm in Veleda's arms, and yet insubstantial, as though she belonged in this sweeping endless place while Veleda had already become part of the world of the living again.

"Yes," Sattia said. 'But it was a joyful death, for I died as a warrior." She spoke with the same calm detachment Dumonorix had shown. "The fighting went on after you were killed, but the rest of the tribes grew fearful of Caesar's wrath and left the Eburones to stand alone. Caesar has laid waste to our lands. Those who have not been killed have been driven away. When Roman javelins ended my life too few of us were left to defend the land from trespassers. Now the Romans are encouraging people from other tribes to take over our fields. They are even offering them safe escort into our country."

Veleda's hands clenched in the darkness. "And Amborix?"

"Our king," Sattia said with a gleaming smile, "still lives. They have not been able to corner him. And you," she went on. "You are not through with the realms of the living after all. You are going back."

She laughed at Veleda's surprise. "Oh, I can see it quite

clearly. The colors of unfinished business hover about you.''

"I must.'' The words had power in them. Even as she spoke Veleda felt herself moving, being pulled in one direction, while Sattia was pulled in the other. Life was still present in this infinity of black sky. In the midst of all these souls traveling from one world to the next, its breath surrounded Veleda, as sweet as the Season of Buds, and its inevitable force carried her away.

Her farewell to Sattia was lost between the darkness and the stars.

21

TENTATIVELY VELEDA OPENED her eyes and sat up. The first sight that met her eyes was the thick convoluted shape of a yew tree.

She was within a grove of them, their dark green leaves rustling above her head as if they were welcoming her. Gazing at the thick-set trees, she smiled sadly. It was fitting that Bast and Anu had chosen this particular place to set her back within the realm of the living. Yew trees were sacred, one of the seven Chieftain trees protected against axing by penalty of death. They did not grow to the towering heights of oak trees, but they were older, far older. It was said that they never died. With each year their wood convoluted and thickened, eventually growing so dense it resembled iron more than wood.

The yew stood for sacred mysteries. It represented Mother Anu's death aspect, as well as symbolizing eternity. In placing her here, the Mother-Goddess had sent her both a message and a blessing.

Slowly Veleda rose to her feet. The air was warm, unexpectedly so, and beyond the dark leaves of the yews, the other trees were rich with green crowns of rustling leaves. It had been winter when she died; now it was summer again.

"Caesar has been putting the fighting season to good use," Mau told her. The cat was here, just as she had expected him to be. Sitting on a fallen branch, black again, he was grooming himself vigorously, smoothing the white fur on his chest into order after the journey. "He went to Albion while you were dead," he said between licks. "To conquer the tribes there."

"I know," Veleda felt herself grow distant, the yew trees of this world receding before the magic-tinted forests of the other. "I saw Dumonorix in the Otherworld."

"In any case," Mau went on philosophically. "Caesar is in Rome now, and there is some good to be gained from his expedition to Albion. The tribes of Belgae have kin among the tribes there, do they not? Well, many of them are making that abominable water journey to this land to help fight the Romans. They will rally to you, and that is good. You need as many warriors as you can get to replace all those who have been killed."

Veleda nodded absently. A sudden thought struck her. It was a question so basic she wondered that it had not occurred to her before. "I cannot very well have a child by myself," she said to Mau. "I'll need to choose a man, and that will be no simple matter if it's to be done in secret."

Cats could not laugh, even magical cats. Yet Veleda was certain that she heard Mau chuckle. "There are many things you will need to be concerned about," he said in a purring voice. "But that, human girl, is not one of them."

Hori prepared himself to go into battle once again. On this morning, it took little effort, a revelation he knew boded ill. He had seen other men become this way: their faces took on a distant expression and they behaved in far too nonchalant a manner before the coming battle. Invariably, they died.

Thinking of that, Hori forced his wandering thoughts into focus. However tempting it might be, he could not afford to become one of those uncaring men who walked willingly toward death. And yet the constant struggle to keep one's wits and body alert, to struggle to survive one battle after another, was exhausting. Even for the most hardened soldier, the thought of setting down the burden of survival and slipping into that pleasant dangerous state could be sweet. Perhaps if he had only himself to think about he might have been one of those who gave in, but not now. He had others whose fate was tied up with his: men who were friends as well as countrymen and comrades. He could not afford the luxury of laying down the weight of living, not while he led his company of archers.

Or at least, those whom the gods had decreed should not yet die. On through the freezing winter and into the heat of summer, the fighting had continued. Despite the frustrating and inconclusive battle at the sacred grove of the Eburones, it still seemed that things were turning in Caesar's favor. Caesar's hair and beard were still long—Amborix had not yet been captured—but the barbarians were sufficiently cowed that the governor felt confident in embarking on his expedition to Albion.

Then, as swiftly as summer storms descended on this country, the balance had shifted. With stunning speed the tribes that had been fragmented by the legion's relentless onslaught drew together. And not only the Belgaic tribes.

Hori's efforts to learn the Gaulish tongue had won him friends among the warriors of those tribes that had allied themselves with Rome, and thus he heard things, as much perhaps, as Caesar himself, though the latter was in Rome and safe from whatever might happen here. Hori's comrades among the Aedui muttered that tribes were taking weapons out of hiding and turning to battle once again, even those who had submitted themselves willingly to Rome. Every day there was a new skirmish to be fought, another disturbance to be quelled, amidst growing whispers that a new resistance was forming.

There was a reason for the change. Hori sensed it. It haunted him in his dreams. His sleep was troubled, ridden by images he could not understand, leaving him to wake more tired than when he had laid himself down to rest.

"Amon-Ra's greetings upon you this morning, Hori."

Hori looked up, forcing a smile. "And upon you, my friend."

Seti lowered himself with a grunt. Pulling out his quiver of arrows he began to examine each one carefully, squinting along the shafts and muttering to himself.

Hori watched him. "We must be careful today," he said.

"Today?" Seti glanced up sharply. "We must be careful every day. What is different? Ah." He drew in a sharp breath. "Has Bast sent the cat to you again?"

Hori shook his head. Involuntarily his fingers touched the amulet of the Cat-Goddess that hung about his neck. "My bones are just warning me is all."

The plump Egyptian snorted. "My bones scream warnings at me from dawn to dusk. They keep telling me it's time to leave this accursed country."

"Tell your bones to resign themselves." Hori grinned wryly at Seti's expression. "At least until your term of enlistment is up."

Seti nodded glumly and returned to examining his arrows. "You're right. We can't all be Caesar, traveling back to Rome whenever the mood strikes us."

"He didn't go back because he wanted to," Hori said. "He went because he had to. They say that if he hadn't, all the power he has built up for himself in Rome over the last few years would have been taken from him. He has aspirations beyond killing barbarians in Gaul, you know," he added drily.

Seti spat at a fly that had landed near his knee. "His aspirations don't mean donkey dung to me. All I aspire to is to get back home alive." He peered at Hori. "Are you certain the cat has not appeared to you again?"

When Hori shook his head again, Seti sighed. "A swarm of bees was sighted yesterday. The Romans say it's a bad omen, and everyone is going about as nervous as a flock of washing women at the Nile when a crocodile is about."

"The people of this land," Hori said reflectively, "believe that bees have a secret wisdom that comes from the realm they call the Otherworld."

"You mean the place they go to when they die." Seti shrugged. "Perhaps the High Priestess who was killed among their holy trees sent them." He glanced about to make sure that no centurions or legionaries were nearby. "I've heard talk that there is a new High Priestess," he added in a lowered voice. "The officers say it's a rumor and they get angry if they hear it spoken of, but everyone in the ranks is whispering that it's true. You must have heard it."

Hori looked at him. "She is not new."

"She has to be." Seti glared, insistent and uneasy at once. "The other one was slain. I saw her fall myself. Your arrow was true, Hori. Caesar rewarded you for it."

"I wish," Hori said softly, "that it had not been mine."

"I know that." Seti laid a hand on his comrade's arm. "And I know you have been haunted by it. But Hori, it was your arrow. You did your duty, and why should that trouble you? The woman was nothing to you. Surely her shade has not been following after you, not with you being under the protection of Bast."

Hori ran a hand across his brow. It came away damp. The heat in these forests was not like the heat of home. In the Black Land, the sun was a blazing presence but a dry one. Here the sun's rays gathered moisture from the air, creating a heat dense and humid that drenched one's body in sweat at the least exertion.

"Her shade does not need to follow me," he said.

Seti regarded him with a troubled frown. "What do you mean?"

Hori did not answer.

The Germans crossed the Rhine River that formed the boundary between their territory and that of the Belgae, leaving their deep wild forests to see the High Priestess who had returned from the dead and listen to her words. They were huge men, as untamed as the land that was their home. They bore no love for Caesar and his legions. The Romans had not attempted a true invasion their country, but the stinging defeats the Germans had suffered at their hands had not been forgotten. Such dishonor must be expunged.

In the remote area along the Rhine, they joined an ever-growing collection of tribes. The Nervii and the Aduatuci, the Treveri who still burned with the loss of their king Indutiomarus, and the brave pitiful remnants of the Eburones. From the marshy regions of the coast, the Morini and the Menapii came. All were tribes who had surrendered to Caesar only after savage battles. They had never ceased to chafe under the bonds of their defeat, and it took little to bring them here.

Most surprising was the presence of those who had made peace with Rome early on. The tribes of Belgae whose chieftains had refused to join the ill-fated confederation now repudiated their cowardice. They had surrendered out of fear, deserting oaths to their own kindred in favor of survival. Now they returned to the fold, drawn by the force of the Otherworld and its emissary, driven to regain the honor they had lost by willingly forfeiting their freedom.

Even from beyond Belgaic territory, allies of Rome who had never raised a sword against the invaders answered the summons of the High Priestess. How could they not? In death the gods had taken her to the Otherworld, and then sent her back to the realms of the living. Surely Caesar and his ten legions, as potent an army as they were, could not stand against the power of one who had been touched by the gods.

The Arverni gathered. Commimus, one of their nobles, had befriended Caesar, but now he turned away from that friendship and brought his people with him.

Divitiacus's tribe, the Aedui, also responded to the call for freedom. The faction that had supported Dumonorix hurried swift and eager to the meeting place, and they did not come alone. Many who had once supported their king slipped away to join them. Divitiacus was powerless to stop them. The gods were no longer the source of his power; Caesar had taken over that place, and Caesar was in Rome.

When all these tribes had gathered in their thousands, Veleda came out to address them.

The silence that fell over the people when they saw her was absolute. To those who had known her she looked just as she had before; to those who had not she seemed a woman as mortal as any other. Until they saw her eyes.

Veleda's eyes had possessed power from the moment the outland Goddess touched her as an untried girl. That power had grown with her Druid training and the weight of the passing years. It had been strong enough then. Now it was something altogether different. Dreams and visions glittered in her eyes, shining with the power of the moon, the moon that was sacred to both Anu and Bast. The hands of the Goddesses rested upon her shoulders, they clothed her in a mantle of silver. The glow of the Otherworld hovered about her, and if any person there doubted that she had indeed been touched by the profound power of the Shining Ones, it took only a look to convince them otherwise.

Veleda gazed out over her people. For indeed, they *were* her people, no longer a collection of tribes united only in their thirst for disharmony but a single enormous family, each member of which was committed to a goal more important than life. Once she had despaired of seeing this day. Now, with so much blood spilled and so many gone to the Otherworld, it had finally happened. But had it come in time?

"All of you have heard of Dumonorix, Chieftain and Druid of the Aedui," she began in a carrying voice. "Let me tell you the words he cried out when the Romans slew him, the words Dumonorix himself told me in the Otherworld."

The hush that held the people, and the Aedui in particular, was profound. Frozen in their places, they stood as if

Dumonorix himself had appeared before them. Their eyes fastened on the High Priestess, wide and unwavering, and it seemed as though they had ceased to draw breath.

Veleda held them in her sight. " 'I am a free man of a free nation,' he shouted before they slew him. The Romans, foolish as they are, thought only they could hear him. They thought the words died with his mortal body. But they were wrong. The skies heard him, and the land. Our Mother, whose breast he watered with his blood, heard him. And most important of all, the souls of every man, woman, and child of every tribe heard him.

"We heard his words here"—she touched her breast under which beat her heart, the heart that Bast and Anu had restored to life—"and though so many of us did not know it at the time, we know it now. We, too, are free—no matter how many legions profane the sacred earth of our country. And while life flows within us, we must fight to protect that freedom, to protect what we are."

A rustle went through the people, rippling with barely contained force. Veleda's eyes were two swordblades fresh from the forge, blazing white hot with rage and blood red with passion. Her voice rang out like the call of a battle trumpet.

"Caesar fears us, for understanding us is beyond him. But we, my people, understand him all too well. His absence from our land is a gift from the Shining Ones. He is the sap that keeps the branches of his army together. Without him they are vulnerable."

She found herself beginning to repeat the words Anu had said to her, and had no idea how her face had suddenly altered, as if the Mother-Goddess Herself was speaking through her. But though she could not see herself, Veleda felt the Goddess, felt Her power flow through her, tinting each word with an irrevocable truth.

"There is an opportunity here," she said, and it seemed as if she was speaking directly to each person in this enormous gathering. "A moment in which fate may be altered.

But time is fleeting and such opportunities rare. They pass as swiftly as the lives of mortals before a Goddess's eyes. Now is the moment to stop Rome. Now is the moment to throw these ten legions from our land for all time. This is our last chance, my people. There will not be another.''

They heard her, but more importantly: they believed her. Their voices rose in a chorus of howls and roars. "Listen to She Who Travels Between the Worlds," someone bellowed, and the whole assemblage took up the title suddenly given to their High Priestess, shouting it over and over.

The sound reached past Veleda to the ears of the Otherworld itself.

The people did not know how truly they had described her.

The skirmish Hori had warned Seti about bloomed into a full-blown battle with terrifying speed. The legate commanding the legion to which the Egyptian archers were attached was to blame. The scouts had warned that there might be a greater number of barbarians than first thought. But when the scouts could not provide proof that this was actually the case, he decided to wipe out the small band of renegades.

The legate was young and inexperienced, newly arrived from Rome and given this commission to advance himself, as were many other well-born young men. The more experienced tribunes might have dissuaded him, but they did not. They needed a victory. Since Caesar had left Gaul there had been far too many clashes with far too many tribes, and a disturbing number of them were not ending well.

So they plunged after the small company of barbarians, who were clashing their shields and taunting them to fight, and soon found themselves fighting indeed, and desperately. More warriors appeared as if by magic, and more after that. They were a terrifying sight as they leaped up from thickets and copses the Romans had thought contained nothing more dangerous than rabbits or deer. Most were naked but for their arm rings and torques. Their unbound hair flew over their shoulders as they screamed out their blood-chilling battle cries and charged into the fray.

Hori, at the head of his archers, found himself in the mindless flow and ebb of dealing death and trying to escape it at the same time. The centurion in charge of his company yelled out orders, but as the battle grew in intensity, Hori lost sight of him. The overeager officer had made a dreadful mistake in allowing the men to be engaged in such terrain. As any seasoned legionary knew, fighting in a dense forest was beyond foolhardy. The trees fragmented the legions' force, making it impossible to coalesce into the disciplined ranks that Caesar had utilized with such success.

Caesar, however, was not here. If he were, this debacle would never have happened.

Inevitably, the combat broke apart into widely scattered separate clashes between small groups of men. Abruptly Hori found himself in the midst of one of these isolated struggles. He was not certain how he had gotten there; the massive trunks of these alien trees loomed all about him, and the clamor of the battle was strangely muted. The rest of his company was missing, save for Seti and Ahotep.

For a heartbeat the three men stood panting, then all at once the trees came alive with barbarians. They rushed out to face Hori and his companions and they numbered far more than three. A score of them pushed through the trees, heedless of the branches that tore across their naked flesh. Their soul-chilling yells curdled the air.

"Retreat," Hori shouted. But it was too late. Even as he spoke the barbarians surged about in a circling movement that cut off any chance of escape.

The warriors closed in as the jackals of home gathered about a hurt gazelle in the deserts of the Red Land. Their teeth shone through the thick sweeping mustaches in savage grins, as they prepared for the kill. Death was in those barbaric faces, and the three archers saw it clearly. In his own way, each one prepared to meet the jackal-headed god

Anubis, guardian of the journey to the land of the dead. It was not a good thing to die in a foreign land, far from the priests of the House of Life who prepared the dead for proper burial, but there was nothing they could do.

Hori dropped his bow and drew his shortsword. It would do little good, but if he was going to die he might as well do it fighting. He glanced behind a burly warrior's shoulder, looking for Anubis. Everyone knew that the god of the dead appeared to those who were about to die, waiting to take charge of their *kas* and guide them away from their discarded bodies. But there was no sign of the god's distinctive form: the powerful man's body topped by the jackal's head with its glowing preternatural eyes. Perhaps Anubis had no power in this foreign land. But if that were so, how would the *kas* of Hori and his companions ever find their way?

The tribesmen Hori had sighted on let out a mighty roar and charged. Immediately the others followed suit. Hori let out a roar of his own. "Farewell, Brothers," he shouted above the voices of the oncoming warriors. "Anubis guard you. I will see you beyond the Field of Reeds."

He raised his sword, and in the instant before the clash, a dark shape streaked down from the trees overhead, and with an ear-piercing yowl, landed directly on his shoulders.

By some miracle of the gods, Hori did not drop his sword. Hori staggered, caught off balance by the unexpectedly heavy weight of whatever had leaped on him. Stunned, he tried to grasp what had happened and react to it before the enemy warriors fell upon him.

But the warriors did not fall upon him, any more than the weight atop his shoulders fell off him. They had halted in their tracks, freezing as if the fist of a god had struck them. Their eyes were huge. Behind him, Hori heard twin gasps from Ahotep and Seti. Reaching up with one hand he tried to dislodge the source of this dismay on the part of both foe and comrade. His fingers encountered silken fur. With a lithe movement the creature leaped off his shoulders and into his arms, forcing him to drop his sword.

Hori looked down at what he held. The great orange eyes of the black cat stared back at him. Bast's messenger had returned.

22

THE TWO GROUPS OF MEN RE-garded each other in confusion. They were enemies, bound by their oaths to try and kill each other. Yet the astonishing arrival of the cat held them back. For the men from Kemet, who clearly understood that the Goddess Bast had sent this cat, to react in such a way would be expected. But they were utterly nonplused by the response of the barbarians.

Edging up to Hori, Seti whispered hoarsely, "You know something of their ways. Do they hold cats as sacred as we do?"

"I have never heard so," Hori whispered back. After that one amazed glance at the cat he had returned his gaze to the warriors. He dared not take his eyes off them. At any moment whatever was holding these savages back from attacking might release them from its grip.

Behind him Ahotep's dry voice said, "Well, it would appear that they have some feeling for this particular cat. It's plain to see he is the only reason we are still alive."

Hori nodded in agreement. Delicately he tried to release the cat from his arms, but with equal delicacy the animal set his claws into the man's arms, making it quite clear that he intended to stay where he was.

The barbarians had begun murmuring amongst themselves. Hori caught snatches of words, but the discussion was too soft and hurried for him to make sense of it. One of them, a huge man with an auburn beard and hair flowing past his shoulders, took several strides forward, his pale blue eyes glaring intently. He raised his huge sword.

The Egyptians tensed, but the cat began to purr: a loud deep rumbling that caused his whole body to vibrate against Hori's chest. Involuntarily Hori ran a hand over the soft fur, and the creature butted his head affectionately against the man's chin. At this, the warrior lowered his sword. He gestured roughly.

"Come," he said, speaking slowly, as if he were not certain the Egyptians would understand him. "You come with us." He gestured again to illustrate what he meant.

Seti nudged Hori, hissing, "What did he say?"

"He wants us to come with him."

The cat leaped gracefully out of Hori's arms. Putting his tail straight up, he minced in a circle about the three Egyptians, then advanced toward the barbarians, who all stared at him in motionless silence. He circled them, too, paused, miaowed loudly, and set off through the trees. The barbarians looked from the cat to the men from Kemet. They stepped back, forming a path. The red-haired warrior gestured again, pointing at the cat. The animal had stopped and was looking back at all of them.

"You come," he said again.

Ahotep, normally imperturbable, clutched Hori's arm with tense fingers. "Death is one thing," he said urgently. "But torture is another. If we go with them they will sacrifice us to their gods. You know the stories."

"And they may only be stories." Hori studied the waiting barbarians. "I have never heard of anyone who was actually killed in the way our men whisper about."

"Still," Ahotep insisted. "If we are to die, I would rather meet Anubis here than hanging on some barbarian tree with my guts dangling and my throat cut."

The cat let out a loud miaow. Equally impatient, the warrior jerked his arm at the three archers. "I say you come," he repeated.

Hori looked from Ahotep to Seti. "We will not be

harmed," he said with finality. "Bast's messenger is here, and it's obvious we are under Her protection, else we would be dead already. We must go with them. And anyway," he concluded with a shrug, "what choice do we have? If we refuse to go and the cat leaves then they may kill us, indeed."

Ahotep took his hand from Hori's arm. "I see your point." He muttered a curse beneath his breath. "But I pray to the gods that these savages will look at things as sensibly as you do."

Warily, with Hori in the lead, they went toward the barbarians.

The warriors took their weapons and closed in around them, guarding as well as guiding them. The trees grew thicker and more massive, the brush more impenetrable. No legionary could have found his way through such terrain, but the barbarians trotted along easily, following trails that were invisible to the Egyptians' eyes until the faint twisting tracks were pointed out. And ahead of them all went the cat, slipping back and forth as if to check on each man in this little group he had forced together.

"I still say we should have killed them," one of the warriors growled as they walked. "They are archers, and it was an archer's arrow that slew the High Priestess."

"Perhaps it was," the red-haired man growled back. "Which is all the more reason we should take them back to her alive."

"Sado is right," another said. "We should kill them. For all we know, it could have been one of these very curs who shot the arrow."

A huge man with flowing black hair and beard streaked with gray spoke up. "Whether it was or wasn't is not important. The High Priestess is alive now, and that's what matters. And the cat is her creature. It's clear she wants these men spared."

"Exactly," agreed the red-haired warrior, emphasizing his point with a fist against his thigh. "The gods have a hand in this. It's plain as the cock on a bull. We'll take them back and let the High Priestess decide what's to be done. It's the only sensible thing to do."

The tribes gathered by the river became aware of the party's approach long before it reached the actual encampment. Sentries posted throughout the woods called out, seeming to the Egyptians to have appeared by magic. Prisoners were not taken in battles with the Romans, and the sight of the three men in legionary garb excited considerable comment and questioning.

But the warriors had few answers to provide. The red-haired man in the lead pointed to the cat, and only said, "It is the High Priestess's will that they be spared."

Gradually the forest began to thin, opening out to broad expanses of meadow. Suddenly the river was before them, broad and serene, fringed by tall stands of trees on either bank. It was not as impressive as the river that gave richness to the Black Land, but then no river could take the place of She Who was the Mother of all Rivers. Still, this foreign river was an impressive sight, oddly comforting for men who had spent all their lives beside the sweeping current of the Nile.

The gathering of people on the near banks was immense. To Seti and Ahotep, most barbarians looked essentially the same, but Hori had begun to know the people of this strange land. He could somewhat distinguish between one tribe and another, and what he saw staggered him. A true resistance was forming here, encompassing far more tribes than even Roman spies realized.

Ahotep and Seti, unable to tell one tribe from another, could still count. They looked gravely at Hori. "The legions are doomed," Ahotep said.

The red-haired warrior gestured at the archers and pointed to the encampment. "You go there," he said carefully. "With us. No harm come to you."

"I understand," Hori said. "We will go with you."

His rendering of the words was heavily accented, but

quite acceptable. Startled, the warriors gaped at him, their eyes widening in astonishment. "He can speak like a civilized man," exclaimed one.

In spite of the tenuous position he was in, Hori had to smile. "The Romans say the same thing when they encounter a barbarian who can speak Latin," he remarked to Seti and Ahotep.

With the auburn-haired warrior in the lead and the rest of the warriors flanking them, the three Egyptians entered the camp. They walked past a seemingly endless array of staring eyes and murmuring voices. The people jostled to get a better look at them. Hori saw distrust and curiosity on many faces, hatred on still more. Seti and Ahotep walked just behind him, and though both were silent Hori could feel their terror. It wrapped about him, as vivid as the hostility directed at him from the rows and rows of staring faces.

They were taken to a small hut and, to their surprise, brought cups of river-cooled mead to drink. "Wait here," the red-haired warrior told them, and left.

Seti peered out through the doorway of the hut. "We could escape," he suggested. "They haven't even placed guards on us."

"They don't have to," Hori pointed out. "How in the name of Hathor could we make our way past all the people in this camp? And even if we could, where would we go?"

Seti listened, sighed in glum agreement, and took a deep gulp of mead.

As the men from Kemet waited, Mau went in search of Veleda. He found her as he had known he would, some distance from the encampment, alone in the sacred grove. She had not accompanied the warriors to fight the legion. There had been no need. They had gone out with her blessing, secure in the knowledge that they would prevail.

And they had. The detachment had not been entirely wiped out, but most had been slain while the rest fled in confusion and disarray. Veleda had seen it. Seated on the long soft grass of late summer, she held a scrying bowl on her knees. Filled with clear water, it was the means by which those initiated in the mysteries could witness events as they were happening. Veleda scarcely needed it though. Since her return from the Otherworld, she had been blessed with even greater powers of seeing. Or perhaps it was that her certainty was greater.

Shifting a little, she stared down into the water. The surface had rippled with her movement and as it stilled, she watched intently. Her ability to see was greater indeed, and because of this, she knew there was something missing from her sight on this day; something she had not yet been permitted to glimpse.

Soundlessly Mau came up beside her. "Come back to camp," the cat said without preamble. "There is someone you must meet."

The distant look left Veleda's eyes. So this was what had been held back from her. "The Goddesses have sent him, then," she said with a curious mixture of resignation and excitement. "From what tribe is he?"

Mau scratched at a flea that had had the temerity to alight on his magical skin. "You'll see soon enough."

He pranced ahead of her on the path that led back to camp, refusing to answer any more questions, waving his tail high above him in the way he did when he was pleased about something. Veleda followed him. She was not nearly so pleased. In truth, her thoughts were jumbled far more than she cared to admit, even to Mau. The man waiting for her would hold the key to both her life and death. It was a heavy burden, for him as well as for her.

As they neared the encampment, Mau turned back to Veleda. "People will descend on you with questions like a horde of biting flies," he said. "I would suggest you not answer them until you see the one I have brought you."

Veleda eyed him. She had questions of her own, but long years of being with Mau had taught her to recognize his every mood. She nodded silently, and they entered the place where the tribes had gathered. Many had already seen her coming. They rushed to meet her, drawing those who had not along with them.

Cries of "High Priestess" rang out, accompanied by so many questions and explanations they all ran together into one long garbled spate of noise. But one word stood out clearly: prisoners. A prickle of unease ran along Veleda's spine. She regarded Mau suspiciously, but here, in the midst of all these people, she knew it was useless to address him. He would say nothing to her, not even in his close and secret way of communicating in the midst of others.

Ardicco shoved his way through the people. "Lady," he said above the voices. "We have brought back some prisoners from the battle. We would have killed them and brought back only their heads, but your cat appeared to us and made it plain that he did not wish us to. I thought we should pay heed to him."

Veleda inclined her head. "That was wise of you, Ardicco. Many men would not have listened as you did. Come, I will speak with these prisoners."

Ardicco made no effort to conceal his relief or delight at the High Priestess's praise. He exchanged triumphant glances with the men who had accompanied him, then followed the High Priestess, who was already following her cat.

Mau slipped ahead of them, weaving through the legs of the crowd. At the doorway to a hut he stopped, waiting for her to catch up, then darted inside.

Veleda made a gesture for everyone to remain outside, and stepped in after him. "One of them speaks our tongue," Ardicco called out as she entered.

The interior of the hut was dark after the brightness of the day, and Veleda paused to let her eyes adjust. Three legionaries were facing her. Their eyes were fixed on her, and they were so utterly still they could have been standing at attention for Caesar himself.

Mau made an impatient noise in his throat, scampered

straight up to one of the men, and leaped into his arms. For the prisoners, the swift movement seemed to break the tension. They relaxed slightly, though none of them took his eyes from Veleda. The one to whom Mau had gone absentmindedly stroked the cat's fur as he watched her.

Momentarily speechless, Veleda stared from the legionary to Mau. The cat stared back. *Here he is*, he said into her mind. *Do not look so shocked. You could do much worse. This is a man from my own land and he follows the old ways. He knows how to respect cats.*

Veleda fought to recover herself. *But I*, she said back to him, practically hissing the words into his mind, *am not a cat. And this man is an enemy.*

The cat regarded her unblinkingly from the legionary's arms. *He is the one my Mistress has chosen. She has Her reasons. Would you question Her now?*

Instead of answering, Veleda fixed her gaze on the man. So this was a man from Kemet, the land of Bast and Mau. And Sekhmet. With an effort she focused her attention away from the leather jerkin and tunic of a Roman legionary and concentrated on the man himself. He was somewhat taller than many of the Romans she had observed over these last years, though he conspicuously lacked the height of her own people. His skin was the darkest she had ever seen, made even darker by the dirt and grime of battle. Despite the muddy coating, there was an unusual red tint to it, like the coat of a finely groomed chestnut horse. He was lean and at the same time muscular, in the way of men who fight for a living.

But when Veleda looked into his eyes she understood beyond any doubt the reason Mau had brought him. The man's gaze was black and liquid, and he withstood her searching of the souls behind his eyes calmly, almost as if he expected it. Most surprising of all was the awareness in those dark eyes. He glanced from her to Mau with keen understanding, as if he knew they were communicating, though he could not hear what they were saying. She sighed inwardly. There was power in the man; Bast had indeed chosen well. There was nothing for it but to accept his presence.

"I am told one of you speaks our language," she said.

Mau butted his head against the man's chin as if prompting him to answer. "That would be me, Lady," he said, saying the words with obvious attention to their pronunciation. "Though I speak it poorly. I am still learning."

She gave him an enigmatic smile. "Learning is a road that never ends for those who are wise." For the first time she looked at the other two men, assessing and dismissing them with equal quickness. They were companions to the chosen man, nothing more. Mau had probably saved them for no other reason than that they were from his land. "Tell your comrades," she continued, "that you are welcome here. Under the ancient laws of hospitality, you will not be harmed."

The chosen man answered her with great care. "Lady, we thank you for your kindness. But"—he hesitated— "may we know the reason we were spared? And why we were brought here?"

He addressed her with respect, which pleased Veleda. His was not the typical attitude she had seen in Romans, most of whom could scarcely credit that women were capable of holding positions of honor, much less power. Because of that, she answered him honestly. "It is not kindness that has caused you to be spared. You fight on the side of Rome, which makes you our enemy. But nothing is ever as it seems in the world. There are reasons beyond reasons, and in time, they will be explained to you."

She turned to leave. Mau leaped out of the Egyptian's arms and followed her. As the two of them left the hut, they heard the voices of the men break out in a hurried discussion in their own tongue.

That evening, as dusk washed the river in swathes of indigo and rose and people gathered around their fires to eat and tell stories over cups of mead, Veleda sent word for the man who spoke the language of the tribes to be brought to her.

Ardicco and another of the men from the party who had brought in the prisoners accompanied him to her hut. The strangers had been allowed to bathe and the man now looked quite different. With the grime removed, the reddish tint in his skin had taken on a smooth sheen, and his dark liquid eyes seemed brighter. He was clothed in his linen tunic, having removed the heavy leather jerkin and legionary's helmet. His hair was cut short in the Roman style, its color a dense thick black that blended harmoniously with his reddish brown skin.

Veleda motioned him politely to a stool. "What is your name?" she asked him. When he told her she struggled to pronounce it. The sounds did not lie easy on her tongue and she could see him restrain a smile at her efforts.

She did not volunteer her own name and he did not ask, waiting in silence for her next question. She regarded him for several moments. "Your skin is very dark," she said at last. "Is it because the sun in your land is so strong?" She already knew the answer to this; Mau had talked to her often about the fiery heat of the Black Land. But she was curious to know what he would say.

"Yes, Lady," the man replied. His voice was soft and well modulated, despite his apparent awkwardness with her tongue. "The sun is the king of my land, as the river is its queen. My people worship the sun. He is one of our greatest gods."

"Ah." Veleda nodded. "To us also, the sun is a god."

Hori looked pleased, and to her surprise, interested. "I was told this by others of your people when I first began to learn your tongue," he said eagerly. "They also said you hold rivers and springs sacred because the spirits of your Goddesses reside in their depths. A great river flows through my land, and we, too, hold this river sacred. She is our very life. I think, Lady, that your people and mine have much in common."

"Once, perhaps." Veleda's tone was cool, a counterpoint to his warmth. "But the Greeks have ruled in your country for ages upon ages, and the Greeks hold women in little esteem. Your people have taken on their ways. I doubt that the ancient rulers of your past would be pleased to see this. Your Goddesses are certainly not."

She watched Hori for his response, and the Egyptian watched her back. His dark face was suddenly expressionless. Was he shocked that she knew so much about his land? If so, he did not show it. "New ways are coming upon our land," he said carefully. "But for myself, I prefer the old ways."

"Yet you sold yourself to the Romans so you could join their legions and come here to rob us of our own ancient ways, the most important of which is freedom." Veleda spoke sharply. She could not keep the words back and had no desire to. Emotion had brought them out, but it was also a test of sorts; she wanted to hear what he would say.

Hori looked away from her, and his dark eyes grew haunted. For a long moment he said nothing. "If I had known the things I would see in joining the Romans," he said softly, "I would have chosen differently. But Lady, I am nothing more than a man. As long as the gods permit me to live, I can only learn through the experiences life gives me. Only the gods can see beyond the days of a man's life and know what those days will bring to him."

"You are wrong." Veleda's anger left her, and her voice was filled with quiet finality. "Even the gods do not always see as you think they do."

He looked back at her, still without surprise. "You speak with them often, then."

"When they wish it."

"And the cat." Hori glanced about the hut as if waiting for Mau to appear. "His magic is intertwined with yours."

She favored him with a slight smile. "He has been with me long and long."

"But not this evening."

Veleda shrugged. "He's a cat. He comes and goes as he pleases."

The tension between them had subtly eased, and they sat in silence for a time. The scent of wood smoke swirled heavily on the warm air, borne by breezes from the river. Dusk was fading into darkness as night came on, though the noises from the vast camp that stretched all about the hut had not diminished. People still talked and laughed, children shouted, and dogs ran past barking. In the distance horses whinnied as they were turned loose to graze for the night.

Hori felt a pang of homesickness, sharp as the stab from one of his own arrows. The sound of so many people gathered together was a piercing reminder of the Two Lands. Except for the difference in language, he could have been strolling through the twisting streets of Thebes as evening drew towards night.

He thought of Seti and Ahotep. When the warriors had come to take him, Seti's round face and Ahotep's thin one had mirrored the same expression: silent dread. They had begun to believe the courtesy shown them was genuine, and they were indeed under the protection of Bast. But as he left them, Hori could see that they were convinced their original fear had come to pass. They would all be tortured to death, beginning with Hori.

But Hori himself had been unafraid. The moment he had seen the High Priestess a weight had been lifted from his heart. There was not the least doubt in him that Bast had returned this woman to the land of the living. The Goddess's reasons for doing so were as much a mystery as to why the priestess had appeared in his dreams, or why his arrow had been the one that had killed her.

But she was here now, and wrapped in power. It glittered all about her, so brilliant a blind man could not have missed it. Gold burnished her, as it had once clothed the ancient queens of the Black Land. Her waist was encircled by it, and earrings and bracelets gleamed at her ears and on her upper arms. A thick torque of solid gold—the mark of her office—glowed about her neck, partially hidden by her unbound red hair. Her slightly tilted eyes were as green and mysterious as the forests of this strange land, and when Hori looked into them, they seemed just as endless.

Veleda had grown into her dignity, as her father Raricus had seen she would so long ago. The gangly awkwardness of youth was gone. Her body was strong and her features broad. She was not light and lithe like the women of Kemet. There was nothing slender or small about her, but Hori was drawn to her nonetheless. She possessed a beauty as foreign as this land, and yet the presence of Bast seemed to breathe along with her.

"I have seen you before, Lady," he said very quietly. She stared at him, and he tried without success to see what lay behind her eyes. "When the legion of Quintus Tullius Cicero was besieged during the winter," he went on, "I watched you sometimes."

"Ah." Her voice was soft, her broad dignified features still unreadable. "And where else have you seen me?"

Now Hori found it difficult to meet that deep green gaze. "Your face was sent to visit my dreams. Before and after." She did not ask him what he meant, and so he had to tell her. "Before and after I killed you."

"Ah," she said again, still soft. "So it was you."

Silence followed. Hori waited. His heart had begun to beat faster, yet he was still calm. She could demand his death in return; surely it was her right. And perhaps that was the heart of it. Maybe Seti and Ahotep were correct, and the cat had led him here for that very purpose.

The silence stretched, until Hori finally said, "What will you do with me, Lady, now that you know?"

"It is no longer important." Veleda's smile was as strange and sad as her eyes. "It was all a part of the pattern."

"I do not understand, Lady."

"Nor should you." She studied him. "But you have been touched by power of your own. The dreams should have taught you that. You said you keep to the old ways. Does this mean you revere the Goddess Bast?"

Hori was not amazed that she knew of Bast. After all that had happened, there was no amazement left in him. "I have worshipped Her all my life," he said, and pulled out his amulet to show her. "My mother is one of Her priestesses."

A kind of lightness came over her face at his disclosure.

"And is it permitted to ask," he said cautiously, "how you, Lady, came to know of the Goddess?"

Veleda smiled.

And so, they began to talk. Before either of them realized it, dawn was brightening the edges around the door flap of the hut.

23

OVER THE DAYS THAT FOL-
lowed the men from Kemet were
absorbed into the camp. Their acceptance was tentative, and more
than a little wary on both sides, but
gradually things began to go easier.
Despite their uneasiness, Ahotep
and Seti had the good sense to fol-
low Hori's example and reciprocate the courtesy shown
them with courtesy of their own. Their respectfulness, so
different from the arrogance most of the tribal people had
experienced from Romans, won them a grudging approval
that slowly began to turn into friendliness.

Surrounded by speakers of the Gaulish tongue, Hori's
proficiency in the language rapidly grew. He served as
translator for his companions, and Seti and Ahotep slowly
began to engage in their own efforts to communicate, a
gesture that further earned them the good opinion of their
captors.

Delegations of warriors from Albion continued to arrive,
swelling the numbers of those already camped along the
river. Armed and ready for battle they came eagerly, offering themselves to fight in the cause of freedom. The tribes
they belonged to were kin to the Belgae and each group of
new arrivals was welcomed with feasts and rejoicing. Druids accompanied them, both to invoke the protection of the
Shining Ones for those in their charge and to see the High
Priestess who had gone to the Otherworld.

As was customary, Veleda met with each Druid, and one

morning she was delighted to see a face she had not seen since the days of her training on Eire.

"Eponina!" Arms outstretched she went forward to embrace her old friend.

The fair-haired woman returned the embrace with hesitancy. "High Priestess," she murmured. "It is an honor granted by the gods to be in your presence."

Veleda stepped back. Eponina's formal shyness was like a drenching in ice water. Her friend from long ago was a full Druid, clothed in the power of her calling, and yet she could scarcely meet Veleda's gaze. The barrier between the worlds seemed higher than ever, leaving her profoundly separated, from this world and all those who truly belonged to it.

"So, my friend," she said, trying to restore her own balance as well as Eponina's. "Do you still snore?"

The Druid looked at her. Slowly her dark blue eyes widened, and then she drew herself up. "Lady," she said with ringing authority. "I do not snore. I never did. It was an imp of the air that you were hearing all those nights. Or perhaps it was the cat that trailed you everywhere like a shadow."

Veleda laughed. It was a free joyous sound, the first true laugh she had uttered since she returned, and for a long time before that. "Ah, Eponina," she said, "It's glad I am that you are here."

The men from Kemet watched as this gathering of warriors grew larger and larger. The tribes from Albion were unfamiliar to them, but they knew enough of the Gaulish tribes to recognize that longtime enemies had joined together, camping side by side in harmony, practicing their swordcraft as fellow warriors rather than blood foes. The thing that Caesar had always scoffed at had happened at last. The tribes were unifying, and not just the Belgae. This new confederation included tribes from all over Gaul, even the huge blond Germans from across the river.

To Seti and Ahotep it was a sight as awesome as it was

fearful, and they watched with growing concern. "Caesar needs to return from Rome," Seti muttered to Hori. "And he had better do it quickly."

Hori was silent. He had spent much time talking with the High Priestess, whose name, he had learned, was Veleda. It was not her true name; that knowledge was kept a closely guarded secret from the time one was born until the day she died. This made remarkable sense to Hori. His people also set great store by the power contained in names; the fact that these people did too only strengthened the opinions he was already forming about Veleda and the tribes of this wild land.

"Do you think it right," he asked, "that the Romans march over these people's lands and make slaves of them? All so Caesar can enrich himself in gold and power?"

The other men both stared at him. "It's the way of the world," Ahotep said impatiently. "You are no green youth, Hori, but a man charged with leading others. You know these things for yourself."

"We signed up to fight for the Romans," Seti added, casting an uneasy glance about him. "Not to make judgments about the rightness of their battles."

Hori met their eyes. "Perhaps it's time we started. In truth, I'm finding that we have more in common with these people than we ever did with Romans."

"You've been spending too much time with the High Priestess," Ahotep told him. "She favors you, and her powers are great." He paused, eyeing Hori speculatively. "She may have put a spell on you."

"She has not," Hori said with such authority there could be no doubting it. "And even were she inclined to, there would be no need. I see and hear with my own eyes and ears. If there is magic guiding my wisdom, it is not from any priestess or god of this land."

"From where then?" demanded Ahotep. "For this is strange talk indeed that is coming from your lips."

Hori's eyes were bright and deep. He fingered the amulet

about his neck. "Who else would gift me with Her knowledge than Lady Bast, the Goddess my mother and all her mothers before her have devoted themselves to? How can you doubt it? The cat is Her messenger. Why else do you think he came to us?"

"He came to *you*," Seti pointed out. "We were just fortunate enough to be there when he did. Whatever power is at work here, it does not concern Ahotep or I. All we want is to leave this place alive." He glanced at the thin dour-faced Egyptian for confirmation, and Ahotep nodded in agreement.

Hori leaned forward. "Tell me you have not had doubts about being in this land, that you have not grown tired of the endless slaughter. You, Seti, have you forgotten all the times you whispered to me about how we do not belong here?"

The plump man could not meet Hori's eyes. "I have not forgotten."

"Well, you were right. We should not be in this land, fighting battles for rulers who are not our own. I see that now. Bast's messenger was a sign. We have been in the service of Sekhmet, and it is time to stop, before She claims our souls."

"You speak of ancient days and ancient Goddesses," growled Ahotep. But he, too, was faltering before the intensity in Hori's dark eyes. "The Romans do not know of Sekhmet. Even in Kemet Her worship is being forgotten. Why even speak Her name?"

"Sekhmet is the Goddess of war. And I, who keep the old ways, have not forgotten what it is She thrives on."

"Blood," Seti said slowly. "Lakes and lakes of blood. Well, She'll be having her fill of it if She's been accompanying the legions. But what would Sekhmet be doing in a foreign land?"

"We came here." Ahotep lifted his gaze and stared at Hori. "And so did Bast. But what do She and Her Sister want of us?"

Hori shook his head. "I don't know. But I do know this: fighting for Rome is not the answer."

The speaking of Her name called Her. Hori, who understood such things, should have known better. But caught up in this new place, he had not paid sufficient attention.

The Dark Goddess stirred, drawn by those who had spoken of Her. She moved slowly, bloated with blood and power, but inexorable nonetheless. She listened to these sons of Her land speak about Her, and She grew angry. She also saw what mortals could not. And that made Her angrier.

She cast about for a means of stopping what had already begun. She found it quickly. The people in this huge land of trees and mountains and water did not know Her. Yet, all unknowing, they served Her. It was not difficult to seek out those whom She could work to Her will. . . .

As the men from Kemet talked and watched, they, too, were being watched. One of the warriors from the original party that had captured them sat nearby, oiling and polishing his weapons. He could not hear their words, and would not have understood them if he could, but his eyes narrowed anyway, and the expression on his face was grim.

There were those who were able to show genuine courtesy to the strangers, and those who could not. Sado fell into the latter category. To him it did not matter that the three men were not Roman. He had wanted to kill them before and Ardicco had stopped him. He wanted to kill them now, but of course the will of the High Priestess prevented it.

"Look at them," he growled to a friend who had just sat down to polish his own sword and battle-axe. "Lolling about like chieftains from a visiting tribe. They're *Romans* for Lugh's sake."

His friend glanced at the outlanders. "She Who Travels Between the Worlds says they're not. What makes you think you know more than she?"

"I don't say I do," Sado snapped. "That's not the point.

What difference does it make what country they come from? They wear the uniform of legionaries and fight for Rome. As far as I'm concerned, that's good enough reason for them to die.''

The other man looked thoughtful as he carefully rubbed oil into the blade of his axe. ''You make sense,'' he admitted. ''Although many people are coming to like them. They have good manners, certainly better than any true Roman I've met. The leader even speaks our tongue, rather than arrogantly insisting that we learn Latin.''

''And will you still speak so kindly when they escape and lead the legions straight to us before we are ready?'' At his friend's silence, Sado nodded in satisfaction. ''The High Priestess should have decided their fate differently. That's what I say. She may be able to travel to the Otherworld and back, but she is still High Priestess, and presiding over sacrifice is her duty. That's what we should do with them. Give them to the Raven Goddess of Battle.''

''Atur!''

Sado's friend looked up at the familiar sound of his wife's voice. There was a certain relief in his face as he gathered up his weapons and rose. ''There is merit in what you say, Sado,'' he said. ''But there is also the wisdom of the High Priestess. By all the Teutates, you make my head hurt. We'll talk on this later.''

He walked off in answer to his wife's summons, leaving Sado alone again. Grim-faced, the warrior went on polishing his sword blade, though the task was already finished. His eyes had gone blank as his hands rubbed the polishing cloth back and forth, back and forth, along the shining iron. He had not said it to Atur, but his head ached, too. He scarcely noticed it. He was listening too hard to the voice that had suddenly entered his thoughts.

Kill them, it whispered seductively. *They must die.*

Divitiacus knew he would have to do something. The strength of his kingship was crumbling under his feet like

sand pulled away by an outgoing tide. It had begun with
the death of his brother. Many blamed him for the way
Dumonorix had died and had not forgiven him for it. Looks
followed Divitiacus wherever he went—not the respectful
ones given a king and Druid of the Aedui, but glances filled
with blame, even open hostility. The comments had been
soft at first, whispered from one person to the next. Then
they had grown louder, bitter with the tang of freedom lost
and blood spilled in support of the wrong cause.

Now Caesar had left the land Divitiacus himself was beginning to refer to as Gaul. His going had further weakened
the tenuous state of the Aeduian king's rule. People were
turning away from him in ever-increasing numbers, drawn
by the voices of those who had long counseled against the
dangers of embracing Rome. Once Divitiacus could have
stilled those voices by pointing to the prosperity and safety
of his people and their lands, but no longer. The return of
the High Priestess from the Otherworld had changed all
that, and now it was the very tribes that had befriended
Rome who stood in danger. A massive revolt was forming
under her guidance, and if the Romans were swept away
by it, the collaborators would suffer.

Caesar could not have chosen a worse time to return to
Rome. But then, he had little choice in the matter. Divitiacus was still enough of a Druid to remember how often
gods interfered in the affairs of mortals. Perhaps the outland
Goddess of the High Priestess had twisted the situation in
Rome, timing Caesar's problems to coincide with Veleda's
return. Regardless, his absence had worsened Divitiacus's
own position. The Roman commander had become his bulwark, his surety against those who opposed him. Even the
ghost of Dumonorix could not get past the security of Roman strength and Roman might.

But now the tribes were gathering, shouting vows that
echoed from the remote border between the Belgae and the
Germans to the calm settled farmlands of the Aedui, and
the voices of the dead were joining them. If the High Priest-

ess came back, would others? Dumonorix's face still haunted his older brother's inner sight. Divitiacus saw him as he had been in the bold laughing bloom of manhood, and as he had been in death, stretched upon the bloody sand, his face frozen in that last expression of defiance. Would Dumonorix return at the head of an army of the dead, crying out to avenge himself against the brother who had chosen Rome over the bonds of blood?

The thoughts chased each other in the king's head like rats in a storehouse emptied of grain. Days passed, and he grew silent and gaunt, hollow-eyed with lack of sleep and his awareness of the people's hostility. When the few chieftains who still remained loyal to him came to discuss the gravity of the situation, Divitiacus was ready.

"We must act," he declared with some of his old power. "Without Caesar these Romans are fools. They are incapable of truly understanding the danger here."

"And what can we do about it?" one of the chieftains demanded. "Every day more of our kindred slip away to join . . . her." He hesitated, as if the very speaking of the High Priestess's name might draw her anger to him.

His uneasiness did not escape Divitiacus. "We will do the obvious, and stop this sickness before it spreads. Gather all those men who are still wise enough to see that our future lies with Rome. I will convince the legate of the legion stationed here to join us. Together we'll crush this High Priestess and her revolt. It will be a fitting gift for Caesar when he returns, and the best way to convince the Aedui that I am still their king."

It was time.

Veleda sensed this in her bones, a deep and secret knowledge that told her the circle was closing and the next part of the pattern must be woven.

Her resistance to Hori as the man she would lie with was long since gone. She had looked into his heart that first night and had seen, as Mau said, that he was a good man.

His allegiance to Rome was not a part of what he truly was. For some time it had been weakening. His days in the encampment and with Veleda were close to cutting the final ties that bound him to the legions. Yet the thought of severing himself from his duty was not easy for him. He was a man who respected his oaths, even if they had been taken in ignorance and lack of understanding. Veleda honored him for this, although there were other matters that concerned her far more.

On a day that fairly sang with the swelling of life, Veleda asked Hori to accompany her for a walk. They left the crowded tents and huts of the encampment, wound their way through the large herds grazing in the meadows near the river, and entered the forest of giant trees that stood guard over the camp.

They went far into the forest. It was the first time Hori had accompanied Veleda so deeply into these great woods. Not even when he, Seti, and Ahotep had been taken from the battle had it seemed that their captors led them along such trackless ways. Veleda was quieter than was her wont, and after a few attempts at conversation, Hori fell silent. There was a purpose to this day. He could feel it swirling in the sweet tree-scented air. It spoke to him in the breezes and peeked out through tiny glades that appeared unexpectedly amidst the dense forest.

Hori appreciated the sight of these small clearings set like jewels in the dark woods. Sunlight slanted down through the openings in the trees, affording him a brief glimpse of the sky. He yearned for those moments. In Kemet the sky was the Goddess Nut, and She was as vast and open a presence as Ra, whose holy eye was the sun. An Egyptian lived his life under the blue arch of Nut's body, but in Gaul it was different. Tree canopies as impenetrable as a warrior's shield hid the sky here. It gave Hori a closed-in feeling that made every sight of blue, no matter how brief, welcome.

From the corner of her eye Veleda watched him as they

walked. To her people she had said nothing of what she planned this day, not even to Eponina, with whom she had reawakened the closeness of their former friendship. Sexual intercourse was not forbidden to Druids, only to the High Priest or Priestess, whose chastity was considered a gift to the Shining Ones. No one had ever broken that sacred oath. Veleda would be the first, an ambivalent honor at best.

What she did with Hori must be kept secret. The people might accept her joining with a tribesman, but an outlander attached to the legions? Not even for one touched by the Shining Ones could such a concession be easily made. The tribe's quarrelsome natures had finally been stilled in the fight for freedom, but this would divide them anew. Even if Bast and Anu had not laid bonds of secrecy on her, she would have made the same decision herself.

As for the act itself, that was another matter entirely.

Veleda led Hori to a glade hidden deep within the majestic trees. Carpeted by moss, and illuminated by occasional gleams of sunlight that glowed and faded through narrow openings in the forest canopy, it was as secretive and private as Veleda herself.

Hori looked about him. "I could almost think, Lady," he said with a smile, "that you wish to be alone with me."

He waited for her to smile back, but she did not. Her green eyes were as deep and dark as the surrounding woods as she looked at him. "You have never asked me why you were spared," she said. "Not since the first day you were brought to us."

"I have not had to." Hori's voice grew very quiet. "Magic connects us, Lady. I have known that a long time."

Veleda continued to look at him. "And have you never wondered if you have a part in the pattern I once spoke of?"

Hori met her eyes. "When it was time for me to know more, I knew you would tell me."

Her answer was oblique and direct at once. "Among our people, there is no shame in lovemaking. It is not a subject to be kept hidden. Men and women take their pleasure freely, and when children result from that pleasure, it only makes the joy greater.'' She studied him thoughtfully. ''Is it that way in your land?''

''Once,'' Hori answered truthfully. ''But these days most people follow Greek customs. Unmarried women even seek out men to be their guardians as the Greeks do. They think it unfashionable for a woman to handle her own affairs.''

Veleda shook her head, but said nothing. The silence between them lengthened into a profound stillness, and when Hori could bear it no longer, he spoke. ''You mention lovemaking,'' he said. ''And bring me to a place hidden from all eyes—''

''Not all,'' she interjected softly. ''Only those of mortals.''

Hori could not look away from her gaze. Visions were swirling in their depths, drawing him in. He saw images both confusing and familiar: scenes of foreign worship mingling with the comforting rites he had always known in the temples of Kemet. The amulet of Bast throbbed suddenly about his neck, filling him with warmth that began where it rested against his throat and spread rapidly throughout his body. The Goddess's presence surrounded him, as sudden and close as an embrace. She bloomed throughout the glade, every leaf and blade of grass shivering with Her power. But most of all, She was in Veleda, gazing out at him through her green eyes, the woman and the Goddess together, and yet each her own entity.

''Lady,'' he whispered, and found himself unable to say more.

Veleda drew closer. ''You will be my first,'' she said, her voice as soft as the breeze. ''Our union has been blessed. Life will blossom from what we do. Will you show me the joy in it, as well?''

Hori rediscovered his voice. He reached out to touch her arms, the flesh firm and warm beneath his hands. ''I will,'' he promised huskily. "In the name of Bast, Lady of Silver Magic, I will."

Afterward, when the fires had been quenched and they lay together in peace, Veleda told him her true name.

Sekhmet was enraged. Not since She had been tricked into drinking a lake of beer tinted to look like blood in the days when even She was young had She been this angry.

The mortal had tricked Her. She, a Goddess, had been deceived by the powers of a mere flesh-and-blood human. Veleda had created wards to protect herself from the sight of others, and Sekhmet, Goddess though She was, had fallen into the trap of not-seeing. Now what She had desired to prevent had been set in motion, and there was no stopping it.

Sekhmet had bothered little with Veleda of late. There had been no need. The threat presented by the mortal had not materialized, for her people had been too foolish to heed her. The gifts of blood had flowed rich and steady, leaving the Lion-Headed Goddess well content with Her decision to favor Rome.

Then Veleda had returned from the land of the dead.

The strength of this irritating mortal was now too great for Sekhmet to attack her directly. But there were others who were far more vulnerable. In Her rage, the Dark Goddess struck at the men from Kemet, using Veleda's own people as the instrument of Her anger.

"It feels as if there are squirrels nesting inside my skull," Sado complained to Deuaus, a Druid known for his healing abilities. "Someone has put a spell on me. I'm certain of it."

The Druid studied him with cryptic hazel eyes. Sado was a man vain of his appearance, but now his hair and beard were uncombed, his eyes bloodshot and heavy. "What have your dreams been like?" Deuaus inquired softly.

Sado grimaced. "A voice rings in my head, asleep or

awake. But I can't make out the words. It's been this way ever since"—he stopped suddenly, his red-rimmed eyes narrowing as a spasm went through him.

"Ever since the three legionaries were brought here," Deuaus finished for him. "Many others have been coming to me and all the other healers with the same symptoms you speak of." He stroked the Druid's egg that hung about his neck. Sado was too caught up in his own discomfort to notice, but Deuaus's eyes were also bloodshot, and they held a distant look, as if he were listening to something far off.

"That does not surprise me." Sado rubbed at his temples. "Can you give me herbs to ease this pain?"

"Herbs will help you for a short time," Deuaus told him. "But they will not cure you. The cause must be wiped out for you to be well again." He was silent for a moment, as if he were listening. "There is evil at work here, indeed," he finally went on. "Those who do not belong among us have brought it. The High Priestess must be protected from them."

"Along with the rest of us." Sado glared at the Druid. "Have you forgotten it was the High Priestess who offered them safety in the first place? She bid us make them welcome under the law of hospitality."

"An evil influence caused She Who Travels Between the Worlds to do so." Deuaus's hazel eyes were blazing, a red tint burning in their depths. "She is in danger. We must protect her."

Sado rubbed harder at his temples. "But how? Tell me what to do, and I will do it."

Deuaus stared into the distance. He cocked his head, then nodded, and returned his reddened gaze to the warrior. "The Goddess of Battle is angry," he said. "She must be appeased."

All over the encampment similar conversations were taking place. A bloodlust was arising in all the people, and there could be only one end to it. Sekhmet swirled over and through the chattering, gesturing men and women, whispering gently to some, shouting fiercely at others, but planting the same murderous urge in each. Seeing the fruit of Her efforts, She laughed. Her magic was taking shape beautifully, moving as swift and deadly as the plagues She had once sent over Kemet when the Nile was low.

How easily influenced these folk were! They thirsted for blood almost as much as She did, and hatred for Rome pulsed in their veins with the heat of desert winds. It was this hatred which made them so vulnerable. What a simple matter it was for a Goddess to slip inside the cracks of such intense emotion and twist it to Her own ends.

Of course, there were some who resisted the clouding of their vision, but that was to be expected. Sekhmet was not overly concerned about these few. There were more than enough others to balance them out. . . .

The voice battered at Eponina's thoughts, flying about her head with dark wings that beat fiercely at her ears, trying to make her listen. She would not. Calling upon all her strength, she thrust the intruder away. There was wrongness here, a feeling of death and blood that weighed as heavy as a ninefold curse. Eponina had always possessed a unique awareness of the Shining Ones; it was this quality which had brought her to the attention of her tribal Druids in Albion as a child. Now that awareness told her that the voice ringing about her head belonged to no *Teutate* of either this land or her own. This was a foreign deity and one whose presence here was ill-omened.

Yet, she appeared to be the only person who realized this. All around her people were gathering in little knots of conversation. They called out to her as she passed, seeking Druidic approval for what they were discussing, but Eponina did not answer. She had tried talking with some of them, but had soon given up. They did not hear her, not even her own Brothers and Sisters of the Oak. The glazed

look in their eyes was universal and frightening, the whites
tinted with a red stain. Madness hovered in the air, stinking
of the coppery scent of blood.

Eponina knew the source of this madness. It was the
alien *Teutate*.

At last, she came upon a few others who had not yet
fallen prey to this spell. Surprisingly, they were not all Druids. They clustered together, staring at Eponina first warily
and then with relief when they saw the clearness in her
eyes.

"Where is the High Priestess?" she asked in a low voice.
She dreaded the answer, dreaded hearing that Veleda, too,
was caught up in this madness.

"We do not know," said an old man whose white hair
covered the Druid's torque about his neck. "We have been
looking for her."

"What is happening?" a woman holding her infant son
gasped. "People are calling out for a sacrifice, but they are
acting so strangely. Their words make no sense and their
eyes—"

"A spell has been laid upon this camp," Ardicco the
red-haired warrior said, his eyes going to the Druids for
confirmation.

Eponina nodded. "It has, and we must remove it before
its evil purpose is accomplished."

"Has the High Priestess done this?" someone else asked.

"She has not," the old Druid said firmly. "Something
else is responsible." His wise faded eyes met Eponina's.
"But only the High Priestess has the power to stop what
has begun. We have used our arts to find her, yet they have
failed. She is shielding herself from us; I don't know why.
Now you must try. You were friends as girls, and you are
friends now. Perhaps she will reveal herself to you."

"I'll do my best," Eponina promised, and hurried off.

The voices in the camp were growing louder and angrier.
Seti and Ahotep had drawn together and were watching
with growing concern. Up until now they had been unable

to hear what was being said. However, the grim looks on people's faces and the tension in the normally boisterous encampment were all too obvious. As voices rose, they began to make out words. Their uneasiness grew.

"Where in the name of all the gods is Hori?" Seti muttered. "I think it would be wise if we went into the woods. Quickly."

Ahotep was staring at a huddle of burly warriors. They stared back at him, their eyes burning red in the strong afternoon sunlight. "What good will it do to run?" he asked resignedly. "They know these woods the way we know Thebes. Wherever Hori is, I hope he's safe. Because I don't think we'll be, at least not much longer."

"And things seemed to be going so well," Seti said despairingly.

Ahotep had no time to answer. The group of warriors had started toward them. As they walked, others came up, advancing on the two men in an inexorable wave of hate. They looked at the two Egyptians and saw their loved ones: husbands, fathers, sisters, wives, parents, children, their bodies twisted in pools of blood, or their feet shackled and heads bowed under iron collars as they were led into slavery. In that moment Seti and Ahotep became Rome, became the representation of the force that had killed so many and destroyed the very balance of the world.

"Take them," a Druid roared out. "The Goddess of Battle is hungry. Let us feed Her, and let us do it in a manner that these Romans, who call us barbarians, will appreciate."

Eponina set aside the bowl of water. She had scryed into its clear depths, searching for some sign of Veleda, but without success. A sudden commotion in the camp seized her attention, and when she rose to her feet to look, she saw two of the Egyptians being borne away. Their dark heads stood out amongst their captors, contrasting sharply in the vivid throng of red and blond hair of those who held them.

There was no more time. Eponina rushed into the woods. If Veleda was not in camp, she had to be somewhere among the trees, unless she had gone back to the Otherworld. Eponina prayed that she had not, that she had stayed in this world, so that she would hear her friend calling to her and reveal herself.

Scowling, Divitiacus urged his horse forward. The stallion went reluctantly, as weary as his rider. The king stared down at the rippling black mane. There were moments when he would have gladly changed places with his horse, trading the complicated burdens of being a man for the simple burden of carrying a man.

Divitiacus glanced about him. Not nearly as many Romans were accompanying his Aedui supporters as he would have liked. Without Caesar, the commanders did not pay as much heed to him, an observation as bitter as the cold looks from so many of the king's own folk. The only thing that had helped him was the fact that Commimus, chieftain of the Arverni and a longtime ally of Caesar had turned against Rome and rejoined his fellow Gauls. Armed with news of the defection Divitiacus had gone to Caesar's commander Labienus. Finally agreeing that something must be done, Labienus ordered a detachment commanded by a young tribune named Volusenus to accompany the Aedui and assassinate Commimus.

This had not been a popular decision among the Aedui. Divitiacus had to forestall efforts to warn the tribes about his advance by threatening to lay heavy curses on any man who attempted it. Perhaps his threat had worked, perhaps not; given his current situation it was hard to tell.

At any rate, the army he had gathered was making good time. There could have been more legionaries, but those that were here were seasoned fighters. This force composed of Romans and Aedui would be enough to destroy the fools at the Rhine River. Divitiacus had told himself that repeatedly.

He dared not believe otherwise.

*   *   *

"Veleda!" Eponina tore her way along the winding deer trails. "It's I, Eponina. Veleda, answer me!"

Abruptly she stopped herself. She was acting out of panic, not with the reasoned wisdom of one who had been trained in the mysteries. Nuadu, their old teacher, would be sighing and rolling her eyes at such a display. Closing her eyes she began again, but slowly, concentrating on her inner senses. She focused them, honing her awareness to a single seeking blade. Still, she could detect no trace of Veleda. Her friend did not want to be found, and her magic was powerful enough to ensure that she was not. There was not even a sign of the everpresent cat that shadowed her everywhere.

Refusing to give up, Eponina went on through the trees, heedless of direction, allowing her senses to guide her. Her eyes remained closed, her feet found their way over roots and through thickets by feel. Suddenly she halted as if she had come up against a wall. At the same moment, a familiar voice called out to her.

Eponina's eyes flew open. She was surrounded by trees, but just beyond them she could see a tiny glade, all but hidden by the massive trunks. Rays of late sun glowed down through the leaves and burnished by a shaft of light Veleda was throwing on her tunic and leaping to her feet.

With her was a man, one of the three legionaries she had ordered spared.

The knowledge registered in Eponina, but she shoved it away for later examination. There was no time to think about it now. Veleda was already by her side, motioning for her to come. The High Priestess's eyes were blazing, the scent and feel of power inundating the air about her. She clearly knew what was transpiring in the encampment without having to be told.

"Hurry!" Veleda said urgently. "Or we'll be too late."

24

EPONINA ASKED NO QUES-
tions. Neither did the man. All three
of them concentrated solely on running. And ahead of them all darted
the fluid form of the cat.

The wicker cage in the meadow
where cattle and horses had been
grazing was almost finished. Bound
hand and foot, Seti and Ahotep watched silently, held by a
terror too great for words. Hori had insisted that the tales
of giant wicker structures crammed with victims and then
set afire were fabrications, created by Caesar and his officers to make the tribes so fearsome the legions would fight
desperately not to fall into their hands. But as the hastily
constructed cage rose into the air, the Egyptians saw that
Hori—wherever he was, perhaps dead already—had been
terribly wrong. They could not know that Hori was right
and it was Sekhmet who had planted the idea in the Gauls'
minds.

Smoke stung the air. A bonfire was being kindled near
the wicker cage, sending flames crackling into the air. To
the terrified men the entire camp seemed to have gathered,
appearing not as individual people but as one giant face
twisted with hate, eyes blazing red. Out of that featureless
mass, a cluster of strong men flanked by Druids suddenly
appeared. They seized hold of Seti and Ahotep, hauling
them to their feet. Dragged toward the means of their death,
the Egyptians lost sight of each other. Separated by tall

muscular bodies, they were denied even the small comfort of being together as they were pulled through wave after wave of shrieking voices and shoving arms.

But inevitably, Seti and Ahotep arrived at the same destination. Roughly they were shoved inside the cage, wincing as the thin strips of freshly peeled wood cut into their flesh. The structure swayed dangerously, threatening to tip over with their weight. It had been put together so quickly it barely held the two men. But it would serve its purpose.

It was impossible to speak in the uproar; even the voices of the Druids, who had begun their chanting, were lost in the din. Seti and Ahotep fastened eyes, bidding one another farewell, as the first of the flaming brands was drawn from the fire.

But the bright end of the torch did not touch the bars of the cage.

Prepared for death, waiting for Anubis to show himself, the Egyptians did not at first grasp that death had not arrived after all. Bewildered, they stared about them. Slowly they realized that the ear-splitting clamor had stopped. The silence was as crushing as the weight of the voices had been. Ahotep nudged Seti and pointed with his bound hands.

The High Priestess stood at the edge of the woods. Her eyes were tightly shut, an expression of rapt concentration blanketing her features. Only the Egyptians seemed to see her, and yet the power she had called forth raced from her, leaping and crackling as sharply as the bonfire, which was now making the only sound to be heard.

A cloud seemed to sweep over the people, and when it had passed, they stood in its wake, blinking and dazed. They looked about them, their eyes no longer blazing with that eerie red light, like beasts staring in out of the night. The Druids standing near the wicker cage glanced up, saw the structure and gaped at it and the men inside in astonishment.

"What has happened here?" one of them gasped into the silence, and then answered his own question. "A spell was laid over us."

He went to the cage and began undoing the thongs that held the two men prisoner. "Come out," he said gently. "The madness has passed. No one will harm you."

But the Egyptians hesitated, reluctant to leave the dubious haven of the cage for the unknown terror that might await them next.

Then Hori spoke in the language of Kemet. "Seti, Ahotep," he called out. "You are safe now. Come out."

The men craned their necks in astonished relief. "It *is* Hori," Seti said incredulously. "He's with the High Priestess." He and Ahotep clambered out of their would-be pyre, assisted by the very men who had shoved them into it moments earlier. The warriors' demeanors had changed utterly. Shamefaced, they cut away the bonds of their erstwhile victims, muttering apologies as they did so.

The enormous crowd of people watched silently, even those too far away to see. There was not a man or woman among them who was not as ashamed as the warriors untying Ahotep and Seti. The law of hospitality was sacred, and the two men had been granted safety under that law, legionaries or not. Now that safety had been violated. Only by the intervention of the High Priestess had a disaster that would have weighed heavy on the honor-price of everyone present been averted. No one understood what had happened here, and it seemed that only the High Priestess could explain it.

The weight of their shame and confusion was crushing. It rolled over Veleda like the sea at high tide, filling her with anger for what Sekhmet had nearly wrought and what she, though she had been fulfilling her own sacred task, had almost allowed to happen.

"What was happening here?" Hori demanded. "Why were my comrades nearly killed?"

Eponina gave him a long speculative glance. "An evil

spell was laid over our people, but some of us managed to resist its influence.'' She turned to Veleda. ''Thank the gods for leading me to you in time.''

Veleda nodded absently. Her gaze went to Mau, silently asking where he had been, why he had not warned her.

The cat's tail lashed angrily against his sleek flanks. *There is only one of me*, he fairly spat into her mind. *I was busy guarding you, adding my power to yours to protect you from whatever mischief Sekhmet might try. I cannot see everything at once, and I cannot see into the mind of a Goddess. Not even my Mistress, Who is Her Sister, can know all of Sekhmet's thoughts. She tricked us both.*

Well, it's up to me to deal with it now, Veleda retorted. She looked out over her people. ''A black enchantment was practiced upon you, my kindred,'' she called out, and for all the loudness of her voice, its tone was still gentle. ''Do not fault yourselves for it.'' Her eyes went to the gathered Druids. ''Especially not you, my Brothers and Sisters of the Oak. This was a magic that came from outside your ken—''

Abruptly she fell silent. To those who watched her, her face went blank, her eyes staring at places only she could see. Hori started to speak to her, and Eponina instantly nudged him. ''Be silent,'' she hissed. ''Can you not recognize power when you see it?''

Veleda was not aware of either of them. A vision was arising. Beyond the Druids, and above the bonfire and the wicker cage, her sight revealed it to her. She saw the rows of marching men, saw their weapons glinting in the slanting rays of the day's last sun. Divitiacus was there. His fear and hatred struck her like a blow. He reeked of things unclean. His souls were heavy with the stench of betrayal.

Veleda shook herself and lifted her arms to the sky. Her voice rose to a ringing shout. ''The dark spell is gone, but the hatred that left all of you open to its power is not. Do you still want death, my people? Then go out to where Divitiacus, the betrayer of his oaths, is coming with his masters the Romans! They are two nights' journey from our camp. Slay them, but bring the king of the Aedui back to me. To give him the death of a warrior in battle is an honor he does not deserve. Bring him here, and let the gods pass judgment upon him!''

The people's subdued mood vanished under the strength of her words. Here was something they could understand. Let the Druids hammer out matters of magic and dark spells with the High Priestess. Romans were a flesh-and-blood threat that a man could deal with. They shouted out their approval in voices tinged with relief. Seti and Ahotep had understood little of what Veleda had said. They stiffened at the new clamor, but they were all but forgotten now, no longer the object of the people's rage.

As the preparations for battle went forth, Veleda turned to Eponina. ''Will you bring the strangers to me?'' she requested softly. ''And later, you and I will talk alone.''

She looked at Hori as the woman nodded and left. ''You must leave us,'' she said to him quietly. ''You and your companions are no longer safe. She who has found you once will find you again. I will give you gold and provide you with honorable men to guide all three of you to the coast, where you may take ship for your homeland. I would not see you come to harm.''

Hori's dark eyes smoldered. ''After what has passed between us? I cannot. Seti and Ahotep must go; I understand that. But do not ask me to leave you. I do not know this 'She' you speak of, but I do know this: we are bonded, Lady. Bast wishes it so.''

''Bast wishes you safe,'' Veleda said. ''And you do know the one I speak of. She is Sekhmet.'' She nodded at Hori's expression. ''Now you see why you must leave.'' Her own eyes blazed. ''There is not enough blood for your people's Dark Goddess in Her own land, so She has come to mine.''

''Drawn to the land where She would find blood in plenty.'' Hori made a sign to protect against evil, though his eyes did not waver from Veleda's. "Still, it changes nothing. I cannot leave you, especially now that I know of Sekhmet. We have created life together—" He almost spoke her true name, but did not. "Lady Bast ordained what passed between us. It would dishonor me to abandon you. Your people are not the only folk who hold the price of honor dear."

Veleda looked into his face and swallowed her sorrow. She had told him much, but she not told him everything. He did not know how short her time in this world would be. "Bast would want you safe," she said gently. "And there is only one way to do that."

Her gaze left his, as Eponina returned with Ahotep and Seti in tow. The two men were bedraggled and bewildered. The instant they saw Hori they broke into their own tongue. Hori talked with them, reassuring and explaining. Then Veleda spoke.

"I am shamed by the violence almost done to you," she said. "But there will be a battle, and you have a choice to make. I can send you away in safety, or you can return to the legions. Whichever path you choose, you will not be harmed in the taking of it. Even if you decide to return to the Romans, you will suffer no hurt. At least," she added, "until you are back with them."

Hori translated to make certain they understood. The men absorbed his words in silence, looking from him to Veleda to the activity of the great camp as it prepared for battle.

"Have we not seen enough of fighting?" Ahotep asked at last. "We have discharged our oaths faithfully, but we are Egyptian, not Roman. This is not our war."

"And what of the omens," Seti put in. "I told you long ago, Hori, that we did not belong here. How much more proof do we need? First the messenger from Bast, and now Sekhmet: working Her darkness upon these people so that they nearly killed us. I say we take the gold and the offer of safe passage this priestess offers us and leave. It's time to go home."

"Both of you are wise," Hori said. "In this land, there is nothing for you but death."

Seti's round forehead creased. "You seem to be speaking only of Ahotep and I. Why is that, Hori?"

"Because I can't go with you." They were still using the language of Kemet, but Hori sensed that Veleda understood anyway. He could feel the weight of her green eyes, but she said nothing, did not seek to argue with him.

"What do you mean you can't go!" Seti and Ahotep burst out almost in unison, their voices vying with each other. "You will not be spared any more than we would be!"

"Please," Hori said softly. "I am bound to stay. But you, my friends, you must go."

Ahotep and Seti exchanged glances. Seti's plump jaw set. "Not without you," he said stubbornly. Ahotep nodded, equally firm. "We have been through too much together to split up now. No, Hori, we leave as we came. All three of us, or we do not go at all."

Hori's eyes met Veleda's. Now he understood why she had not interfered. He was caught between honoring her and honoring his friends. But *she* wanted him to go with Seti and Ahotep. If he refused, and they remained as a result of that refusal, then he would be putting his comrades seriously at risk. It was a choice that tore at his heart to make.

"So be it," he said, aiming his words at Veleda, rather than Seti and Ahotep. "If there is no other way to convince you, then I will do as I must."

Sekhmet called upon the winds to carry Her away. Her plan had failed, but She was not as furious as She might have been. The taste of blood was still in the air. It would be spilled in plenty, and She swept off to the place where it would be. Blood, after all, was blood.

Divitiacus had badly misjudged the hearts of his men. The nearer they drew to Belgae territory the less enthusiastic they became. By the time they entered into the broad dark forests, their eagerness to fight was eroding as rapidly as their faith in Divitiacus's plan. Yet they stayed, held by their oaths and by their confidence in the Romans who accompanied them.

It was a confidence that was ill-founded. In passing through the dense woods, the orderly ranks of legionaries strung out and separated among the trees. If Caesar or one of his more experienced generals had been in command such a mistake would never have been allowed to happen, particularly not after the disaster that had befallen Sabinus, Cotta, and their legion. But Volusenus had allowed eagerness to overcome caution. He wanted to get this matter over with quickly, so he could return to the comfort of his quarters.

Divitiacus, however, saw the risk, and he grew nearly frantic at its implications. The trees were nearly impenetrable, the column stretched out and splintered, when he sent his stallion charging up to the tribune. "Have you lost all sense!" he shouted. "Call your men together. Get them in close formation. You are begging for us to be attacked!"

Volusenus eyed him tolerantly. "You're nervous as a virgin about to be poked for the first time, Divitiacus," he said. "I've sent out your own men as scouts and they've reported nothing amiss. As soon as we come across a decent spot in this gods forsaken wilderness, we'll camp for the night. Then in the morning, we'll take care of Commimus, and scatter this rabble he's joined up with."

"You iron-headed fool," Divitiacus snarled. "We cannot wait—"

At that moment, the enemy tribes struck.

The battle was swift and savage and quickly over. Many of the Aedui fled, to return later and give their oaths to the rebel cause. Largely left to fend for themselves, Volusenus and his legionaries—spread out and disorganized, too isolated from one another to form the safety of close ranks—were slaughtered to a man.

Only Divitiacus was spared. A cordon of warriors converged upon him, twisting his sword away and taking him prisoner. Shouting in triumph, they began dragging him off through the trees. As they did, the desperate king called upon his powers.

Divitiacus was not a fool; he knew full well what awaited him. His heart told him he deserved it, but his mind screamed at him to live. He obeyed his mind. He was still a Druid, and that was the one thing that might save him. Closing his eyes, he murmured words under his breath, secret words that would summon up a fog to envelop and carry him far from his captors.

Nothing happened. The men continued to yank their captive along the dim forest trail. It seemed that the Shining Ones had turned their faces from Divitiacus indeed, and with good reason. Yet he kept whispering the words that might avert his fate.

Then a presence reached out for him. Divitiacus had felt it before. He had heard that harsh laughter twine through his mind. He knew this was no *Teutate* of the Aedui, or of any other tribe in Gaul. Blood surrounded this foreign deity, crusted with the deaths from old battles and shining and wet with the deaths from the new. To Divitiacus, none of it mattered. He still wanted to live. He welcomed the strange Goddess.

A red mist swirled up, encircling the Aeduian king in its folds. The men who held him let go of his arms with cries of fear. When they recovered themselves, the mist was gone, and so was Divitiacus.

News of Volusenus and his detachment's destruction spread throughout the lands the Romans called Gaul. From there the word flew southward to Rome and the ears of Caesar. By then, there was other news to accompany it. The Carnute tribe had made an attack on the largest of the Roman grain depots in the town of Cenabum in central Gaul. The garrison had been completely overrun, a number of Roman traders killed, and all the storehouses seized. The success of the venture had drawn the surrounding tribes into the revolt, swelling the number of rebel warriors even more.

Caesar was appalled to hear of these events, yet he could not act on them with the immediacy they required. The political maneuverings he was engaged in were as crucial to his future as his control of Gaul. Rome was in a state of near anarchy. The Triumvirate of Caesar, Pompey, and Crassus that had successfully ruled the empire for years had been broken. The Parthians had murdered Crassus and inflicted the worst defeat on a Roman army since the time of Hannibal. The stability of Rome now rested on the unsteady partnership between Caesar and Pompey.

And unsteady it was. His political opponents had murdered one of Caesar's most effective supporters in the street. When his angry supporters tried to cremate his corpse on a funeral pyre in the Senate House, they burned the entire building to the ground. The public was outraged. General disorder was rampant, and Caesar was struggling to hold onto the power he had amassed as governor of Gaul.

It was not until late winter that the partnership between Caesar and Pompey solidified enough for Caesar to break away and hurry northward to his demoralized legions. By then, the peaceful and long settled territory of Provincia in southern Gaul had been attacked.

Arriving in Provincia, Caesar immediately took charge. He recruited additional men to defend its northern border from the rebels, and then set off deep into Gaul in pursuit of the mysterious High Priestess and the revolt she had spawned. Caesar was not a man overly given to superstition, particularly in these wild lands where the natives lived lives bounded by primitive beliefs and their savage Druids. But even he was made uneasy by the developments that had swept over these lands he had conquered and left in confidence.

The woman had been dead. True, he had not seen her

body himself, but officers he trusted had watched her fall, and the centurion in charge of the archers vouched for the reliability of the Egyptian whose arrow had slain her. Yet the reports were all the same: she had returned from what the barbarians termed the Otherworld for the sole purpose of driving the Romans from Gaul. Caesar found this difficult to believe, but the uniting of the tribes and the attacks were all too real. As for the High Priestess herself, there was only one way to establish the truth of her return.

The dreams came more and more frequently of late, the scenes and images spreading themselves so clearly before Veleda's mind that there were times when she could not tell the difference between sleeping and waking. Faces rose before her. Her father and brothers laughed as they had done when alive. Bormana, who had died of a fever in the bitter cold days of *Ogronios*, the Time of Ice, laughed with them. Ancamna looked at her with deep wise eyes. Sattia came, smiling, and with her, Dumonorix. And all the other dead, so many of them, their numbers beyond counting, the weight of them heavy beyond bearing. They were patient, knowing that her time in this realm was coming to an end, that soon she would join them.

But the living haunted Veleda, too. Hori's face was ever with her. The look in his dark eyes as he bade her farewell was a memory that was not a memory, so fresh and painful was it. He had left and yet he had stayed, for the baby he had helped to create throve in the safety of her mother's womb.

She grew steadily within Veleda. She had taken on a presence of her own now, a small self who moved and shifted as the mood struck her. Veleda's body did not know how short a time was left to it in the world. It prepared for the life within it as the body of any mortal woman would. Her breasts grew full and tender, her waist thickening as her belly, always flat, slowly began to round with a mind of its own. So far the concealing spell she had cast over herself, as well as the loose robe of her high office had hidden the changes, but it would not be long before neither magic nor the flowing folds of softly woven wool would be enough.

Mau had come to the same conclusion. "It's time to start making plans," he told her late one night, when he had come in from hunting. "The eyes of the Druids will soon see that their High Priestess has broken her vow."

"Not just the Druids," Veleda replied with a snort. "Any woman who has ever borne children will soon know I am carrying a baby."

"All the more reason to leave, then." Mau administered several licks to a front paw and thoroughly washed behind his ears. "This friend of yours—you still believe she can be trusted?"

Eponina knew of the baby; after the events of that day, there had been little choice but to tell her. Mau—ever practical—had suggested killing her to keep the secret, but Veleda had refused. Friendship aside, there was no need. She had seen into the other Druid's heart and she knew Eponina would not betray them.

"Eponina can be trusted," Veleda said flatly. "And I will have need of her when the time comes." She gave him a wry glance. "She'll make a better midwife than you will, my friend."

Mau stiffened his whiskers. "Perhaps," he conceded. "But you have my protection, and that of my Mistress, as well as your own Goddess Anu. How can that compare to what a mortal can provide?"

"There is no comparison." Veleda smiled at the cat's affronted mien. "For a creature of magic who has lived as long as you have, you seem to know little about childbearing. Women need other women at such a time. I am mortal, too, you know." Her smile faded. "For a while longer anyway."

Mau rubbed his long sleek length against her. "Never mind," he said in the purring tone that he reserved only when he wished to be affectionate. "Let the woman come if it pleases you." He went still under Veleda's stroking hand. His orange eyes took on a far-off air, seeming to look through the walls of the hut and beyond. "This is a good country. There are many places we can go where we'll be well hidden from the eyes of others."

Absently Veleda continued to stroke the cat's thick soft fur, thinking of the events that had brought her to these remote heights. The conglomeration of tribes had grown steadily, swelled by great numbers of men who had only recently been fighting for Rome. One of them was a charismatic young chieftain from the powerful Arverni tribe named Vercingetorix. On hearing the news from Cenabum, Vercingetorix, serving as an officer in a troop of Gaulish cavalry under Caesar, departed to join the call of the High Priestess. He brought along a group of followers whose numbers rapidly grew into the thousands as the tribes of central Gaul mobilized to join those of the north.

The instant she saw him Veleda knew this tall, powerfully built chieftain with the bright red hair had been chosen, just as she had been chosen. Vercingetorix was a born leader of men, and as fearless and astute a commander as Caesar himself. Nobles who were older and more experienced, such as Amborix and Commimus, willingly followed him. In this, they and others were encouraged by the High Priestess's all-important endorsement. At long last, the tribes had a leader they could unite under, a man powered by the mystical presence of the Druid who had returned from the Otherworld with the blessing of the gods. It was a potent combination.

Yet this hard-won unity soon faced its first challenge with Avaricum, capital of the Biturges.

Avaricum was almost completely surrounded by a river and a series of impenetrable marshes. The only access lay through a narrow stretch of land protected by a solid wall of timber and rock. The *oppidum* itself was of surpassing beauty; even Caesar had named it the most beautiful town in all of Gaul. Not surprisingly, the Biturges were opposed to burning it, as they had burned at least twenty other towns in order to rob the Romans of both shelter and supplies. They pleaded with Vercingetorix for the chance to defend their capital, and he in turn, came to Veleda, accompanied by the king and nobles of the tribe.

So strong was Veleda's seeing that the state of *sitchain* was unnecessary. "You must tell your people to leave," she said sternly to the tribal leaders. "Abandon Avaricum and burn all its stores to prevent them falling into Roman hands. Those who stay within the *oppidum*'s walls will die. The omens favor Caesar in this."

Some of the Biturges took heed of her words, packed their belongings and left. But there were those who did not. The independent nature of the tribes was asserted yet again, as most of the townspeople, devoted to their lovely home along the river, decided to remain and fight. As Veleda had foreseen, Caesar and eight of his legions besieged the town, overran it, and massacred the inhabitants, sparing not women or children or the aged.

It was a sobering defeat, but there was a purpose to it. The High Priestess had warned against the defense, Vercingetorix had echoed her, and all those who had listened had survived. The tendency to splinter apart from a single goal, as the doomed inhabitants of Avaricum had done, was quelled, opening the way for a victory far greater than the defeat of the town had been.

Vercingetorix, Veleda, and their huge army of followers now traveled deep into the territory of the Arverni in central Gaul. Flushed with victory Caesar led six of his legions after them. Winter was a brutal time to wage war. Spring was late in coming this year and snow still held the land. It was time to destroy the upstart young chieftain and the demon priestess he followed so the weary legionaries could return to their warm quarters.

But Caesar and his men were marching into a territory waiting to engulf them. The heartland of Gaul was a sanctuary that Roman influence and might had never truly penetrated. Since earliest times the region's central location had determined the entry routes into the land as a whole. The terrain was forbidding, providing a refuge for those who understood the ways of the towering plateaus and broad uplands.

Caesar's objective was the Arverni's capital, Gergovia, a fortified mountaintop in a rugged region of extinct volcanoes. The town stood atop a plateau twelve hundred feet above the plain, surrounded by steep wooded slopes. It was a place that seemed impervious to assault. Yet Caesar was confident that it would fall to Roman discipline and the ingenuity of his engineers and their siege equipment, as Avaricum and so many other barbarian strongholds had fallen.

With Gergovia in sight and the Romans hard on their heels, Veleda called Vercingetorix and his officers to her. "Do not barricade yourself behind the walls of your *oppidum*," she said. "In that way leads disaster. Spread our warriors out along the slopes and hills and watch for opportunity. Do this and Anu will bring us victory."

Vercingetorix was a man whose blood ran hot with the fire to defeat Rome. But he was also a canny commander who recognized the ring of truth when he heard it. When the force of magic accompanied those words, they were even more potent. He listened to Veleda.

The Romans' attempt to close on the stronghold failed. Their carefully ordered front, famous for its discipline, collapsed and became a rout. Waves of shouting warriors attacked from all sides, driving four legions of panicked soldiers down the steep slopes to level ground, where the two remaining legions rushed to their aid and stopped what had become a panicked retreat. Over seven hundred men were lost, nearly fifty of them centurions.

It was the worst personal defeat Caesar had ever suffered. Given the tenuous state of matters in Rome, it was one he could ill afford. But Caesar had not held onto his position as governor of Gaul by being weak-hearted. Many and long were the nights he spent brooding, not on the disaster but on how to turn it to his advantage. When he emerged from his seclusion he had formulated a new strategy. He would have to lure Vercingetorix from his stronghold to defeat him, a difficult task perhaps, but one that could be accomplished if handled properly. As for the High Priestess, her hold on these people would not be broken so easily. Hers was a destruction that would require more subtlety.

"I still think you should tell our Brothers and Sisters of the Oak," Eponina said. "This child was ordained by the Goddess, after all."

She and Veleda were following a deer path through the forest. The trail twisted and climbed toward the mountains, the towering limbs of the fir trees reaching up to the sky in lacy rows of green. It was cool in these woods, though the day was warm. The air was alive, redolent with the smells of earth and sprouting plants. Patches of snow, crusted and stubborn from the ice of winter, still clung here and there, but spring was loosening the hands of the Cold Season and soon they would be gone.

Veleda laid a protective hand on her belly as they walked. "That would not be wise. This war we have begun is at a turning point. The tribes who have held back are rushing to join us now that Caesar has been driven from Gergovia. Even the Aedui have turned their backs on Rome. If it were to come out that She Who Travels Between the Worlds is now carrying a child she created after lying with a man from the legions, there is no telling what might happen. It is too great a risk."

"What would it risk? You told me, and I understood. Others would understand, as well. The hand of Anu is in this. She has blessed what happened between you."

Veleda smiled sadly. "You have been a good friend, Eponina, and I am grateful for it. But I fear your wisdom may not be shared. I have striven all my life and beyond for the tribes of our land to unite. Now that it is finally happening, I'll do nothing to jeopardize it. Besides, the Goddesses themselves warned me to say nothing.''

"So we disappear until your time comes.'' Eponina frowned. ''While everyone believes that you have gone into the mountains for a sacred retreat. It seems to me that the greater risk lies in your being gone for these next months. The people rely on you for guidance. Vercingetorix relies on you.''

"Sebbaudus possesses the wisdom of his age and his nature. Like you, he resisted the evil that took over so many others in the camp by the Rhine. He is a good man and a far-seeing Druid. He will make a fine Chief Druid.'' Veleda walked in silence for several moments, while Eponina regarded her thoughtfully. Before the other woman could speak, she went on. ''As for Vercingetorix, he is as careful and canny as a wolf in winter. He will not act foolishly.''

"That is fine for Vercingterox,'' Eponina snapped. ''But what about the Romans? Caesar is still smarting from our victory at Gergovia. What if he attacks while you are gone?''

"He won't.''

There was a note in Veleda's voice that made Eponina stare at her. ''What have you seen?'' she asked sharply. ''There is something on you today, Veleda; I know it. You have been acting strangely all morning. And the cat—'' she glanced about, her blue eyes searching the trees. Mau had been with them since they left Gergovia, a silent and constant presence. But now, there was no sign of him. She swung back to Veleda. ''What knowledge has your vision brought you? Tell me.''

Veleda had stopped walking. A bottomless sorrow shone in her green eyes. ''This,'' she said very softly.

25

THE SOUND OF DOGS BEAT against Eponina's ears. Their voices rose in a chorus of baying and barking as they rushed toward the spot where the two women stood. Off to the left the brush rustled wildly, then parted. A doe pushed through. She was panting, her liquid eyes distended and frantic as she ran for her life.

Veleda looked at her and for a fleeting instant the animal paused, flanks heaving, her dark stare fixed on the woman. *Go*, Veleda said to the doe. Eponina heard the words clearly, though the High Priestess's lips had not moved. *They will not want you any longer.*

Thundering hoof beats came hard on the heels of the dogs. Snorting and blowing, a cluster of horses crashed through the trees with far less finesse than the panicked doe. Eponina was a Druid; she knew the sense of danger. The men who approached were not Romans but there was peril here nonetheless. Omens had hovered unseen all morning. The doe had already vanished into the trees and she snatched at Veleda's arm, urging her to do the same.

But Veleda would not move. Solid as one of the ancient firs that surrounded them, she stood, waiting for the riders. Eponina released her arm. "Will you use your powers then?"

Veleda did not answer.

The hunters came on, pulling up their lathered mounts as they saw the women. The horses stopped reluctantly,

tossing foam from their bits, their hooves flinging up clods
of the soft forest floor. The dogs charged on after the
quarry, returning at the sound of the horn, clamoring in
protest but obedient. From the backs of their restless sidling
horses the men ringed Veleda and Eponina. They were nobles; jeweled torques glinted about their necks, and their
bracae and mantles, though splashed with spring mud, were
fine and colorful.

"Commimus, my lord," Veleda said calmly to one of
them. "Out hunting, I see."

"Lady." The chieftain inclined his head in respect. He
was a noble of the Arverni, Vercingetorix's tribe, one of
many chieftains who had once supported Rome, though he
had joined the rebellion late, along with his retinue. A troubled expression sat heavy upon his bearded features and he
had difficulty meeting the High Priestess's gaze. "The dogs
struck the scent of game, but as you see, we have lost our
quarry."

"Have you."

Veleda's tone discomfited Commimus even more.
"Lady," he said uneasily. "I do not know what you
mean."

"Ah, Commimus." Veleda's smile was ironic. "But you
do. The thought is there in your mind, as plain as the torque
about your neck."

The other men looked at the noble questioningly.

"Forgive me, Lady," Commimus mumbled. He twisted
on the saddle pad, turning from the High Priestess to his
companions with obvious relief.

"This is an opportunity that has been sent to us by a
Teutate, and we cannot ignore it." The words were rapid,
tumbling from his lips. "Eventually, the Romans will defeat us. They have all the other times. In dream after
dream, I have seen it, ever since I joined this ill-fated revolt. The few victories we have had so far mean nothing.
We will be destroyed, and Caesar will reserve his worst
revenge for men like us, men who once oathed to him,

and then broke those oaths. There is only one way to save ourselves."

"But my lord," one of the chieftains said, drawing up his stamping mare. "The High Priestess! How can we—"

Commimus's eyes were fierce, afraid, and determined all at once. "We have no choice. You know that. For the last month we have talked of how we might go back to the Romans without being seized as traitors. Here is the means. Indeed, it is the only means. Think of how we will be greeted, if we bring her back with us. Not even Vercingetorix would please Caesar as much."

Eponina's blue eyes flashed. She drew herself up, fastening her stare on each of the men in turn. "How dare you." Her voice started low, swelling steadily with her fury. "The High Priestess stands before you, and you say you will give her over to the Romans? Not while I am here you will not. She may refuse to use her powers against you, but I will—"

"Eponina." Veleda laid a hand upon her arm. "Do not. For the sake of our friendship, I ask this of you."

Eponina whirled on her. "Why? How can you ask such a thing after they have said what they will do!"

"There has been enough death covering our land. I will not be the cause of more, not when it means a Druid causing harm to our own people."

"They deserve the harm!" Eponina's rage was unabated. "They are breaking their oaths. They are betraying you! Exile beyond the Ninth Wave is the least they should suffer."

"Eponina," Veleda said again. "Please. This has been foreseen. You know that. And so does Mau. Do you see him?"

The Druid did not need to look in order to answer. "I do not," she said angrily. "But it proves nothing, least of all, why you should give yourself over to these dog's tongues who call themselves men."

Veleda was silent. She wanted to explain, and she feared

that if she did her own anger would overwhelm her. Even with her Druid sight, Eponina could not know the depth of her friend's struggle. Yes, Veleda wanted to use her power! She wanted to blast these cowards with words that would shrivel them smaller than the clods of mud beneath their horses' hooves. Indeed she had started to do it, when Bast spoke to her. The familiar voice thrummed through her mind.

Do not, my daughter, She said. *It will avail you nothing. This one is deep in the hold of Sekhmet. The moment in time has passed. You must take a new path.*

"Lady," Commimus said awkwardly to Eponina. "Your courage is as great as that of the High Priestess. You may go from this place. We will not hold you."

"And why should I do that?" Eponina said coldly. "Aside from the fact that even creatures like yourselves, who have forfeited all honor, would not dare to kill a Druid."

Veleda touched her shoulder. "Accept his offer, soul-friend. Take your freedom and go. Freedom is a precious thing, too precious to lose because of me."

Eponina glared at her. "These rotting piles of horse dung have no power to take my freedom or anything else from me. I am freeborn, and I make my own decisions. I will stay with you, Veleda." She blistered the men with her blue stare. "And let them try and stop me."

"Very well," Commimus said with a sigh. "Then we will take you both to Caesar." He still could not look at either of the women easily, particularly the High Priestess. "Forgive us," he whispered again. "Forgive us."

Veleda's eyes were terrible in their calmness. "No, my lord," she said in a voice as terrible as her eyes. "I will not stop you. But neither will I forgive you. You have made this choice. Live you with the consequences."

And so it was done. Commimus sent one of his men galloping off to find where Caesar was encamped, while he and the others took their prisoners out of Arverni territory as rapidly as they could.

After the defeat at Gergovia, Caesar had taken his six legions on a forced march to the north and set up camp along the broad river that ran through the territory of the Lingones, one of the few tribes still friendly to Rome. Labienus had fought his way back upriver with his four legions to join him. Now the governor was busy recruiting additional cavalry and infantry from the German tribes that had not joined Veleda, luring them with promises of plunder when Gaul was defeated once and for all.

For the men who hurried through the rough and wild terrain of the Arverni lands with their precious captive, it was a journey fraught with terror. They had embarked on this course of action for the sake of their survival and that of their kin. They were determined to see it through. But this was no simple matter. To seize any Druid, much less the High Priestess, and consign her to the Romans carried dreadful risks, in the Otherworld as well as this one. For reasons known only to her, Veleda had not called upon her awesome powers to destroy them, and only that convinced them to go ahead.

A prudent man had to weigh the costs, pick the winning side. Thus had Commimus counseled them, repeating in turn what the Shining One who had visited his dreams had said to him. But someone else had echoed the words of the strange Goddess, someone mortal. And he had done it so convincingly that the Arverni chieftain had finally come to believe it. When Veleda, Eponina, and their captors neared the Roman camp, Veleda saw the man who had aided Commimus's betrayal.

Divitiacus.

Flanked by sentries, he stood outside of the massive earthworks that enclosed the encampment, waiting. He had aged greatly since the night Veleda had first seen him in her vision in the stone hut on Eire so long ago. His hair, once bright as the sun, had faded to a dirty brown streaked with gray. The piercing blue eyes were puffy and veined with red. The bold, handsome king who had welcomed Rome long before Caesar's sandals ever touched this land had become a man bloated with the weight of nightmares, fear, and broken oaths.

Veleda looked down at Divitiacus from the horse they had given her to ride, and to those who watched, it seemed that she was the victor and he the captive. "Do you think that you have won anything here?" she asked him in a voice cold as a sword blade plunged in ice.

"I have won you." The king straightened up. As keenly as anyone else he felt Veleda's presence and how it diminished him. He sought to regain himself, in his own eyes, as well as those of the men around him. "You are a prisoner of Rome, Lady, while I am a free man."

Veleda's laughter shocked everyone but Eponina. "Free is something you will never be, Divitiacus. A dark Goddess holds you prisoner, and She will be crueler to you than any Roman could ever be to me. But even more: you are prisoner to yourself. There is a terrible burden upon you, O King. I do not envy you in the bearing of it."

"Your words are air," Divitiacus snarled. "They carry no more meaning than the wind."

"Ah, but Divitiacus," Veleda said with her icy smile, "the wind has great meaning. You, who were once a Druid, should know that. I have journeyed upon the wind, and it has shown me much." Her eyes narrowed upon his. "Your brother, for one, and your hand in murdering him."

Divitiacus paled. "You know nothing of that," he whispered.

"I saw him in the Otherworld, Divitiacus." Veleda's voice was as merciless as her eyes. "Lie to yourself, if it pleases you. But I know the truth."

Unable to prevent himself, the king took a step away from her. He raised a hand, almost made a sign to protect against evil, then jerked it in the direction of the camp.

"Take her," he said harshly. "Caesar is waiting. I will lead you to his quarters."

The governor's stronghold had been constructed with all the organization that went into each of his camps. This camp, though, was bulging at the seams with men. Ten legions of infantry and several thousand cavalry comprised a large enough army, but these were also mingled with vast numbers of servants and drivers and auxiliaries. All of them created a clamor too self-contained to take note of even so important an arrival as the High Priestess. Centurions shouted to legionaries and cavalry officers, horses and mules and wagons clattered by towering German auxiliaries dressed in gaudy finery. Few paid any heed to the small party that rode through its midst with Divitiacus walking in the lead.

Caesar's large tent faced east, the direction Romans found most favorable. The sentries who surrounded it stood at stiff attention, watching the chieftains and the two Druids approach with flat hard eyes. Divitiacus was apparently well known to them, for the sentries at the doorflap stepped aside.

"You may enter," one said. "He is expecting her." As he spoke, his gaze strayed to Veleda and remained there. Indeed, he and his companions could not take their eyes from her. Unnoticed she may have gone in the rest of the camp, but these men knew who she was. And the knowledge terrified them. Torn by their duty and their fear they waged an obvious struggle to remain at attention, as Veleda, Eponina, and their captors dismounted.

The head sentry raised a hand. "Only you and . . . she," he told Divitiacus. "The rest must wait here."

Before Divitiacus could move, Veleda strode in ahead of him, head high, moving as though he were not there. Inside the tent she paused, staring at the man who had risen to greet her.

"Ah," said Caesar softly. "We meet at last."

Veleda was silent.

"You have done well, my friend," the governor said to Divitiacus. "But now that you have succeeded in having her brought to me, I would speak with her alone."

Divitiacus looked uneasily from Veleda to the Roman. "Caesar," he began, "I do not think it wise—"

"My friend," Caesar broke in gently, "there is nothing to be concerned about. Leave us now."

It was courteously said, but a command nonetheless. And Divitiacus, though a king in his own right, obeyed. Under Veleda's contemptuous gaze he departed from the tent.

Veleda turned her attention back to Casear. Not since the day he had executed Ancamna had she seen him. So long ago that day seemed, and yet the sight and scent of her foster-mother's blood washed her memories red, as vivid as if it had just happened. Hate rose in her, but she stilled it with all her formidable power to be calm. This Roman was not a man to be bested by uncontrolled displays of emotion.

Caesar was studying her with brown unreadable eyes. "You," he said to her with surprising mildness, "are supposed to be dead."

Veleda looked at him steadily. "I was."

He digested this in silence, and the two leaders took each other's measure. Veleda hid a smile as she took note of the Roman's clean-shaven face. Amborix had never been captured. The king of the Eburones was still alive, still fighting Rome, and Caesar's vow to neither shave nor cut his hair until Amborix was in chains had apparently been forgotten. She stared into his brown eyes and her smile widened.

Surprise flicked over Caesar's features. Deliberately he turned away to pick up his goblet of wine. "Yes," he said casually. "I'm aware that your people see little difference between the two states. Divitiacus has told me of your Otherworld, where you enjoy yourselves as you did in life. If you die bravely, that is." The condescension in his tone was subtle and unmistakable.

"Divitiacus is a poor choice if you wish to learn about the ways of this land." Veleda glanced about at the tent's sumptuous furnishings. Beneath her feet there was even a piece of mosaic floor Caesar carried with him from camp to camp. "But then, you care little for that. Your only interest lies in conquering us and stealing our wealth."

The governor nodded. "That is quite true. Divitiacus has served me well for that purpose. And he is loyal to Rome."

"He is loyal to himself, great Caesar." Veleda's voice matched his in condescension. "He follows at your heels because he is afraid to do otherwise. It will not help him, though. Death is waiting for him. He was trained as a Druid, and he knows this for himself."

"Death is waiting for all of us." Caesar took a swallow of wine, savoring the taste in his mouth. "You have cheated it once, Priestess. You may not be so lucky again."

Veleda's chuckle took the Roman off guard. He was suddenly and forcibly reminded of the High Priestess who had preceded this one: the woman whose execution he had ordered. Strange, he had not thought about her in years, since the day she died, in fact. But there was something eerily familiar about this new priestess, this raw-boned woman with her red hair and ungainly height. Physically, she did not resemble her predecessor, but the air of dignity, the depthless eyes, were the same. Most of all, there was that disconcerting and frustrating sense that he was trying to hold a conversation with the fog.

"Ah, if you only knew how lucky and unlucky I am," Veleda said, and let out a hearty laugh.

Determined to keep control, he said, "The one who filled your place before you spoke as you do. But I ordered her death, and she went to it like any other woman." He smiled. "After all," he added confidentially, "you did not truly die that other time, did you? With only the two of us here, you can admit it. It was a Druid trick, wasn't it?" His smile vanished. "What is not a trick is that I can easily order your death, and for certain this time. It is within my power to do so.''

"Is it?" Something came into Veleda's eyes: deep and hard, and so piercing Caesar had to fight against dropping his gaze from hers. "Not all things are within your power, Commander of the legions. Much as you desire them to be. It is easy to conquer a land; it is harder to control it. Already you are finding that out for yourself."

With devastating accuracy she had precisely echoed the sentiments Caesar had recently expressed to his own officers. He regarded her thoughtfully. "Tell me, Lady, what would you do in my place?"

"What you could not do, and never will. You do not understand the soul of this land, Caesar. With all your soldiers and all your power, you are a stranger here." She paused, staring at him. "Just as you are in Rome. It is your fate."

"Truly." Her words had taken Caesar aback once again. He poured more wine to cover his discomfort. Of course she had heard of his troubles at home, he reassured himself. Even in this remote land, the network of tribal gossip was highly efficient. "You are uncommonly perceptive, Lady," he said. "But since you are credited with having the sight of an oracle, you should be." He gave her another of his measuring stares, the kind of look that made most men drop their eyes. "I will offer you a bargain of sorts. Use your gifts to see my future, and I may spare you."

Veleda's eyes did not turn from his. "You cannot spare me, Caesar. It is not within your realm to do so. But I will speak to you of your future anyway." She drew closer to him, and Caesar, Governor of Gaul and Commander of armies, had to call upon all his discipline not to back away. "Power waits for you, man of Rome, in all its forms. You will taste its sweetness and its bitterness. You will see the beauty of it, and the ugliness. And in the end, it will kill you."

Caesar's fingers tightened around the stem of his goblet.

Here was truth. Spoken from the mouth of a barbarian, a woman who presided over a religion as bloodthirsty and backward as her country. But it was still truth. Caesar was an astute man; he recognized the sound of it. "Will I rule this land?" he asked tensely.

"You will rule more." Her eyes were distant and cold. "Rome will bow before you. The world will know your name. You will live forever."

"You just said," he reminded her, "that the power I gain will kill me."

Veleda smiled. "It will."

"Then it must be that I will live a very long time." Caesar laughed and slammed down his goblet. "No matter. Your words have amused me. Yes, I will spare you."

Veleda's features were utterly impassive. "You would have done that anyway. It is not in your heart to kill me. You have seen too much death, and you will see more. You need me alive. Executing the High Priestess who came before me was in your best interests. Executing me is not."

This also was truth. Caesar could not deny it. Being in this woman's presence had already convinced him of her use to him alive. As a rule, he had nothing but contempt for the Gauls' habit of allowing women to lead them. But even he could understand how men would follow a woman like this one. There was a power about her, a presence different from anything he had ever encountered. It repelled and drew him at once.

He had spent years in this cold wet country fighting these stubborn barbarians, and it was still not over. Never could he have admitted it to his officers, but he was tired of blood, tired of the thousands upon thousands of these foolishly brave people sprawled in the graceless postures of death. Perhaps the wisest thing would be to kill the woman. The power in her was too great. It could not be controlled.

But she would make a noble captive in Rome. With her bearing and demeanor she would attract enormous attention, and Caesar needed that attention. She was uncivilized now, but she would gradually come to take on Roman ways; everyone who came to Rome did. Then even his enemies would have to concede that this fierce female leader of her savage people had been tamed by great Caesar's mercy.

Yet, aside from all the logic there was another reason that defied all sense. He simply did not want to add this ungainly woman with the clear far-seeing eyes to the countless numbers of the dead.

"You are an interesting woman," he said. "And Rome will find you as interesting as you find Rome." He waited for her to react, and was somewhat disappointed when she did not. "For that is where you are going," he went on. "I cannot allow you to stay here; we both know this. You will be exhibited before the Roman populace, and then I will give you as a gift to one of our greatest houses, someone with whom I wish to gain favor, of course. You will spend the rest of your days as a slave, Lady, but a well-treated one. And you will be alive."

He turned as if to summon the guards, but suddenly swung back to Veleda. "If you have truly seen that I will conquer Gaul, why, in the name of the gods, have you not counseled your people to submit? Had you only done so, things would have been so different. For all of us." He waited impatiently for her response.

Velda could see the impatience swirl about him, and she took her time. "But Roman," she said gently. "You were not listening. I said you would rule in this land. I never said you would conquer it."

Caesar glared. Abruptly he called for his sentries. "Take her," he said when they came in. "I will make arrangements for her confinement and that of the woman with her. She must be carefully guarded." He looked at Veleda, forced himself not to glance away from those enigmatic eyes. "She has a long journey to make."

* * *

The tavern was small, dimly lit from a central fire and heavy with smoke and the odors of beer, sweat, and roasting meat. Hori sat by himself in the corner. He stared at the cup of wine that had been set on the rough wooden table before him without seeing it.

By now, Seti and Ahotep were well started on the long journey home. Hori had not gone with them. He could not. For the sake of seeing his friends safely off, he had accompanied them to the coast and bid them farewell, this time brooking no arguments. Then he had done the only thing he could to see Veleda again. He had started back to rejoin the legions.

He knew the Romans would welcome him. His return from the barbarians would be hailed as a miraculous feat, a testament to his cleverness and courage. It would occur to no one, not centurions or legionaries or auxiliaries, that his was not the escape they all thought it to be. They would never realize his true purpose, and in marching with them he would find his way once again to Veleda and the child she carried. He did not question the danger or the logic in following his course of action. The knowledge that he must do this thing was as constant and right as the Nile in the Inundation.

For days Hori had walked, staying in taverns popular with Romans so that he might hear the news. In such a way had he learned of the fighting in the territory of the Arverni and that Caesar had gathered all ten of his legions there. He traveled inconspicuously, wishing to attract as little attention as possible. He was grateful for the generous share of Veleda's gift of gold that Seti and Ahotep had pressed on him, but he used it sparingly. He was even more grateful for the bracae and mantles the warriors had given him and his comrades to wear on the journey to the coast. They were plain garments, the clothing of common men. They attracted neither the notice of Romans nor natives.

On this evening, as he rested his feet after another long day of walking, Hori listened to the gossip circulating through the smoky recesses of the tavern. Roman garrisons had spread throughout this part of the land and soldiers from the one nearest the tavern had come to drink and eat. They talked loudly about the fighting and their speculations on what Caesar would do to defeat the rebels. In their garrisons they were nervous and wary, but in these dim confines, with wine to loosen their tongues, their voices rose in anger at Gaulish stubbornness.

Hori looked up as the tavern keeper's wife brought his dinner: meat and bread and wheaten porridge. She returned his glance curiously as she set down the plate. "You wear our clothes, although you are not of our land," she said to him in Latin. "But neither are you Roman. Where are you from?"

Hori took a sip of his wine, watered, as the Romans liked it. He saw that the group of legionaries at the next table had stopped their own conversation and were listening closely to this exchange. Earlier, when they had come in, he had heard them mention their journey to the coast. For some reason Hori had focused on that; he did not know why. He had lingered while the Romans were served, waiting for an opportunity to present itself.

The Romans were eating their own meal, still studying him with suspicion. He smiled at them, though his answer was directed to the woman. "I'm Egyptian, and I belong to an auxiliary troop attached to the legions. The Eighth, to be exact. Or at least, I served with them until the rebels captured me. Now I'm on my way back."

The men's eyes went wide. "You were captured by the barbarians?" one of them breathed. He exchanged glances with his comrades and sat forward on his stool. "By Mithras, I've never heard of anyone that happened to who lived. How did you escape their savagery?"

"With great difficulty, Centurion." Hori was keenly aware of the innkeeper's wife. She was refilling the legionaries' wine cups, and he could feel her disdain, wordless but rife with contempt. He wanted to turn to her, to explain himself in the Gaulish tongue. Instead, he grinned at the Romans. "It's quite a story," he said. "Would you like to hear it?"

Hours later, with many cups of wine between them, Hori and the legionaries were still talking. He had told the tale of his captivity, crafted out of truth and a great many lies. His listeners could not tell the difference, nor did they want to. Hori fed the beliefs he knew each one of them nurtured, embellishing the stories with details that convinced the Romans of their accuracy. To add to their admiration, Hori modestly let it slip that his arrow had slain the High Priestess, an act rewarded by Caesar himself.

The reaction to this disclosure had intensified his feeling that he must glean all he could from these men. There had been an odd silence, followed by an explosion of chuckles, raising of cups to one other, and sly glances.

"So tell me," Hori said, touching his own lips to the rim of the cup. He did not drink; he had refrained from that for some time, his head remaining clear while those of his companions fogged. "Why are such capable soldiers not with their own legion?"

The Romans grinned at each other. Unlike most men whose voices rose with drink, these men had begun to talk more and more quietly. The man who answered him was the centurion, and he spoke barely above a whisper. "We had an errand to perform, a very important one. Ordered by Caesar himself. We're on our way back to tell him it's been done."

The food and beer and wine suddenly clenched together in Hori's belly. With an effort he forced an expression of mild interest onto his face and kept it there. "Truly? And what could be more important than fighting the barbarians who have endangered our rule in Gaul?"

The centurion laughed. "Let us say we had to deliver—someone. And because of it, there may not be much need for your archery skills when you join up with the Eighth again. I have a feeling that these barbarians will soon be too disheartened to go on fighting.''

"That could only happen if that female Druid who started this rebellion were captured." Hori pretended to drink more wine. "And by my gods, I don't believe she even exists. I saw no sign of her when I was a prisoner. Vercingetorix is the leader of the Gauls. The High Priestess is only a myth.''

"She's no myth,'' another of the men said.

Hori grinned. "Why, you're beginning to sound as superstitious as the natives. I've already told you I killed her.''

"These Druids are tricky demons,'' the centurion said wisely. "They don't even have the honesty of a good Roman to stay dead.'' He looked at the others with bleary sternness. "But we have said enough.''

"Oh, come on, Silius,'' one of the legionaries said. "We can tell him. After what he's been through, he deserves to know. He'll keep quiet. And think about it: this is the very man who Caesar himself thought had killed her.''

The centurion poured himself more wine. "Very well,'' he growled. He propped his elbows on the rough table, glaring at Hori. "But mind me well, this is between us. Now listen: the king of the Aedui took the woman captive in Arverni territory and brought her to Caesar. We all thought he was going to have the creature executed, this time for real. But he's canny, our commander. There's no one cannier. He came up with a far better plan.''

"One that must be kept secret,'' another man added.

Hori shook his head, affecting an air of outraged astonishment. "I killed her. She fell with my arrow in her.''

"Evil magic,'' Silius said. "These Druids excel at it. But the barbarians must not know about any of this.'' He looked about as he spoke, satisfying himself that the tavern keeper and his wife were nowhere near.

"That's easier said than done,'' Hori pointed out. "Barbarians seem to find out everything, especially what we don't want them to.''

"Ha. They haven't found out about this. And they won't. Not until Caesar is ready for them to." The centurion emptied his wine cup, wiped a hand across his mouth, and grinned. "She'll be taken to Rome, but there is a spectacle planned for her first. An exhibition, you might say. Caesar plans to strip her naked except for her chains, and show her to everyone in the port town as the slave she'll be in Rome. He's already sending an extra detachment there to quell any disturbances. But I think he's just being careful. She'll be shown, hustled onto the boat, and away before anybody can react.''

"Whew." The utterance was forced, and Hori was relieved that the tavern was too dark and the Romans too drunk to notice how he had paled. "That's quite a revenge.''

Silius laughed. "Oh, indeed, it is. The magical High Priestess of the tribes will be humbled for all to see. Word of it will travel from the coast through the rest of Gaul like a plague.''

"Wouldn't it be more effective to carry her in a procession from the Arverni lands to the coast, letting the people see her along the way?'' Hori wished desperately that this had been done. The tribes would have risen up in a fury and rescued their High Priestess.

"And have Vercingetorix lead his rebels against us in one attack after another, until she escapes in the confusion?'' Silius looked disgusted. "Caesar is not that foolish. No, this is the better way. The rebels will still learn of the woman's fate, and it will demoralize them so greatly this alliance of theirs falls apart. They'll be easy enough to conquer when they've returned to being quarrelsome and at war with each other, as well as us.''

It was true, and Hori was chilled with the knowing of it. It was all he could do to keep from dashing out of the tavern, but he forced himself to wait. Acting too quickly

would be disastrous; it would only arouse the suspicions he
had worked so hard to lull. So he sat on, pretending to share
in the Romans' delight, pretending to drink, while they got
drunker and drunker. Finally he rose quietly from the wine-
spattered table, slipped past the befuddled legionaries, and
out into the night.

26

THE PATTERN HAD ALMOST come full circle. Seventeen years ago, Veleda had come to this harbor along the coast. She had been a girl then, eager and unsure, on fire with the will to unify her people as the outland Goddess had asked her to. The harbor had been a simple place then, a stopping place for the tribes who wished to trade with the Venetii and engage passage for themselves and their goods to Albion, Eire, and places beyond, including Rome itself.

Caesar had changed all that. After his defeat of the Venetii, he had turned this once quiet *oppidum* into a crowded port heavy with the influence of all things Roman. It bustled with activity. Traders of all countries walked the streets that the Venetii warriors, laboring as slaves under legionary overseers, had enlarged. The ancient fortress walls had been torn down to make way for villas belonging to wealthy Roman citizens, and temples were springing up where tree shrines to the local *teutates* had once stood.

Through a narrow opening in the wooden hut, Veleda looked out into the darkness, watching another night take shape. She treasured these transitions, so rhythmic and constant, knowing how few of them were left to her. The moon was already visible in the crescent shape of a sickle. Bladed and sharp was the Goddess in Her crone aspect. It was fitting that She should appear this way, a reminder of how swiftly one's mortality passed. On such a night had Mau come from the Otherworld. And now he had gone back. It was a sign Veleda could not misread. He had done all he could for her in this realm.

"There is still time." Eponina's voice broke into Veleda's thoughts. Kneeling by the fire, she poked the reluctant flames into life and glared at her companion. "We can use our skills to contact other Brothers and Sisters of the Oak. They will come to us, and bring warriors with them—"

"No." Veleda's voice was pitched softly so the guards outside the hut would not overhear, but there was inflexible power in it. "All that would accomplish is their deaths. With you, it's different. You can still be free, Eponina. Please, let me save you."

"I will not." Eponina's tone was equally firm. "I have told you that."

Veleda sighed and looked out at the night again. The restless sound of the ocean was borne to her on the breeze. If she craned her neck she could make out the shoreline and the tall shapes of the boats moored along the docks. There, too, the Romans had replaced the round coracles of the Venetii with their own vessels. All those years ago, she had boarded a simple hide boat to leave her homeland. Now a great Roman trading ship waited to take her away again, this time in chains.

The baby would be born in the city of Veleda's enemies, the people she had devoted her life to fighting. The thought brought a grim twist to her lips. So this was how Bast and Anu had contrived to keep the tribes from discovering that the High Priestess had broken her vows. It was a bitter strategy; under Roman law, this daughter would be a slave. Freedom, that most precious of gifts, would be denied the child, unless Eponina succeeded in rescuing her from Roman captivity.

Veleda glanced across the tiny room at her soul-friend. Eponina was still crouched beside the hearth, her tall body hunched over as she poked at the flames. The firelight glinted off the blond hair that lay unbound over her shoulders. In truth, Veleda did not believe that slavery was the path for her daughter. Plainly, the Goddesses had sent Eponina to her to prevent that. Veleda might wish to save her friend from danger, but Bast and Anu saw things differently, and so did Eponina herself. As for Veleda, she had seen little since her meeting with Caesar. It seemed that the Goddesses were taking her gifts from her, as They had taken Mau. In preparation, perhaps, for her own departure.

Outside the hut one of the two legionaries currently on guard paced by on his rounds. His sandals crunched on the rocky ground, as stolid as the man himself. Caesar had devoted great care to the men charged with guarding his important prisoner until she was taken aboard the ship that would carry her to Rome. They were unimaginative and seasoned soldiers, devoted to duty and impervious to the superstitious fears that plagued so many of their comrades.

Veleda listened to the man who had just passed. His footsteps faded and paused, as he walked a little ways out from the hut. She heard the familiar sound of a man relieving himself, then silence, broken only by the sound of waves and the distant voices of people in the town. She waited for the steps to return, and knew they would not. Eponina lifted her head, staring. She rose to her feet, moving swiftly to join Veleda by the narrow opening. The Druids looked at each other. Death was on the wind, sudden and sharp. They both smelled it.

The other guard completed his circle of the hut and halted as he failed to meet his companion. He started to call out, but the name he tried to speak abruptly became a soft strangled cough. Silence fell again. Eponina jumped as the door was pushed open, but Veleda stood motionless. She did not smile, and yet her eyes shone with a welcome as deep and warm as midday sun.

A figure she had not thought to see again in this life slipped inside. His tail straight up, Mau trotted briskly to her, and Veleda knelt to stroke him.

"Mau," she said softly. "You came back."

Of course I did, he said into her mind. *And see who I brought with me.*

"You," Eponina gasped.

Veleda looked up, her eyes widening. Hori was entering, laden down with the weapons of the two guards he had killed. "I could not leave," he said before she could speak. His voice was flat and hard, his accent very strong, a clear sign of his distress. "My countrymen left safely, but I could not go with them. And by the gods of both our lands, I am glad I did not."

Veleda scowled. "By not listening to me, you have put yourself in danger." *And you have let him*, she added accusingly to Mau.

The cat sat down. *Listen to him*, he said.

"It's you who are in danger," Hori shot back. "Let me tell you what they have in store for you." Swiftly he described his conversation with the Romans. His words were harsh. This was not the time for soft and courteous persuasion; the next set of guards would be coming to relieve these two, and all of them must be well gone by then.

"She will not leave," Eponina said wearily. "I have tried and tried to convince her."

Hori dropped the weapons with a clatter and went close to Veleda. "What purpose will it serve for you to sacrifice yourself now? Stripped naked with your rounding belly, you'll not be a symbol of freedom and defiance, but an object of shame, a priestess who has broken her vows. Caesar will rub it into your people like salt in an open wound."

Human girl. Mau's inner voice was like a purr inside Veleda's head. *My Mistress and Anu wish your daughter to be born in freedom, not in a place where men have overturned the Ancient Laws of Motherhood, giving fathers all rights over children, while their own mothers have none.*

Veleda stared into the knowing orange eyes. *I thought They had left me*, she told him painfully. *I thought this was Their will.*

Foolish human girl, the cat purred. *Never would that happen. But now it is time to accept the help of others, for your sake, and that of the babe.*

Hori and Eponina had stood watching this silent exchange between woman and cat, the Egyptian with impatience and the Druid with respect. "Veleda," Hori broke in. "There is little time. More guards will be coming at any moment, and if they discover what has happened to these two, we are doomed."

"He's right," Eponina said. "If we're going to act, it must be now."

Veleda nodded. Her eyes were clear again, seeing far. "Yes, it is time," she said. "I will escape. We will all escape. And you and I," she added sadly to Eponina, "must leave our home behind us." She saw the opposition in her friend's eyes and went on. "If I remain it will only cause more blood to be spilled, and blood without purpose is a waste. Perhaps it is always a waste." She was silent a moment, looking into Mau's fathomless eyes. "This"—she laid a hand over her belly—"is what I must think of now."

The two legionaries from the nearby garrison finished off their wine, paid for their meal, and left the tavern. Slowly they sauntered through the darkness, bound toward the hut where the prisoners were confined. They did not hurry; it was still early, and there was no reason not to let their comrades stand their full term of duty.

Suddenly one of the legionaries stiffened. "I see something," he cried out. Metal clanged against the quiet sounds of the night as he and his companion drew their swords. Drawn by the commotion a handful of their comrades piled out of the tavern, yanking out their own weapons as they shouted out questions.

Deep in the shadows Veleda raised her hand and murmured several words. The Romans faltered, swaying dizzily and rubbing at their eyes. Suddenly one of them began to laugh. "See what he has called us out for," he hooted.

"Look! Look there!" He bent over with laughter as the other men peered at a large cat that had just stalked out of the darkness. The animal paused, staring back at the legionaries with regal disregard for their scrutiny. He passed on and was soon gone from their sight.

Chiding the guards, the others went back inside the tavern. The two legionaries continued on their way, the one who had raised the alarm still grumbling that he had seen more than a cat. When they arrived at the hut, they found their comrades dead and the hut empty.

Sekhmet's shrill laughter wounded the sky. *I have won,* she exulted. *Even You can deny it no longer.*

You have succeeded in the spilling of more blood, Her Sister said. *But You have not won.*

Say You so? The Lion-Goddess's blazing eyes were incredulous. Their fiery yellow depths were tinted crimson with the enormous amount of blood She had consumed. *You are a fool, gentle Sister. The mortal and that brat she carries have fled this land forever. The unity You set her to achieve is no longer. Look*—She thrust a hand out at the earth below—*the Romans are destroying the people You allied Yourself with. Yet You say I have not won!*

Bast smiled. *You always were shortsighted,* She said.

The Romans were carrying the day. The backbone of the revolt—this last and greatest bid for freedom—was broken. Vercingetorix's stronghold, Alesia, had fallen, and the slaughter of its defenders was rampant.

But Divitiacus was not sharing in the fierce exultation of his Roman allies. He had been surrounded by a group of his own tribesmen who had gone over to the rebels, and now, knowing that both they and their cause were doomed, they were determined to take their despised king with them.

In desperation, Divitiacus called upon the foreign Goddess. Once before, She had come to save him. Perhaps She would do so again.

Help me, he cried out silently.

And the Goddess answered him. Her voice rang through his head, drowning out the cries of dying men and the savage yells of his own kinsmen who had gathered to kill him. *Not this time, mortal*, She said. *You are a man without honor, and you have served your purpose. I have no more need of you.*

When the swords flashed at Divitiacus there were so many blades they blotted out the sky.

Sweat covered Veleda's naked body in a fine sheen. Her hair lay over her broad shoulders and strong back in long damp tendrils. Squatting in the timeless pose of giving birth, she strained, her muscles standing out against the smooth pale skin. Through the great contractions that shook her body in an ancient rhythm, she was dimly aware of Eponina's arm supporting her, of the Druid's voice both soothing her and calling out encouragement.

The baby was ready to depart the safety of her mother's womb. Every shred of Veleda's strength and power was now devoted to bringing her forth. An enormous spasm rolled through her. She strained even harder as Eponina cried, "She comes. Push now, push hard!"

The walls of the comfortable, tidy hut that had been home to them for the last four months suddenly receded. The brilliant vistas of the Otherworld shone and danced before Veleda's sweat-blurred gaze. They were vivid, so clear that for an instant, she feared the Goddesses would take her as the baby was born, not giving her the chance to hold this child she had nurtured and carried and was now striving to bear.

But Bast and Anu were not so cruel. Tiny and wet, covered with the fluids of birth, a perfectly formed girl-child emerged into the world, swiftly caught by Eponina's skilled hands. And yet, the time remaining would be short. As the baby left her, Veleda felt her own life force go with it.

Another contraction went through her, and the afterbirth came. *Soon,* she told herself, *soon.*

Distant in her exhaustion, she settled back on her pallet of furs, watching Eponina wash the child. She spoke and her voice was a thread of sound. "Give her to me and fetch Hori."

Eponina understood. Veleda had told her long ago of the price she would pay for this child. Her blue eyes brimming with tears, the Druid laid Veleda's daughter in her arms then went outside to where Hori had been impatiently waiting.

Veleda stared down at her daughter. So warm she was, and so fragile. Such a tiny human person to bear the weight of future ages and obligations. "I am about to be freed of my burdens," she whispered to the puckered face. "But yours, my daughter, yours are just beginning. I am sorry."

Unblinking, the baby returned her mother's gaze. Her eyes were dark, as the eyes of all newborns are, but the expression in them was like no child Veleda had ever seen among the many births she herself had assisted at. There was awareness in her daughter's eyes, a wisdom that did not belong in the face of one so newly come into the world. Vaguely she realized that Hori and Eponina were beside her. Hori was stroking her damp tangled hair, his black eyes even blacker with grief.

Veleda made herself speak. "Eire is a good place," she whispered. "We have been made welcome, and the Romans will never come here. I have seen that. Raise my daughter on this Holy Island as she should be raised. In the old ways."

Hori and Eponina were giving her their oaths, but to Veleda their voices were thin and insubstantial, twining around her ears like tendrils of mist. "I give this child the name of Damona," she said, and the baby smiled at her.

Veleda saw love and regret in those unworldly knowing eyes. She was gripped by the same emotions, with such force, she almost cried out at the pain of it. *This I swear to you, my only daughter*, she said into the child's mind. *Never will I be your mother in this world. But never will I leave you.*

The baby smiled again, her understanding glimmering in Veleda's fading consciousness. Veleda smiled, too. "Thank you." Her voice was so soft Hori and Eponina had to lean forward to hear.

She wanted to say more, but suddenly Mau was there, rubbing his head against her face, though neither Hori nor Eponina appeared to see him. "Well, human girl," the cat said gently. "It's time to go at last."

Veleda found herself outside the hut with Mau beside her. The sturdy walls had become transparent as a mountain pool. Inside she could see Eponina and Hori huddled over a body that lay on a bed of furs. It was an empty shape, devoid of meaning, and it took her a moment to grasp that there was the form that had once housed her.

Eponina had taken the baby from her mother's arms and was holding the child close. Over the Druid's shoulder Damona was looking straight at Veleda, as if the walls did not exist for her, any more than they did for Veleda herself.

She smiled as the woman and the cat walked into the trees.

Author's Note

The histories of the Celtic people who inhabited what would one day become France, Holland, and Belgium are as elusive as the mist. Much is known about the language and customs of the Celts in Ireland; Rome never conquered Eire, and thus the people's way of life remained intact. Gaul, however, was completely defeated, her people and religion assimilated into Roman customs and ways until the very language of the Continental Celts disappeared. Today it is difficult to recreate the people who inhabited the rich lands of what would become the Roman province of Gaul.

Julius Caesar described the tribes of Gaul as bloodthirsty childlike savages practicing large-scale human sacrifice. Later accounts depict them as noble heroes of an idyllic, near-mythical civilization. The truth lies somewhere in between. When he wrote his famous memoirs Caesar had his own agenda. In order to gain public support for his lengthy and expensive war, it was essential that he present the Gauls as savage barbarians in need of the "civilizing influence" of Rome. The Celtic tribes, in fact, boasted a sophisticated culture with an ancient and extensive trading network that stretched from Greece to Egypt to Rome itself. They built roads, devised prosperous farming methods, created astonishingly beautiful artwork, and in general lived within the framework of a rich, though carefully defined, class society.

However, the tribes were a quarrelsome people, constantly at war with each other, and they may indeed have practiced human sacrifice. Impulsive and notoriously undisciplined in battle, Celts were joyously eager to die in combat, and these characteristics played a large part in their downfall. In his determination to conquer Gaul, Gaius Julius Caesar built his ten legions into the greatest military force in the known world. Against such an army the exuberant tribal warriors, each bent on his own personal victory, had no chance. The battles that took place between Celt and Roman occurred as I have shown them. For their descriptions I am indebted to Ramon L. Jimenez, author of *Caesar Against the Celts*, and to Caesar himself for his *Conquest of Gaul.*

Many of the characters in this book actually existed. Divitiacus and his brother Dumonorix were indeed at odds with each other over collaboration with Rome, and I have relied on historical accounts to describe Dumonorix's brave death. The fate of Divitiacus is more uncertain. The Aeduian king suddenly and mysteriously disappears from all mention, and it is widely supposed that he may have been assassinated. It is not inconceivable that he could have died at the hands of his own people, as I have depicted.

Vercingetorix is also a real figure: a national hero in France, and the man who came breathtakingly close to driving Caesar from Gaul. To prevent further slaughter of his people, he tragically and bravely surrendered himself to Caesar after the defeat at Alesia. He was sent in chains to Rome, kept starving and imprisoned in a dungeon for seven years, and then strangled at Caesar's order in a lavish public display.

As for Veleda herself, she is as shrouded in mystery as her people. Tacitus in his *Histories* mentions a woman named Veleda who was a "prophetess" of the Bruceteri tribe in the time of Vespasian (AD 69–79). She was described as a virgin ruling over a wide territory and was so powerful that she not only represented her tribe in political negotiations, but also was venerated as a near Goddess. Veleda is a Celtic name that means *seeress*, and scholars have speculated that the word could be a title rather than a name. Other than that, very little is known. Even the spelling of her name varies; I have gone with the most common form.

Wherever possible I have tried to use words from the little that survives of the language of the Gauls. Some of the expressions that describe religious practices are from the ancient Gaelic of Ireland, but since Eire did host Druid colleges of learning, such words would probably have been a part of anyone educated on the "misty green isle." The word *oppida* was used by Caesar to describe the large fortified towns of his foes, but the history and usage of this term is murky. Evidence suggests that the Gauls themselves used the word, so I have included it in the text.

The tribes of Gaul were a well-traveled people and there is historical as well as archeological evidence to support long-term trading contact between pre-Roman Gaul and Egypt. Cats had long been held sacred in Egypt; they belonged to the Goddess Bast, and even in the days of Greek and then Roman rule it was an offense punishable by death to harm one. Non-Egyptian traders brought the first cats to the European continent, most likely stealing them from Egyptian ports, for the law forbade taking the precious animals away from Egypt. Still, cats were rare in the time period of this novel, and were completely unknown in Northern Europe. Regrettably, Mau is a creature of imagination, though the inspiration for his character comes from my own outspoken cat Yuri.

Sarah Isidore

AVON EOS PRESENTS
MASTERS OF FANTASY AND ADVENTURE

THE GILDED CHAIN:
A Tale of the King's Blades
by Dave Duncan   79126-9/$6.99 US/$8.99 CAN

THE DAUGHTERS OF BAST: THE HIDDEN LAND
by Sarah Isidore   80318-6/$6.50 US/$8.50 CAN

SCENT OF MAGIC
by Andre Norton   78416-5/$6.50 US/$8.50 CAN

THE DEATH OF THE NECROMANCER
by Martha Wells   78814-4/$6.99 US/$8.99 CAN

PROPHECY: BOOK FIVE OF THE BLENDING
by Sharon Green   78811-X/$6.99 US/$8.99 CAN

World Fantasy Award-winning Editors

Ellen Datlow and Terri Windling
Present Original Fairy Tale Collections for Adults

"Unusual and evocative . . . [the] series gives the
reader a look at what some of our best storytellers
are doing today."
Washington Post Book World

RUBY SLIPPERS, GOLDEN TEARS
77872-6/$6.99 US/$8.99 Can

Original stories by Joyce Carol Oates, Neil Gaiman,
Gahan Wilson, Jane Yolen and others.

BLACK THORN, WHITE ROSE
77129-2/$5.99 US/$7.99 Can

Featuring stories by Roger Zelazny,
Peter Straub and many others

SNOW WHITE, BLOOD RED
71875-8/$6.50 US/$8.50 Can

Includes adult fairy tales by Nancy Kress,
Charles de Lint, Esther M. Friesner and many others.